WHEN THE BUTTERFLIES COME

A NOVEL

BY

ROSEMARY LIGHTFOOT NESS-BITNER

THE SECRET AND THE BUTTERFLY and its companion book, WHEN THE BUTTERFLIES COME, expose the impotence of our financial institutions' regulatory framework and courts when pitted against a committed wrongdoer. The books were inspired by a matter of civil litigation. All characters, events, and conversations are fictional, the products of the author's imagination, or used fictitiously. Any resemblance to actual characters living or dead, events past or present, localities or conversations is entirely coincidental.

A caution and disclaimer

There are opinions expressed in these books which are not those of the author. They are expressions of the characters' beliefs and convictions only. Some or all of these opinions, particularly those of Marty towards married women and their children, and David's opinions and actions concerning a wide range of matters, some readers may find offensive. They are presented as part of the narrative to illustrate the depths of depravity and sociopathic disorders of the characters. They are in no way intended to convey the feelings or attitudes of the author.

The author holds deepest sympathy and highest esteemed regard for the victims of the sociopathic characters. It is the author's hope and intent that, by these illustrations, the reader will gain an appreciation of the presence of the evil forces that lurk in some minds, craftily disguised as normal. If you are squeamish about offensive material, especially cruelty to insects, animals, and people, or if you are offended by characters' offensive behaviors and expressions of strong opinions about controversial subjects, you are advised and cautioned to not purchase this book. If you are a child under the age of eighteen, do not purchase this book as it contains erotic adult content.

DEDICATION

To loving.

Table of Contents

GLORIOUS BUTTERFLY

David put an ether-soaked handkerchief over Marty's nose and mouth. She struggled briefly while he held her arms. Her thoughts were of a woman crazed. *What's he doing? Where's my bunny?* She struggled and gasped for breath. The air was intoxicatingly cool and she was suddenly overcome with dizziness, falling unconscious. David had timed his attack perfectly, just after Marty exhaled so she breathed the ether in deep. It was only fifteen seconds before she succumbed.

When Marty woke she was sitting on a hay bale naked. Her hands were bound behind her, ankles chained together, and her mouth covered with duct tape. Her head was groggy, and she shook it to dispel this surreal happenstance. *This must be some kind of joke, but I don't like it. David's way out of line doing this kind of shit!* She squirmed and groaned to free herself, but her struggles were of no use. She looked up to see David standing about three feet from her, out of kicking range. She shook her head up and down, then gyrated back and forth as if to demand that he free her at once. He stared at her like a man transfixed. It was that faraway look he sometimes lapsed into. After a little while she stopped struggling and stared back at him, as if requesting an explanation. He was expressionless, staring as if she didn't exist. She glanced off to the side and saw both her diamond and her pearl necklaces hanging from a nail on the side of the barn.

He finally spoke.

"Marty, I have the utmost respect for you. You are not an ordinary woman. Most women are silly creatures. They are selfish, vain, incredibly boring, pathetic beings who go through life focused on trivialities and obsessed with petty jealousies. They are insufferable company for men with ambitions and purpose. They do not know their purpose for living. They concern themselves with who among their circle of nitwits lunches with whom, who attended whose parties, and who said what to whom. They are maddeningly boring, despicable, narrow-minded beings that men are made to suffer.

"You are different, Marty. You identified your life's purpose early. You understood a woman's purpose is to please a man, and you made the most of it. You are like your mother that way. You both figured out that you could make considerable fortunes by shamelessly plying your best asset. You both mastered the techniques of feminine guile to get men to do your bidding. You, even more than your despicable mother, learned how to conquer men with your cunt. I salute your genius. My purpose was to harness it for the good of the firm. You can appreciate that.

"But there's something you should know. You have a tiny scar on your right little finger. You had a little nub of flesh there when you were a child, didn't you?"

Marty remained silent, but David held a knife up to her nose, threatening her if she refused to answer. "Well, didn't you have it removed?"

She nodded, suddenly afraid. *I don't know where this is going but I don't like it.*

"I noticed your nub when you were a little girl. You were at Dad's house in Rondel Hills, bouncing a ball with me. Remember?" Marty shook her head. "Well, that's okay. I remember. That's all that matters. I knew someone else who had that same nub on the same finger. He had his surgically removed too. Do you know who he was?" Again, Marty shook her head. "It was Dad, Marty. I saw his nub when I was a boy. One year I was sent to summer camp, and when I came home, Dad's nub was gone.

"You and I have the same father. You didn't know that, did you? You are not Joseph Maloney's daughter. You're Marvin Sustack's. You and I are half-brother and sister." David paused to let Marty absorb the information. "It's okay, Marty. I don't hold it against you that you're beautiful and I'm ugly. Our mothers were different and they determined what we looked like, not Dad. Dad was handsome. You're beautiful. Your mother is beautiful. My mother was ugly, and therefore so am I. Nature worked out that way for us."

David stared at Marty before he continued.

"We have a serious problem. We're brother and sister so we're not supposed to fuck together, but we did, vicariously. We broke a mitzvah. And you broke another mitzvah when you fucked Muscle Boy. You broke the one that forbids a betrothed to fuck someone other than their betrothed. You shouldn't even fuck your betrothed until after you're married by a rabbi. I see you're shaking your head to everything I'm saying. Is that because you're not a Jew? These rules don't apply to you?"

Marty nodded.

"Ordinarily, that would make a difference. Since your mother is a gentile, that makes you a gentile. Jewish law shouldn't apply to you, but you're not ordinary. Dad treated your mother like a wife at the office. She wasn't an ordinary shiksa. She was more like an office wife than a shiksa. By Susan being Dad's office wife, you're the daughter of a woman who sought to become a Jew. Dad wouldn't marry Susan and let her join the tribe through marriage. It's complicated, Marty, so I don't expect you to understand everything I'm saying, but Dad wanted Susan for his wife. But for Mother, he would have married Susan.

"Dad loved Susan and you more than he loved Mother and me. Dad pushed us aside to be with Susan and you whenever he could. You probably don't remember that, do you? Dad loved your mother so much he tied me to her through his will until she dies. Can you see why I think of her as Dad's wife, which makes you a Jewess from my perspective even though no rabbi would agree with me? Susan, Mother, and Dad all hurt me, Marty. You and I need to correct that. That brings us to why we're here, and why you're chained up."

Marty shook her head vigorously.

"According to the ancient tribal rules of five thousand years ago, when someone comes into contact with a corpse, we must have a red heifer sacrifice. That's a heifer with not a single hair on it that is not red. Sometimes people used to cheat a little. If a heifer had some white hair, they'd just pull out the white hair, figuring the priests wouldn't notice. In our circumstance I figure although you're not an actual corpse, your soul is dead. That's just as bad as being dead, Marty, and maybe even worse. You are a hopeless base whore, forever committed to whoring. That makes your soul a corpse. I know that for sure because you just fucked for diamonds and betrayed your future husband. I think of Bob as a son, and I didn't like watching you betray him."

Marty looked at David and rolled her eyes as if she thought he'd lost his mind. *David's one sick asshole. First he gets his jollies learning about my innermost feelings, and then he watches me while I fuck Muscle Boy. Now he says everything I did for the company, which he paid me to do, was immoral. What next? Will he spank me? I haven't felt this alone and abandoned since Mother sent me to boarding school. I wish Bob would come along and put a stop to this craziness. Where could he be on a nice weekend like this? I wish I hadn't told him to stay away.*

Men! They surprise you when you don't want to be, but when you need them around they're off doing something else. Damn it! This isn't fun anymore. I can't think straight. Just wait until David takes this tape off my mouth. I'm going to give that little prick a piece of my mind. After all I've done for UGGA, for him to treat me this way. He got loyalty from me—bottoms-up loyalty. I fucked my ass off for UGGA. Where's the loyalty from him? Nobody should treat their best employee this way. Why is he doing this to me? When do I get my necklaces? Where's my floppy-eared rabbit?

And would someone shut those fucking pigs up? They're so damn noisy. I wish David would hurry up and feed them so they'd shut up. Where did he go? David, I can't see you. You can't just leave me sitting here like this. I can't think with those pigs grunting like crazy, and I can't speak.

David! Come back here. What are you doing? Where are you?

CHATAT AND QORBANAT

Marty's situation was precarious. A day that began with promises, fun, and games suddenly turned weird and scary. The hot late-summer-afternoon sun beat down on the prairie. The air was still, the humidity cloying. There was no breeze or sound except for the occasional cry of a magpie or the shrill "tuhweeee" of a male red-winged blackbird standing watch on a cattail at the edge of the barnyard pond. She'd arrived casually dressed in blue shorts, sans underwear, expecting to give David an obligatory hug for his magnanimous generosity. She accepted David's pearl necklace as an offer of good faith and now she trusted his good intentions. She was told she was being reinstated with a raise in pay, a diamond necklace, and a floppy-eared rabbit. Best of all, she'd be reunited with Bob, her lover and husband-to-be. On the drive over to David's, she'd wondered what other company would set her up like this and pay her this well to fuck her brains out. She ignored David's reversal of policy regarding office romance. She overlooked his previous temper tantrum when he learned of her engagement. She desperately needed to believe she was lucky in business and lucky in love.

But now events took an unexpected turn. She listened carefully when David instructed her to be still, to fully comprehend the events which were about to transpire. Before that day she had no idea that she and David shared the same blood, nor could she imagine her half-brother's innermost thoughts that their common blood made her a potential rival for Marvin's assets should she ever correctly piece together her parentage. Too late she realized that, to eliminate the risk of a contest for their father's assets, David needed to get rid of her.

She suddenly saw the world through David's sinister eyes. She was twenty-eight years old. Her allure would soon fade. She'd carried the firm's sales on her back, literally, for the past few years, but her results had plateaued. She expected to marry David's new prized salesman. Now she understood that David considered her a threat to his plans. Marriage to Bob could result in the two of them striking off on their own in a different direction, or, with her voracious sexual appetite, there was no telling what turmoil his new sales leader might have to deal with if he married her. Sales could suffer. Suddenly, too late, she realized that possibly David had his own designs on Bob. She shuddered and quivered, realizing she was likely a mere pawn in a very dangerous game. Fear shot through her blood. She now knew she was undoubtedly way over her head into something very dark and foreboding.

David saw all along that it was risky to allow events to progress naturally without intervening. He'd already talked the entire matter over with Dolly. He and Dolly concluded that he needed to maintain control of the company and events, but he also needed a righteous rationale in his own mind to commit a heinous act. For that, he reached far back to his historic roots and plucked an ancient mitzvah from the Torah.

David stared at Marty sitting on her hay bale, no doubt hoping he'd snap out of his madness. She was bound and gagged, completely at his mercy. He would do all the talking. It was his ritual; she was merely an instrument of his penitence. Her role in God's mitzvah was to compliantly accept God's will, to be quiet and play her proper role. It was time for David to involve her in his fantasy ritual, never before practiced in human history with anything other than a red heifer. David realized that Marty probably thought he was insane, and from a psychological sense that worked to his advantage; otherwise, she might have offered even more resistance than she did. David knew he wasn't a madman. He knew himself well. He was a willful, motivated murderer with a penchant for sadistic terror. In David's mind, Marty was no different than the helpless butterflies he tore wings from as a child. He had long before lost all feelings for the sufferings of others, be they insects or humans.

"Marty, in our religion, when someone defiles God we must atone. The way to atone is through sacrifice. Our religion stopped this practice about two thousand years ago when the Romans destroyed our holy temple in Jerusalem and murdered over a million Jews. Rabbis tell us sacrifices are forbidden now, but I don't believe that makes the practice invalid. I made an altar in my basement. It's hidden behind a bookcase with a secret button that opens the wall to access it. It's a modern altar, with gas-fired burners and a hood that vents to the fireplace chimney and takes the smoke out. I can't feel purified unless I make a sacrifice.

"I built the house and altar facing east, toward Jerusalem, where the ancient priests sacrificed before the Romans destroyed our temple. Today, we'll make our offering together. It will purify us from our sins. It will be a chatat, or sin offering. You will be absolved of your sins by participating."

Marty was dumbfounded by what she heard. She looked at him as if he were mad. She only half heard what David said as her mind blocked his voice with thoughts of her own. *Is David mad? It sounded like he said he was going to absolve me of my sins, but how could he? And why am I bound up this way?* Then her mind came back into focus and she listened carefully to what her murderer was saying to her.

"Marty, this particular offering also atones for contact by a member of the tribe with a dead person. I'm not real clear on this. Maybe it was to absolve people who committed necrophilia, or maybe it was just used if somebody touched a dead person. I'm no expert on this five-thousand-year-old stuff. But as I explained, your soul is dead so you are morally lifeless, and that's kind of like being dead. In this special case, we must use a red heifer to atone for our sins like they did between five thousand and two thousand years ago.

"I especially need to do the red heifer offering because I staged today's events. That was wrong of me. I already knew you'd lost your soul. I watched you lose it years ago. In fact, I paid for much of your debauchery. I entrapped you, another sin for which I must atone. This is called the Qorbanot offering. It's rare and special. We're going to be the first ones to do this in two thousand years. What we're doing is really special. I hope you are as proud to be part of this as I am. Unfortunately, I don't have an actual red heifer to perform this offering with and our faith doesn't have priests anymore, so I've decided to substitute you for the heifer and myself for the priest. Pretty clever, huh? Substitutions weren't permitted in ancient times, so this won't be exact, but trust me. I'll do my best. Stop shaking your head and squirming, Marty. I'm your big brother. You need to listen to me. I know what's best here.

"Your hair isn't red but a dark brown, with a patch of red, which looks like it comes out of a cowlick. In a proper sacrifice, the mitzvah says I should have only red hair. I'm not going to remove all your black hair and just leave that little patch of red. I figured out a better solution. Since you are not a real heifer in the first place and since you only have a little patch of red hair, we're going to read the mitzvah from left to right like gentiles read the newspaper, instead of our accepted way from right to left. It'll be okay, Marty. This won't be a kosher sacrifice anyway, since you're not a hoofed animal and I'm not a priest from two thousand years ago, but it'll get the job done. I hope God will know we made a good effort. To make your hair uniform and perfect without blemish, I'm going to first remove your red cowlick plug. You'll be like a black-haired human version of a red heifer but without any red hair. That way, you'll still be without blemish, see, but you won't have all red hair like a red heifer because you're not a heifer in the first place. The more I read the Torah, the more I realized that the key to the sacrifice was to remove all signs of blemish, so I don't think it matters too much that you have black hair instead of red hair. I know this may sound confusing to you, Marty, but don't worry about it. Trust me, I'll get this done and God will be proud of both of us."

With that pronouncement, David pulled on a rope running through the pulley block attached to the rafter of the barn. Soon, Marty hung upside down above the hay bales. As she became more terrified, she started squirming and struggling in earnest, which was useless. When David grabbed her hair, she was helpless to stop him. What would be unthinkable to a normal person, David believed was normal. He believed it was his duty to God to proceed.

He took a very sharp knife and extracted a circle of skin and hair from her scalp, removing her streak of red hair. He looked at her scalp carefully, as a surgeon might assess an incision, satisfied he'd removed all her red hair as blood trickled down Marty's cheek.

"Now you are without blemish. You are perfect in the eyes of God."

He watched her look at the blood dripping onto the hay bale as she looked at the floor. He could see in her eyes when Marty realized she was under the control of a madman and that David was going to murder her. David could tell her was heart racing. He felt smug knowing he had her trapped like a rabbit cornered by a venomous snake. He enjoyed the sensations of her terror as he continued explaining his ritual to her.

"Now, Marty, before I perform our next step, I want to explain that by participating in this ritual, your body will be freed from sin. Your bodily sacrifice will be accepted by God. When the Messiah comes and rolls up the earth and releases the spirits of the dead to come to him, to be reborn on the Temple Mount in Jerusalem, your purified body will reenter another body somewhere in the universe, of which God is the great master. I should be saying some prayers about now, but I don't know what they would be. In fact, I hardly ever go to temple, so rather than try to make something up which could screw this up worse than it already is, we'll just get on with it.

"Your spirit might not know eternal peace, Marty. It might leave your body and go deep into the earth where it will reside with the spirits who seek sin and debauchery, who reject God and embrace the ways of Satan. While your pussy—or cunt, as you often call it—will never again know the pleasures of penises and tongues, it will live forever in the minds that follow your chosen path. Whenever a Monarch butterfly opens and closes its wings as it flies or draws sustenance from a flower, those who see it will know your spirit is in that butterfly and their minds will enter your world. They'll imagine their tongues and penises are inside you, and their minds will embrace your free spirit. I don't know where your spirit will go. I can only proceed as my voices instruct me. As your voices dictated your behaviors, mine ordain what I do."

He could feel Marty's shock as she struggled violently to free herself, but to no avail.

David smiled and chuckled to himself as he watched Marty writhe in her agonizing horror. After she'd exhausted herself, he explained the procedure he would use to murder her.

"I want you to understand the elegant procedure for the sacrifice. I'll slit your jugular first. It's humane and painless. You'll barely feel it. Your blood will drain onto the hay bales. I will give you a little push after I slit your throat, so you'll feel a swinging sensation. You'll become dizzy as you bleed out. Your blood will sprinkle on the hay, which the animals will eat.

Death will be very peaceful. You should appreciate the irony of swinging upside down while you bleed out. After all, you *are* a swinger."

David let out a much louder guffaw as he looked into the terrified upside-down eyes of his victim. "Then," he continued, "I'll eviscerate your corpse and remove your gut pile. The gut pile is not part of the sacrifice, so I'll feed it to the pigs. You might get a little laugh out of this, Marty. I extended the names of Gut and Pile to Guta and Pileo, so they wouldn't feel diminished by being referred to as Gut Pile."

David laughed out loud in maddening, self-absorbed hysteria when he caught Marty's barely audible plea to God as she begged for David to have a heart attack or get hit by a lightning bolt.

David caught his breath and resumed the narrative of his concocted ritual.

"Guta and Pileo are my two biggest pigs. The smaller one I called Scraps. He'll get what Guta and Pileo leave for him. After eviscerating your corpse, I'll render your flesh into oversized buckets, and then I'll take your bodily parts up to the altar in the house. I'll put you to good use, Marty. Your flesh will roast as I pray for atonement to God. Your flesh, including your glorious pussy, will be chopped into small portions and fed to my dogs and pigs. Your bones will be ground into fine powder and small chips by my wood chipper. They'll be used as fertilizer for the roses in the gardens around my house.

"The roses will thrive on your bones, Marty. Just think how exciting that is! Bob once told me he loved a girl named Rose when he was in high school. He mentioned that you resembled her. It will be fitting and beautiful for the garden roses to draw their nutrients from your bones, Marty. When Bob sees those roses reaching for the sun, I'm sure he'll recognize their beauty. Maybe he'll even relate them to you somehow. I'll smash your teeth with a hammer after I saw them from your jawbones. I'll scatter your little tooth fragments in the pen where I keep the guinea hens. They'll store them in their crops until they are worn away from grinding the grains they eat.

"I promise I'll keep our sacrifice a secret, Marty. Don't worry. I've processed other bodies before. I've already planned how I'll dispose of your car. It's not likely that anyone will think you came here to repent and join me in a sacrificial ritual, but in case someone does, they won't find any proof. You can rest easy about your clothes and the hay. The goats will devour your clothing and your shoes, and the sheep will eat the hay. Your necklaces will go back to my safe deposit box where they came from. They were gifts Dad gave to Mother, so they belong on my side of our family. I'm sure you'll agree that's fair.

"Finally, Marty, I sincerely thank you for your exceptional service to UGGA. You helped build the company and never complained about your duties. You did everything I asked of you and more. No firm ever had a more dedicated, loyal employee. Your efforts were deeply appreciated. Oh, and Marty, try not to worry about dying. Nothing we do matters as long as our wealth ends up glorifying God and Israel. Our souls and our assets all go to the same place in the end. Nothing else matters. What you are doing is good and noble." David laughed while he delivered his mock compliments and honor.

Marty became delirious from blood loss, quickly succumbing to her hopeless situation and resigning herself to her fate. Then Marty stopped hearing David's laughter and instead heard the voices that guided her past behaviors.

"Do not bemoan your fate, Marty," said Miss Promiscuity. "Your spirit will join with ours and tempt many young girls to follow your example. They'll wear the Monarch tattoo as their badge of debauchery, as you did. They'll seduce many boys and husbands, and your beautiful spirit will guide millions of mortal souls."

"Yes," Miss Iniquity chimed in. "You'll dance and romp with us, your spirit sisters, in the thought realms of many femmes. We'll instruct them in temptation's ways. We'll nibble their nipples with our tickles of pleasure. We'll fill their titillated twats with consensual cocks and teasing tongues of the men they seduce. Together with us they'll feel the nirvanas of countless orgasms. Our egos will radiate in the glories of their seductions, and we'll revel in the havocs they unleash. You'll see human behaviors you never before thought possible. Lovers will betray their betrothed. Some will even murder their mates to free themselves to come and dance with us. You'll see! Death is just the beginning of your merriment. Your body was but one of many we succored with pleasure's nourishment. Our debauchery is ecumenical and eternal. Satan loves us, and all who wish to join us are welcome. He's in our DNA. We are his eternal spirits. Place your thoughts with us and our pleasures as your body dies. Come away with us and be loved by us."

Marty waved her hand as if to shoo her imaginary friends away, her mind spinning. *But I don't want that life anymore, even in death. I've lived it. I am wretched because of it, and I am possessed by lusts I want to control but cannot. Go away. Stay out of my mind now. Be gone, all of you.*

In advanced delirium, she mouthed incoherent thoughts as her brain struggled with its loss of blood. *Bob, know I love you with my whole heart. I hold you in my arms, my love. I know what love is now.*

Her mind short-circuited and wandered. *Where's my floppy-eared rabbit? I want to hug my bunny. How can I save fifteen percent or more on my car insurance? Life and death seem irrelevant to anything. Nothing matters anymore. Why does that black sheep stand upside down looking at me?*

The last thoughts Marty had as her weakened bloodstream pulsed her life onto the hay bales were of her and Bob, lying in their pup tent in Shenandoah Park and looking up at the stars. She prayed silently. *Somehow let me meet Bob again, and let me have a monogamous life with him. Forgive me, God, for all the marriages I've destroyed. I am sorry for everyone I've hurt.*

David, now thinking Marty dead, undid the duct tape from her mouth and freed her arms, only to tie them in front of her torso. He placed the hook of the block and tackle lift under the arm tie and lifted Marty's body for rendering. As if by some miracle, she was not yet dead. David placed his ear next to her mouth to hear the barely audible words she whispered with her dying breath.

"Bob, darling, I pray for your happiness as my soul goes away. I will love you forever after death and for eternity. Live, Bob! Live and love again. Go to Barbara. Find her and love her with all your heart because she loves you so much. I was wrong to take you from her. I could not help who I was. Forgive my body. My soul will find yours and we will be together again someday, I swear it. Good-bye, my love." Marty embraced monogamy in the moment of her death.

David stared vacantly at the barn wall while he pulled on the rope and lifted Marty's body. Each pull reminded him that no one had ever loved him, furthering his loathing of those who experienced the emotion. As Marty peacefully expired, a small white butterfly came and rested on her earlobe. It stayed for a while with its head poised over her ear canal, sharing its magical secret with Marty's still-conscious brain.

"Marty, do not despair. You will not die—not now, not ever. I am the voice of the Eternal Spirit, and I am here with the Spirit's message of comfort to help you pass through your moment of distress. As soon as your body on Earth dies, your spirit and all your loving goodness and sensuality will instantly reawaken in a new body in a new place in a new world. In your new life, you will have a mother and father who love and nurture you. You will have the identical appearance and will experience the same identical emotions that you now have in your present body, and in your new body and new world you will reunite with Bob. He will be with you. He will always hold you. He'll be forever in love with you, married with you, and you will have two beautiful children.

"Your new body and your new life will extend far longer than life on Earth. You will be sexually active for five thousand years in your new universe, and you will experience inter-universal travels and pleasures you cannot imagine. You will live the meaning of the word nirvana, and your sexuality will experience endless gratification from Bob. Your family will adore you. Your happiness will be their source of happiness as well. There is no sin in your new universe, no violence, nothing to covet, no reason to bear falsehoods, and a benevolent god to worship. You will be the loving goddess of goodness of your new planet. Your surroundings will be identical to Earth's because you will live in a parallel universe to Earth. In your new world, you will discover happiness beyond anything here. From your next universe, you will go on to countless other universes and you will never die. Come away with me now, Marty. Trust my message from the Spirit and trust in the magic of the butterflies. Be not afraid. Let go."

"I'm coming with you now. I am ready to leave Earth. I am unafraid. Oh, Bob, my dearest love, hold me close and never let me go." Marty mouthed her last words on earth as the little butterfly fluttered away.

After David disposed of Marty's corpse and he'd prayed for atonement of their sins, he donned one of his late mother's dresses, flat shoes, and a wig made to look like Marty's hair. He drove her car to a park-and-ride lot and from there rode a courtesy bus to the airport, carrying a garish accessory handbag. At the airport, he walked into the terminal and kept walking from the north-side to the south-side terminal doors where he exited. He took a cab to a gas station near his farm, where he walked into the ladies' room and walked out dressed as a man. The women's clothes and handbag were now stuffed into a large shopping bag from a sporting goods store. David walked home from the gas station, took the women's clothes and bag to the barnyard, and fed his dress, the large bag, and Marty's edible attire to his goats.

Walking to the house from the barnyard he was joined by Dolly, his favorite sheep.

"Today was busy, Dolly," he said to the animal. "We accomplished a lot, and we concluded the Marty episode. She did her job of distracting Bob from corporate finance deals. All his old contacts are stale now. Don't let today's events upset you. She was only a goy. Her mother is a goy so she was a goy. Dad made a mistake bringing her into the world. I only corrected his error.

"We need to stay true to our Khazarian heritage, Dolly. We disguised our goal and who we really are. We tricked the slut into working for us, just like Dad duped Susan, only we weren't stupid. Dad fell in love with a goyish girl. I didn't. Marty no longer had a purpose. Like all goyim, she was only here to serve us. It was time to throw the used-up goy girl away. We're selling nationally now, Dolly. We can't build a national firm on the back of a single whore. UGGA has very high ethical standards, and we needed to keep up our outstanding corporate image. Just don't tell Bob what you saw today. It's our secret."

Dolly stood there, chewing grass.

"We also need to keep our secret from the rabbis. If one of them comes into the barnyard, don't say anything to him. Our ritual flunked kosher. I didn't use a clean sharp knife, and I kind of sawed on her neck instead of doing a clean cut. That's why Marty struggled for a while before she died. I didn't use a healthy heifer either. No rabbi would approve of using a human being instead of an animal. The tribe doesn't do sacrifices anymore. I'm not a qualified kosher slaughterer either. I've never done a kosher killing. I've never even seen one or studied it. I'm not sure I did it correctly. Also, I don't think there's anything in the Torah where you're permitted to feed a sacrificed human to barnyard animals. In fact, I know we're not allowed to sacrifice people in the first place. This would really upset a rabbi, so mum's the word, okay?"

Dolly stood there, chewing her grass.

"What else could I do with her, Dolly? I figured since the business needed to get rid of her and since she and I were both sinners, it would be a neat idea to sacrifice her and bless her soul, even though I'm not a rabbi. I kind of killed two birds with one stone. I remembered to ask God for forgiveness for my sins and for screwing up the sacrifice by using a human being instead of an animal, so we might be forgiven for what we did. Hopefully we'll get lucky with God. I'll pray again next time on Yom Kippur to make doubly sure God isn't too upset with us. Hopefully God will understand I tried my best. Actually, what we did was probably some kind of first. We might have made history. Just promise that you will never breathe a word of this to a rabbi, Dolly. I don't think any of them would be happy about this, and that wouldn't be good."

Dolly stood there, chewing grass. David knelt beside the animal, put his arms around her neck, and began sobbing. He buried his face in her wool and smelled her musty scent.

"Don't look at me that way, Dolly. It had nothing to do with you. I'm not going to sacrifice you. I had to get rid of her. Don't be upset with me," David pleaded with the sheep for understanding. "Her mother would have nagged me to hire her back at the firm because of the deal we have, but I didn't want her anymore. I think she had a personality disorder, Dolly, and possibly some mental issues," he said as he touched the side of his head with his index finger. "People who work for UGGA need to be in tip-top mental health. Her mind was upside down, especially today. Ha-ha! Can't you see that's funny, Dolly? I made a joke. That completes the first part of my plan. Now it's time to move on. I did my best for her and always treated her first-class. I prayed for her future in the world of the spirits, I prayed to God for the forgiveness of her sins, and I thanked her for her service. I did for her what every good employer would do for a trusted and valuable employee."

David's chest heaved as tears rolled down his cheeks onto the ground. "I'm not a bad boy, Dolly, honest. I'm good. Sometimes I hurt people and it feels good, but afterward I know I did something wrong. But I can't help it. I love you, Dolly. You understand me." He kissed Dolly's forehead and stood up.

Dolly stood there, chewing grass.

"Please don't be upset, sweetheart. I only pretended to fuck her. She needed to think the whole experience was believable. You saw me use Muscle Boy in my stead. I didn't do anything with her. She meant nothing to me, honest. I never cared for her as I do for you. I apologize if the scene upset you."

Dolly stood silently, chewing her grass.

"Honestly, Dolly," David pleaded, "she was disgusting, not beautiful like you. I never would have entered her female part, honest. Listening to her talk about whoring made me certain I needed to be rid of her. Anyway, she had an upside-down view of the world." He chuckled. "I'm going into the house now. I know the wife isn't here, but I had a hard day and I'm tired. I'm going to watch a good fight and go to bed. You sleep with the other sheep tonight. I'll bring you into the house tomorrow."

He kissed the sheep's forehead a second time and went into the house.

PATS

Bob was at his desk when he heard the door handle move, its slow downward motion almost imperceptible. *That's David. He never knocks first like everyone else, but I guess that's his prerogative. He does own the place, after all.* But it was annoying that he dispensed with common courtesies. Bob rationalized David's behavior as that of a man looking in on his 'son,' but that didn't fully explain it.

Everyone noticed the creepy way David opened doors. They joked about it. He opened doors so softly he often went unnoticed by those on the other side. Bob's door opened a barely noticeable half inch. David peered inside and listened for a moment before he entered. This was a routine entrance for him. It was his silent pantomime act, but it lacked the dramatic theatrical music that gave audiences the creeps.

He missed his calling. He should have been a government spy. His eyes met one of David's looking through the slightly cracked door. *Yep, that's David all right.* Bob grinned. *Always sneaking around, looking in on people, listening.*

David quickly slipped into Bob's office in a movement resembling someone trying to escape a stakeout. Quickly and ever so quietly, David closed the door behind him. In his flair for the dramatic, he made every entrance appear to be a matter of extreme secrecy and urgency.

It had been a week since anyone at the firm had heard from Marty. Bob wasn't making as many sales calls as he normally would when he was in Plaintown, and he hadn't been on the road. He was baffled and hurt by Marty's behavior, but he still missed her terribly. He agonized over her and worried why he hadn't heard from her. His mind spun on a rat wheel.

Did I say something that offended her? No, he dismissed that. Marty was thick-skinned, a tough, fun-loving cookie. If something he said bothered her, she would have told him. *Was there foul play? But who could want to hurt her? Could someone from her past, a former lover or estranged wife intent on settling an old score, have harmed her?* That seemed too implausible. Yet the thought of foul play continued to dog him.

She'd taken time off before but never this long without calling anyone. Barbara and Susan noticed Bob's mood change. They were astute to changes in office morale. There were office whispers that Marty was in love with Bob. Staff members speculated that she got cold feet; she was too footloose to become a married woman and likely balked when things got serious. The other women couldn't see Marty as a motherly, stay-at-home type. She was too much like a free-spirited butterfly. She lived alone and valued her privacy. Living alone was essential when a woman needed to manage several affairs simultaneously. Speculation ran rampant; anything from Marty meeting up with an old flame, to being spirited away for a romantic vacation.

Just like that, Marty was gone. It made sense to the women who knew her the longest. No one filed a missing person report, which might've given Marty and the firm unwanted publicity, but no one really knew what to think. No one knew for certain any reason for her disappearance, and she hadn't given anyone a hint she was leaving. It was mysterious, even for her. David did his best to minimize the staff's concerns, chalking everything up to Marty's penchant for carousing. He sought to allay Bob's anxieties and replace them with jealousy.

"It's been a week since anyone has seen or heard from Marty. I just thought I'd ask if you could think of why she's not calling into the office or why she's staying away. Did you have a disagreement about something? Did she mention anything to you about running off for some reason?" David asked.

"I haven't heard. I have no idea why she hasn't called. I thought we'd hear from her by now," Bob replied. He was a bit despondent. Marty was always on his mind, and he couldn't compartmentalize his worries about her absence, which left a hole in his heart. His mind constantly returned to thoughts of Marty and the life they would have together. If he could cut off his arm to have her back, he'd gladly make the trade.

"Do you know who saw her last?"

"No. Barbara saw her about a week ago. Marty took some of her things home with her and told Barbara she'd be staying at home for a while. I don't know about anything after that. Shouldn't we call the police?" Bob's voice betrayed his anxiety.

"Well, I did think of that. I talked to Susan about it, and she thought we should give it a little more time, just in case Marty's off somewhere and wants to have privacy. Therefore, I haven't done anything. If her mother isn't too worried, I guess we should just wait and see if we hear from her."

"Why do you and Susan believe Marty wants privacy?"

"Well, you don't know her as well as we do, or for as long as we have. She's had some lovers in her past. She tends to attract men, and she has been known to go off with a man for a period of time. She has a history of being quite a romper, you know." David imparted, looking chagrinned.

Bob didn't like hearing about Marty's proclivity for love affairs, but he had to ask, "Just how long has she stayed away with a man in the past?"

"Hard to know for sure, what with holidays and long weekends. I'd guess maybe ten days or so would be on the long side of her absences. A week away isn't out of the norm."

"This is above my pay grade. I don't know what to think. You and Susan decide about calling the police. I'd like to know she's all right though. I hope you two don't sit on it for too long."

"Okay. Thanks for sharing your thoughts. Try not to worry about her. You know how it is with some women. Men just kind of come and go into them—into and out of their lives I meant to say, sorry. They get excited about a new man, but then he gets stale and they're off after a newer one. Some of them never know what they want. I guess that's why we call them cunts." David gave a little chuckle. "By the way, I noticed you've slowed down some. Is that because you miss having Marty around?"

"I think so. I'm very fond of her. She was a great help to me."

Both men were only telling half-truths. Bob wasn't about to tell David he intended to marry Marty, especially now that she might be off with another man somewhere. No man likes admitting his girl was whisked away by another man. There was also that thorny executive memo about office love affairs. He'd clearly violated the policy. David was not about to tell Bob he knew about their plans to marry, and he certainly wasn't going to mention he was a murderer.

"How about coming over to my place in the morning and meeting me at my barn? There are some things I'd like to talk over with you. I like being in the barn, away from everything. It's a quiet place to work."

Bob often met David at his home on the way into work when he was in Plaintown. They had a routine of meeting for an hour in the morning to discuss the markets and everything affecting securities' prices, from politics, to economic policies of the Federal Reserve, to cyclical pressures in various industries, new technologies, women's fashions, the weather, and anything else incidental to the markets.

As Bob pulled into the driveway the next day, he saw David in his barn dressed in overalls, boots splattered with animal dung, and a big straw hat. Bob wore a two-piece suit and wingtips. He joined David in the barn, who was perspiring heavily.

"Hello there. I'm moving some hay bales by the front door of the barn so I can just push them out with my feet and close the barn door on wet mornings. That way the animals can get to the hay and the inside of the barn doesn't get wet. On warm nights, I want to keep them outside. When it rains they can stay under the shed over there, but they'll need hay. I want the bales where I can just push them outside where they'll still stay dry under the roof overhang. Could you help me lift some bales and move them up near the big sliding door?"

Bob happily obliged and soon they were grunting in unison, lifting bales and moving them to the front barn door. After two bales, David stopped to look up toward the house while Bob went to the back of the barn to move a third bale. As he slid the hay bale away from a stable wall, he noticed a small patch of red hair sticking out, about six inches long. Stooping down to pick it up, he saw it was attached to a small patch of dried skin, about the size of a half dime.

Must have something to do with the animals, or possibly it's from a fox that got in here. It's curious. Maybe I'll hang onto it and put it in a framed picture of a fox.

Bob liked foxes, seeing them often in the forest meadows around Milltown. Distracted by his thoughts, he put the tuft of hair into his pocket and forgot about it. David returned to the back of the barn and the two partners lifted and grunted in unison as they moved four more bales close to the front barn door before taking a seat on the bales and looking out at the barnyard. The goats were off on their own playing on a mound of dirt, the sheep grazing on grass stubbles—except for Dolly, the black sheep. That one stayed close to the front door of the barn. Occasionally she'd looked up at the two of them as if to check if they were still there. The other sheep paid them no mind.

"There are a few things on my mind," David began. "First, there's Marty. I can tell from some of the expense reports that came in you two were spending a lot of time together when you were on the road, even on weekends—and you weren't selling on weekends. Now I don't judge people, but you are like a son to me and I just don't think you should get too moonstruck over a gal like that. Fact of the matter is Marty is a slut, and sluts have a hard time staying loyal to one man." David looked at Bob with widened eyes, as if giving a warning. "You weren't thinking about marrying her, were you?" He tested Bob for a reaction.

"Well, what if I were? Even if she had lovers in the past, people change. We developed pretty special feelings for each other. Besides, you encouraged it by sending her on the road with me. What did you expect? She's a brilliant mind, a widely educated woman, and she's so damn beautiful. It's hard to take my eyes off her." Bob was like a fish that swallowed a hook; Marty was still stuck in his gut and he couldn't shake free of his thoughts of her. He needed to bite off the line that tied him to her and swim away, but he just couldn't bring himself to do it. He still imagined a married life with her and a home with happy children.

David recognized his protégé was unable to free his mind of Marty. The younger man was vexed. Some intervention was needed to get sales back on track.

"I understand. These things happen. People fall in love. But Marty's problem, if you call it that, is that she falls in love with every man, married or not. She has a way about her that drives men crazy. Sometimes she has several men after her at the same time. I don't know how she does it. I mean, I don't know how she manages to keep them from knowing about each other, but she does it.

"Every now and then we've gotten calls from upset wives claiming Marty was stealing their husband. We just listen then tell the wives we've got nothing to do with what consenting adults do. We tell the wives to go back to sleep and after a while the husband will get tired of her. That's what we recommend to them. I'm telling you this because I'd like to see you forget about her. She's probably off on the other side of the planet in some exotic hotel with one of her boyfriends, and you can't afford to get mixed up over a whore."

"Stop it, okay? I don't want to talk about it anymore. Maybe I've made a mistake. Let's just leave it at that." Bob still loved what once was beautiful, but what was now remains of a corpse fertilizing the flowers and the barnyard grasses.

"I understand," said David. "Anyone can get romantic notions about a slut. It's natural. Don't worry about it. It will pass. I've always wondered why Marty never made a run at me. I guess I'm just too ugly, too old. I'm not young and handsome like you. Maybe she just figured an old guy like me couldn't keep it hard long enough to make it interesting for her.

"Tell me, were you able to keep it up long enough for her? Did it help you keep it that way knowing she fucked half the salesmen on Main Street, or did that make you want to hurry everything and wash off afterward?" he sneered, as if he'd smelled his shoe after he'd stepped in something one of the dogs left in the grass.

Bob recoiled at David's hurtful vulgarities, but he admitted to himself that he was hearing a valid point. How often since her disappearance had he looked at his phone to make a sales call and frozen? How often had his thoughts drifted to Marty? For long minutes at a time, he would sit and stare at the phone, imagining he was holding Marty's ass cheeks in his hands and licking her honey pot with his tongue. How many times did he picture her sitting on his lap and kissing him with her long soulful French kisses? He knew he needed to snap out of his paralysis of thought, but he was stuck. Marty held his mind in her hands and his heart in her arms.

"That's all I can take of this, David. Let's leave the subject. I'm sure we have more important things to talk about. What else is on your mind?"

Bob was the sort of man that clung to people after they were long out of his life. David correctly identified this trait as the source of Bob's determination. He was still seeing events as the long-ago little boy who desperately tried to hang on to his dead father. Now he wasn't willing to let go of Marty. David resolved that turning Bob's thoughts away from Marty was going to take time and effort.

David put his hand on Bob's back and patted him a few times. After all, what's a father to do when his son is distraught with thoughts that the love of his life is off somewhere in Europe or Asia fucking her brains out with another man? David tried to show Bob there was kindness in his heart, that he could be of great help to his friend and would-be son.

"Life is on my mind, Bob—your life. Life is about time. Time is the most precious thing God gives us while we're here this short while on Earth. I think about you quite a lot, Bob, about your future. I see you as uniquely blessed with a great opportunity to build a huge company and make a vast personal fortune. I have this vision that you will be tremendously successful if you'll keep some things in mind. What I'm about to tell you is extremely important. I want you to take my thoughts and words into your heart, bind them to your mind, and think of them when you go to sleep and when you wake up, for most men do not have the benefit of these thoughts. I give them to you because you are like a son to me, and because you are my best friend and because you are special."

"This is to help me forget Marty, right?"

"No, I can't make you forget her. She's a woman and you're a man. This is about the heart. No man can change another man's heart about a woman. But you will come to forget Marty in time. That's how the mind works. After what she's done, you now know you can't trust her. Besides, the Martys of this world are a dime a dozen. When you are on the road by yourself wholesaling the fund to brokers, you'll meet dozens like her. The world is full of fuck-crazy sluts who want to take a successful man into their bed. Your biggest challenge will not be forgetting Marty but avoiding entanglements with the women you'll meet on the road. Your best defense there is to keep moving from city to city, never staying in the same place too long. No, these thoughts are about you becoming a complete man, a man with a great purpose.

"Most men go through life aimlessly and clueless because they have no purpose. Many take their guidance from their wives who simply want a monthly paycheck. Those men are worse than clueless. The Orientals call such men 'salary men.' I call them stupid. You are not like other men. You have talent beyond measure, and you will have the benefit of my wisdom and guidance. You will be a mensch among men, a leader. You will be the tip of the spear for the firm, our kidon. Your presence and your words will lead other, lesser men to follow you and do as you tell them."

"That's cool, David. Say, tell me something. Why does that black sheep follow you around like she does? I notice the other ones kind of stay off by themselves, but the black sheep stays close to you."

"I don't know why she does that. She's been like that since I got her as a little lamb. I brought her home on a cold snowy night and kept her in the house for a couple weeks until she was strong enough to be outside. She's kind of taken to me, I guess. I call her Dolly. I guess she thinks she's special.

"But getting back to the subject, Bob, what I think we need to do is have a period of time where I give you lessons on how to think like a man. You've never had the benefit of that, and you need that to become successful in this world. What I propose is that, when you're in town and before you go into the office, you swing by the barnyard here in the mornings. I'm usually out here with the animals and it's a good time for me. In the morning, my mind is clear. I feel relaxed and do my best thinking then, here in the barnyard. What do you say? Would you be up for some executive coaching?" David gave Bob a fatherly sort of look, which showed he had Bob's best interest at heart.

"Sure, I'm all for that. I look forward to it."

"That's very good. I think it's healthy for a person to take their mind off matters of romance for a little while and learn something about the world around them. Otherwise, you go through life running on emotions and not understanding how the world works. These executive lessons won't take too much of your time. When we're finished, you can get back to thinking about romance again. Maybe you'll even send some smoke signals to Barbara, the Indian girl. I can see you two have eyes for each other. She's quite a beauty. I can't understand why Marty would go absent without leave and give that squaw an opportunity to get together with you" David said as he gave Bob a couple pats on the back.

EXECUTIVE LESSONS

So began an intensive period of executive mentoring sessions whereby David sought to groom Bob for the responsibilities of UGGA executive management. David claimed the key to being a successful executive was to understand the proper way to view the world and the actors who played their respective roles in the grand mosaic of life. By topic are the messages of wisdom imparted by David.

Time, the First Lesson

"Time is God's greatest gift to you. You need to make the most of the precious little time you have on Earth. When Adam made his huge mistake of listening to Eve in the Garden of Eden, God punished him by commanding Adam to atone for eating that apple by working his ass off for the rest of his life. That's the world's first mitzvah, the very first order God gave to man, so it must be important.

"Anyway, you need to be working every day, except God gives you a day off every week. That's called Shabbat, or Sabbath. You get a break. You're supposed to go to shul, if you're a Jew like me, or I guess the rest of you are supposed to go to church or do whatever you do when you get a day off. But taking a day off or honoring Shabbat puts you in conflict with the first mitzvah. You're not supposed to get time off, so even God tries to fuck up your mind and waste your time. You must always be on guard against wasting time. Now I know for a fact that a lot of guys skip out on shul to go to football games or just to lie around and watch TV. I'm not sure if God takes you to the woodshed for not going to shul, but he might. You've got to watch out for God. If you don't listen to him, he can fuck with you. Anyway, the first mitzvah is about time management, and I've got some great thoughts about it.

"Look, God lets some guys get away with watching football games and just goofing off on Shabbat. They don't pray all day and God doesn't kill them for being slackers, so it must be okay with him if you kind of get the jump on these slouches by actually working on the Sabbath. That way, you're honoring the very first mitzvah and you can get ahead of guys who take the day off. Now, this kind of contradicts the mitzvah that you're supposed to go to shul on the Sabbath, but there's also a way to get around that. See, on Yom Kippur, we Jews get to atone for all our screwups for the year. There's a period in the service right near the end of the High Holy Days where the rabbi yells, 'The gates are closing!' That means you have a limited amount of time to get to the shul and pray for God to forgive you for all your screwups all year long! It's kind of like the two-minute warning in football.

"So what I always do is time it to the exact minute. At the last five minutes of the service, I barrel into the shul parking lot in my Cadillac and come to a screeching stop right in front. Usually there's a guard there, so I jump out of the car, put on my yarmulke—that's Jewish for skullcap—and then I scream at the guard, telling him I have a life-or-death emergency. I hand him the car keys and run into the shul just in time to see the rabbi closing the curtain on the holy of holies. I bow my head in prayer and scream out, 'Forgive me, God!' I act like I'm really sorry in case God is watching me.

"Then the gates close. I've atoned and I'm forgiven, see. I'm good for another year. The big plus about doing it this way is I don't have to waste a lot of time listening to the service, time I can use wisely by studying stocks. And there's a second big plus. The guard keeps my car right there in front of the shul, so since I'm also the first guy out, I just jump right into my car and take off. Then I go to the delicatessen where all the other Jews go and break the fast with them by ordering a double-sized pastrami sandwich.

"The point I'm making is you've got very little time on Earth to make money, so if you can find little ways to cut corners to give yourself more time, then cut those corners. Another example is taking a shower. You can save a good fifteen minutes every other day by just throwing on some deodorant instead of taking a shower. Just think about it! Fifteen minutes a day times one hundred and eighty-two working days works out to having an extra 3.79 days a year to do something important, like calling salesmen and telling them to sell the UGGA fund! Over ten years, that's an extra thirty-eight days! Just think of the edge you'd have on other guys you compete with if you had an extra thirty-eight days of sales every ten years!

"Even when you go to the grocery store you should think about making every second count. Take those plastic bags they put on those little stands around the store. They expect you to waste your time every time you pick something up, like a bunch of carrots or a head of lettuce. They want you to get the carrots, and then walk around looking for the bag rack. Then you're expected to take one bag and put the carrots in the bag. Then you walk to the lettuce, pick out a bunch, and then walk back to the bag rack for a bag to put the lettuce in. Don't waste your time. Just take the roll of bags off the bag rack and carry it with you in your cart. When you go to check out and there's a line in front of you, don't waste your time. Just go to the service desk, hand them what the groceries are worth and walk out with your groceries.

"You can apply this same relentless scrutiny to all sorts of things that waste valuable time. For instance, do you really need to shave every day? Do you wear shoes that lace up or loafers you can just slip into? How about going to restaurants instead of grabbing a sandwich?

"Examine your driving habits. If you consistently drive ten miles per hour above the speed limit, chances are no cop will bother you, unless you're in a school or church zone, because the cop makes more money nailing the guy who's going twenty miles an hour over the speed limit. So when you just kind of zip along peppy on the gas pedal instead of driving like a slow-motion barge, you rack up saved minutes.

"Stop signals and red lights are the same way. You come to a red light, you slow up a little, and you look up and down the cross street. You see there's no cop and you can beat it across the intersection before an oncoming car can hit you, so you go for it. You just saved probably a full minute or two. Beating five red lights every day gains you five minutes a day. Three hundred days of driving a year and you've just saved twenty-five hours that you could use making sales calls! See what I'm driving at?

"Driving in stop-and-go traffic is another time waster. There wouldn't be stop-and-go, bumper-to-bumper traffic if there were no communists in the first place because they make all these rules about driving carefully and stopping when you have an accident and exchanging insurance cards and licenses and registrations. If there weren't so many communist obstacles to getting around expeditiously, people with big tough cars and trucks could just push these idiots in their tiny little tinny cars right off the road. If those tin car douche bags knew the big cars and trucks could just shove them off the road, they'd drive a lot faster so they wouldn't get hit in the first place. Then traffic would flow smoothly.

"Unfortunately, the commies have taken over the country, so you need to do the next best thing on your own. You need to buy an old Cadillac, one of those iron battlefield tanks they used to make in the 60's or 70's, or an old Ford pickup truck. Those old Caddies and those old Ford trucks last forever, and you can get parts for them. But the reason you need to have one is they scare the living shit out of other drivers when they see you driving anywhere near them. They can tell from looking at your car that you won't give a second thought to ramming them if they get in your way or if they won't let you cut in line. I have one, as you know. I even took a sledgehammer to the rear passenger doors to bang them in so it looks like I just don't give a shit about having accidents with it. It scares the crap out of people just to look at my car.

"Here's another thought on stop-and-go driving. Sometimes on a freeway there's a shoulder lane. You're supposed to stay off it unless there's an emergency. Well, an emergency is how *you* define it. Squandering God's greatest gift, the gift of time, creates all kinds of emergencies. Suppose somebody is late to work because of traffic. Then maybe something doesn't get built on time and somebody ends up dead or injured, or maybe somebody can't get to a doctor's appointment on time and the doctor gets upset and goes off and plays golf, and then cancer doesn't get diagnosed on time. Do you see what I mean? These communists have fucked up the entire world, but you can't let them get away with wasting your time. The way to beat freeway traffic is to either use the shoulder you're not supposed to use, or turn on your headlights and blow your horn while you bang into the back bumper of the car in front of you. Wave your hand wildly and scream while you do this. Other drivers will get out of your way and you'll eliminate a lot of wasted time.

"When you drive and someone cuts in front of you, just speed up and pass him so you get back in first place. Always see your time as more valuable than the other guy's. Once there was this redneck in a brand new pickup truck; it was one of those Dodge Rams. Well, he passed me, so I passed him. Then he made a huge mistake. He tried to pass me again, so I rammed the side of his Ram with my Caddie. Well, he starts flashing his emergency lights and waves me to pull over, which I did. He pulls up in front of me, kind of half on the shoulder of the road and half in the driving lane. I sit in the car and wait. He gets out of his truck and starts walking back to me, carrying a baseball bat. Well, I can see he thinks he's going to smash my windshield in, and maybe my head too, so I just sit and wait until he gets real close. Then I gunned the car and drove straight at him, like I was going to run him over. You should have seen him dive all the way over to the side of the road. I blew the horn as I drove by him. He was screaming and swearing, but I just drove off. You just can't let people waste your time and get away with it.

"There's one other thing about driving that's important. Every once in a while, a cop will follow you and flash his lights for you to pull over. You know you're about to get a ticket, right? Well, there's a way around getting a ticket. First, you need to prepare in advance. Buy about ten or fifteen candy bars, and take the wrapper off one of them and leave it on the front seat next to the wrapped ones at all times. Got that? Okay, I see you are nodding your head yes.

"Now, once you know the cop is behind you, slow down. Drive very slowly, almost imperceptible slowly, and slightly weave the car back and forth on the road, like you've got control of the car, but it's actually kind of hard for you to stay in control. Got it? Okay. Then, you look for something to run into as the car slows down, like a tree or a telephone pole, or somebody's parked car. Just don't ram the car into any people.

"You need to go slowly as you do this, so you don't hurt yourself too much. Ram into something, or if you can't pull over because you're on a freeway, just kind of gradually scrape your car against another guy's car. Then, when your car stops, just fall over on your passenger seat and rub the candy bar on your face around your lips and make a mess. Hershey's chocolate bars are great for this.

"When the cop comes to the window, just lay on the seat like you are passed out. The cop will open the door and shake you. You act groggy, like you passed out. Then you mumble 'sugar' just repeat that one word a couple times, and very feebly point to a candy bar. Now, the cop will think you have diabetes and he'll panic. He'll shove a candy bar into your mouth. You eat some of it, and then you slowly act like you're coming back to life. You thank the cop for being such a savior. Tell him you think he might have saved your life. Cops like hearing that. "Tell him you're sorry for the inconvenience, that you noticed there's something wrong if you don't get sugar every once in a while. You've meant to see a doctor about it, but you haven't had time to get in to see one, you've been working so hard to make money to pay your back taxes to the city that employs the cop. You're trying to be a good citizen so the cop can get paid so he can feed his wife and kids.

"Soon, you'll have the cop feeling so sorry for you he'll be crying right along with you. Then, offer him one of your candy bars in case his sugar ever gets too low. By then, he'll be glad to let you drive off without a ticket. I've done this routine twice and it's worked both times.

"A great way to reduce wasted time is cutting in line when two lanes of traffic are trying to merge into one lane. The commie time wasters will always be happy to sit in the longest, slowest-moving lane, so the correct move is to pull out of the slow lane, get into the fast lane or pull onto the shoulder, and race ahead of all the slowpokes. Here's where having an old Cadillac tank-type car is a huge advantage. Most drivers will let you get back into line when you've reached the front because they're afraid you'll smash into their new plastic car if they mess with you.

"One objection to having an old clunker is that they use a lot of gas, but they really don't. The gas other people waste by sitting in line in their new mileage-efficient cars waiting to go nowhere is actually a cost for them and a time-saving opportunity for you. You just roar right up to the front of traffic lines and jam yourself right in there. Sure, some people will blow their horns at you, but they're just jealous because they didn't have the chutzpah to do it themselves. A lot of them just blow their horns and scream to impress their wives anyway, so just ignore them. Always carry a ten-foot piece of surgical hose, a hammer, and screwdriver in your car. If you forget to stop at a gas station and run out of gas, you can always stop next to one of those little plastic cars, punch a hole in its gas tank, and siphon off some gas into your car. If you get good at this, you can avoid gas stations entirely and save even more time."

Bob looked at him askance. "It sounds like you make a lot of friends driving like you do."

"I don't care about friends. I don't have any, I don't need any, and I don't want to make any. Friends slow you down. They have ideas about things and their ideas are never as good as mine. That reminds me about avoiding slowing down while you are driving, like when you come to an intersection and there's red lights stopping you, and you are back behind the first car at the red light. Well, say you're going to be turning right, or left for that matter, onto the cross street. Now you've got a choice. You can sit there like a schmuck or you can take the bull by the horns. If there's no building on the corner, just grass or small shrubs, you don't have to sit there and suffer through this intolerable communist waiting around bullshit. You just turn the car's wheels into the curb and gun the motor. That jumps the car up over the curb and you can cut across the corner and get where you're trying to go while all the schmucks just sit there waiting for the light to turn green. It's the Occam's Razor principle."

"I always thought Occam's was about using the fewest assumptions to solve a problem, getting the most likely answer that way."

"Well, you'd be wrong about that, or Occam was wrong. It doesn't matter. The whole point of Occam's Razor was to solve the problem. Just get her done, see? My way gets it done."

"Okay."

"Getting stuck in a long line of cars because some repair crews are working on the road and they've closed down traffic to one lane is another situation you need to know how to manage. Most people just sit there patiently and wait for the line to move along at a snail's pace, but that's a huge time-wasting mistake. The proper thing to do is make a hard right turn onto a neighborhood street. Then race as fast as you can down the side street, make a left turn at the first cross street, and race through the neighborhood for about ten or twenty blocks. Turn left again and race back onto the road ahead of all the suckers who waited in line. You save all kinds of time by using this tactic."

"But in neighborhoods there could be little kids playing in the streets. Shouldn't you drive cautiously?"

"Hell no! Never slow down just because it's a residential neighborhood. If some little kid is in the street, that's just the democrats teaching that kid to be irresponsible. Those kids have democrat communist parents who haven't taught them to respect the rights of drivers to rule the streets. Now I'm not telling you to run over the kid. That could get you into trouble. It might even be expensive. There's a simpler way. When the kid is out in the street, you just drive around him. Just bounce the curb and drive through the kid's front yard, see. You don't even slow down. The kid won't even notice anything is happening. You might tear out some bushes and flowers and you might put tire tracks through the yard, but that's unimportant. The important thing is to save time. The key to doing this move successfully is to take the curb one wheel at a time so you don't knock the front end out of alignment."

"That's quite a lesson. I never would have thought of it."

"You're learning very valuable things. You'll appreciate it more after you've practiced these tactics yourself. Here's another one you should employ to keep ahead of communist time wasters: intimidation. You should keep this in your repertoire. We've been discussing them for a while now, so I want to make sure you're getting the concept, so answer me this. When you see a bunch of people running a marathon to raise money for breast cancer, crippled kids, multiple sclerosis, or to commemorate some kind of historic event, like the Boston Marathon, what do most people see?"

"Well, everybody sees a worthy cause and public participation, a community bonding sort of thing."

"Exactly right," exclaimed David, "but that's not what's really going on with these things. They're really communist community organizers who are trying to fuck up everybody's minds and lull them into la-la land. Their real goal is to disrupt normal business commerce, snarl traffic, and keep people from thinking about making money so they'll become more dependent on the state and therefore vote socialist because socialists are just about legitimizing the theft of stuff from hard workers and giving free stuff to lazy bastards. It's just glorified bullshit and it's not what God wants to go on here. It's about justifying, in the minds of the people, the notion that it's okay to be lazy and dependent upon others, and that's plain wrong."

The glance Bob gave David was full of skepticism. "But these things are done on weekends when people aren't working anyway. How do you square that with your thinking?"

"Very simply, people are told in Torah that they are supposed to work for six days, possibly seven, a week, not just five.

God worked for six days. Who in the hell do these people think they are, anyway? Do they think they get a bigger break than God? God worked his ass off for six days, and then he rested. He didn't run any stupid marathons. So you see, it's really about justifying idle foolishness, which is all communism is anyway. So now that we understand what we're up against, I'll tell you how I deal with it. You can beat these bastards if you put your mind to it.

"In the trunk of my car, I keep two red flags on little flagpoles, and I also keep one of those flashing red lights you can plug into the car's cigarette lighter. On the floor of the passenger side front seat I keep a bullhorn. Now when I'm trying to get somewhere, even if it's not for business, and I see one of these marathon runs or some stupid parade, anything like that that's designed by these fucking communists to get in my way and slow me down, I just take them head-on.

"I get the flags out of my trunk and put them in the holders I have mounted on the inside roof headliner of the car. The mounts are just inside the rear windows, so the flags stick out of the car and make it twice as wide as it actually is. Then I plug the red flashing light into the cigarette lighter and stick it on the roof of the car. Last, but very important, is my bullhorn. Now I'm ready to take on these communist bastards. I flip on the flashing red light, flip on the car's emergency flashers, and start driving straight at them while blowing the car's horn.

"When I'm right on top of them, I roll the driver's side window down and yell at them with the bull horn. 'Clear the road! Clear the road now! This is a civil emergency! Your lives are in danger! Get off the streets! Go home now! Lock your doors and close your windows to avoid radioactive fallout! Take shelter in your basements! Cover your children with lead shielding and put up ten gallons of fresh water! Run! Run now! Run for your lives! Ahhh, they're coming!'

"I have all of this written on a little three-by-five card I keep in the glove box, so when I come up against communist craziness, I'm prepared for them and I know just what to say. I have another variation of my 'get off the road now' program based upon an imminent meteor impact. I tell them to get into their cars and drive out of the city as fast as possible. Come to think of it, I should get one made up for a tornado strike too. Anyway, can you see what I'm talking about? Your time is worth more than their efforts to waste your time."

"What happens when you do this? Does anybody get hurt?"

"Nah, it's just a lot of fun to see them scramble to get away. I never actually run into anybody. They're like cockroaches in the kitchen when you flip on the lights. After they run for it, I just pull off to a side street, take down the flags and the flashing light, and keep going where I was trying to go in the first place. Sometimes cops will show up, but everybody is so hysterical and incoherent the cops just scratch their heads and go off somewhere to get a donut. Anyway, if the cops ever stop me, I've got that covered too. I'll just tell them I heard there was a big disaster on a shortwave radio that I somehow picked up on my car radio by a freak radio transmission. That should work.

"The way I see it, I'm keeping God's law, except for driving on the Sabbath when I do this on a Saturday. For the gentiles, Sunday is the Sabbath, so I don't have any Torah rule violations when I run at them on a Sunday. So I'm good with God on this program. Well, if a cop stops me on a Sunday, I just tell him these people were attacking my religion, which tells me I've got to work on Sundays, and they were intentionally blocking the way. I have the right to use the road on my Jewish workday.

"The only time a cop stopped me because of this he just threw up his hands and drove away, so I'm sure what I'm telling you to do is okay with the police, the Highway Patrol, FBI, CIA, NSA, the Homeland Security manuals, U.S. Army intelligence manuals, the Outer Space NASA Planetary Discovery Regulations Manual, the French Foreign Legion Marching Orders, the South Pole Penguin Regulations, and the Universal Dog Catchers' and Cat Neutering Manuals. So you see, there're all kinds of rules and obstacles people will come up with that are designed to waste your time, but if you think straight about these things, there's always an exception. Your job is to think of the exceptions. Just remember to always think outside the box. Your time was given to you by God, and the communist bastards have no right to waste it. Keep on thinking like I do and you'll go far in this life."

With the conclusion of the lesson, David gave Bob a pat on the back. Bob departed for the office with the understanding the two would meet up for drinks later in the day.

Money, the Second Lesson

"Money is the second greatest gift that God gave you after time, which is a terrific gift if you don't waste it. Without time you wouldn't have been born because being born took time. And you also wouldn't need to know anything because you wouldn't have time to learn anything in the first place. So now you need to learn about money, which is the next most important thing after time, about which you now know everything. Now before you can know what money is, you first have to know what money isn't. When somebody gets a paycheck, does that mean he's made money? No, it doesn't. He hasn't made any money at all. When you go to the store and pay for something with a check or a credit card, are you paying with money? No, you aren't. There was no money exchanged in either transaction, no money at all."

Bob cocked his head and looked at David as if he had an extra head. "Well, are all these people who work for a paycheck or who buy stuff with a check or credit card just nuts?" he asked.

"Well, yes, they are nuts. As a matter of fact, the entire world is nuts. I'm the only person in the world who has a sane mind when it comes to money. Dad explained this to me very thoroughly, and since he's died I've done a lot more thinking about money and have refined my thinking about it. Now I've got it completely understood like no one else in the world. So when you understand what I'm about to tell you about money, you'll have a huge advantage over everybody else in the world too.

"I already told you what a no-good slimy son of a bitch Woodrow Wilson was, so we don't need to go over the creation of the Federal Reserve and income tax and how mistaken those two abominations were. Since the creation of the Fed and income tax over a hundred years ago, no single politician, president, senate, or congress has put forth legislation to repeal those betrayals of the peoples' trust, with one exception. Every congress and every president from Wilson to the present turned their back on the people of the United States of America. When people figure out how badly they're screwed, they will scream for change."

David was excited and spitting out his words as he continued.

"According to section eight of Article One of the Constitution, the article that defines the powers of the legislature, it's congress that has the powers to coin money and regulate the value of the coins. President Jefferson warned that it was dangerous to have a private bank in charge of the nation's money. He gave that warning thirty years after he wrote the Declaration of Independence. Think about that. A key founding father of the country, after only two previous presidents, worried enough to warn the people about losing control over their money. The control over money was in the peoples' hands, not a privately owned bank's as we have now. No congressperson except one since Wilson, coalition of states, or president has introduced a law or Constitutional amendment to overturn the Federal Reserve Act, nor has any state of the United States been able to overturn that wrongheaded legislation through the federal courts. We're stuck with a privately owned bank, The Federal Reserve Bank of the United States, exactly what Thomas Jefferson warned against. It controls our currency using laws that make us use printed paper fiat as if it were real money, which it isn't.

"Why and how did this happen that, in the time from September to December 1913, the American people got screwed out of having power over their own money? Dad explained that there were concerns at the time about bank runs and failures highlighted by the collapse of the Knickerbockers' Trust Company in the year 1907. The house banking and currency committee wanted to create a centralized system of banking so reserves could be marshaled to give credit to troubled banks so as not to have runs where depositors panic and take their money out and collapse the banks. That's what used to happen when banks made bad loans. Now they make the dumbest loans ever and citizen taxpayers must pony up their wealth in higher taxes and higher prices to paper over bankers' messes. The dollar was gold-backed then, as were treasury bonds. That had to change, so the bankers' sales job went to allow for a 'flexible' currency. And the currency had to be managed by smart dudes behind curtains who could spot trouble and prop up troubled banks, kind of like the Wizard of Oz behind the curtain makes everything wonderful in the Emerald City.

"It was a charade, a contrived takeover of America's banking system by J. P. Morgan, part of a long-term plan to steal gold and silver from the American people and move it into the hands of the wealthiest families of the world. Dad said Knickerbockers' failure was a manufactured crisis because their clearing firm, National Commerce Bank, failed to clear Knickerbockers' securities transactions during a market drop. But it happened for no good reason, as the National had over sixty million dollars of deposits at the time. It had plenty of market muscle to absorb Knickerbockers' trades, but Morgan saw a chance to eliminate competitors by declaring Knicker-bockers' insolvent. Bank runs of the time ruined many Morgan competitors and Morgan, with government help, propped up the financial system and restored confidence in the surviving banks, especially the Morgan bank. He got the government's goodwill and the inside track on bank legislation.

"Morgan, along with a group of wealthy private families, including the Red Shield Rothschild group, the Rockefellers, the House of Windsor, and the wealthiest families of Italy and France, successfully bought off the peoples' representatives in the house banking and currency committee to pass the Federal Reserve Bill out of a committee to a voice vote the night before Christmas recess. Few congressmen were even there, and most had been drinking. But they passed the legislation to find out what was in it. Dad believed these committee members got big payoffs for screwing the American people. They took away the peoples' power over money in exchange for payoffs, and in violation of the Constitution. The people didn't fight that legislation. They didn't get to read it ahead of time. Why not? When the government intends to steal from the people, they always lie about it and never publish the proposed legislation in advance. People tend to be ill-informed and disinterested. When people insist on being stupid, somebody will always steal from them.

"Louis McFadden, congressman and chair of the house banking committee, tried hard to derail the Federal Reserve. He blamed it for causing the Great Depression in order to consolidate its powers. He blamed the Fed for financing the communist Bolshevik Revolution. Dad swore that McFadden was a great champion of the American people. John F. Kennedy was a champion also, by his pocket veto of the Coinage Act of 1963, but unfortunately that pocket veto resulted in Kennedy's death. True champions can't be timid. A true champion must stand up and fight evil head-on. Dad regarded McFadden and Kennedy as champions.

"Dad liked jazz and rhythm and blues. He loved the song 'Louis, Louis' by Richard Berry. Most people think the song is about a lovesick sailor at sea, pining to get into the pants of his girl on the beach. Dad didn't think so. He thought Berry understood the scam that was pulled on the American people with the Federal Reserve Act and was expressing Louis McFadden's frustration at not being able to overturn that wrongheaded law. Berry was a genius. His song tells people to go back to how things were, back to the honest money Kennedy wanted before they murdered him.

"When Kennedy was murdered, who benefitted the most? Johnson became president, bankers controlled the people with fiat money, the military industrial complex got lots of freshly printed fiat money to fight the Vietnam War, and the socialists got money for Great Society programs. The war and the social programs were a gigantic waste of resources and a huge bust. Berry called it before it happened, according to Dad. Berry's song worried the bankers, and they got the FBI to investigate. Dad said that was a ruse. The FBI just wanted to portray the song as an assault upon the morals of our youths. It was a J. Edgar Hoover obsession, or so that was the flap over the song at the time, but that wasn't it at all.

"The FBI has never given a damn about morals. With the slimy, filthy, cock-sucking blackmailer J. Edgar Hoover in charge of the FBI you'd have to be a lunatic to buy into that morality bullshit, but the FBI did its best to protect the bankers who control congress and the President. The powers that ran the country then didn't want the public to understand the meaning of the song. The public still doesn't understand the meaning of the song. The public doesn't understand anything.

"Politicians who try to be champions of the people can't get anywhere in a banker-controlled country. They can't get anywhere because the American people are too stupid to get behind honest leadership for their own good. People would rather watch reality shows like *Dancing with the Stars*, or the NFL, anything that doesn't make them think. Americans aren't going to know what money isn't until the day they no longer have a country. They are that stupid. They are lazy idiots being eaten alive from the inside out. They have a vampire squid's beak sucking the life out of them, stealing their wealth and making them into debt slaves.

"Dad thought the Fed was put together by the top bankers to suck out wealth over generations. They permanently installed their families in the top one-tenth of one percent of wealth in the world and screwed everyone else. In effect, there's a leech sucking the wealth blood from the American people, and by world fiat central banking with international currency reserve holdings and swap lines, the world's people.

"I've now explained what money isn't. If Americans don't soon get it that they don't have any real money, the Russians will drop nuclear bombs on our cities and the Chinese will invade and kill us all. Then the whole country will be populated with Chinese and Russians, and our country's daughters will all become sex slaves to the Arabs and the Chinese because those people know what money really is. Am I making myself clear? If there's something you don't understand, just ask."

"Well, sort of. You're sounding a bit extreme. Tell me again what real money isn't."

"Real money isn't paper. It's not a credit card balance. It's not numbers in a checking account. It's not what the government wants you to think it is. The dollar is not real money. It's a piece of the country's debt. It's a fraction of the debt the country owes. The dollar is not redeemable in gold or silver. It represents a tiny part of the bad loan assets the Federal Reserve carries on its balance sheet. Your non-money paper dollar is your fractional ownership of some sub-prime auto loans, sub-prime mortgages, government debt, and any other crap paper the banks unload on Mother Fed when the banks can't meet their regulatory requirements for loan performance against their highly leveraged tiny base of bank shareholder equity. It's not rocket science.

"A dollar is a debt chit in a giant worldwide pyramid debt scheme. The dollar, the euro, the yen, the Swiss franc, the Canadian dollar, the Hong Kong dollar, the Aussie, the kiwi, the yuan, and all the rest of them are all debt chits in a worldwide 'fuck the little guy' debt scheme. Honesty and morality are on one side of a seesaw board and fiat money is on the other side. When fiat goes into ascendance, morality and honesty descend. Honesty and fiat money are opposites.

"Okay. Well, then, what *is* money?" Bob asked sincerely.

"Money is gold and silver and nothing else."

"What about platinum, oil, diamonds?"

"Just gold and silver," David replied with force.

"How do you get there?"

"Simple. Since the dawn of man, gold represented the god of the sun, the god of daylight, the greater god, whereas silver represented the goddess of the moon, the goddess of night, the lesser god. Those concepts of worshiping gold and silver by relating them to celestial deities is ingrained in the innermost consciousness and sub-consciousness of mankind all over the world. Central banks use gold, the greater god, as their base plate bedrock asset to give them credibility with other central banks. Upon that gold they can have their member banks engaging in lending activities using paper chits and pretending there is gold behind the paper for domestic money use, which isn't true. Silver is the people's money, the lesser money for all us mud slops who are not central bankers. Silver is the metal people turn to when they realize the central bankers are screwing them by foisting a 'paper is money, wink-wink, nudge-nudge' scheme upon them.

"There's an old saying, probably started with the German Yids. It says, 'You can fool some of the people all of the time.' That would apply to today's Americans, for they truly are a crowd of dummies. The next part of the saying goes like this: 'You can fool all of the people some of the time.' Today, that applies to the world at large because all the world's peoples are using paper money presently. The last part says 'But you can't fool all of the people all of the time.' That's where we're going next."

"You mean what the people will do when they realize they've been had?"

"Exactly right. The day is fast approaching when people will see what money isn't. They will see the elites as modern imperialists, only modern elites don't use an occupying army like the Brits did in India and America, or the French in Indo-China and Africa, or the Spaniards in Central and South America, or the Portuguese in Gao and Brazil. Modern elites use fiat money to enslave people by getting them into debt, owing currency back with interest, and then undermining the debtors' ability to repay by setting up competition for the project the debtors borrowed against. The NAFTA Treaty and Trans-Pacific Trade Partnership are cheap competition American workers cannot beat. Debtors see a decline in price realized for product or service sold, and debts carried by debtors become impossible to repay. Debtors borrow more to stay afloat. The political class sells their constituents up the river as debt slaves for money obtained from the bankers. It's a scheme to keep labor working cheaply for capital.

"Debtors are trapped, like coal miners in remote towns in the 1800's and 1900's. They worked their butts off, had no transportation, little free time, and they were always exhausted and sick, so they shopped at the company store. They kept getting deeper in debt and couldn't get out. There's even a song written about that called 'Sixteen Tons.' People will figure out that the currency they borrow from banks to live, to buy houses and cars, and to go to college with is simply modern-day imperialism. They are trapped in their debts, like impoverished coal miners.

"They are like the cockroach that goes into a roach motel. The roach feels great going in. It eats the poison and can't get out. It dies. Debt is like that. It feels good borrowing money, but then the interest you must pay is like poison and you can't get out of debt. Financially speaking, you die. The people who buy the debt, the high-yield products, can't get out either. Police, firemen, teachers, and other public employees are all trapped in its grip because their pension plans own a lot of it and the debts will be worthless when the system revalues currency and debt, when the system returns to real money. Everybody bought this shit from the insects, high yield, guaranteed, blah, blah, and blah. It sounds great until the debtor can't pay. It's like an eight-lane freeway running into this shit and a goat trail trying to get out."

"David, who are you calling the insects?"

"The financial planners who sell packaged products to dummies. They prey on the unsuspecting, like lice, ticks, and mosquitoes, all sucking blood, the money, from people who don't realize it's happening. The people are so dummied down by the financial media into believing that the Federal Reserve and the banks will always have some kind of safety net for them or control of the markets, they might as well be dead corpses getting eaten by bugs. Americans have been duped by the media, academic monetary theorists, underwriters who package products, and the insects who sell products. The public believes if they do what the insect says they will retire, but that's all bullshit.

"The scam depends upon keeping markets levitated using foreign currency carry trade, like the yen dollar swap. Banks borrow in yen, use the money to prop up the market with high-frequency trades and derivatives, short down the yen for a cheap payback, puff the markets, sell product, and get fees. It's a scam. Take an ounce of sugar, spin it into cotton candy. It looks big and wonderful until the kid takes a bite out of it. Then it's small, real, and sticky messy. Buyers won't get out, just like cotton candy. It only works in the imagination, not when someone takes a bite and wants their money back."

"And the debt load? How is that a scam?"

"This debt pyramid is a giant Ponzi scam. If the people aren't taking on enough debt, or if they try to pay down their debts, the bankers force the country into a war and have the entire country go deeper into debt. The only way out is to throw off the yoke of debt."

"How?"

"People see that the markets aren't working right. The bond and stock markets are artificially propped up with derivatives. Those are options, futures, and things like that, where a little money controls lots of assets. Derivatives on indexes push whole markets around, but there's a hitch. Before a dealer writes a derivative, the customer needs to have a margin account. The customer needs to put up collateral for the write, which he borrows from the dealer in the form of short-term treasuries. Eventually, the Fed runs dry of short-term treasuries to loan to the dealers and collateral dries up. Asset values collapse. Little people lose their life savings and pension plans, inheritances, whatever. Big guys screw little guys, like always.

"Unrest from the bottom rungs of society will metastasize and spread outward and upward. It will get ugly. This happens once every five generations, like the eighty years that passed between the First and Second World Wars, and then another fifty years passed until we got into the Korean War." David conveniently forgot facts, times and dates when he tried to make a point. "The whole system will be torn up by the roots and replaced with a new monetary system, shoving the old one aside. To put trust into the new system, at its outset banks will need gold for their foundation and silver for coinage for the people. Money must once again be trusted."

"I get that, but why do you say there may be civil unrest?"

"You hear hundreds of politicians blather about what the other guy did wrong, about why the other party is the wrong way to go. You hear endless talking points by these politicians and by the guests on the idiotic TV and radio talk shows, but none of these panderers—and they are all idiots and panderers—ever talk about the real problem which plagues the nation. The problem is simple to define, yet none of these politicians or blatherheads will define it."

"And that would be what?" Bob seemed intrigued.

"The entire world is using dishonest fiat money. All this paper money has counterparty default risk, the risk that some government—America's , Italy's, France's, China's, Japan's, California's, Chicago's or whoever's—will fail. They all owe each other. When one fails, it sets off a daisy chain. They all fail.

"This risk of global default exists because fiat is the antithesis of constitutional real money, which is silver and gold. The Founding Fathers knew real money was the key to sustaining the republic because it keeps government honest and makes government work for the people instead of making people work for the government like we have now. They knew what they were doing. It's simple.

"The financial crisis of 2007 and 2008 was the tip of an iceberg, the first hint of the Great Fiat Currency Crisis that will follow. It was only sub-prime mortgage and mortgage-backed securities markets getting rattled, along with minor shakes in equity markets. Look at it as a minor tremor before big earthquakes."

"But I thought the TARP program and the Quantitative Easing, Operation Twist, the Fed blowing up their balance sheet with four to five trillion of garbage paper they bought off banks' balance sheets solved all that. Bailouts worked. Not true?" Bob asked for clarification.

"Nowhere close. The 2007 to 2008 financial crisis was just the first inning of a nine-inning ball game. The bailouts bought banks some time to restructure their criminal activities and put a backdoor escape in place for the next round. Banks and regulators all know the bail-outs didn't solve the problem. That's why they passed the Dodd Frank legislation, so the brokerage firms could duck under bank holding company umbrellas and continue issuing junk loans. Under Dodd Frank, the banks' subsidiaries' assets can be seized or 'bailed in' in our coming currency meltdown. It's spelled out in the customer agreements of the big brokerage firms, and banks and trust companies that operate under bank holding company umbrellas. It's there, but the public doesn't read, doesn't want to know the truth," David continued.

"Which is?"

"The Great Fiat Currency Crisis was merely postponed by the bailouts. Bad debts were not written off, and bank execs never went to jail for fraud. They got bonus checks for fucking everybody with more taxes, higher prices, and for protecting the wealthy from the little guy understanding the truth. Problem loans are still there. Banks can't use generally accepted accounting or mark bad loans to market. That would wipe them out. They must pretend everything is okay, but it isn't because people can't service the debt of the loans they have and the government can only service its debt if interest rates stay low. The world economy is like the HMS Titanic, doomed to go under. Right now, water's coming in the lower decks. The guys in charge are saying everything is okay, but that's a lie. People will drown.

"The dollar is a debt chit on a bad loan portfolio that's taken in trade based on confidence only. The treasury notes and bills are collateral for repro trades, where both parties agree to unwind in a week or a month, whatever, but it's a way to keep assets inflated and put cash in the hands of irresponsible parties so they can make their next payment and extend the day of reckoning. Chinese, Arabs, Persians, Russians, and many others don't want to get stuck holding dollars or any other fiat currencies because the debt load is steadily dragging the entire world into a great depression. Many countries will default on their debt, many will have worthless currencies. Dodd Frank law permits the bank holding companies to throw their subsidiaries into FDIC for liquidation and all bank subsidiaries' customers' assets will be in receivership, with the derivative counterparties being first hogs to the trough."

"Which means?"

"Which means the people with bank checking and savings accounts will see their savings seized, like they did in Greece and Cyprus. This means customers of brokerage firms will have their accounts frozen and securities liquidated at huge losses and the proceeds seized. Pension and assets of trust companies in bank holding companies will see their assets frozen, liquidated, and seized as well. The world economy will seize up. There will be no ATM withdrawals, no credit cards will work, no groceries will be on the shelves. Law and order will collapse. Americans will come face-to-face with truth. They've been played by the bankers. They went off constitutional money in 1913 and now they're going to find out what a hell Woodrow Wilson led them to. Both political parties went along with this scam for over a hundred years. Both parties thumbed their noses at our Founding Fathers. They played along because they got rich. Hopefully they'll change and push for honest money and get rid of the Fed, the IMF, the World Bank, and the imperialism that goes with it."

"Will the people go after the bankers?"

"Not at first. They will need time to figure out how they got hosed. Remember, they're not smart in this area. First they'll blame anybody who has money. History will probably repeat itself. The goyim will blame the Jews and raise hell with us Jews before they come to their senses. Then they'll go after the real culprits, the bankers. They'll go after all bankers, regardless of race, creed, sex, or religion. That's what secular law teaches kids in school these days. We must be politically correct. I'll believe it when I see it, but that's the hope.

"When will the people wake up? When will they challenge banker rule?" Bob's question required a thoughtful answer.

"People usually react to conditions after the fact, not before. That's all they are capable of doing. They are really herd animals unable to think for themselves. They're willing to look the other way when somebody is engaged in corruption or abuse, as long as it's hurting someone else and they can't see it hurting them directly. They'll put up with a president who is a serial rapist if he promises them a bigger paycheck, even if he raids their Social Security trust fund so he can pretend he balanced the budget.

"They'll even allow a radical terrorist to occupy the White House and commit treason as long as they think he's not hurting them directly, as long as the damage he's causing won't show up until a few years into the future, as long as the NFL is on TV. They'll let a president bomb the crap out of some little country, or let the Marines knock the snot out of some shithole on the other side of the world for the business the defense contractors get. As long as what the government is doing is to somebody else and it doesn't affect them directly, people tune out and watch football.

"Think back to Vietnam. No one cared about the place until body bags started coming back. That made it real. People started thinking, 'Holy shit! These are real dead bodies. These guys went off to this little place on the other side of the world and came back dead. This could happen to my kid or my boyfriend! Oh my God! What are we doing? Oh fuck! We've got to stop this!' Only when people saw the consequences of not knowing what was happening did they pay attention.

"There was a college experiment where a guy was strapped to an electric chair. Students were brought into a room where they saw him through a two-way mirror. The professor conducting the experiment told each student the experiment was important. He had to know how much pain the guy in the chair could take. He told each student to turn a knob that sent electrical juice into the guy in the chair. A student turns the knob and the guy screams. The professor has the student turn up the juice and the guy screams louder. Many students participated in this experiment, and almost all kept increasing the juice to the guy. As long as it was the other guy getting hurt they didn't give a shit. That's the lesson here. The guy in the chair never actually got shocked, that part was all faked, but nine out of ten students had no conscience about torturing the guy in the chair. Almost everyone went along doing as they were told. Few challenged authority.

"The key to being a leader of dummies is to make enough of them think you're looking out for them. Make them believe they are special and above it all while you're screwing the shit out of them behind their backs. Political people excel at this. They fool the poor into voting for them by promising to give them free stuff, but the poor end up with their dignity stolen and their kids losing respect for their parents. The middle class thinks that beating up some little country is a great idea, but the cost just make them poorer and some of their kids get killed in the process. These are outcomes of dishonest money at work.

"Every voter who uses their vote to try to advantage themselves at the expense of the other guy instead of using it for what they believe is the best for the country is just an asshole with the right to vote. The people have lost sight of the integrity they once demanded of their leaders. As a result, we have slimy political pricks but no leaders. When change comes, integrity will return. That'll be after the monetary situation gets straightened out."

"But how will people know their currency isn't real money?" Bob's question was as much a probe about when as it was about how.

"It sort of happens slowly, and then suddenly. Right now, a lot of the people think their money is backed by gold or silver. That illusion is perpetuated by phony gold and silver trading and inventory reports. The exchange covers its ass by saying in disclaimers that they get their data from warehouse operators but they can't vouch for the veracity of the data. So what you have is reports that count warehouse receipts as ounces of physical products in possession that haven't been delivered yet. Two warehouses can each claim they own the same ounce. Foreign nations will sniff it out first. They'll want actual physical metal, and they won't want dollars or paper contracts that promise them they have some metal secretly stored someplace. The bankers try to play the old 'Guess which walnut shell the pea is hiding under' county fair game with their allocated bullion accounts. Country by country, people and institutions will wake up and demand physical possession of actual metal."

"What makes the public wake up?"

"Could be a metal warehouse can't stop a delivery notice because they have no metal, or people hear it through the grapevine. Maybe they have a friend in Europe or China who explains that their money isn't backed by anything. Then they wake up and start asking questions. Another way of finding out is some guy's wife complains that meat costs more, and that the price continues to rise. Maybe he tunes her out because all women can get bitchy and he knows that, but then he goes to pick up his favorite six-pack for the NFL game on TV Sunday and he notices that the price went up twenty-five or thirty percent from the week before. He goes to the checkout register and asks the clerk if there's a mistake. The clerk says no mistake and his manager is standing there nodding. Now the guy suddenly remembers what his wife was bitching about and he gets a cold chill. He realizes for the first time he's not making enough to keep up with the increases in cost of living.

"His most important costs—beer, gas, and dog food—are way up. He gets this terrible fear that his wife is right about this money stuff and suddenly the lightbulb goes off in his brain. He's getting screwed! Medical costs, food, insurance, clothes, movie tickets, sports tickets, even the cost of feeding his beloved dog are out of control. He panics. He gets home and asks the wife how much money they have. She tells him, 'Not much!'

"He sees he can't get much interest on their measly five thousand bucks, so the banks can't help him. He calls his union boss, wondering when his next pay raise will be. No luck there. Then he remembers from somewhere in the deepest recesses of his cranium that his grandfather once gave him a few silver dollars and told him to hang onto them because the government couldn't print them like they can print paper dollars when they want to have a war or when they want to give freshly printed money away to people who never want to work. His granddad told him those silver dollars had to go up, and by

God, go up they did! Gramps was right! Gramps never could get his prostate to work, he walked with a limp, and he couldn't see well, but the old buzzard understood what money was. The old buzzard saved their ass for a few months, but then what?

"Now our guy reads about money and how the Fed screwed him. He sees stuff on TV about buying gold and silver coins. He's ready to learn. What he learns makes him angry. He's ready for monetary change. When he puts in a day's work, busting his ass, he wants the money he makes to hold its value, like the real money Granddad gave him.

"That's how it begins, one guy at a time. After a few guys get it, they tell others and the word spreads like wildfire. Men get off their couches at halftime and cry out, 'The dollars the U.S. Government is pushing on us aren't good enough to buy my dog his fucking dog food! I'm getting rid of dollars and buying gold and silver!' There's a collective rallying cry of an indebted nation and a screwed population. It happens like that."

"So real money is what?"

"It is that which holds value, is portable, and is readily accepted in trade and commerce. Gold and silver qualify. And if it's not acceptable under an imposed fiat currency scheme, then a black market will *always* develop apart from contrived fiat-imposed marketplaces, and the black market will always grow to become the dominant market until the fiat-controlled market capitulates and becomes a marketplace that accepts real gold and silver money. That's the history of these things. It's not rocket science. Gold and silver are eternal, like the sun and the moon. Paper burns or it decays, gets eaten by insects, and loses value.

"What makes people wise up?"

"It's hard to explain. It's like when a change in the weather happens. It's when life stops feeling good. Everybody just kind of feels it. It's like at the end of a party when you've had so much to drink that you can't even get it hard to screw the prettiest girl there, even though she's begging for it. You know the party's over.

"It's simple to understand honest money. Ancient Hebrews understood it. In Proverbs, there's a verse about society needing honest weights and measures. That means when somebody works and gets paid, they must get paid in something that represents equal value to their work. They must get paid in silver or gold coins because precious metals will hold value over long periods of time—that is, if the bankers aren't fraudulently manipulating the market price of it to artificially hold down the price of the metal. They do their fraudulent manipulations by selling paper ounces short on the commodity exchange to hold the price down while they take delivery of the physical metal into their own vaults. This scam will not go on forever. Competing exchanges that require physical delivery are already competing with our exchange. Price control will go to the physical market and the paper market will follow. This will happen during the period when the currencies reset their prices to the metals or when the currencies are replaced with new metal-backed currencies. When the little guy wises up and the price of silver resets sharply higher, he'll have to pay a lot more for the silver or work a lot harder for it. When the financial landscape changes, the bankers will own all the metal and they'll screw the little guy, like they always do."

"How is the little guy getting screwed right now?"

"By working like a fool. The husband and his wife are both employed in part-time jobs and forced to accept dishonest weights and measures, dishonest money, for honest work or product. The little guy must work for his paper dollar, but the government doesn't have to work for their dollars. They issue a bond. The Fed prints dollars and gives the dollars to the government for the bond. This circle jerk is all computerized and digitized. The value of the little guy's efforts or product sold is diluted, eroded, and debased by the unlimited creation of fiat dollars by government borrowing.

"The current system is abused by politicians who pass laws that favor their donors and funnel fiat government money into all kinds of nefarious schemes. They pay college professors grant money to study stuff like what time of day bugs like to fuck or how some ancient battle was fought. Really? Who gives a shit about crap like that? Or they'll have wars like Vietnam and Iraq so neocon fucktards can get money to defense contractor buddies. Or they'll spend money on nuclear bombs, enough to blow away civilization ten times over when they only need to kill everybody on Earth once. How many times can you kill dead people? Only governments that don't have to earn the money they piss away do insane things like this.

"It's cheap government money for the rich and well connected, and it's high-interest money and never-ending debt servitude for the great unwashed masses. It leads to horrible waste of resources and gross misallocations of capital and talent. It destroys savings. Diminished savings diminish capital formation. The economy carries a debt it can't service or repay. We have a depression. We have World Wars Three through Six. People die. Cats sleep with dogs. Men turn wives into whores and sell kids out to pedophiles because that's the only way the family can make money and survive. Humanity reverts to savagery. We may end up with another asshole like Hitler as a result of the folly of fiat money."

"Can't the central banks change course?" Bob wondered aloud.

"In a word, no. A government that uses dishonest money has no interest in serving the people who elected it. The only interest is in perpetuating the system.

"To perpetuate the system the political class and bankers employ Kabuki theater. They'll insert a magical shyster president who promises to unite the races only to later divide them, things like that. The problem with that agenda is it's the wrong one. Race relations are neither the problem nor the cause of divisions, only the symptom of the deeper division between those who control money and therefore power pitted against the ninety-nine percent who don't. Dishonest money is the sole cause of the problems that America faces. It's all Woodrow Wilson's fault. The culpability must be laid where it belongs. Every other issue is a minor irrelevant sideshow. It's that differential. The Kabuki part is the sideshow of division and the 'us against them' mentality the political class instills with divisive social programs like Obamacare. All these things are subterfuges intended to distract from the truth, which is that the political class is adamant not to allow the people to have real power which only comes about when people have real money."

Bob stares at him for a moment, then asks, "Can't the public vote for a change to honest money?"

"They could try. If they understand the issue it could happen, but the odds are against that. The voting system is rigged for change to lose. The established powers in both political parties will work together to thwart the idea. Unfortunately, few politicians understand the message that needs enunciation. Americans' votes don't count anyway. The political class contracts the software companies to program the voting machines to continue the status quo. Votes don't matter.

"Fundamental change doesn't occur by established means because established means themselves, the voting processes, are corrupted by those who have power. Power is an aphrodisiac. It's very hard to voluntarily give up one's own power and too easy to rationalize keeping hold of power regardless of the misery it causes. Fundamental change occurs from the bottom up, like it did in the first American Revolution."

"You said first as if you expect a second. Isn't there a way for the existing system, especially through the Fed and the banks, to right things internally?"

"It's too late for that. They used to print money and cause inflation, and then they'd raise interest rates and invert the yield curve, making short rates higher than long, causing a credit crunch and a recession. That would move things toward a perceived normalcy for a while, but the aggregate debt load on the system kept rising. They can't do their one-trick pony act anymore. They've gone so far into money printing and monetization of government and other bad debt that they now ride a tiger. They can't get off. Interest rates are stuck near zero. If they raise rates, bank loan asset values drop and wipe out the equity of the banks and the Fed. They must keep asset values artificially high to prevent systemic collapse. They are cornered. Their stimulating efforts failed.

"Instead of raising short-term interest rates, which would immediately cause the worst depression in the history of history, they keep short rates artificially low and keep buying poor quality debt from banks that are choking on it and creating more of it, with more printed money. It's not a healthy central bank with money creation checked by gold and silver backing of money. It's the opposite of what the Founding Fathers made into constitutional law.

"Bankers do great as long as the Fed stays in business and the public gets screwed. The Fed says inflation has something to do with labor costs, while prices of beef and everything else are doubling. People will go along with fiat money insanity for a while, even for generations, but then people come unglued because they can't make it. They raid stores and steal stuff, they cheat on their taxes, black markets show up, riots break out, cops get shot, and civilization unravels. You can only water down ground beef for so long, you can only put less in the cereal box for so long, and you can only put your thumb on a scale for so long until people figure it out."

"Then what happens?"

"People see they're in trouble. Those who misled the public for generations, who went along with Keynesian economics instead of going back to Say's Law, where money is honest and only used for transactions, not deficit government spending, are in more trouble. Banking policies that prevented clearing out unhealthy businesses and consumer debts get scrapped along with the Fed and its member banks."

"Where do you think we're headed?"

"We're headed forward to the past. The past is our future."

"What past?"

"The same one all fiat monies and their banking systems have. Take the German Weimar Republic. The country had crushing war reparations debts and impossible future payment burdens. The United States and the western nations of Europe and Japan have crushing debts and impossible future payment burdens. The German people thought they could escape the problem. As individuals, they took on more and more risks. They bought stocks which went up for about three years in a grand finale market top blow off. The market gains kept them even or ahead of the depreciation in the Deutschmark. The market players could pay for their groceries for a while, but toward the end that all changed because their currency collapsed.

"In mark terms, a German who had a million marks in their markets saw his value increase to nine million marks in the last two or three years of the rise. The mark wasn't gold-backed at the time, but the U.S. dollar was. When the German economy went through its collapse, their currency collapsed with it. The German who now had a nine-million-mark valued portfolio had to sell his stocks for marks and convert marks to buy dollars or gold to get money for food. The mark was legislated to be worth nothing and was replaced by the Rentenmark. When the German converted his marks to dollars, he lost ninety-nine and nine-tenths percent of his wealth. He lost everything. German companies went bankrupt along with the country and its currency.

"The dollar we use for money, like Weimar's mark, is no longer gold-backed like it was before the Fed got its grip on America's economy. Americans' incomes, like the Germans who lived the Weimar disaster, can't keep pace with the rising cost of food, health care, and essentials. The dollar is being devalued in real goods and services like the Weimar mark was. To cling to their wealth, Americans put their money in the stock market, like Weimar Germans did. Americans have employee retirement pension plans, individual retirement plans, trusts, individual wealth, all invested in the stock market. Financial planners, the insects, cheer Americans onward with high-yield products, partnerships that use leverage, mortgage debts, equity loans, margin accounts, exchange-traded funds that use leverage, just about anything imaginable to reach eight percent returns. Americans are told they'll get eight percent a year if they stick to their insect's plan.

"They're not told the Fed is a hollow corpse, that banks will fail from bad loans, that people will have to swallow negative interest rates on money they keep at the bank, or that the insects need to recalibrate their financial planning models to assume a negative two percent interest rate instead of a positive eight percent rate. It's all set up for a terrible destruction of wealth. America today has eerie similarities to the Weimar Republic. It's like a jet flying over an ocean that loses power to its engines. It doesn't end well.

"The insects blather that diversification will prevent a collapse, but in a systemic credit contraction all assets, stocks, bonds, home values collapse similar to what happened in Weimar Germany. We want to believe that somehow we are different, our markets are different, our money managers are smarter, but when I look at the underlying conditions, our situation is no different now than their situation was back then."

"But the Weimar was a creation after the Great World War. The Germans lost the war. America has won its greatest wars, World War Two and the Cold War."

"Yes, but no. You see, when there's a war, no country wins, economically speaking. There are costs on all sides and huge debts are incurred to fight wars. The winners have the costs of rebuilding the losers to avoid never-ending strife arising from defeated peoples. Look at the Marshall Plan, McArthur's rebuild of Japan. Look at West Germany's costs to absorb failed East Germany. Our Middle East adventures weren't cheap either.

"But I digress. The point is, regardless of the source of the debt, it is the size of the debt that matters. America, indeed the entire world, is crushed by staggering debt burdens. Most do not see the predicament the Fed has them and it in, nor are most prepared to survive an economic collapse that could mirror the Weimar collapse."

"What can they do about it?"

"First they must see the risk. We're talking about crowd psychology. After the Titanic hit the iceberg, the captain's main instruction to his officers was not to let the passengers panic. People in authority never want people under their control to be alarmed, and that's natural. It's necessary for the people to stay docile to maintain control of them. Lifeboats went away half-empty while people partied on the decks. Two-thirds of the passengers died that night because they didn't know the risks, and the men in authority told them there was no need to panic. If the guys in charge were honest, another seven hundred people would have lived.

"Financial markets aren't the same as ocean liners sinking, but the psychology of crowds is the same. Americans are constantly reassured everything is fine, that the Fed will always back-stop the market, that there's no reason to think your insect-created plan will not succeed. It's like a crowd believing a sinking ship will miraculously get them across seven hundred miles of ocean when it's dead in the water. People need to see the risk is that their plan will not get them there, that insects don't know what they are talking about, and it's time to make sure they survive when the economy goes under. In other words, make sure you have a seat on a lifeboat."

"And the seat is gold and silver, right?"

"I'm afraid so. You see, unlike the Titanic, where one-third of the people survived, on the USS Lollypop America, only one person in a hundred owns gold or silver. Financial survival rates among Americans will be lower than the life survival rates on Titanic."

"Do you think that will happen here?"

"It's happening and it's past the point of no return. It's like that ship. It's time to get off. Our top political leaders are career crony kickback artists, serial rapists of the nation, and slimeball influence peddlers who sell off the nation's interests for payoffs from big donors or foreigners. Politicians run for office saying we need serious conversations about reforming Social Security, welfare, defense, government waste, whatever, but none speak to the truth which is that things are dire because we have dishonest money. Once elected, no politician wants change because of the pensions, benefits, and kickbacks they can get by cooperating with the bankers' lobbyists to screw the public. Nothing will change until...."

"Until the public changes things from the bottom up," Bob chimed in.

"Bingo! You're a fast learner! I'm proud of you. You're one American in a thousand who understands what money is and what it isn't. People understand that the United States is based on three branches of government. Like a three-legged stool, we have a legislative branch to make law, an executive branch to enforce law, and a judicial branch to interpret law. As long as those three branches exist, everything should work out somehow and the country keeps going into perpetuity, right?"

"Right!"

"Wrong! If a three-legged stool has nothing to set on, if it floats in midair detached from Earth, can you sit on the stool?"

"No."

"The stool without a foundation or floor to set upon is useless. Similarly, a government with three branches but without a solid foundation to set upon is also useless. The necessary foundation for the United States to survive as a sovereign nation is honest gold and silver money as the constitution prescribed. Honest money is the floor the three branches of government must stand upon. No floor, no government. Without honest money, all you have is corruption in government and society on all levels. All Americans become con artists trying to get more dishonest fiat money than the other guy. Civility collapses, dignity flees, and ethics are scorned. What's left is a nation of depraved, dishonest people who live in fantasy worlds. Family life disintegrates. Sin is glorified. Debt piles up until it chokes normal life like weeds choke a lawn.

"Eventually, maybe soon, a change occurs that sweeps away the country that once was and replaces it with something authoritarian. People stop wondering where they will go for their next vacation to piss away their fiat money. Instead they wonder how they will eat. Summer turns to winter, socially speaking. Change is forced on the people. When the slave master knows the slave accepts substandard rewards for labor, the slave master knows he can push the slave harder. When the slave master can give dishonest money in return for labor, the slave master knows the entire nation is weak. The people will eat dirt if the slave master tells them to. They'll starve and accept corruption because they have lost their backbone and their guts. They want to be taken care of by their slave master, even for just one more day. They are screwed until a leader emerges and rallies them to demand change."

David raised his index finger and wagged it in front of his eyes. It was a wag of admonition, like a cat's tail twitches when intently watching a mouse, waiting to strike its paw.

"If the people choose change, the change times will not be happy times. Misery like never before seen on Earth will descend. Causes of pent-up frustrations will get pulled up by their roots and destroyed. People know that when less than one percent of the people control over ninety percent of the wealth, something's wrong.

"Frustration boils over into anger. There's two ways to ease those frustrations. Either the one-percent changes the rules in their own disfavor, which history shows will never happen, or the ninety-nine percent revolt. Anger boils if the one-percenters let time pass and the ninety-nine percenters see no change. Then an 'us against them' mentality takes hold, a cause is born, and a leader emerges. The ninety-nine percenters channel anger into vengeance, and the one-percenters discover they ride a tiger of their own creation but can't get off. This is when Madam Defarge gets her lists and scratches off names as the mob puts the one-percenters under the guillotine and their heads drop into the bucket."

"There will be a revolt, or a revolution?"

"No. There could be an authoritarian power grab, but the Second Amendment prevents that. If there's one revolution, there will be three of them. The first will be the war of the ninety-nine percenters against the one-percenters. The ninety-nine percenters will win that one, because that's human against humans and the ninety-nines have ninety-nine more people than the ones. They overcome the police state spy world set up by the ones."

"Why would there be more revolutions after that?"

"Before the revolution, the ones invented robots and machines with artificial intelligence because a machine can work cheaper than a ninety-nine, even a Chinese ninety-nine. So the next war will be between the machines and the ninety-nines that survive the first war."

"Who wins this second war?"

"The surviving ninety-nines win again."

"But if machines can outthink people and not need any rest or food, and if they are advanced enough to replace themselves, how can people beat them?"

"Easy. Male human warriors have a prime driver. Machines reproduce because their software tells them they need replacing, but humans reproduce because males want to pass their genes along. Human males have a primal drive to fuck that machines don't have. Machines don't have pussies. It's the same reason humans conquered other animals to control the planet, to feed and shelter their female pussies. Men love pussy."

"What if the one-percenters, the elites, win?"

"Then the one-percenters, the elites or Illuminati as some call them, will enslave the ninety-nines. They'll set up concentration camps. They'll divide the population into those who will be willing slaves for them and those who will not be. The unwilling, about half the population, will go to the camps. They will be worked to death or murdered outright, like in the Soviet Gulags or in Nazi concentration camps. Pastors, priests, rabbis, and clerics will be murdered because the progressives don't want religious opposition. All National Rifle Association members will be disarmed, rounded up, and murdered because the progressives do not want armed resistance to communism. All teachers and professors will be screened to see who was not progressive enough in their classrooms. Those who flunk these tests will be executed because progressives cannot tolerate anyone who voices contradictory thoughts to their dogma. People with learning disabilities or handicaps, people who are old and sick, will all be exterminated by the progressives because their utopian society cannot afford the costs of this excess baggage. All media people and journalists will also be given litmus tests. Those who were not progressive enough will be murdered. Families will be separated between willings and unwillings. One-percenters don't care about the morality of this. They don't need God. They believe they are God. They believe they know what's best for us."

"That sounds chilling. How can society ensure the one-percenters do not win?"

"Simple. The ninety-nines need to vote to protect their Constitutional rights, their rights under the Bill of Rights, and their foundational God-given right to honest gold and silver money. More than anything, a return to honest money takes away the powers of the central government to usurp the public wealth to control the people. Honest money chokes off the lifeblood of dishonest government. If government wants a social program, they must put it to a real cost benefit analysis and an honest public vote, same with a war. An honest vote makes people think. 'Why should I vote for my government to do this when my church or my local school district can do it better? Why do I want to spend my hard-earned silver money to kill people on the other side of the planet who are minding their own business?' Honest money leads to honest discussion and honest disclosures, like what will it cost me, who'll make the money, and how much?

"If the ninety-nines weave a web of truth, demand honest money, stand firm for their rights, and communicate with modern media, it becomes impossible for one-percenters to escape the web. They get caught in their lies and control schemes. Their puppet political candidates and communist false promises get snared in the web of truth. When there's dishonest money, it's impossible to see the truth. The costs of lies, programs, war nonsense, all of it, is too difficult to quantify. It becomes next year's problem or next generation's problem. It's like drinking alcohol because the government is telling you it's better for you than milk, but the day of reckoning, that next day, presents you with the true cost. One day the people wake up and say, 'Oh my, what have we done? We are ruined. We had a great country once, but we were foolish and we didn't hang onto it.'"

"This seems like profound thinking, David. Assuming the ninety-nines win, what will the third war be about?"

"That's after all machines are gone, and all the one-percenter are gone. That ushers in an era of disintegration and tribalism. Over half of the ninety-nines will be dead from nuclear bombs and radiation. It's the messy times. Maybe only one-percent of the ninety-nines survive. The remnants of humans left fight each other to survive."

"What makes you think the richest one-percenters living right now won't come out on top?"

"Because they won't, that's why. They're no different than insects. I know something about insects, so pay attention. An insect has a tough outer shell called an exoskeleton. The insect thinks that shell will protect it from everything, and it almost does. But if you take a big spider and put it up against the insect, the spider often wins. It finds a joint or chink in the insect's armor and rips into it. The spider eats the helpless insect."

"Rich people aren't insects, David."

"They behave the same way. They use money as their exoskeleton armor. They buy islands, big ranches and houses, hire bodyguards, go to far-off places they believe will be safe when the economy collapses. They have panic rooms and bunkers, yachts and airplanes. All these things are like an exterior protection from the mobs of the disaffected who feel they've been screwed by the system. The mob is like the spider. It watches and it waits for its opportunity, then makes its move.

"The insect can't get away from the spider's woven web and the wealthy can't escape the mob. The mob gains control of communications, intelligence, supplies of this and that. The elites must make a move sooner or later, and then the mob gets them. Maybe the rich have a weak joint or chink in their armor, like a sick kid or a surgery they need, or a property that needs repairs. Life events, normal everyday issues occur, and then the rich expose a chink in their armor. Then the mob makes its move. European monarchs thought they were safe from the mob. Roman nobility thought they were safe. Wealthy Carthaginians believed their money could buy protection. The monarchs, nobles, and wealthy were all wrong. Today's elites think they are safe. That helps them rationalize that it's okay to screw the mob by denying the mob honest money, but rationalization is all it is. It's not real safety. Real safety is honest society and honest money, and that means the elites must yield power to the mob by returning society to honest money. How that happens, I can't foretell."

"What happens to the survivors of this apocalypse you're predicting?"

"Civilization will be gone. Survivors will return to Stone Age times but with modern assault rifles, airplanes, and submarines. This war will go a long time, maybe a thousand years until all weapons are used up, rusted, or jammed. Then people will fight with clubs and baseball bats."

"Why will they keep fighting?"

"Civilization will have broken down completely and people will revert to animal instincts. Every man will want a harem of women so he can control the most pussies. It will be a time of relapse into old prejudices and hatreds. Society will fracture into tribes. Black people will kill white people and vice versa. Brown people will be in the killing business also. Political correctness will evaporate. The only political correctness will be honest money. A person can pay or they can't. Fundamental mercantilism with honest money will be the only source of social harmony. Since earliest times, mankind has found a way to see a difference in another human being from himself and use that as justification to kill. It's human nature.

"Outside of mercantile harmony, wherever it exists, civilization will collapse. Blood will run in the streets of America. Groups will function in an 'us against them' world. When the chaos comes, be especially vigilant about the jihadists of the Muslims. They're smart and dedicated to winning power. They teach their young to love dying for their cause. Don't try to reason with them, avoid them.

"Times will be like when I was a kid at military school before I figured out that if I broke my arm I could get out of all the bullshit. They had this game they made us play called capture the flag. There was a big field with two poles at opposite ends. Each pole had a flag on it, one red and the other blue. The red team was supposed to capture the blue flag and the blue team the red one. If you got tagged by the enemy team, you went to the enemy prison until the game ended. It illustrates two things. First, old guys like to watch young guys run their asses off. Second, from the time a boy is a child in America, he is made to think of other guys as enemies. He's hardwired. The third thing—I told you there were three things—is the prison concept. If you didn't get sprung from prison by your teammates, you didn't get lunch."

"Really, David, this sounds crazy!"

"Not crazy. Fact. But I outsmarted them all. While the instructors were refereeing the game, I sneaked off the field and ran to the mess hall and ate lunch. Then I went to my bunk and missed the whole exercise. You need to think a little faster than the guys who make the rules. Don't go nuts over ideological causes. Try to get along and keep a low profile when society crumbles."

"But the blood in the streets stuff. That's crazy," Bob exclaims, unconvinced.

"No, it's how humans are. Especially the ones brought up to believe they are somehow superior to others, and that covers almost everybody. No mother brings her kid up to think he's mediocre and stupid. All mothers and fathers see their kid as a winner. The kid gets hardwired to beat the other kid. It's not a big leap to think it's okay to join a group that wants to go to war with another group. The next big war will be local turf wars. Clubs, gangs, affinity groups will bond together to kill others. They'll have local prison camps where they torture and rape, like capture the flag games, only nastier. Be smart and avoid the insanity as best you can, because once you're dead you can't get laid afterward. Life's fun stops.

"There's no turning back. Civilization was destroyed by Woodrow Wilson when he took the country from honest money to debt-based currency and allowed taxes on income with the IRS, to make sure the Fed got paid interest on the money the government borrowed. That was and is the deal. Once a society starts down the path to socialism, it goes all the way to the end, to the complete destruction of capital formation, complete surrender to corrupt government demigods, complete abandonment of morals, and complete acceptance of evil. Only after society has filled itself with socialism's drivel to the vomit point, to the point where people crave decency again, will society go back to honest money, honest trade, honest government, and honest morality.

"It's a process, like an ocean tide coming in and going out. No one person can fight it. Live in the moment, be aware of it, and sense when it changes. Do not get caught on the wrong side of it. The tide can drown you. Don't think too far ahead here. Remember, you're in the money management business. Try to live through the revolt of the ninety-nines and the upheaval and disintegration that follows.

"After the turmoil, there will be years of deep depression, not ten years like the Great Depression, but twenty to fifty years of hardship for mankind. People will lose all notions of civilization. Groups of people will form for self-protection and survival. Groups will form pacts to hunt down and kill other people for their food, lands, guns, ammunition, precious metals, even their women and children. The human race will devolve into cannibalism, diseases of all sorts. There will be mayhem and wars, even nuclear wars."

"Who's going to come out on top of this mess?"

"It'll be kind of like Russia when the Tsar fell. There was a fight between the White Russians who wanted some kind of a republic with capitalism, personal rights, and freedom. The Whites fought the Red Russians, or Bolsheviks, who were worthless goon squad communist thugs. Thugs who want to steal, cheat, and lie always win over honest people, unless the honest people take the cocksuckers head-on."

"Head-on how?"

"Why do you think progressives are trying to take Americans' guns away? It's because they want to be able to steal everything from people who work for a living without a fight. It's a desperate attempt by the one-percenters to maintain control of the ninety-nine percenters. The one-percenters want to use the government to take everything that belongs to everybody. Guns do not kill people, only people kill people. If a guy wants to kill somebody and he can't get a gun, he can run people over with a car or use an axe, or a chainsaw, or he can poison them. A killer finds a way.

"The reason for the Second Amendment is so people will always have protection from the tyranny of government. Government is controlled by the one percent who can buy the politicians. They like it, they want it, and they want more of it their way. Liberals tell you the Second Amendment is so you can have a rifle to go deer hunting. That's not true. The Second Amendment has nothing to do with deer hunting. The Second Amendment is the peoples' protection from their own government getting rabies from listening to idiots like Diane Feinstein. By liberal logic, we must also ban cars, knives, baseball bats, hammers, electricity, swimming pools, ropes, chains, bathtubs, and even stepladders because they all kill people. By liberal logic, these items are no different than guns, so we should all revert to our naked state in the Garden of Eden.

"But wait! Shortly after the Garden scene, Cain killed his brother Abel. Now Cain didn't have a .45 pistol to do that, so it must be that people kill people, even if there are no guns. So guns can't be the problem. We should also take away all machines, by liberal logic, because the machines will be out to get us some day. When you see a machine, you should shoot it before it gets any funny ideas. When we sleep at night, the machines are thinking about how to take over. All machines are no-good fucking bastards that should be shot. Don't trust them!

"When the president says he wants to ban guns, what he's really doing is tossing out a canard because what he wants is to take away everything you have, everything you have worked for all your life, all your wealth. He wants to give away everything you have to the one-percenters because he works for the one-percenters, not the ninety-nine percenters. He doesn't want America to exist anymore. He wants a communist state with all wealth controlled by the one percent, his buddies, crony friends, and nobody less. He wants to take everything so you can't leave anything to your children.

"We already have communism in American cities. Balti-more, D.C., Chicago, Detroit, Milwaukee, Philadelphia, San

Francisco, Newark, and a dozen more places that aren't American cities anymore. They're communist toeholds in a worldwide communist movement. Many who live in these places don't give a hoot about America or rule of law. They want free stuff. They want to rip off stuff from anybody who has anything. They don't want to work for it. Those who might want to work can't because the system has imprisoned them and they can't get free of it without honest money, so they vote for amoral, unprincipled politicians who help them rip stuff off from people who are stupid enough to work or build a business. These people do not care if the people they elect are thugs, murderers, thieves, or whores. All they care about is putting somebody in office who will help them steal stuff until there's nothing left. It's societal cancer.

"The country will go through a hundred years of communism, complete immorality and depravity, until someday a hundred years from now a small group will form and rediscover honest money, religion, family, good neighborliness, truth, honesty, morality. These things go in some kind of cycle I don't fully understand, but I know it's there. Right now we are headed into the morass or abyss phase of it. Corruption, prostitution, murder, theft, human trafficking, drugs, money laundering, all sorts of badness will be well rewarded. Just be aware of where you are in the cycle. Don't try to change it, but do try to make money on it. If you can beat the bastards at their own game, great, but don't stick your neck out. Until this social malignancy passes, until the government stops aiding and abetting it, you need to have guns, lots and lots of guns.

"People need to tell their president, 'Forget it, pal. We see your falsehood for what it is. Put your phony moral outrage away. Be a man instead of a useless dipshit with mental health problems and congenital lying issues. Work on the real problem of dishonest money, and societal stresses and psychotic behaviors will evaporate. Honest money will do more to stop gun violence than any laws you could pass. Use your bully pulpit to tell the truth and do some good. Work for the ninety-nine percent, bring back honest money, get rid of the Fed, and put America back on the gold standard. Make the dollar as good as gold again. It'll be hard, but so what? If they still have their Constitution, Americans can do anything, even a hard depression. Get society back on an honest footing. Stop politicking and tell the truth. Stop playing golf and do honest work like the rest of us. Remember, the truth is what is so, and the truth is so what! It's not rocket science, Mr. President, you asshole.

"Liberals are the most dangerous people because they believe they know what's best for everybody. They're like privates trying to tell a general how to run an army. They don't know what they're doing but they presume they have some God-given right to fuck around and change what's working. They've never built a business or created anything except stupid movies. They don't understand the concept of 'live and let live.' They always need to be fucking around with everyone else's lives and businesses because they don't know what else to do with themselves. The irony of it all is that most of these leading liberals are fuck-crazed movie stars who have the lowest IQs of the entire human population. But there are so many people who are just as fucked up as they are that they go to see the movies. The idiot movie stars make so much money they buy politicians who want to make the world even more fucked up. That's how movie stars run the country and the world.

"Can you imagine making a living by pretending you are somebody else? Jumping into bed with all kinds of different people? Can you just imagine all the diseases and mental problems these movie stars have? They are all nuts, and they have the money to put other insane people into public office. So here we have these stupid idiot movie star liberals running the country. No wonder everything got so fucked up!

Remember this, it's important. Stupid dummies like power just as much as we smart people do... maybe even more. The whole country is an experiment in progressive idiocy managed by Hollywood, and they don't care that they are screwing up the world forever."

Bob thought about it for a little while, and finally said, "That sounds dire. What about the police? Won't there be enclaves of safety when the world comes unglued?"

"Maybe. Thomas Jefferson said people needed guns to protect themselves from the tyranny of their own government. Maybe he meant mobs too. I don't know. He might have though. When civilization cracks, you can forget the police, as they'll be overwhelmed by the crimes. Many police will capitulate and transfer their allegiance to the vandal elements, just like the mercenaries sold out their Carthaginian rulers in the Punic Wars. A hired soldier has no loyalty to the one hiring or the country hiring. There's no citizen sacrifice in a volunteer army. It's going to be extreme times going forward because we've allowed extreme idiots from academia to mismanage the world's economy for over a hundred years without honest money.

"Jefferson also said, 'The tree of liberty every so often must be nourished with the blood of patriots.' But he only got that half right. The tree of liberty doesn't care whose blood it drinks. Trees can't think, just like mobs can't think. The tree of liberty will do just as well if it drinks the blood of scoundrels, nitwit economic academicians, system manipulators, and goon squad puppets and politicians. Jefferson didn't know trees can't tell blood types.

"Dishonest debt spending created present demand at the expense of forward demand. Debt service from past borrowings used to bring demand forward can no longer be serviced, meaning the interest can no longer be paid. The result is a breakdown of the financial system, defaults of governments, banks, parties and counterparties to derivatives that every player kidded themselves into believing would protect them. When the system fails, there will be no food or goods on the store shelves. Riots and looting will start it off."

"Won't the elites avoid the breakdown?"

"No. Were the Romanovs spared when the Bolsheviks took down the monarchy? Were their children spared? In the French Revolution, the monarch and his court members were not spared. When things change, the mob seeks revenge for being screwed. They want to hit back. People in the Old West used to hang cattle rustlers. There were no niceties and few trials. Mob justice comes quickly. Mobs have one or two leaders, agitators, and everyone else joins in. Morality goes out the window.

"When the aristocrats were in charge of Europe and Russia, they made rules to favor themselves and screw the serfs. They were sociopaths who justified their ways by hanging around with other sociopaths. They had grand parties and winter palaces, and places to go away and play, but the poor were never invited. The wealthy never shared. They thought they were entitled to their sociopathic lifestyles. Today you have the government officials, the top bankers, the Fed, and the top one hundred or top one thousand families in the world, who are all filthy rich and powerful. They make the rules and laws to screw the little people just like aristocrats of old.

"Today's sociopaths are cut from the same cloth as the old aristocrats. They have exclusive getaway meeting places like Davos, and they have their yachts and mansions. They have politicians in their pockets, and they believe they are entitled to perpetuate this."

"But many of these played by the rules. They earned it. They created businesses. They succeeded," Bob challenged.

"Yes and no. They buy legislation to make it possible to get and keep monies that the little guy can't participate in. The rules and costs of access to these loopholes are beyond his means. There are minor differences between the big political parties. The little guy just gets a Kabuki theater show called an election, but nothing changes. The wealthy own both parties and nothing changes until the little guy revolts. Then the mob does the same thing to the modern wealthy it did to the old aristocrats. It turns them out, except for the English monarchy which struck a compromise, or it offs them like it did the Romanoff family.

"The nations of the world are fed up. They see America can print dollars and exchange paper for stuff they produce. They have had it with the current post-Breton Woods system where the dollar was supposed to be as good as gold. Nixon broke our word on that deal way back in 1973. The world no longer has honest trade. Our military enforces our theft now, just like the Roman army did two thousand years ago.

"The dollar is just a piece of paper now and it will get eaten by the markets like breakfast toast. It's not gold and everyone knows it. Other countries want to use gold and silver, and they will have their way because they now own the gold and silver. Bankers will go along with their wishes because there's money to be made financing growth in low-cost production nations.

"Who would you finance if you were a banker? Some guy in China who works his ass off for next to nothing, or some guy in the United States who demands minimum wage, Social Security, welfare, food stamps, subsidized housing, etc.? The American lifestyle is running smack dab into a wall, like an egg that's going to go splat."

"What can I do about it?" Bob inquired of his mentor.

"I don't know. Some people will build a bunker and stash food in it, but the mob will find them. Maybe you'll see a solution while things are happening. Just try to be flexible. Be willing to eat your pets. Just be aware it's going to happen.

Maybe after three-quarters of the world's population has exterminated itself, order will return, but that could take fifty years.

"It's taken a hundred years of Woodrow Wilson's policies, every government's policies since, and Keynesian economics to get things to this impossible state. It may take many decades to get back on track and have a civilized society with honest money functioning again. It may take fifty years before people will trust any form of centralized government after the present system comes unglued. You should buy lots of whiskey and get some good books to read. Dig up Woodrow Wilson's body and drive a stake through the betrayer's heart. Make creation of dishonest money punishable by death again, like the Constitution prescribes. Shut down the Fed, strip the bankers of all ill-gotten gains, and make them do community service for all the lives they destroyed."

"Sounds radical, David." Again, Bob sounded skeptical.

"Returning to honest money and banking like the Founding Fathers prescribed in the Constitution isn't radical. Our current system is what's radical. The Founding Fathers were geniuses. If we follow their prescribed path of honest money, America will forever be the strongest nation, the beacon of freedom for the entire world. If we continue on the socialist path we are on, we'll end up in a shithole like Venezuela. No food, no toilet paper, nothing. No input, no output, nothing. Just shit. Compare the Founding Fathers' result, which is America, to what the shithead Saul Alinski preached, the guy who cheated his way through college and spouted communist nonsense. His outcome is Venezuela. Take a good look at the difference between the products of capitalism and socialism. It's there for all to see and compare. It's inconceivable to me that any political leader would let that Alinski moron's thinking get into their head, unless of course they don't give a shit about being dishonorable or about selling the country's interests for their own self-enrichment.

"As long as people believe that fiat currency is money, you need to think of ways to outsmart the government. If the government can cheat by just printing dishonest currency, which is not an honest weight or measure given for honest work or product or service, then you have to out-cheat the stupid fucks who vote for the government that is cheating you. You need to be okay with that because by voting for a government that perpetuates fiat money, people are electing to perpetuate a fraud on you, on your honest work. Get it?"

"I think so."

"Never cheat on your taxes—the government will nail you for that—but you can avoid getting ruined in the mess the bankers have made. Avoid all the stocks they promote. Stock promotion isn't new. It's a way of taking huge gobs of wealth from idiots and transferring it to the already wealthy. Usually it's done in stock issues that people don't understand. It's some high-flying technology or magical biology company that's going to change the world. I'm not saying these companies won't change the world. Some of them will, and you can even see it happening with some of them. The problem is they get heavily promoted beyond common sense and they may never make enough money to justify what people pay for them.

"When you hear everybody buying this or that company and the talking heads on TV are speaking about it all the time, gushing over their next new product or service, then it's likely over, or over enough to avoid it. I watch some of the talking head shows sometimes. They never make sense to me. They talk about this neat new idea or that one, but never about the balance sheet or the earnings or the market size. They just gush away and every night it's a new story. Some of the women on these shows chatting about these companies look to me like they're having orgasms right on TV over this crap. They wear sexy outfits and salivate over crazy stories about what some company is doing. They remind me of when I was a little kid and me and my friends used to go into a closet and jerk off together. It felt good and all that, but we never accomplished anything except getting ourselves excited. We never knew any more about anything than we did before we started jerking off. Those TV stock promoters are kind of like that, jerkoffs in front of a TV camera.

"An example of a new technology stock everyone went crazy over was RCA. After World War One, the government released airwaves for commercial use. RCA was there with television sets. It was new, so everybody was going to have one. Information was going to open up the world. Well, the stock went up lots, like 60 percent per year for some years. It reached $114 per share, split adjusted high. Then the leverage came out of the market. People had to pay off their loans. The stock went all the way down to two dollars and fifty cents, for a loss of 98 percent. People had mortgaged their homes to buy it. Brokers went broke on it. People killed themselves.

"Today is no different because people and their fear and greed are never any different. Today there is leverage in the whole world, with governments, companies, and individuals leveraged up to their eyeballs. When the markets ultimately resolve this craziness, there will be dramatic declines all over the place in stocks, bonds, and real estate. People will jump off buildings like they always do. That's another thing. When this is happening, and afterward for a year or two, do not walk close to any tall buildings because some idiot who's committing suicide might land on you.

"The Western world is so dumbed down the people who commit suicide don't even do that right. They know they are slowly being replaced by machines, yet when they commit suicide they jump off buildings or shoot themselves. Just think about that for a minute. If machines are the enemy, why not get even on the way out? I heard one time where Elvis Presley shot his TV because it was bothering him. And every now and then you hear about some office worker or college kid throwing his computer out a window, or a football player, who wants to keep things private, throwing his cell phone into a river. Well, those people are on to something. They're getting rid of a machine that's trying to control a human life. See?

"Take it a step further. Every shrink who counsels nutty people should tell their suicide patients that they can make the human population better off on their way out. Instead of jumping off buildings or shooting themselves, take a machine or two with them when they go. They could drive a car full speed into another car or a bus or train. 'Fight back! Destroy some machines when you check out!' should be a sign posted in every shrink's office. Now the exception to this is when you find a machine that's a true friend. Are you getting this?"

"Yes, I think so." But Bob sounded unsure.

"Okay. I'll explain some things we do at UGGA to beat the communists and their machines. Payroll is supposed to pay on the first business day of the month, but it never happens. We always pay as late in the month as possible. That's why I keep the old card-fed computer. Mrs. Rodriguez or Barbara could do the payroll by hand in thirty minutes, but we have this procedure, chiseled in stone, that the payroll must be done by computer to make sure it's accurate.

"It's a combination computer and card shredder. When we put data cards into it, some always get shredded. Then we have to redo the payroll a few days later, after our in-house technician fiddles with the knobs and the trays and cleans out the shredded cards. The company that made it went out of business, so nobody knows how to repair it properly. To make sure the computer knows we mean business, we slam it a few times with a hammer. The computer room is moldy because the air conditioner is old and it leaks. This causes the computer to frequently short-circuit. We use bleach to clean the mold and spray some bleach on the computer in case there's mold in it. We blow-dry the computer's electronics with a hair dryer before we run it again.

"Can you see the genius of this system? Every month, like clockwork, the payroll is at least two weeks behind schedule. The business keeps the bank float on payroll money. When you multiply cash float for two weeks, times twelve months, times twenty people on staff, it works out to a delay of four hundred and eighty person days of pay not going out. So, at two hundred and fifty work days per year, the business gets almost two years' use of one employee's monies each year. Figuring interest at four percent, the business gets another two weeks of one employee's income in interest each year. Multiply that by ten years because that machine is over ten years old, and I figured this out ten years ago, the firm gets about twenty weeks of one employee's work for free! The machine pays for itself! The employees always get angry with the computer technician, but never at me. I screw them and get away with it! Pretty neat, huh?"

"Amazing!" Bob answered, but looked to be deep in thought.

"Well, it doesn't stop there. Every employee contract has provisions that they don't understand. They only get paid salary or pension for a completed month worked or entitled to at the end of a month survived. So, every once in a while, somebody quits to get married, or they die in retirement. That means we don't pay them for a partial month. So if some gal gets married at Christmas and quits the day before, we can screw her out of her December paycheck and get about twenty days of free work out of her. Same for June weddings. I always encourage them to get married toward the end of June, just to make sure it doesn't rain on their wedding. So they listen to me, and then I don't have to pay them for most of June. Good thinking, right?"

"But what about a wedding present from the company, or a going-away present?"

"No chance. If they invite other employees to the wedding, the employees can give the bride something. The company just sends a card saying they'll get a mystery gift and it'll be sent to their new address in one week. That way everybody thinks it'll be something wonderful, like a new set of silver or something, but we just send them a picnic set of paper plates and two sets of plastic knives and forks. Can you see the fiat money game as I do? It's totally adversarial. Do all you can to squeeze down your fiat payout and use the savings to buy real silver. Beat these bastards at their own game."

"I see how you think."

"Good. These little things add up. Always, when you take out a subscription to any kind of research service, put down that it's for personal home use because it costs less. Look at it this way. A business is constitutionally defined as a person, so why should any person get a better deal than another one? These communists think businesses should pay more than individuals because they believe it's their moral right to screw businesses. You need to screw them back every way you can. Have your wife join some wholesale buyers' club so she can get your stuff wholesale instead of paying decorators. Decorators don't know anything about decorating anyway. Open a business out of your house, even if you're only reselling used diapers. That way you can write off some house expenses too.

"Keep office rent costs down. What I did one year is I had the building put a chandelier in our front office. Then I tried to clean it myself, but I failed. I pulled it down off the ceiling and I fell on top of it and cut myself in a few places. I had some bruises, but I didn't break any bones this time like I did when I was a kid trying to get out of staying at a military youth training camp in Arizona. I screamed like a crazy person, ran into the building lobby where there were people all around and screamed for the building manager. I had blood all over my shirt. I yelled they were trying to kill me and I needed an ambulance and a doctor. Well, an ambulance came and took me to an emergency room. I told the doctor I was traumatized by the experience and got that on the report, so they were really anxious to try to settle with me. I threatened to sue them for not putting up the chandelier properly. I told them I'd settle if they cut our rent in half for five years, which is about what their legal fees would be to fight a liability case. That's how you can keep your costs down, see?"

"I think I'm starting to get it."

"The Securities and Exchange Commission auditors are people you need not fear. Their audits give you another opportunity to keep your costs down and screw the public. They're government people who fly around the country, look at different cities, eat at nice restaurants, stop in and chat about the fund and then sign off on stuff, go to a night club or a strip joint, and go home and collect their paycheck. They are worthless communists. They check on how much of a staff's time is spent working on the fund itself and how much is spent working on the investment advisory management company and on the underwriting company.

"Here at UGGA, we do a two-week study every year where everybody works for the fund and nothing else. Then we have the fund's financial officer certify the number of hours worked on the fund. After the certified time study, everybody catches up on all their work for all the other companies. This way we can charge expenses to the fund for about two to three times what hours are actually worked on it on an annual basis and we get the work done on the other companies for free. I create a report for the communists to sign off on. It tells the fund's shareholders they are getting communist government approval for the screwing I'm giving them. The bureaucrats that I pay fees and taxes to support make up rules that cost me money to put worthless people on government payrolls that cost me more money. I even the score. I give back to the public the craziness in government they vote for. I have the proper perspective. Everybody who works for the government is a worthless, subsidized leech, pretending to do something worthwhile.

"Fund commission trades are what people in the trade call 'soft dollars.' They are higher-cost commission trades than trades done at a deep discount firm. The government allows the higher trade costs on the sham theory that the fund gets research from the brokerage firms and the higher-cost trades are a legitimate way of paying for the trades. Little research would survive if it were put on a cash basis. Soft dollars gives us a loophole we can drive a truck through. We can use soft dollars as kickbacks to a broker-dealer for fund sales. All the dealer has to do to cover his ass is send you some newspaper clippings or something he picked up out of a magazine so you have something in your files to show the regulators the dealer gave you research, when in reality you paid the dealer for sales. So the fund's shareholders get to pay some of their money in higher trade costs for you to get more sales so you can have more assets and make bigger management fees. That's a neat concept, huh?

"Always make sure that whatever you do, you're indemnified for it. What I like to do, as a condition of employment here, is make each employee sign as part of their contract with the firm that they indemnify me for anything I do. They don't know what it means, they don't have a lawyer, and they want the job, so they sign the indemnification clause. In all my years I've only ever had one gal ask me what it meant. I just told her it was standard language and not to worry about it, so she signed it. When I have clauses like that and a regulator starts in on me about fining me or the firm, I just tell them that the employees have indemnified me and if they go any further, I'll bankrupt some of these women with no husbands and children at home to support and that the regulator will throw them out in the street. That scares the hell out of them because they don't want bad publicity. Like I said, they just want a paycheck like all good communists. So I promise them not to do whatever it is that's bothering them, and I actually stop the practice that has them upset, but only until I get a different regulator. Then I just go back to doing what I always do.

"Remember this if you remember nothing else. Fiat money, by its dishonest nature, makes all transactions in fiat money dishonest transactions. Transactions between governments are dishonest as well as transactions between private parties. The person giving a good or a service knows he's getting dishonest payment in return. He knows the fiat currency script has a finite value because it's fast becoming worthless, so what does he do? He cheats on what he's supposed to give you! The builder builds a shoddy house. Your doctor doesn't give a shit about you. He checks you to make sure you've got a heartbeat, then fills out his insurance forms. Dentists tell hygienists not to clean your teeth too good. They want you to get cavities and have root canals and implants. Vendors of all goods and services only care about their insurance liability for the crap they sell you. Lawyers just want to run hours on you. They don't care about what's true or whether you win or lose. They are jaded. They think everyone in society is a scumbag or a criminal, so why should they seek out truth? The days of honorable lawyering are history. They just want to get paid. It doesn't matter who pays them, so they take bribes. There's no quality, no pride, no service after the sale, no truth, no goodwill. With America so debauched, what difference does it make at this point in time?

"The government hogs off the wealth of the nation by printing crap paper and people know it. No one of integrity gets to be president because both parties put up con artists who agree with the banks to continue the fiat lie. People become slothful because they accept that the government will look out for them, even though their standard of living slides into the toilet. Even whores don't give you your money's worth. If you want good whores, you need to go to Venezuela or Cuba, remember that. Communism has those places so fucked up their economies have already collapsed and the women there fuck for practically nothing.

"You can't believe in anything or anybody. The Bank for International Settlements is behind this whole charade. They're a bunch of high-stepping rich pricks with headquarters in Basel, Switzerland. That bank is the instrument of the wealthy. No longer do the kings field armies to conquer others. What we have now are just militaries for showboating, not for real fighting where millions are killed. The wealthy are the new kings of power, and they use the fiat system to keep their power by bleeding the world's peoples through deficit government spending, giving the largess to their cronies.

"You have morally bankrupt people in positions of government power. Their job is to steal money from the people and give it to their wealthy friends. Banks that should fail stumble onward, crazy schemes and projects get funded while honest ideas starve from lack of funding. These crimes against the people go unpunished, never prosecuted. Prosecutors are paid off not to prosecute. The Justice Department looks the other way until the statute of limitations has passed, and the people are told it's all too confusing. That's hogwash, of course. The top people know what's going on. They know the Fed needs to be audited and put out of business. They do their ridiculous annual swan song at Jackson Hole. It's madness and it needs to stop. It's just one of dozens of central banks controlled by the Bank for International Settlements. People are terrified to stand up to this ungodly wealth-stealing enterprise and so it will continue until...."

"Until the system falls of its own weight?"

"Yes, unfortunately, until wild animals roam the streets, cats sleep with dogs, and cities burn from people looking for firewood to keep warm. The only way systems change is from the bottom up. There was a poet who once said it all succinctly: 'Enjoy your pineapple, munch on your grouse, for it will be your last meal, bourgeoisie.' The guy was Russian with one of those unpronounceable names. I don't understand why Russians can't just use names like Tom, Dick, and Harry like normal people do.

"That poet predicted the boiling up of a popular revolution that reordered society. Russia became a huge mess because they went communist. The Red Russians killed the White Russians and the Russian people lived through a hundred-yearlong mistake. They're fucked up over there from living under all that snow.

That can happen here. When the people revolt against the Fed and the bankers it's likely they'll turn communist. They are numb from watching *Dancing with the Stars* and the NFL and so dependent on government they've stopped believing in themselves.

"Remember, money is the most hard won, most fought over, strongest motivational driver in the world for most people. I'm not talking about what motivates the religious types or moonstruck lovers here, just ordinary people. People fight to their deaths over money. They sell their children and wives for money when their needs are strong enough. This is usually a lesson best learned by example. You can't appreciate how important money is until you've experienced a really rough patch and you have no money.

"A day of reckoning will soon dawn upon America. The rest of the world will not take a paper dollar that's been printed up, or brought into existence by a bank loan, in exchange for their oil, gold, lumber, metals, or labor. That's going to end just like it did for the Romans. The Romans paid an ounce of gold coin for a thousand bushels of grain. After a time, the Romans clipped a quarter of the coin off, declared it had the same value as the unclipped coin, and demanded the same thousand bushels for it. When conquered peoples resisted, the Romans killed them. It was rule by extortion. The whole scam collapsed, the empire died, and people who worked cheaper took over.

"The same will happen to America. We don't invade countries to make them safe for democracy. That's bullshit. We invade them to make them take the paper dollar for whatever they have that we want, or we kill them, just like the Romans. A day of reckoning will usher in profound changes. Take retired school teachers and other government employees. They live large in today's economy. They get fat pensions. They spend freely on travel and indulgences because they are confident their unions will keep that pension money coming forever. The rug will be pulled out from under them when the dollar gets rejected. Their underfunded pensions will be reduced or eliminated and the costs of everything will rise sharply for them. Their gravy train will go off the rails. Teachers were once dirt-poor, but they loved to teach kids and help them along in life. But liberal democrat policies and unions made teachers well-off. Now they teach kids communism and attitude. They care about their pensions, not the kids. Kids can't even read or write in cursive anymore. They can't think their way through simple math problems. American teachers couldn't get work in China."

"That might be because they don't speak Chinese," Bob interjected.

"Don't be a smartass. Pay attention. You need to under-stand the dangers of information and computers and how they can capture all the people of the world. My thought is that the insects, the financial product sales people, have corralled people's money into financial products. Then one day, the markets' computer systems will magically glitch and people won't be able to get their money. That will be an excuse for the government to close the markets and the banks, declare martial law, and eliminate elections. The guy in the White House becomes king and the first thing he does is kill everyone who can think. Then you'll have a nation of total dummies who watch the NFL and drink heavily. Then the top guy will sell America to the Chinese or the Muslims. Democracy ends. Then, the Chinese will kill the top guy too."

"Why?"

"Because the Chinese killed millions of people during the Mao years and they also killed our navy at Pearl Harbor. I'm just saying, you need to plan for this contingency. Long ago you could count on the Pope to rally his troops to defend America against the Chinese and the Turks. America was started by righteous high quality people like the Pilgrims, the Knights Templar, Ted Kennedy, Marilyn Monroe, General Custer, Alan Greenspan, Al Capone, Davy Crockett and the Pope, but now the world is all mixed up. People can't think straight like I can. The country has no morality and the Pope has no cojones. He flies around blathering about global warming, while billions of Christians and Jews are getting slaughtered by fanatics. He should be lobbying world leaders to bring back the gold standard, educating people about how honest money breeds better morality; but, not this guy."

"David, the Chinese didn't bomb Pearl Harbor. That was the Japanese."

"What difference, at this point in time, does it make? If one of those countries doesn't try something, the other one will. You need to keep an eye on them."

"And, the Pope didn't start America."

"Well, too bad for him. He missed out on a big market. Don't try to sidetrack me.

"When most people make money, they can't contain themselves. They have to show it off with big houses, expensive cars, fancy clothes, exotic trips, and so on. That's a huge mistake. When you make money, keep it a secret. Never sow seeds of envy in others' minds, for when society collapses they will come for you and your money. They will pester you for loans they'll never be able to repay. Then when they can't get a loan from you, they'll steal from you or even kill you for your money if they think they can get away with it. That's how nuts people get over money. Invest what you earn in UGGA, never spend a dime.

"Once upon a time a kid could work hard, save his money, and buy a baseball glove. He felt good about that. He'd accomplished something. Now everybody buys on credit because they can't save. There's no reason to save when the currency buys less next year than it does this year. People borrow to buy right now. They're in debt and they must pay interest on it. It's great for the banks. They make slaves out of everybody. If we had a gold and silver real money system, everything would get better. America today is just a big whorehouse where everybody scams everybody else. Fiat money turns everybody into whores. America is a nation of whores. Shame on all of us.

"Do good things with your money when it will help bring about good things. Help a kid get educated if the kid wants to learn things, but don't squander your money on kids or people who have crazy idiotic notions or vague ideas that money is the key to success for them. It isn't. Brains are the key to success.

Brains is always more important than money. If someone has no brains but wants to work hard to succeed with some good direction, it's okay to help them. In any kind of help case, help a little at a time and watch the progress. Encourage, but never lavish money. Money is no substitute for determination and self-accomplishment.

"When a deal is promoted to you, and you find yourself all excited about it, feel your emotions rising, never commit your money at that time. When you buy a stock, the prospects for the company and the risks it faces should scare the living shit out of you. Then and only then should you begin to commit money. You will always know the outlook for an investment better on the day you sell it than on the day you buy it. It's like a woman. When you get that first kiss you think it's going to be wonderful, but after you live with her for months and years, you see her warts, smell her farts, get a better idea of what she's really like. Stocks are like that too.

"Here's something else you should remember. It has to do with crowd psychology and money. When one truth is spoken amongst a thousand lies, as loud as they may be, we as humans now have the choice of lie over truth. Unfortunately, most times lies win over fact because humans are psychologically more comfortable with mass thinking than following the least favorable opinion. Thinking requires hard work and time, plus a rooting out and discernment of the facts. It's much easier for the human to succumb to the lazy nature of assumption that one thousand people must be right and one person therefore must be wrong.

"Most people are hardwired to join in with the crowd, for that is the course of action which is most instantly gratifying. In the markets and on market talk shows, this crowd behavior can be the underlying driving force for periods of time, particularly during times of easy credit expansion. It is important to look for investments where the crowd is not looking—nay, where the crowd and the media are giving you constant reinforcing messages that your thinking is terribly wrong. You must, to be successful in the long term, know that what you are seeing and hearing in these crowd-shouting genres is all driven by an underlying sponsored lie. It may be that you are being baited to merely buy a good company but at an extreme valuation, or you may be getting set up to buy that which a big seller has the objective to offload onto the mindless unwary. You are best off to work away from the crowd even though it is unpopular and even sometimes without joy, as the money the crowd throws at these promotions can indeed make prices rise for a time, even a long time, but that is not investing in the purest sense. It is a form of joyriding and it tends to end badly for those who go for the ride.

"When it comes to relieving a society of real money, the bankers employ several tactics you need to understand. The easiest way to get someone to part with something that is extremely valuable is to make them believe it is worthless, which is what these tactics are designed to do. These propaganda tactics are easily recognized, for they have been repeated through the centuries.

"The first is called demarketing. It's the opposite of marketing. They are methods which are employed to make gentiles believe their gold and silver assets are worthless. News media, which is controlled by the government, begins a propaganda campaign. They tell the public that diversification no longer includes the metals because the metals aren't money anymore. This isn't true of course, because central banks and banks that operate in the commodity markets all seek to own gold and silver. The propaganda tells the public that gold and silver are too volatile to own. This is designed to scare people away from owning value and instead direct them to own overvalued garbage that insiders and large clients wish to unload on the unsuspecting and witless. Unloading is done by sticking the insiders' selling shares into financial products that get distributed to the public by the insects.

"Another tactic is to short paper gold and silver on a commodity exchange, particularly the COMEX, which does not enforce its concentrated position limit rules, and simultaneously purchase large quantities of physical bullion at bargain prices. This tactic is used as a risk-free measure by the large operators because their paper shorting can be covered by a force majeure declaration whereby the commodity exchanges are closed and the outstanding short exposures are covered at prior day's closing prices before the price goes up. This is classic market manipulation to the detriment of the public.

"Another tactic the commodity exchanges used in years past was to change their rules midday. They may raise margin requirements or stop taking buy orders if silver or gold start rising in price and they risk losing control of the market price.

"Other tactics employed include having media pundits and talking headline readers continually emphasize the terrible outlook for the metals, telling people to bring their worthless precious metals into the nearest coin shop and exchange their two-hundred-year-old heirlooms for valuable paper currency which was freshly printed by the billions on worthless rag paper only yesterday. They say this baloney while they orgasm over some hot new idea company that won't be around in five years. You can feel insanity grip the public mind-set when a demarketing program is in full swing.

"Another tactic is to influence accounting firms to issue qualified opinions on the companies that market operators want a position in, even though the companies may not have factored receivables or sold their royalties, patents, various assets, measured ore or reserves forward to get operating cash. The effect of doing this qualified opinion tactic is to scare the shit out of most investors and advisors who will not look beyond the qualified opinion into the operating history or the current position of the company. That's because there's always going to be some dipshit lawyer who will sue if the price of a particular stock declines. An advisor sees himself in front of an arbitration board with a lawyer screaming, 'Didn't you see the qualified opinion?' Of course you did, and you looked a lot deeper than that, but lawyers specialize in making points by acting like hysterical clowns with rabies. You could have a company with equipment assets and ore they could sell forward, and no debt, but those factors usually will not be considered by the typical investor or advisor. The typical advisor will be scared, thinking a qualified opinion might give fodder to some asshole lawyer who wants to sue him if things don't work out, so that advisor is scared off and passes up a bargain. A skilled market manipulator, in cahoots with unethical management, can short a stock down to a pre-agreed price with little actual purchasing going on because of the qualified opinion. Then a deal is done that gives the advantages to the operator and management and dilutes the ownership of the existing shareholders. This tactic gives the skilled market manipulator a great opportunity to pick up valuable assets on the cheap.

"Remember, these tactics have been perfected by market operators and central bankers to governments over centuries and they depend upon a gullible public. All the rules and regulations, all the loopholes within them and how to use them to best effect, all these factors are designed to give market operators, corporate insiders, and bankers the advantage. They make the rules and control the game. It's like taking candy from a baby for these guys, or raping an innocent young maiden. Maybe that's why the Fed is located on Maiden Lane in Washington, D.C., come to think of it."

"Couldn't other countries, like China, come up with competitive parallel systems to clear international trade and settle commodities on a cash basis, instead using paper to play the game?"

"Yes, they already have them, but I think it will take them a while to become as adept at stealing from the public using these methods as American bankers already are."

"Meaning a few years?"

"No, actually, I'm thinking it will take centuries. All the rules, the ins and outs of the opaque bullion markets, knowing where all the bones lie, so to speak, these things are taught over generational lessons and those secrets are tightly guarded. I think the Orientals may try to compete, but I believe it will take centuries for their crooks to get as good at stealing from the masses as ours. I'm talking strictly about the financial markets. The top Chinese guys are powerful political thugs and they already know how to screw the living shit out of all the ordinary Chinese. The top Chinese could also become as good at stealing from the financial markets and the bullion markets as our crooks if they hired some of ours to show them the ropes, and if our crooks can see where they can make more money working for the Chinese than for the West's crooks. In that case, the Chinese could eat our lunch in a year or two.

"Make sure you understand the structure of financial institutions. See the world through their eyes and you'll avoid a lot of headaches. Banks are especially important to understand because they control the markets and the games played on the public because their lobbyists control Congress, the White House, and all the agencies. Bankers are clubby. They sit on lots of corporate boards and divide up huge bonus pools. When one bank blows up, the top executives just get big golden parachutes and the public gets screwed. For example, in the TARP program during the financial crisis, the public was told we needed to rescue the banks instead of letting them fail, so the government approved the Taxpayer Ass Ripped

Program to give big bonuses to the top bank executives for screwing the public, and the public bought the lie.

"After the last financial crisis, the banks figured they could get away with an even bigger crisis and screw the public even more. They got Washington slimes to pass the Dodd Frank law, which lets the banks rip out their depositors and any other account within any other subsidiary of a bank holding company. This is called a bail-in scheme. The bankers set it up after the last crisis by reorganizing themselves into bank holding companies. The latest scam scheme means people who hold hypothecated accounts in a bank's subsidiary company, like their brokerage subsidiary, or their trust subsidiary, or their bank subsidiary, can have their assets seized to satisfy the holding company's derivative losses to a counterparty. So it's important that when you open an account at a brokerage for the firm that you be positive that the brokerage does not have hypothecation clauses in the customer agreement. Few people read agreements or understand them. Bankers count on that.

"This new arrangement allows bank holding companies to take enormous risks with their clients' assets. It encourages banks to offer high-yield products with all kinds of junky assets in them and to take tremendous risks on their trading desks. If banks win, the top guys get paid big. If banks lose, the public holds the bag. Many banks are actually just hedge funds now, except the public doesn't get a cut of the performance fees. Those are called executive bonuses.

"You'll get a whiff that the end of the banker games is close at hand. All their insider information and high-frequency trading has to come at the expense of the public. The watchdogs who are supposed to protect the public will just sleep through the public rape until there's a mistake somewhere. Some trade blows out and there's a derivative bust, and that's when the watchdogs start to sniff. That's when the banks will eat each other. Some bankers will mysteriously disappear or commit suicide. That's already happening. That's the cover-up part. Then some bank confesses to criminal wrongdoing. That sets off the civil class actions, and then the public loses confidence. Humpty Dumpty falls off the wall and goes splat. That's Mom and Dad's retirement, a broken egg with no nest. The nest is the dollar. People stop believing in the currency. It's the 1930's all over again, but on steroids.

"The new scam makes life great for the insects. They point to products that will supposedly meet the plan they sold to Mom and Pop, without explaining derivative risks or hypothecation to them. Those requirements come from future regulations after the next financial crisis exposes this disgraceful sham. Regulators are always chasing the horse that already left the barn. Then there will be the usual hand wringing that everything was completely unforeseeable, that there was never any legislation to regulate derivatives and so forth. Of course, this is total bullshit for the public to swallow. But those regulations will only come after thousands of people first commit suicide and millions lose everything because of these banker con artists. I'm telling you this so you don't get the firm sucked into it. Know your account agreements. Avoid this shit.

"If I come up with any more good examples of how money affects people and how you should view money, I'll make sure to let you know." David offered Bob a knowing smile. Then he looked far away and nodded his head as he concluded his lesson on money.

Women, the Third Lesson

"Women are the third greatest gift God gave you, but he made a mistake. Women are an accident. God was clueless when he made that first woman. I've tried to analyze women from many different perspectives, you know, like I would a stock. I've worked hard at this and given it a great deal of thought, but it's extremely complicated. There are some differences between women and men, and there're even some differences between women. However, there are also some commonalities, so I'll start by telling you what I know for sure, and then we'll get into areas that are more complicated. Okay?

"Okay."

"All right. First I've looked at what the Torah has to say about them. The first woman came out of Adam's rib, but maybe not. How they got here is confusing. Some rabbis say there was one named Lilith who was a woman put here before Eve was taken from Adam's rib. If Lilith was a real woman who didn't come from Adam's rib, then she was put here first as a person who might have been equal to Adam. This was likely problematic for God if it were true because Lilith was probably some kind of a mouthy bitch Adam couldn't get along with, so God had to get rid of her somehow. Lilith might have been the first feminist and God had to go back to the drawing board and come up with a woman a man can get along with.

"If the Lilith story is true, then the Eve story about her being taken from Adam's rib makes sense. God wanted women to be somewhat like men, sort of grateful to men for their existence, so he had the first woman in the book of Genesis come from a man. Think about that for a minute. This is huge. It's a big concept.

"If it weren't for the men to get women pregnant with children then there wouldn't be any more people on the planet and Adam would have just died an old man with no kids. So God must have wanted lots of people. That's why he made women, so there'd be lots of people. Maybe we have one less rib than women do, I'm not sure. But if we are short a rib then that's because God wants us to marry women so we can get our missing rib back. I think God likes to see what people do. That amuses him, so the more people the funnier things get because most people are fuckups. If God just wanted more people, why didn't he keep Lilith around? That's a key question. The answer has to be that God wants women to be obedient and subservient to men. That must be right or else the Torah is wrong, and the Torah can't be wrong. We have to conclude that women are here to produce more men until we can figure out how to reproduce men without them.

"The planet is half full of women. It's a real predicament. We can either totally ignore them or we can try to understand our problem and work with it. If we ignore them, they get all moody and upset about being ignored and drive men nuts. When they say something, you have to pretend you're listening to them and that what they're saying is worth listening to, even though it probably isn't. This results in a tremendous waste of your time, which you'll remember is the most important gift God gave you, but if you ignore them they start working on driving you nuts. Then you'll end up wasting even more time. Some guys try to escape from this conundrum, if only for a few hours, by begging off on Sundays and watching football. Some even watch football on Sunday, Monday, and Thursday nights, and college football on Saturdays. Then for the rest of the year there's baseball, basketball, and some guys also watch hockey and the Olympics. The really lucky guys are the ones who can shake the wife off for hunting and fishing trips, or escape into a garage and work on a car.

"We know we're stuck with them and we know they are emotional and tough to shake off, so we need to understand what drives them so we can keep them from catching us off guard. Women are sneaky as hell, so it's important that you learn from me what they're all about. Otherwise you'll end up with one of them screwing your life up, so pay close attention here.

"I've made one profound observation about human women. They are not like any other female group from any other species on the planet. Other females, like sheep and goats or deer and elk, don't wear makeup. Even female monkeys and apes don't wear makeup and those animals are supposed to be kind of like us. Monkeys and apes don't seem to have any trouble procreating, so there must not be a reproductive need for human women to wear makeup. This leads to only one conclusion: Human women wear makeup to impress other human women. They need to feel that they are better-looking than the other women they know. That's the only conceivable reason.

"So you always need to tell a woman she looks nice, no matter what. If you're with one woman and other women are around, never tell other women they look nice. If you do, your woman will go nuts buying even more makeup. A better idea is to wait until you are alone with your woman, and then tell her those other women all looked like shit compared to her. That will get you a peaceful day or two. Look at those as bonus days.

"Another thing that makes no sense is women wear high-heeled shoes. They walk around like crippled animals, off balance, subjecting themselves to twisted and broken ankles. They fuck up their feet so badly they often need surgery. Their behavior is unfathomable and yet almost all of them do it, unless they're naked native women running around barefoot in some undeveloped country.

"Then there's the way human women like to dress to show off their tits. They wear dresses that are guaranteed to make them catch colds because their chest is exposed from their neck to their belly buttons, and there's this flimsy bit of cloth that sort of covers up the middle and outside half of their tits but lets you see the inside half. They call it the 'plunging neckline' or the 'plunge your eyes down to my pussy' look, or something like that. I guess they're not sure if they should wear anything to cover their tits or not, so they compromise.

"You must act like you never notice this look, and you never comment about it. Even if your woman asks what you thought of another woman in the half-a-tit dress, you must tell her that you didn't notice the dress or the woman wearing it. Now when a woman is nursing a baby, she will usually hide her tits, which is really weird because that's when her tits are the biggest. So when her tits are kind of normal-sized, she tries to accentuate them, but when her tits are naturally full, she tries to hide them. I need to do more tit research and study the way women think about them. It's a very mysterious area, and very few men have put a lot of serious research into it. I've thought about applying for a grant from the National Science Foundation to study tits, and I may still do that. I'll keep you updated on the idea.

"When women wear a skirt or dress they don't sit with their feet on the floor. They sit with their legs crossed so you can look way up their legs, almost all the way up to their pussies. It's very hard to understand them. I can't imagine why they are always showing off their body parts like they do. This is a very hard area for me, but I'm trying to tell you what I know about them. Every young man needs good advice and guidance from an older man in this area.

"Women love to talk a lot. You can tell that just by being quiet. If you're in a restaurant, just listen for a while. Before you know it, some woman will start laughing like a screaming hyena. Then everybody will start talking louder and all the women will start shouting. It's always the women who make it impossible to hear yourself think in a restaurant. They talk all the time about stuff that means absolutely nothing. Mostly they talk about how pissed off they are at other women or about some guy who said or did something.

"They never talk about what the markets are doing or what kind of deal they can put together. They'll talk about babies and birthdays and funerals, like how nice somebody looked in their casket, if the guy was a goy, or how nice the widow looked at Shiva, if she's a Jewess. They'll even talk about the food they ate at the reception after they put the poor stiff in the ground, can you imagine that?

"If they talk about how a baby barfs up its food or shits after they just put a fresh diaper on the little bastard, you need to pretend it's all very fascinating. If they talk about their fucking cats and how the damn things tear up their furniture, you have to try hard not to let them know that they're nuts for having cats in the first place. You need to let them think that it's all just fascinating.

"Listen, this is really, really important. As an UGGA executive, you need to understand that nothing escapes their attention. The female organization is a giant information gathering and dissemination machine, like a combination vacuum cleaner and leaf blower. Gossip goes into one end, gets spun around, sliced and diced into total nonsensical bullshit, and then when you'd least expect it, like at a cocktail party, or in an important meeting, little balls of gossip crap and flying monkeys come blowing out of it. That's the women's way of disseminating information.

"Never tell any woman what you're thinking. If you make that mistake, they'll never forget it and they'll never let you forget it either. Everything you think about has to be top secret around a woman. Never even hint at what you're thinking about. If you give them a hint about something, it drives them totally nuts and they will not rest until they do the same in return.

"You could say 'I thought that so and so was thus and such,' and sure as hell, a year later, after the facts and opinions have all changed, the woman will zap you with a 'But I thought you said!' kind of shot into your composure. They'll hit you with a zinger when you are off guard and helpless. They're very crafty that way. Think of them as airplanes circling overhead always ready to drop a bomb on you. They like to remember stuff you say or do so they can use it against you later. Have you ever watched old German war films where Hitler bombs the crap out of everyone? You should. That's the closest men will ever come to understanding how women go about deploying what knowledge they have attained about them to bring them to their knees. Never say anything to a woman except to tell them they look nice.

"They like hearing that. You can say 'yes' or 'no' to some things, like if they ask you if you had lunch or not, but be careful. Even the simplest thing can get you nailed. Like if you tell a woman you had lunch, she'll start in on you. 'Who with? What did you talk about? Was his wife there? Why not? Why wasn't I there? How are their kids doing? What do you mean you didn't ask? What do you mean you don't give a shit about their kids? What kind of monster are you? You just go out and get your own dinner!'

"'Okay,' you say. 'Okay!'

"'What do you mean you're going out by yourself? Don't you want to take me with you? Fuck you!'

"Can you get it? Can you see how the least little thing you say can be used to torture you for an entire month? Then they won't let up on you until you buy them something so they'll look better than some other woman. Now you can see why some guys join the Marine Corps. It's so they won't go nuts listening to a woman. Some guys would rather take their chances getting killed.

"It's best to lob women a marshmallow to chew on when they ask a question. If she asks, 'Did she have a hat on?' or 'Did they drive their new car?' you say, 'I didn't notice.' That way you don't have to hear her say, 'Well, did you know she wore that same hat last week to play bridge? Didn't she look silly in it?' Or 'When will we get a new car? What do you mean our car works fine? What do you mean you don't give a shit if it's an older model? I guess you're married to me because I'm old too, huh? You're a monster! Why can't you turn that fucking football game off?'

"You see what I mean? Just tell them you don't know or you can't remember anything and you'll have a more peaceful life. Just try to think of yourself as part of the sofa and move as little as possible. Keep your head down. It's important.

"Never, ever have a drink with a woman. That's really asking for trouble. If she's your wife, she'll get a little buzzed and she'll start grinding on you about all the things that are wrong with you and your home and your life, her parents and her siblings, her pets and her preacher, then she'll move on to her gynecologist, and all her other doctors. She'll complain that her flowers didn't bloom right and that the butcher didn't cut the meat right and that so and so was a terrible bridge partner, and that the dress she just pissed away your monthly income on doesn't fit her right.

"She'll tell you it's all your fault that the kids got bad grades, and that one of them has a mental problem because you told him a bedtime story where Bambi got shot or about how the baby and the cradle fell out of the treetop, or how the wolf went after the three little pigs. She'll even complain that the grocery store had the wrong kind of toilet paper and it's your fault that the house ran out of it because you spend too much time in the bathroom so she got the cheaper kind and now it scratches her ass. Trust me. When you take your woman out for a drink you will get an earful.

"Now it's much worse than that for you if you have a drink with a woman who is not your woman. Then all hell breaks loose. One of her girlfriends is going to see you sitting at a bar having a drink with another woman who is not your woman. If she is crying while you're sitting there with her, then you were either being a monster to the poor woman or you were sympathizing with her and helping her get over a rough patch. Either way, you are in huge trouble.

ROSEMARY LIGHTFOOT NESS BITNER

"If your woman's girlfriend spy reads the scene and determines you were being a monster, then you are reviled for hurting one of the girls. You'll end up sleeping out in your car on the street and you won't even be allowed to bring the car into the garage. Your dinner will be thrown out on the lawn for you, without a plate. Doors will be slammed in your face and your kids will be told to never speak to you again. You can't go and apologize to the other woman and make it all right, because she was crying about something entirely different, like just two minutes before found out her cat got run over by a car or something, but it doesn't matter. Nothing really matters. You are in the doghouse, buddy, and you're going to stay there until your woman drags you back out to bitch to you about how one of her girlfriends said something about her to one of her other girlfriends.

"If you're having a drink with a woman who's not your woman and the snoop sees her smiling or laughing, then you are totally fucked. You were running around on your woman. You were luring that woman into bed with you. You've been meeting her secretly for years. You're a low-down dog and a terrible monster. It's back to sleeping in your car and eating your hamburger or hot dogs off the grass again. Never mind that the woman just got a phone call a few minutes before from her kid, who told her how he put a frog in his teacher's desk drawer and the frog jumped out and the teacher ran out of the classroom screaming to get away from the frog and you were only meeting the woman to plan a surprise birthday party for your wife.

"The truth doesn't matter to women. Their emotions are all that ever matter. They just want to have some reason to constantly be hysterical. Your woman will never believe you're telling her the truth, and even a week later, when your woman confirms with some other members of the female organization that you really were telling the truth, it still won't matter. All that matters is that you were seen with another woman in a bar. That's what your woman will remember for the rest of her life and she'll never forgive you. The only thing worse than having a drink with a woman who is not your woman is going to a bar and having a drink by yourself. When the spy sees this, you've had it, buddy. You were planning something and not letting your wife in on it, or you were waiting for some mystery woman, or you just got caught embezzling and you wanted that one last drink before the auditors checked the inventory accounts and you committed suicide.

"Whatever your reason for being there it's wrong. Now you're out sleeping in your car and eating chicken noodle soup off the grass. You wish you could trade places with the family dog, but that's out of the question. The dog did nothing wrong. The dog is now sleeping on your side of the bed and he's even been elevated to higher status at mealtimes. He's allowed to eat off the table. You get to eat off the grass with the worms. Maybe you try to explain that you were just waiting for an old buddy from college who came to town and you hadn't seen him for ten years. It won't matter. Your woman will never believe you.

"So what can you do when you want to have a drink? You do what I do. You drink discreetly where the women can't see you. You go to a liquor store and buy a bottle and you drink it while you're driving around in your car. That way all you need to worry about is the cops. If they nail you for drinking while driving, and odds are low on getting nailed for that, then at least the cops will tell you what the deal is, what the punishment is, and when it's over. Sure, you might have to watch some horrible movies of traffic accidents with people who got their guts splattered all over the place and you might have to fork over a few hundred bucks, but that beats listening to a woman grinding on you and driving you nuts for months or years until she can't even remember why she's pissed off at you.

"Those are some of the basics to keep in mind about women. They apply to all women. Remember always that women are trivial, vain, selfish, gossipy, thought-challenged, and steeped in jealousy of other women. Parties, who talks about whom and who entertained whom and who wasn't invited, are all matters that concern them greatly, almost as much as which male is presently dipping his wick into which woman's pussy, especially their own. Now that we've covered that, let's get into the more complicated female subtleties you're going to run into.

"Let's say you're at a dinner party and you are seated across from some guy's wife. She goes to eat the olive from out of her martini glass, but it falls off the toothpick and hits her on the chest as it rolls down into her brazier. You're the only one who sees this and she knows you are the only one who sees this. Now, what you need to do next will depend upon the behavior of the woman. If she gives you a big grinning smile, that's your signal to go into rescue mode. She wants you to stand up, throw your body across the table, hold her shoulder to keep her steady and with your other hand reach down her bra and get that pesky olive out of there. That way she saves herself the trouble of having to get up and go to the ladies' room because she might have been paying close attention to a conversation at the table. That woman will be very grateful and she will thank you for the help, later.

"In the same identical situation, if the woman looks away from you. Kind of off to the side, that means she needs help but is too embarrassed to be up front about it. She expects you to get up, walk around the table behind her, quickly reach down her bra, grab the olive and eat it yourself so no one will see she's so shaky from the booze she can't get the olive from her glass to her mouth. She'll also be very appreciative for your assistance and she too will thank you later.

"Again, this time you're across from a young winsome, full breasted, gorgeous woman who has a boyfriend next to her that has no brains and he's ignoring her. When that gal looks you in the eye as she drops the olive into her bra, you're actually getting an invitation to fuck her right then and there. She's hot to get your dick into her and she doesn't want to wait until later. That gal wants you to come up with some excuse, no matter how feeble, to get her the hell out of there and take her to some room in the hotel or even the ladies' room and fuck her brains out. That's definitely the signal you're getting from her and you need to move fast.

"Make an announcement that you have something very special to bring to the table and you need her specific help to go with you to go get it. Now, there's absolutely nothing to bring to the table, so you take her to a liquor store, grab a bottle, go to a room, drink half the bottle with her and fuck her, then you take the unused half bottle with the two of you back to the table. You explain that there was a whole case of this stuff, but somehow somebody stole it. The two of you were everywhere looking for it, kind of like a snipe hunt, but all you could find was this half-bottle.

"Now, when you put some deep thought into each of these women's behaviors, like I have, you can only come to one conclusion. When a woman indicates distress to you at a cocktail party, she's really trying to tell you she wants to get laid. They all want to get laid, kind of like chickens with a rooster, but they have their different ways of giving you the 'I want to get laid' signal. When you get that signal, you need to move on it fast, before some other guy gets it. This is your big advantage. Most men don't understand women as well as I do. I'm glad you're paying close attention and getting this. It's important.

"One subtle signal they sometimes give off is when they want you to punch out their boyfriend or husband. Let me give you an example. You're at a picnic. Her husband is at the grill making hotdogs. He hands her one with relish and mustard and onions on it. She shakes her head. He persists and shoves it at her and yells something at her, like that's what she told him she wanted. Now this sort of thing happens a lot with women. They change their minds on a dime and it's always some guy's fault for not realizing they've changed their mind, even though the woman never said a word about it. So now this guy is pissed off because he has this hotdog and she doesn't want it. She holds up her hands to him, waving him off like a carrier pilot gets waved off on approach from his landing signal officer.

"That's your clue that the woman's husband has crashed and burned. She's now more pissed off than he is over that fucking hotdog and she wants somebody to rescue her. At this point, you need to run up to him and give him a man-to-man chest bump, or a double-hands-on-chest shove that knocks him back a few steps, preferably on his ass. Now you're a hero to that woman because you got that nasty inconsiderate bully off her. This move really works best after you've had a few beers because if he comes back at you, you're going to have to knock the crap out of him, and if he knocks the crap out of you it helps if you're too stoned to feel anything.

"I know this seems like a big to-do over whether or not a hotdog has relish on it, but to a woman, this means everything. They want to see in their crazy warped tiny minds that no matter how old, how ugly, how stupid they are, there's this knight in shining armor who will rush to their aid and save them from eating a fucking hotdog with relish on it if they don't want it. Remember that.

"It was never about the hotdog. It was about the woman getting some man to understand her, which was impossible for that poor bastard because nobody can ever understand women in the first place. If you time your move right and nail him before any other guy does, all the women will think you are their champion. They'll think you understand them, even though you don't, and even though they don't understand themselves. But they won't give you any grief about anything for a few weeks because they'll believe you tried to help them somehow by knocking some poor bastard on his ass.

"They'll never remember why you did what you did, just that you did it. Your own woman will probably ask you why you did that. You just need to tell her, in a manly way, 'It was the right thing to do.' Sometimes this response to a woman's signal can land you in jail overnight because the police want to make sure you've cooled off before they let you out. If that happens to you, just get a good night's sleep and a big breakfast before you go home."

"There's one special breed of woman you need to be especially careful with. Never do business with one of these because they are nuts. They call themselves feminists because they see the world inside out and backwards. Instead of being soft, warm loving creatures that want to have babies and please a husband and have a good home, they want to live for the sole purpose of making men miserable. They want to fight and bitch about everything and basically eradicate men from the face of the earth. They must all be mentally ill because their top leader instructed them to do everything possible to repel men, to keep men out of their lives. This leader of theirs came up with this really sick idea that to keep men away from them they should make their pussies smell as terrible as possible; so she instructed them all to stick dead fish in their pussies and ride around in bicycles instead of cars, to kind of grind the smell of a stinky fish into their pussies on a permanent basis. You can't do business with women like that. If you listen to them long enough they'll let it slip out how much they hate men for whatever reason. Some will try to conceal themselves, so you have to kind of smell around their female area while being inconspicuous about it. If you get that fishy smell, you could have a feminist, so be extra careful.

"One day in your UGGA investment career you will certainly run across this situation. You will make a call to talk to one of your clients. The client could be a man's wife or it could be the husband, no matter. The wife will answer the phone. You'll ask how things are doing, you know, usual small talk. Then, all of a sudden, this woman will start crying. That's what they do best, cry. She'll confide in you that her husband has stage four cancers in some organ, like the prostate, stomach, colon, liver, or all of his organs. She'll start crying. Now, here's where you can really get some terrific business. See, most guys will tell her how sorry they are to hear this terrible news and they'll tell her if she needs anything to just call and they'll do whatever they can to help her. But, that's the wrong thing to say. If you're smart, you'll take my advice on this.

"See, the real reasons the woman is crying are that the guy will die and won't be bringing home a paycheck anymore, and secondly, she won't be getting schlonged by her old reliable meat organ anymore. See, in truth, women don't love men in the first place. They're just like ungulates. They just want the guy to hose them and then they don't want him around the rest of the time. They'd rather be playing bridge with the girls or going to some stupid garden party or lunch with their girl-friends. Except for the necessary schlonging and money coming in, women don't want men around. Here's what your correct response needs to be to all her crying:

'Wow! That's terrific news, Molly. Soon that piece of dead wood will be dead for real! Right after we get him buried, I'd like to take you out for a martini at your favorite hotel and then fuck your brains out. You're a real hot number and I can't wait to get into your pants. I'll take you on a celebration trip to Paris and we'll just party until we drop. What do you say? Have we got a deal?'

"See, that kind of response puts you in a whole different category from all her other friends. Now she can look forward to continue getting schlonged and she can have some hope that you'll replace the corpse's lost income. So, you've solved her real-world problem instantly. Your move is to get with her as soon as possible after he dies. Don't even wait until his body cools before you bang her. Tell her you just can't wait for formalities. Then, get his insurance proceeds invested in UGGA. After that you need an excuse to stop seeing her because schlonging a client is against some ridiculous rules. Schlonging is okay as long as assets go up, but if they go down the woman can turn bitch on you and sue you for duress and mental stuff, which they can fake really well in front of an arbitration panel because they are all nuts anyway and arbitration panels are just as crazy. So, after you've banged her a few times and gotten her money, you're better off to drop her because once she's a client the rules kick in. This is valuable advice and a great insight into female psychology, so don't forget it. Do you think you can be a good company man and answer the call of duty to help a woman in distress?"

"I don't know about that one, David. It sounds a little sordid."

David didn't like the sound of that. It smacked of impudence. He verbally retaliated. "Well, life is one sordid run of the gauntlet. That's not it with you, though, is it? It's Barbara, that Indian girl in the front office, isn't it? I've seen the way you steal looks at her and I've seen the way her eyes light up when she sees you. Is something going on with the two of you?"

"No, David. It's just your imagination working overtime," said Bob. But, to David's trained ear, Bob sounded unconvincing.

"Well, in any case, remember this about women if you remember nothing else. Just always be ready to give them the servicing they are all looking for and don't try to understand them. Just think of yourself as a dog they grab onto for a good humping. You can never understand them, so don't bother trying. You'll just drive yourself nuts. Always have an escape plan when you're with a woman. You can lose them in the crowd when you take them to a football game; or you have to leave dinner early because you have too much work to do; or you need to meet the guys at the gym; or you must go to the library. Better yet, take her to the library with you and when you're there tell her to get lost. She can't scream at you in a library. Just never stop thinking of how to get away from them. It's important to understand that when dealing with women you are in a constant state of war."

After Bob drove off for the office that day, David sat pensively on a grassy rise at the edge of the barnyard. All was quiet. The sun approached midday and the animals and birds were resting. Dolly ambled over to David and lay down beside him. David reclined on his sheep and rested his head on her back. As he looked up at the clouds and scratched the animal's head, he talked to her.

"It's time to think ahead, Dolly. We can't let this Bob fellow have control of the game we play, can we? Do you have any bright ideas?'

Dolly, of course, said nothing. The sheep didn't even make her 'Bah' sound. That's one of the things David liked about the animal. No back talk. No contradictions. No mistaken communications, ever.

"This thing could take any of several paths, Dolly. With the deal we made with Bob, it's unlikely that he'll up and quit. He's not the sort. He sticks to his goals. That's going to be a long-term problem for us, sweetheart. Probably I gave away more than I should have. I could kick myself for being impulsive. So here you and I are, just sitting together in the barnyard.

"There's always a move, Dolly. You know that. You know I've been thinking about this. I won't let you down. Don't worry. I'm true to my roots. There's one path I foresee this taking, and I can make our move now, so I guess I better start working on it. Who was that girl Marty said she whored around with here in Plaintown? Didn't she say something about making a pornographic movie and going to orgies with her? It was Rita, wasn't it? Yeah, I remember her name was Rita. Do you remember a different name?"

Dolly lay there chewing a bit of grass.

"I need to figure out who this Rita is and give her a call, Dolly. Tomorrow the Mrs. goes away on a trip to France for three whole weeks. Tomorrow night you can stay with me in the bedroom. Would you like that, sweetheart?"

Dolly lay there chewing her grass.

THE OTHER LESSONS

China

Bob arrived the next day for another executive coaching lesson on diverse topics.

"China is something you need to know about because the Chinese are going to take over the entire world. I've never been to China, but I read a book about it once, and I watch the news on TV. Whenever something about China comes on, I turn up the volume so I can hear it. It's a world player kind of country, so you'd think we need to know a lot about it, but we don't. They've got about twenty billion people living over there in an area the size of Colorado. They think they are the center of the universe and they all wear stupid-looking gray jackets and carry a little red book around with them. Most of their women wear black skirts and walk around in rice paddies, unless they are wearing black pants. I don't know why their women wear black pants sometimes and black skirts other times, but it's probably not important.

"I once had two salesmen who went there and told me all about it. They said Chinese women are all sex-crazed and beautiful. They got laid constantly. They said Chinese screwed better than American women and that they fuck non-stop over there. I gave those sales reports a lot of thought. They must be accurate; how else can you explain the over one billion people they have?"

"I don't know. Maybe it's because they have a five thousand-year culture."

"Maybe, but I doubt it. They had Samurai warlords and warriors running around the place killing everybody and keeping the population down for thousands and thousands of years. They even rode on horses so they could kill people faster. Those women must have fucked their brains out to keep replacing the population killed by the Samurai."

"Weren't the Samurai Japanese warriors?"

"Maybe, but who cares? It doesn't matter. They've been killing each other for ten thousand years. They even invented steel over there so they could make these terrific swords that cut heads off easier. As a matter of fact, I don't think you need to worry about radical Salafists. The Chinese will eventually invade the Middle East and kill everybody in that country for the oil."

"But the Middle East isn't a single country. It's a place with a lot of countries."

"No, it isn't! It's a big sandbox with camels and Arabs driving around in Mercedes Benz cars between oil wells to gas up. Remember, it's not that important who kills who in those places, anyway. What is important is to never underestimate your adversary, and the Chinese are your adversary."

"But we trade with them."

"Don't let that little detail fool you. It's just a Chinese plot to screw us. Way back in 1841, when the Brits landed in Hong Kong, the Chinese were incredibly naïve. They let the Brits set up trading all over China, which at the time was a split-up place with different strongmen in charge of different areas. This was before the Reds took it over. The Brits got the Chinese women hooked on opium. The Brits were getting silver from the Chinese women in exchange for opium, and then, when the women were totally stoned, the Brits screwed their brains out. That's how Hong Kong Chinese learned English. The Brits showed them how to make heroin and how to smoke the opium pipe. In return, the Brits got laid a lot and they got China's silver.

"The Communists ruined a good thing. They're dickheads who got the people working instead of getting wasted on opium. Now the Chinese want their silver back from the West so they can use it as money again, like back in the warlord days. They'll get rid of paper dollars just like they got rid of opium. Chinese think everything that went wrong in China is the West's fault. They want to settle old scores and make us pay for what our ancestors did to their ancestors.

"They carry grudges for thousands of years over there. They even take special care when they bury their ancestors' bones. When they build something, they dig up bones and rebury them. They're completely nuts over old bones. Once they get their silver back, they'll put the price up to hundreds of dollars an ounce here in the U.S. They'll invade the United States. They'll kill all the men, screw our women, and enslave our children. Then they'll move about ten billion Chinese over here to live in the U.S. Ten or twenty years from now, there will be ten billion Chinese in Africa, ten billion Chinese in the U.S., maybe ten billion in South America, and another twenty billion still in China.

"I'm trying to tell you to learn Chinese; otherwise, you'll be screwed. You don't have to thank me for all this wisdom I'm giving you. It's part of your grooming to run UGGA. If I didn't enlighten you, you'd never learn anything."

Russia

"You can't possibly expect to be the chief executive without completely understanding Russia. Russia is a country that's three hundred times larger than the United States. I guess they need a lot of land to make all the vodka they drink and develop a few decent chess players. The reason Russia is such a problem for the normal world is their peoples' brains are frozen by all the snow which makes their entire culture focus on ice hockey.

"Their nitwit leader is so obsessed by his tiny man complex he rides around naked on horses to pretend he's a big man. He walks down a long hallway in the Kremlin with cameras angled up so he appears bigger. It's like the *Wizard of Oz* scene in the Emerald City.

"The Russian people don't eat right. They have no sunshine so they can't grow vegetables. They have vitamin B deficiencies throughout the entire country. Russians try to compensate for the lack of vegetables by buying vitamin-fortified cereal, but that just leads to bigger problems. Their cows are always freezing to death or getting eaten by abominable snowmen, or yetis, so they don't have enough milk for their cereal. They compensate by putting oil on their cereal instead of milk because they have so much oil it comes out of their water taps.

"Solving Russia's problems will solve all the world's problems. The first thing that needs to happen is the name of Russia needs to be changed from Russia to Not Russia. Then all of Not Russia needs to be divided up into smaller pieces of one square mile each. The little pieces of Not Russia need to be given out to Americans, so each American owns a few square miles of Not Russia.

"Then American construction companies must get interest free loans to buy bulldozers from Caterpillar, because CAT could use the business. These construction companies must bull doze all the Not Russia buildings that have onions on top of them, including the Kremlin building and the surrounding Not Russia government buildings. That would be good because those buildings with onions on them don't look like big square boxes like we have here in America. All the Not Russia government workers must be fired and sent to China. This would be ideal. They are model, top ranked, world class government workers. Since they have Not Russia so completely screwed up, they could leave and screw up another country.

"Once all the stupid looking buildings are leveled, normal, good-looking buildings, like McDonalds' golden arches and Colonel Sanders smiling on a bucket of fried chicken on top of the building, could replace all the goofy Not Russia buildings. Each American who owns a chunk of the new Not Russia would be given a fast food franchise license. This would allow Americans to hire their own personal private contractor armies to operate within Not Russia to ensure that the Not Russian people quickly adapt to America's common sense approach to living the American Dream. With Americans running the place things would happen quickly. Strip clubs, bars, football stadiums, drag car racing, and stock car racing tracks, everything wonderful American would get quickly built. Not Russia would get jump started into the American way.

"As a final step to straightening out Not Russia, all the furniture and jewels of the Winter Palace and all the other palaces and Dachas need to be auctioned off. Those nice things don't belong over there anyway. The Russians don't wear jewels and they don't like nice furniture at all. Their furniture would look great in American whorehouses and those jewels would look better refashioned into pendants that hang the jewels on necklaces. The jewels would hang on the plunge line and rest on top of the cleavage, right between the tits of hot American women.

"The remaining cleanup of the Not Russia mess would take all their military toys on barges to the middle of the Atlantic Ocean. Submarines, ballistic missiles, tanks, ships, all Not Russia toys, would be placed in mid-ocean. Then a group of U.S. Navy destroyers would come and blast the crap out of that Russian garbage and sink it to the bottom of the ocean. That would also give our Navy necessary gunnery practice for the next time we go back to Vietnam. We need to blast the living shit out that place like we should have the first time we were over there. Now that you have a complete understanding of Russia, you can consider yourself wise in geopolitics, which is required to be a top executive."

Politicians

"Politicians are Jell-O in suits with no principles or ethics. This is important to know because when you need to get something done or if you need to get a regulator off your back, you need to figure out the right politician to bribe. The politician will sell his mother for a buck and let you screw his daughter for two bucks, but they play a vital role in society because civilization is messy. If you don't have a guy in your pocket who can slime around in sewers, you can get into trouble. Never hesitate to ask your local politician what it costs to get something done. When you ask, make sure you're stuffing a thousand bucks in his pocket. That way you'll get his attention.

"None of them know how to get anything done. They'd never survive in business. They're not smart enough. You need to work out what you want done with your lawyers ahead of time. You outline what needs to be done, have your lawyer make you a roadmap, then take the roadmap to the politician and pay him off. That's the way to do things. Don't mess around going to zoning hearings or crap like that. Don't bother with school board meetings. All that stuff is a waste of time that never gets results. What gets results is paying off the right people ahead of the meeting.

"Judges are trickier to bribe, but it's doable. Keep in mind that they are politicians in disguise. They want to get bought off on their rulings, but they want to pretend that they're above it all. They're neurotic nitwits with big egos. They wear black robes to feel safe inside their neurosis.

"To bribe a judge without getting clumsy about it, first find out what charity they or their wife are affiliated with. You arrange a big donation to the charity and have the charity agree in advance that it will pay a huge consulting fee to the judge or the judge's spouse. Then you'll get your judge to rule in your favor. Notice I said *your* judge. Once the judge agrees to terms on the bribe, you own them."

Government

"Government is an institutional insane asylum for powerful people who have the most money to hire the lobbyists and bribe the bureaucrats so the little people pay taxes and get screwed. Government is like a child-eating monster. It stumbles along and steps on everything in its path. It sways a little to the left or the right, but it always moves forward. It always gets bigger and does less for the people and more for itself. Its bureaucrats have individual fiefdoms that grow larger by doing less. The only objective of government is to get bigger for the sake of getting bigger.

"If you want to have a frustrating day, call the government. You will be put into a voice messaging system that tells you all the wonderful things your government is doing for you, then you will be directed to a line that tells you there's an hour wait before you talk to a real live human being. When the human being picks up the phone, you will be accidentally disconnected and will need to start all over again. What the country needs is a leader who fires ninety percent of the people who work in government.

"A government is only as effective as the person in charge of running it. Most governments have ineffective leadership and nothing ever gets accomplished, or what does get accomplished is a mishmash of projects and programs that can't possibly work or the private sector would have done it already. When I think about leadership in government, my own personal idol is Adolph Hitler. That guy really knew how to get things done.

"But, David, you're a Jew. How can you idolize Adolph Hitler?"

"Easily. I'm on the subject of leadership in government. Hitler got things done and he didn't let anybody get in his way. He was totally committed to moving his country forward at all times. When he needed to lie, he lied. When he needed to murder, he murdered. When he needed to make a whole population forsake their morality and go forth and murder other peoples by the millions, he did that also. When he needed to find a scapegoat to advance his agenda and blame for his country's past losses and failures, he found one in the Jews, and he got the whole country behind him to commit the murder of millions of Jews.

"The man was a magnificent example of outstanding leadership. Under his leadership, Germany advanced from a terrible depression to become the world's powerhouse. He never lost sight of his goal and never thought for one moment that any deed was too horrible to undertake in order to achieve the goal. He even killed his niece, his lover, because she displeased him. Later he killed Eva Braun, his mistress, before he faked his death and slipped away to Argentina. That's leadership, being able to murder like that to first protect his image and later to silence Eva's knowledge of his escape plans and his legacy. That's true leadership, knowing how to use everybody.

"I wish I could be more like him. I think I could be if I could figure out a way to get control of the country, but I haven't done that yet. And conditions in America aren't ripe for a leader like Hitler. Plus, now there's that dratted social media and the National Rifle Association. Those freedom-loving bastards will fight back. Ideal conditions for a totalitarian America won't happen in my time, but they could later in your lifetime, or in your children's or grandchildren's time. I have to be content to lead a company forward. Whenever I get bogged down with some problem, I think to myself, 'How would Hitler solve this problem?'

"So you would murder people who got in your way?"

"It's not that I wouldn't like to. I'd like to kill half the people who work in the office, but that's a huge step to take without control of the police or the government like Hitler had. In the corporate world and in government, people get murdered all the time. It's happening now and getting swept under the rug. People who trade currencies, interest rate derivatives, and precious metals illegally for big multinational banks somehow mysteriously fall out of windows, or their cars roll down embankments and crash, or they drown in their bathtubs, or they hang themselves, or miraculously find a way to shoot themselves twenty times with a nail gun without stopping from the pain of the first shot. This stuff happens. Planes with important people aboard, people who know secrets that must be kept, crash and those key people die. You can't take testimony from a body part splattered over the ground after a plane wreck, or from a guy who blows his own brains out while feeding squirrels one morning sitting on a park bench in Washington, D.C. either."

"What are you saying?"

"Be aware of these things. In every country there are sociopaths. Power is an aphrodisiac for them, and they will murder to gain and hang on to their power. Seeing their deeds for what they are gives you some sense of when the country will fall into the hands of another Hitler."

"There will never be another Hitler."

"Oh yes, there will be. The next Hitler will be billions of deaths worse than Hitler, because the next one will have the nuclear weapons he or she needs to kill by the hundreds of millions of people, probably billions."

"Are you serious?"

"I'm deadly serious. All it takes is one sociopath to piss off another sociopath. Then bam! One guy nukes the other, but wait! They have a friend who has nukes and the friend shoots off a few nukes at the first guy. Then he blasts those bastards back. Soon nukes are flying everywhere and ninety percent of the world population gets fried. Maybe the USA comes through it all with only two or three cities getting nuked, and we'd be kings of the rest of the world because we have anti-nuke missiles and iron shields and lasers, but that's not why we might survive. Our American babes are so good-looking with such hot pussies that no enemy, not even terrorists, want to hurt them.

"Avoid participating in government. You'll be bombarded with phone calls and surveys. You'll never get any work done, plus you'll spend half your working hours reporting for jury duty. You'll never have time for your own business.

"If you ever go into government, make sure you have a private e-mail service, like in Switzerland or Luxembourg, or maybe the Cayman Islands, or have your own server in the basement of your house like top government people who are above the law have here in the United States. That way, the government and the regulatory agencies can't see what's going on. That way, like the criminal people we have in the American in government who commit treason by selling the country's interests for money, you too can delete things that you did which are illegal and should put you in jail and the government can't get to you. You can lose your e-mails, lie under oath, commit crimes, bribe regulators, and make illegal payments to people all over the world or have them make payments to you. You can sabotage your corporate opponents and commit whatever crimes you feel like committing.

"It's a terrific concept! It's also a good idea to know some mafia guys so you can kill people who know too much about what you're doing. It's better and cheaper than paying lawyers to defend you. Just destroy evidence and kill people who know too much. You leave no trail to follow. You can live on top of the dung pile you made and get propped up by people you bribe in the mainstream media to create the phony image that you're a good-natured person."

Regulators

"A regulator's job is to put you in jail or out of business for no reason whatsoever. They will find any excuse or customer complaint to sit on your business and waste your time, no matter how honest or innocent you are. If you have industry clout like Bernie Madoff, regulators leave you alone even if they have a detailed case dropped in their laps. Regulators are politically sensitive, but they don't know the ins and outs of the industry and they have trouble relating methods of fraud to market developments. They are cozy with big firms they want to get jobs with. They permit these big firms to conceal their litigation histories and criminal wrongdoings from their clients while they screw little firms to the wall to build up their résumés. If you find one that treats you fairly, kiss their ass.

"When they come to the office, be courteous and offer them a glass of water. Do not try to bribe them, especially if there are two of them. If one of them hints that they want a bribe to leave you alone, make sure they're alone. Feel them out and get them to make a demand for money. They could be wearing a wire, so you never make an offer to bribe them first. Sit them down in an office with no access to your computer systems.

"The best way to get the regulator to leave you alone is to tell them to be careful not to touch anything. Tell them there is a mysterious virus in the office and people who have come there from the outside world have gotten ill and died. Tell them you're getting some infectious disease specialists from Russia to fly over in a few days because no Americans can figure it out and the last scientist who came dropped dead in fifty minutes. Then fall down on the floor and roll around a little, hold your head and stomach alternately, and spit up on the floor. Tell them that's the initial sign of it, that it hasn't progressed any further with anyone on the staff yet, but outsiders get those same symptoms and die in about an hour. Get up and walk toward the regulator with your tongue hanging out. Hold out your arms and ask them to catch you and get you to a chair. If they haven't left by then, scream and hold your throat. Tell them it's getting worse. Tell them they need to run for their life. That should do it.

"Some women regulators use their position for husband shopping. Like all women, they are fuck-happy, but these women like fucking the men they regulate. Some carry whips and chains in their briefcases. If one asks you to discuss things after hours or over lunch, she's looking for it. You have a big decision. If you fuck her and she doesn't think you liked her, or if you did a poor job on her, she can make life hell for you. If she likes it, she can make life hell for you as well because she'll want to marry you and have kids. She'll keep coming around to regulate and fuck you to death until you give in and marry her. If you don't give in, she'll throw you in the slammer.

"The way out of that situation is to get sick and stay sick until she goes away. Have Mrs. Rodriguez or Barbara take down her questions for you and have a lawyer with them until the regulator goes away. The other possibility when all else fails and she really insists on talking with you is to have an auto accident. Just drive your car head-on into a truck. Do this in the city so you're not going so fast you kill yourself, but break your nose and an arm or a leg, like a combined speed crash of about twenty-five to thirty miles per hour. Then you can get some sympathy from her while telling her that you can't remember anything. You can even drop your licenses for up to two years until she shakes off. Apply to get your licenses back again after she finds some guy and gets herself married. Be prepared to pass out on the floor whenever you are asked a question you don't want to answer."

David withheld from Bob an incident where he tangled with a female regulator. For reason known only to her, she decided to camp out at the UGGA offices and nitpick every detail of the firm's activities. All transaction blotter books were pulled for her inspection to correlate sales with commission payments to dealers. All regulatory manuals were scrutinized for procedural violations. All investment board meeting minutes were examined. She even called Fund board members to confirm their understandings of the meetings.

David had asked her, "Can you give me some idea when you'll be finished? And, must you sit here in our public lobby when we have a conference room set aside for you?"

"When I finish, and not before! Do not rush me and do not interrupt me again. Until then, make yourself useful and fetch me a glass of water. And, by the way, from what I can tell, you seem to be the only person here who has nothing to do. All you do is buy and sell the market average based upon that silly chart you keep in your little closet. Isn't that right? And you charge fees for this nonsense? You have a lot of gall to run a sham like this, Mr. Sustack."

The woman had humiliated David right there in the lobby in front of the firm's employees. It was clear she intended to camp out a while, and she was not going to be hurried. David was made to feel small and insignificant. His ego was bruised and he had flashbacks to the humiliations he suffered at the hands of his mother. Two days later, the woman's car was broken into and gasoline was poured over the car's interior and the car was set ablaze. Police came and investigated David and his whereabouts that day, but they found nothing and the crime was never solved. The next day the regulator closed her audit books on UGGA, produced a satisfactory report and left the premises. She never returned to UGGA again and subsequent regulatory audits were done in less than a day's time, always with satisfactory comments. David had descended to new sociopathic lows where he was brazen and willing to defy authorities, push back against them when they challenged him, and commit crimes against those officials who got in his way.

Charities

"Charities are organizations created by women to drive you crazy. If you give money to one your name will go on lists and you'll be hounded to death with phone calls and mailings. They'll find out who your friends are. They'll pressure your friends to take them as guests to dinner functions, where you're supposed to be happy about eating a crappy meal and buying useless junk at silent auctions and raffles. Once your name is on a charity's donor list, you'll be on hundreds more like it. They sell your name to other charities because they're all so hungry for money. Think about this. If all the government's wonderful programs really worked we wouldn't have the need for charities, would we? Charities are proof the government's programs are phony bull shit.

"It becomes impossible to get rid of charities. It's like having a pit bull's teeth clamped into your knee that you can't shake him off. They aren't run by smart people. If they were, they'd have all male charity nights and they'd hire some terrific hookers so the men would spend big bucks. Charities are run by women volunteers, so you won't see many hookers at those functions. You'll get a long-winded speaker or washed-up entertainer and a terrible meal. You'll talk to idiots. You'll go home swearing you'll never go again so there's no reason to go in the first place.

"Charities aren't about helping people anyway. They are opportunities for wives to dress up and flaunt their dresses and jewels at other women, and to have a chance to gossip about women who didn't show up. Charity events are for women to go husband shopping or to find a stray guy and get laid. Married women look at these events like they're going to a car dealer to upgrade their car.

"Wussy husbands get dragged to charity functions. They are battleground arenas for women. They slip past you and rub against you or ask stupid questions like 'Did you like the artwork they're auctioning off' or 'Did you like the speaker?' None of them ever ask about a company's financials or about war or football or anything interesting like that. Notice while they talk to you they're trolling their bait trying to get laid. They rationalize this behavior by telling themselves they'll sacrifice their bodies for charity.

"Poor people that these charities are supposed to help get crumbs and drippings from these events. Some entertainer from out of town gets five or ten times more revenue than poor people get. If you want to help somebody work from the heart, then help somebody directly. There's a rub to that. People will pretend to need help when they just don't want to work. The world will always have poor disadvantaged people. If you give them money, you'll breed more of them.

"Poor people breed like rats. They do that so that they'll get more votes so they can screw you out of your money by taxing the shit out of you. A good philosophy is the one Scrooge had before he saw the ghosts of his past in the *Christmas Carol* by Dickens. You feel good when you give to charity, but you do not solve the problems of the poor. There will be more of them tomorrow. It is an unfortunate reality. If Jesus couldn't eradicate poverty, you won't succeed either. You're better off spending money on hookers. You get something great in return, unless it's syphilis."

Doctors

"Avoid doctors unless you're near death and need a painkiller. Most of them are quacks trying to make a buck. The few who know what they're doing work for private billionaires, or they already retired. The rest are just trying to survive the government's paperwork jungle and get out of their practices as soon as they can without getting sued out of business. If the doctor works for a Health Maintenance Organization, he's just a data entry clerk and you're a data file. They only want to keep you alive long enough to maximize the Medicare reimbursements they get for carving into you when you're near death. They look at you as a future corpse on a conveyor belt to their cash register. After they squeeze all the insurance money out of you, you're sent to hospice and then the morgue.

"The days when you could get the doc to come to your house, take your temperature, stick a needle in your ass and give you a shot of penicillin for five bucks are long gone. Witch doctors, faith healers, and marijuana smoking are just as good as a doctor if you're sick. If nothing is working, drink lots of whiskey. If you want to be sure a doctor is prescribing the right medicine and drugs for you, get the prescription, take it back to the doctor, and make him take it first. That's the only way you can be sure the guy is trying to help you and not trying to kill you. If everybody did that, doctors would think twice about pumping everybody full of pills.

"You can't get out of this world alive, but you can make the exit as painless as possible. If you're looking at a big co-payment for an end-of-life procedure and you think you'll leave your heirs penniless by going through with it, and especially if your doctors start saying things like you have better than fifty-percent odds, you're better off just drinking whiskey until you die from the drinking. Remember these insights when you're at life's checkout counter."

Babies

"Babies make me want to throw up. They shit, cry, puke and slobber without caring where the mess that comes out of them lands. You can get their messes on yourself if you're not careful. Lots of times a woman will show you her baby, because she's really proud that something actually came out of her pussy instead of a prick. Her mother and her preacher told her that she was supposed to have babies. She feels like she's a legitimate person because she reproduced herself instead of just screwing her brains out for the joy of it. She wants you to adore her baby, but your correct move is to get away from that dangerous little thing before it goes off on you and ruins your clothes.

"You can be discreet. Tell the mother that you'd love to pick the kid up and have it shit all over you, scream in your ear, or throw up on you, but you can't because you have a highly contagious disease that will probably kill her baby if it gets within ten feet of you. She'll grab the kid and run from you as fast as she can. Another tactic is to tell her you have bad luck with babies. Tell her you held one once and it sneezed on you. That got you so discombobulated you forgot what you were doing and you dropped the baby, and then it kept crying for hours afterwards. That tactic usually works, especially if you've already used the first one about being contagious."

Lawyers

"All I'm going to tell you about lawyers is that you can't trust them, not even the ones on your own payroll. They are all about racking up fees. If there's five ways to strategize a case for a defense or an offense, they will figure out the course of action that is most likely to take the longest and rack up the most fees. When you're in litigation, notice how the lawyers from the opposing sides like to talk with each other after a hearing or deposition. They'll tell their respective clients that they're trying to agree on the timetable for the next step in the case or some such bullshit. What they're really doing is trying to decide what they can do to get the most juice out of the plaintiff and the defendant for themselves. They're officially sanctioned to rob you blind. They'll talk about football or their favorite whorehouses, or the outlook for weather, or swap jokes, but they'll charge you for their time on the phone. They have no empathy for the people they represent, none. If they try to tell you otherwise, they're bullshitting you.

"Lawyers are the worst cocksuckers on the planet. They deal in shit fights between people who didn't have enough sense to talk things over in the first place, but since some people are idiots who want to fight, lawyers make a fortune on them. You can tell how fucked up a country is by the number of lawyers it has per thousand people in the population. America is the world's most fucked-up country because about one person in every three is a lawyer. America is a country where nobody makes anything and people go around suing each other because they have nothing better to do with themselves.

"Be alert for lawyers' dirty tricks. Sooner or later somebody is going to sue you. Lawyers will talk to each other about the case for hour after hour and resolve nothing. Neither side will recommend you settle because that ends their billable hours. They enjoy watching both parties suffer and they keep things stirred up as much and as long as possible. If you are defending, your lawyer will push a template button on a computer and the computer will spit out a hundred defenses. This stuff is all prepackaged, like instant cereal, but your lawyer thinks you're stupid. He thinks you'll believe he went to hours or days of effort to look up all these cases on point and that he's some kind of genius, but in reality he just pushed a button. So he bills you for twenty hours at seven hundred dollars per hour, or fourteen thousand dollars for two minutes' work. That's not the worst of it. His paralegal is the one who actually pushes the button while he's out playing golf and hustling new clients, or he's working on another case while he's billing you for his helper to push a button.

"If you're the plaintiff, or the one suing, your lawyer will make as many false representations as possible to try to exasperate the defendant and bleed him to death so he'll settle and your lawyer will get a contingency piece of the action. That leaves you open to counterclaims when discovery of evidence takes place, which is what the lawyers want—more bullshit, more hours, more misery for their clients and more fees.

"Lawyers belong to the Trial Lawyers Association. Its purpose is to fuck up the country forever by helping members pass laws and regulations and encouraging them to charge outrageous fees to suck the wealth out of the country. After law school, lawyers first spend time interning at the city zoo. They learn trial tactics watching monkeys throwing papers and banana skins in the air and screaming at each other. After interning they join their association. It's a union of ambulance chasers, ghouls, leeches, and argumentative fuckups who give bad advice because lawyers rarely know what they're talking about. They must have a secret pledge amongst themselves to never create wealth, just destroy it by dragging people into the legal process and not letting them out without first getting shaken down for their money or losing an arm or a leg. They have secret meetings with judges called case management conferences where lawyers and judges slime around plotting how to squeeze more money out of their suffering clients. In the good old days, real men settled things faster and cheaper with gunfights. That's when the world made more sense, and it didn't have many lawyers.

"Lawyers don't want to go to court because no one knows the outcome and neither wants to lose. They know that arbitrators and judges fall asleep or go mentally absent during argument and evidence, so the guys who are supposed to decide just don't pay attention. The judge or arbitrator who falls asleep during the proceedings is the smartest guy in the room. He knows it's all bullshit, so why pay attention? A trial is a great time to let lawyers drone on and on and catch some sleep. Judges look at trials as nap time. You might as well throw the case into a washing machine and see what comes out. The entire system is completely useless.

"If you're a plaintiff, no matter what you're suing for, show up at trial or arbitration wearing a neck brace, even if nothing's wrong with your neck. The judge or arbitrators are so dysfunctional they'll just throw money at somebody if it looks like they should feel sorry for them. Even though the petitioner is suing for a bad trade, the arbitrators will throw money at him because they think it might help his neck. If you're the defendant, show up at trial with a minority lawyer or a lawyer who wears a leg cast and crutches because the same principle applies. The arbitrators or judge will give you the decision because they'll reason your lawyer is on a contingency and he needs the money. The best lawyer is one who is near death and they have to bring him to court on a gurney with oxygen and an IV drip. Those guys win cases. That's what you look for in a lawyer. Forget competence. Get a guy who's near death. Old lawyers are good too. They don't like to waste time in court when they can be out on a golf course.

"Never tell a lawyer anything, not even your own lawyer. Whatever they learn about you they'll use against you, even by giving your confidential information to an opposing lawyer so he can come at you with it and your guy can then charge you money to defend you against the other lawyer. The best thing you can do if you get sued is to grab all the money you can and leave the country. Buy a place in some foreign country somewhere in the middle of nowhere, like Wyoming, and hide your money in coffee cans buried in the ground. That way lawyers won't get their filthy hands on your money and neither will the guy who is suing you. Lawyers work the court system to screw you. The only way to beat them is to flee the country. Otherwise, you can work all your life and some bastard will come along and steal your money from you. Your own lawyers will help them."

"David, Wyoming is part of the United States."

"Doesn't matter. Wyoming might as well be another country all together. There's only animals there and they don't tell lawyers or government snoops anything. Animals can be trusted with secrets. People and lawyers can't be trusted. Take my word for it. Get a place in Wyoming."

Military Personnel

"Military personnel are different from regular people. There's no longer a draft so they aren't out there fighting Hitler anymore, and there aren't people running away to Canada to get out of going to Vietnam anymore either. The military is all voluntary now. I read a book once that makes me believe our voluntary military is very dangerous to the country. It had to do with the Punic Wars when the Carthaginians were a world power and had all the lucrative trade routes in the ancient world. The Romans went to war with them over that, kind of like Russia and China are in a low-grade war with the United States today.

"It started with money or currency wars, and then it got into hot wars. Well, the Carthaginians were basically rich Jews who traded around the Mediterranean Sea. They had huge palaces and were fabulously rich. They even sent camels to the Arabian Peninsula loaded with silver and traded one ounce of silver for three ounces of gold. The world always runs on imperfect information, and the Arabs didn't know the value of their gold, but they liked silver because it was shinier.

"Anyway, the Carthaginians hired private army mercenaries to defend their city against Rome. That plan worked as long as the Romans were easy to beat, but by the third Punic war, the Romans were winning. All the while these wars were going on, the mercenaries kept demanding that the Carthaginians pay them more and more to defend the city. Eventually, by the third war, the Carthaginians couldn't pay enough and the mercenaries turned against the Carthaginians and slaughtered a lot of them along with the Romans slaughtering them. So the moral of the story is you can't buy protection, just like you can't buy love.

"So today in the United States we have the exact same Carthaginian situation, with the military being the mercenaries and the Russians and the Chinese and the Muslim extremists taking over the world from us. We're all going to get slaughtered, some by our own military, some by the Russians, some by the Chinese, and some by the Salafists Fundamentalists. We're a lot like those Carthaginians. We're complacent, decadent, stupid, and rich, and we're about to get taken down."

"You told me about the Carthaginians before."

"Well, they had three Punic Wars, didn't they?"

"Yes."

"Well then, maybe I'll tell you about it a third time someday. Don't be disrespectful."

"Okay, sorry."

"Now, where was I? Oh yes. When it comes to the individual military person, you need to recognize that they are willing to risk dying for the security of a paycheck. Most people aren't wired that way. Most people fear being killed and want to put as much distance between the risk of getting killed and themselves as possible, so you have a different sort of animal here, one you shouldn't antagonize.

"Veterans are patriotic. They want to live in a strong America. When they see some globalist give America away to the rest of the world while they can't get benefits for getting their limbs blown off or being poisoned with Agent Orange, they get pissed off. What can happen is, like in Carthage, the active military and the veterans could look at the situation and decide they need to change it to save the country, so stay on the good side of the veterans you meet. Treat them with respect and deference always, and respect the experiences they have had. Many of them have seen horrors that other Americans cannot comprehend, like the working end of a Chinese AK-47 automatic rifle or a Russian 152mm long rifle.

"Females are a separate veteran category. When I was growing up we didn't have many women in the service, but all that has changed. Maybe they're patriotic just like the men are, but I have a hard time with that because they don't have any testosterone that makes them get all fired up to want to go out and kill people. Still, they have some level of training that teaches them how to kill you. They're probably kind of like black widow spiders that kill males and eat them, so be careful when you run into one of them. That's all the wisdom I can give you about the military, the veterans, and the women in the military. As you know, I broke my arm to get out of a military boarding school."

Insurance

"Insurance is not complicated. The companies that manufacture insurance products make sure, with all their legal fine print, that the insurance contract you enter into gives you the lowest possible odds of ever collecting anything. Essentially, insurance products are the mirror opposite of investments. In investments, you put money in and hope it grows. In insurance, you put money in and hope you die or get sick so the money doesn't have to grow to get you paid. The insurance company business model is to take in the money up front, then buy a fancy headquarters building and hire a lot of really sexy broads so the top guys have lots of pussy around at all times, and also buy fancy homes and cars for the top executives and give them huge compensation plans. If it's a stock company, the shareholders also expect a dividend.

"The other part of the insurance business model is the part where you need to pay out claims. To be a successful insurance company, your business model must be to never pay out claims for anything. Hire lawyers to fight like hell to avoid paying claims. If somebody is horribly disfigured and covered by your policy, don't feel sorry for them. Fight them tooth and nail. Fight them until they die. Change judges, change courts, change lawyers, do anything but never, ever pay the victim. You make sure your contracts are ironclad and impossible to collect on. You put in clauses that block the claimant from winning a dime off you. For instance, if it's a life policy, you put in that if the claimant has ever been anywhere within ten miles of a dog, he can't collect because he could have caught a disease from the dog, or that he can't go skiing, bicycling, to a movie with air conditioning, or to a restaurant that doesn't have a complete shutdown and cleaning every hour. You stick morality clauses in there too. If the claimant has ever smoked a cigarette, banged a bimbo, drank two shots of whiskey in the same twenty-four hours, driven over the speed limit, gone off on a hike in the forest, or eaten more than two cookies in a day, then he violated the contract.

"When the poor bastard's widow tries to collect, you find out who his friends were and bribe them to say he did something he wasn't supposed to do. Then you bleed her money down with protracted litigation until she needs to settle cheap. Now, if she won't settle cheaply, you work on driving her nuts, like having some of your office staff calling her day and night with solicitations to all kinds of stupid stuff, like raffle tickets, vacation home time share deals, cruise trips, groups and churches she could join, memorial tomb stones she could buy for her stiff, free rides in hot sports cars even though she's eighty-five. You get the idea. Make her want to take a small amount of money so she can leave town and get away from her phone.

"If you get into the insurance business, make a good business relationship with a sleazy insurance company that operates in a state with loose regulations. Sell annuities. Show that you have a high rating from the rating agencies when you sell your policies. When you have a bunch of policies on your books, keep collecting the premiums as if the policies had a great company behind them, but in your policies you have a clause that lets you resell the policy and the underlying guarantees to pay out money. Sell your book of business to a sleaze company that may fail in the future, but keep the premium and pay the sleaze company only a portion of it. You make all the money for selling the policy but take none of the risk of paying on it.

"I saw a magazine article once where a company did that and the sleaze company that bought the policies failed. It had sob stories about old people and disabled people who had no money, and it railed about how badly they got screwed. It made me think we should be in that business too. There's big money in it, and the people getting screwed don't even know it until they desperately need money. It's not like the investment business where you need to mark the values of your holdings to the market every day so people can see right away that their values are up or down. Also, insurance is not regulated by the Securities and Exchange Commission or by Financial Regulatory Authority, so regulations are made by the different state insurance commissioners. It's hard for them to catch a shady operator.

"When people buy insurance, they should have a sit-down meeting with the top executives of the insurance companies, but that doesn't happen. It's like mutual funds, where people never meet their portfolio managers either. People can only hope that the agent with the big smile and the nice haircut isn't out to screw them. Actually, he might not be out to screw them personally, but they can get screwed by the contract clauses or by their policy getting sold away, or by their company's financial condition collapsing years after they've bought the policy.

"In the health area, we could screw people with huge premium increases. To get a book of business built, all we need to do is lowball the other carriers until we have our client base. Then we raise our premiums until we start losing business. Companies got smart about this and began making employees pay for part or all of their health care. Most people are too lazy or otherwise engaged to keep up with all the changes and the different coverages offered under the different policies, so they just stay with the policy they have. We could raise premiums until people can't afford coverage. Then we could have a plan that lets them pay partial payments until they catch up with what they owe, but if they get sick before they are fully caught up, we could screw them and not pay any benefits. That's a great concept. We should consider insurance as a business line for the firm."

Guns

"Guns are essential to the American way of life. God gave the Ten Commandments to Moses, and then he gave identical copies to Charlton Heston, John Wayne, Charles Bronson, Clint Eastwood, and Oliver North. In those commandments, the second one is the big one that the government bastards are most afraid of. The Second Amendment to the Ten Commandments is the right to have a gun. The reason God got that in there is in case the Egyptians try to get back here and take over America again. It's not theirs anymore, so they can't have it. When they try to get smart with us Americans, it's our God-given right to blow those fuckers away.

"Gun companies are missing a terrific opportunity to make a fortune on the Second Commandment law. Take Samuel Colt, for instance. Sam made a fortune selling Colt .45 pistols to men who had small man complexes during the frontier days. He came up with a slogan that appealed to little guys who were getting beaten up and bullied by big guys. He said, 'My Colt .45 makes every man the same size.' Oil companies expanded on this marketing idea, only they call it segment marketing. Oil companies take the same liquid and put it into different containers and mark up the price. They call it motor oil, transmission oil, brake fluid, windshield washer fluid, and hand sanitizer, but it's all the same stuff sold in different cans.

"Gun companies should combine the genius of Sam Colt and the genius of the oil companies and do serious marketing. They already sell .45 caliber pistols and 9mm pistols, but they need to brand them better. They can have guns with Hebrew on them for Jews, guns with Arabic on them for Salafists, guns with Spanish for Hispanics, and so on. They could sell every woman, regardless of religion, ethnic background, or language, half a dozen guns for their whole family. On weekends, everybody in America could go out in their backyards and shoot their guns off. Americans could organize neighborhood games. Instead of playing cowboys and Indians using little cap pistols like we did when I was a kid, American kids could all use real guns. That way the country would be a lot safer because everybody would become a great shot. When the Egyptians or the Chinese try to take us over, we'll be ready."

Environmentalists

"Environmentalists are people who don't know what an ice cube is. All they do is crab and bitch about how tough life is for polar bears. They go around to grade schools with slide shows of these polar bears floating around on ice bergs and they scare the shit out of little kids telling them the polar bear will drown when the ice berg melts. So, here you have a nation with five hundred million brain washed third graders who are losing sleep because some huckster showed them a half-baked movie of a polar bear floating on an ice cube; and never mind that the damn things can swim all the way across the Pacific Ocean when they work it right.

"The environmental movement is a scam to foist another tax on a bankrupt American public. The scammers want to start a carbon exchange trading marketplace run by their company. Their company rakes off a commission on all the trades. It's not a competitive exchange, so the scammers get fat commissions with the government's blessings. Billions of bucks are in this scam. The polar bears don't get the money. What would a polar bear do with a wad of hundreds or a credit card, anyway? The public and the government don't get the commission money from the trades either. The money goes to politicians that get stock in the carbon trading exchange. They will pass laws that make their theft legal. Environmental stuff is a con job. It's shameful to make third grade kids think polar bears are suffering. Voters gladly bend over and let the scammers screw them without getting the facts. Governments of China and India don't give a shit about a few polar bears, and those two countries are 99.99% of carbon emissions. Check out the facts. I always get my facts right.

"There's a common-sense solution for polar bears. Since there's a million times more ice on the South Pole than there is on the North Pole, and since ice on the South Pole gets bigger by eighty billion tons of new ice every year, why not just move the polar bears to the South Pole? Has anybody ever thought of that? No! Of course not! It's too simple and there's no money in it.

"If the environmentalists really gave a shit about polar bears they would move them to the South Pole. Look at all the ice they would have! Plus, they'd get a bonus. The polar bears would get variety in their diets. All the bears eat are seals and dead whales. If they were relocated to the South Pole, they could also eat penguins. The South Pole is overrun with penguins. The damn things are an environmental hazard because they shit all over the place and they are noisy. It's time to send in the polar bears to clean up the place. We'd get healthier bears. Everybody knows a balanced diet is good for you, so seals and dead whales plus penguins equals healthier bears. When you put your mind to it, there's a common-sense solution for everything."

"That concludes your formal executive training here at UGGA. The rest will be on-the-job type learning. If you have any questions, be sure to ask them and I'll give you my complete answer. You are now free to return to your romantic fantasies of Marty or Barbara or whomever, just don't let a woman interfere with sales."

"Thanks." *I need to take my brain for a shower. I'm glad these sessions are over.*

"Don't mention it. How else would you ever learn anything?"

As Bob drove away from David's barnyard to the office, his thoughts turned to Marty: *Marty, my love, whatever happened to you?* Bob's thoughts were never far from her. He punched his car's dash in frustration. *I feel like my sensibilities were assaulted nonstop for days on end. I thought about Marty the whole time David dumped his view of the world on me. I'm glad I won't remember anything he said.* Nothing eased the ache he felt inside. At unexpected times, he could still hear her laughter, that teasing, mirthful laugh of a woman who loved everything about life and who gave life everything she had.

In the evenings when he was asleep, he could still feel her breathing against his chest as if she were there in bed with him. In the mornings, he half expected her to emerge from the bathroom. Then there was her voice. Bob heard it whenever he was alone. Her voice came from his memory, but he heard it nonetheless. It talked to him as if she were present in the room with him. Life for Bob was as if she never left him, and he began to believe Marty never left him. Her presence, her closeness with him, was something he could never explain to anyone. Other people would never understand a love like this. It was something greater than remorse or pining for a lost love, or a missing someone. She became part of him in that wonderful year, but she left without an explanation.

Bob tried to reconstruct his last days and moments with her, but she left no clue. One moment she was there, full of joy and love, and the next she was gone. He could not imagine or accept that he might never see her again. He wanted her back as she was when he last saw her. What happened to her? His mind first touched madness, then anger, but he did his best to conceal his emotions. If only he could punch the problem in its face and break its nose. But he couldn't do that. He was a man now and there was no definable foe.

He wrestled with his thoughts and struggled to hold her ghost. *I ache for her warmth next to me, for a kiss from her.* He willed her to come back, but his forces of thought were only met by silence. *I don't care if she had the reputation of a notorious whore. I love her, all of her, everything about her. I love her just as she is.* Passions for Marty coursed through his blood. He wore his heart on his sleeve. *How could she do this to me? What have I done or not done to make her leave me? What happened to you, Marty, my darling fiancée? Why can't we be together again?*

He sensed that David read his feelings and understood them in a man-to-man sort of way. He resented David's encroachment upon his feelings, but he accepted that his senior partner was only trying to help. His management lessons of the past three months provided an offensive distraction, but his mind still fixated on Marty.

When David came into the office, he stopped in to check on Bob. "A strange call came in late yesterday. Some woman said she was a friend of Marty's, said she knew Marty for years before she came to work at the firm. Somehow, she had your name. Maybe Marty mentioned you to this woman, I don't know. But anyway, the woman's name is Rita and she said she'd like to meet you and talk with you. Here's her phone number."

"Who took the call?"

"Nobody. Apparently she called after we closed and figured out how to get into our voice mail. She left the message on my machine. I wrote her number down but I erased her message."

"Thanks, I'll call her."

RITA

Rita wanted to meet in a public place, a bar. She told Bob to dress casual. The night after David delivered his message, Bob went to the appointed bar. It was a neighborhood beer and burgers joint, nothing fancy. Rita's eye-popping figure was perched on a bar stool. Her blue eye shadow, deep red lipstick, and plunging neckline invited males to notice. Bob joined her at the bar.

"You must be Rita."

"Yes. And you would be Bob. Thank you for calling me. I am pleased to meet you."

"The pleasure is mine, Rita. I understand you wanted to tell me about your friendship with Marty."

"Yes, I did. Marty and I go way back. We, shall I say, double-dated a few times together. Those were fun times. Marty was happy and footloose then, but there was an incompleteness about her. I could tell. When you came along, she changed. She told me one night that you took her breath away, that you were the one. She was very excited about marrying you, Bob. She loved you."

"You're saying loved, as in past tense."

"Well, yes, Bob. I guess I did say loved. You see, no one knows Marty as well as me. I don't think a man who loved a woman as much as you did should be left thinking things were one way when they weren't. What I'm trying to say is Marty has a disease. It's a psychological disease. She and I have it and we can't escape from it. Men make fun of us. They call us bimbos or whores or nymphomaniacs, whatever. But the truth is, Bob, we can't help ourselves. We love sex so much it affects our judgment and our choices. We easily make mistakes. We can even turn our backs on a man who loves us, who we are in love with, but we can't help ourselves. We need more than one man in our lives. Monogamy terrifies us, Bob. Do you mind if I order another Gibson?"

"No, Rita, go ahead. I'm buying."

"Why thank you, Bob. Bartender, another Gibson, please."

"Make that two," said Bob.

When Rita ordered, a man arose from a table as if on cue and approached Bob and Rita.

"Hi, my name is Phil. I'm doing a piece for the local paper about some of the popular neighborhood bars. You two look like a perfect photo opportunity for my lead segment. Could I trouble you to let me have a few photos? I'm just trying to help the local retailers. Would you mind?"

Rita looked at Bob, then to the photographer, shrugging to feign indifference. "Why not?"

"Okay" said Bob.

The photographer started taking shots. He wanted a few close-ups of Rita and Bob's faces, cheek to cheek; one of them toasting each other; and one of Rita looking very suggestive with the slit in her skirt showing a lot of leg and her arm around Bob. A final request was one of Bob giving Rita a kiss, bending her over backward while holding up his Gibson.

"That was great, you two. Thanks so much."

"Don't mention it." Bob waved the photographer off.

"Marty was telling me true, Bob. You are a very good kisser. I can see why she stayed with you as long as she did. Here's my card. If you want company sometime, I'd like hearing from you."

"Thanks, Rita. But tell me your woman's intuition. Will I ever hear from Marty again?"

"I honestly don't know, Bob. Maybe she just got afraid of commitment. If I were you, since you haven't heard from her, I'd move on."

"Thanks, Rita."

TRACKING

Little Sparrow called Chief weekly to discuss matters of interest to them both: the usual goings-on with the various tribes, reservation issues, Chief's investment interests, and politics. Lately their calls dwelled on the topic of Bob and the disappearance of Marty.

"Bob's been melancholy over Marty's absence. He won't snap out of it. I wonder if there's anything I should do."

"You've begun going into his life, Sparrow. You must do more than just letting him know you are woman."

"What are your thoughts, Father?"

"A man has many voices in his head. Some voice he hears says he wants a woman. But another voice tells him to try to understand why things are as they are. One voice asks if he is doing the right thing, and another asks what he should or should not do. These things matter as much on men's minds as women's, Sparrow. Your Bob is confused now. He was to marry this Marty woman, but now she's gone. She went away suddenly and Bob is disoriented."

"Maybe we shouldn't call him 'my Bob,' Father. He promised himself to another. She may come back."

"You may think that, Sparrow. I think she will not come back."

"Why do you say that?" Sparrow's interest in her father's thoughts was keen.

"She's not back after three months. Police cannot find her. She left no word for Bob. She will likely never be back, I think."

"Do you think she found another man?"

"Not sure. That is only one possibility. There are others. She may have been taken away. She may have something to hide and fears to come back."

"Will Bob always be this way?"

"No. He will change with time, but you could move time faster."

"How, Father?"

"Enter his other minds and find what things trouble them. Help him see what he cannot see, Sparrow."

"But Father, those matters are not my business. I may offend if I start asking about them."

"You must not ask, Sparrow. You must first know what concerns him and then go to him when you have answers to his concerns."

"I do not understand you, Father."

"Sparrow, remember when you were a little girl. I took you on the plains and the forests in the snow and showed you what the animals were doing by looking at their tracks."

"I remember."

"Do you remember when you first saw tracks they all looked like there were senseless crossings of tracks going different directions, doubling back, going this way and that?"

"Yes, Father, I remember."

"Then do you remember when I taught you how to read the tracks? How the wolf followed the deer, how the deer moved with the sun behind it in the morning and back with the sun behind it in the evening? How the coyote track followed after the wolf's track and how the rabbit's tracks stopped where the snow had the brush of the owl? How we figured the time of day the owl hunted the rabbit and how we figured when the deer and the wolf and coyote passed? How the tracks painted a picture for you, and once you saw the picture you understood what happened among those animals that day? How we found the kill the wolf made and how the coyote stood off and waited his turn? I know you remember such things."

"Yes, Father, I remember. But why are we even talking about this, my chief?"

"Because, Sparrow, you must use those lessons I taught you and track the human animals. Once you understand their tracks, you will find the answers to the questions your Bob is asking himself."

"Father, you are most wise, but how do I track humans in a city?"

"The human animal also leaves tracks, Sparrow. He leaves paper tracks. You must first ask why this Marty woman disappeared. Ask why it was ten days before the police were called. Ask why she didn't sell anymore, why Bob sells instead. Ask what changes were made for the people in the firm with her gone. Ask how the money moves and how the internal ledgers change. Ask if you know what everyone's deal is who works there, why they are there, what they appear to do, and what they really do. You must know as much about the firm as Mr. David and Ms. Maloney know. Then you must know how the money moves around in the firm, and into and out of the firm, who gets paid, what they appear to be paid for, and what they are really paid for. Once you have all the questions you can think to ask, then you must also be able to answer them. When you know their tracks, you will see a picture and you will have your answers. Remember, Sparrow, I trained you well. You are the one with the advantage. You are the hunter."

"Thank you, Father."

"You're welcome, daughter. And daughter, be very careful that you track alone and unseen."

"Your concern, Father?"

"The Marty woman disappeared for a reason. That concerns me. Until you know the reason, you must assume it could be anything. Things are not always as they appear to be."

"Thank you, Father. I will track alone and unseen." Barbara felt a chill up her spine.

"You are welcome, my dear daughter. Do you still feel love for your Big Horse?"

"Yes, Father. I know I love him. I have never stopped loving him. When we see each other, our eyes kiss. I love him in my deepest ways, Father, but I am fearful that Marty has entangled him with woman favors."

"I see, but can you tell if she carries a child?"

"I do not see that, Father."

"Then I think things will reveal themselves to you and to him, and he will not be trapped by her favors. I think he will be your man, Sparrow. Eyes do not lie. You have my blessings, daughter. May the spirits bring love and a happy life into your heart." Chief sat back in his massive leather chair, looked up through an open skylight, and drew deeply on his pipe.

"Thank you, Father."

VAULT

Whether by intent or by accidental slip of the tongue, a seemingly innocuous comment caught doubt's tripwire and launched a carefully choreographed dance of suspicion and trust. Both David and Bob were in the reception lobby on this fateful day; Bob to review the vacation schedules of the marketing staff with Mrs. Rodriguez and David to confirm some appointment dates in his calendar with the ones kept by Barbara. When men are talking while at the same time peering at a woman's breasts they may accidentally let a comment escape that reveals a truth or condition.

David, always one to stage-manage events according to his evolving grand plan, was this day a man with a bifurcated mind. The detailed cognitive brain was following Barbara's recitations about dates, times, persons to attend, board agendas to be discussed, securities to be approved for fund purchases, etc., while the casual, all-sensing receptors of the disengaged remainder of his brain were suddenly overwhelmed by lurid beckoning impulses from Eros.

Barbara never wore brasseries. Her breasts were like a nubile goddess's and they invited touching. They were full, firm, and glowed with a warm copper-colored radiance. Her nipples tilted upwards as if they yearned to be rubbed between a man's thumb and forefinger.

From her blouse wafted the combined scents of lilies and feminine body heat. David believed her breasts were underappreciated. He thought it was a waste of womanly bounty for Barbara not to have a man in her life, not to have a man's hands caressing and squeezing those breasts. She possessed an erotic arabesque quality of feminine beauty in those breasts. Their very presence, unadorned by the hands of man, bespoke of male ineptitude and failure of the male organization to appreciate that which beckoned to be touched. Even David's long-held commitment to homosexuality wavered for brief intervals whenever he was near Barbara's breasts. His mind was firmly on them this day, although his hands were not—at least not yet. He was busy complimenting her for keeping his appointments in sync.

"Thank you, Barbara. You know I'm terrible at paperwork. I always forget to write things down and my record keeping is useless."

Barbara responded with a matter-of-fact "You're welcome, David," and went back to what she'd been doing. As David turned from his strategic position behind Barbara's right shoulder, he artfully flipped a paper clip from his appointment book. The metal missile arched through the air over Barbara's shoulder and traveled down into her blouse where it came to rest in the perfect strategic location about three inches below her cleavage above a slight fold on her stomach.

"Oh my goodness, I'm so sorry!" shouted David in a mock fluster of male incompetence. "Here, I'll get it." He thrust his hands down Barbara's blouse. He fumbled around for the errant clip and in a deft faux-inadvertent maneuver he managed to squeeze both Barbara's tits while moving his fingers frantically in search of the elusive clip. She took a deep breath, swelling her breasts, as David's hands groped her. Instinctively, she deeply inhaled David's scent for close analysis by her olfactory receptors, not to give him an enlarged playground as he mistakenly assumed.

There were the normal pheromones of male testosterone. She recognized those instantly. But there were other, fainter, mysterious scents she couldn't quite pinpoint. There was a trace odor of decaying flesh, a faint hint of something related to decomposing rancid ketoses, and a fleeting nearly indecipherable presence of formaldehyde. Mindful of her father's teachings to remember the smells of a place and a person, Barbara exhaled slowly, sifting the molecules of scent as they passed through her nostrils, confirming what she detected when she first inhaled. She committed David's odd smells to her memory. Now finished mentally cataloguing his peculiar essence she moved to disabuse him of his mistaken misogynistic notions.

"Stop it! Just stop. I'll get it. Just get your hands off me!" she screamed. Barbara lifted her blouse discreetly, retrieved the clip from underneath, and handed it back to David. For a woman just molested, Barbara kept her composure. Another lesson from her father was to never flinch in the face of an enemy. When David reached for the clip, Barbara just held onto it and stared into his eyes.

"Do not ever touch me again," said the winsome Cherokee.

There was a long pause, a seminal moment when their eyes met and held fixed to the other's. A message of sorts passed between the pairs of eyes, and David felt a twinge of fear. For a brief moment, he realized this woman was likely more intelligent than he was and perfectly capable of killing him. A chilling fear welled up within him, recalling millennia of adversarial dealings and hatreds. David didn't understand why he felt the way he did, but in that instant, he instinctively knew Barbara represented a hidden mortal danger to him. His skin flushed red. He knew at once that he didn't know anything about her, how she thought about things, how she viewed him and the business, even why she was really there. Everything he assumed he knew about her was somehow terribly wrong and indefinable, yet he was fascinated by the mysteries of her danger and decided right then and there to play along with this newly revealed unspoken threat to his ordered world. He chose to allow it to travel its natural path of discovery and come for him.

Barbara let the clip drop into David's open palm.

. . . .

David was correct to feel fear when he looked into Barbara's eyes. She was not the simple clerical staff girl she portrayed herself to be on her employment application, nor was she merely Mrs. Rodriguez's dutiful assistant. She was the office mystery, the silent ever-present wisp of graceful femininity that everyone depended upon. She made herself important by simply taking upon herself tasks that others were too busy or too lazy to complete. By volunteering to help everyone, Barbara came to know everyone's job functions. She had free reign of everyone's desk and files as a good helpmate should. She was smart and always kept her mouth shut. Now, for the first time, David felt uncomfortable. As his fear receded into reason, he sensed that Barbara likely knew more about the way the office ran than he would have liked. He made a mental note that he needed to respect and be cautious around this newly discovered adversary. Her knowledge of the firm's workings was formidable! The realization suddenly struck him like a bolt of lightning.

Susan even went to Barbara for assistance with the firm's regulatory filings and changes. Susan depended on her to research regulatory changes, interpret the nuances the changes portended for the firm, and ascertain what course of action the firm should take to comply or avoid the newest rules. Her abilities in this area were uncanny. Susan recognized that she had an intelligent brilliance her other administrative assistants did not possess. There was an unspoken knowledge amongst the office staff that Susan relied on Barbara.

There was good reason for Susan's increased reliance. Barbara was a competent learning machine. She kept to herself and worked tirelessly; she never said anything about her personal life, and no one knew who she really was. Barbara told everyone she was Cherokee Indian, which was only half true. Her skin tone was light olive with just a trace of darkening from her minority Somalid gene. Her eyelids were not thick with ancestral millennia of squinting from snow glare. Her almond-shaped eyes had an alluring, life-lifting attraction about them. A glimpse of deep sensuality and mystery escaped through her irises and pupils.

She had the high cheekbones and slight jaw protrusion of her father, but her beautiful, full mouth held flawless Arab teeth, not her father's gapped shovels. They set a perfect bite and sparkled brilliantly. Her dazzling smile made men wonder about their chances, so she modestly concealed it from most men who came through the office. She made an exception for Bob. He was her intended. Her whole face brightened in his presence as if she were experiencing life for the first time. Her eyes smiled and her lips parted to reveal her pearly whites. She had a regular breastbone, not an inverted one like her father's. Her toes were in the same proportions as Caucasian or Negro toes were, without the elongated second one many Cherokee bore. She scrupulously avoided changing clothes in the presence of other women in the office on the off chance that someone would recognize she had notable non-Native features.

She revealed to no one in the Jewish firm that her mother was Lebanese. Her mother was born of a Christian woman who married a Muslim Arab. In Beirut, there is a mixing of cultures unlike any other place on Earth. To many outsiders, this mixing blender seems incomprehensible, but to the Lebanese, to mix is normal. Most Lebanese avoid taking sides with competing factions and simply try to live and love. Barbara's mother was raised in the Christian traditions and faith, even though her father and grandfather were Muslim. Barbara's paternal grandfather explained his daughter's upbringing as a Christian in a Muslim household by saying he was a deeply loving man who would never impose his own religion upon his wife. He wanted her to know she was always adored, loved, free, and never subjugated. After all, they lived in Lebanon during times when society was open and free. Oppression of another's free will was frowned upon. Barbara, her mother, and her grandmother all possessed a mysterious sensual attraction. They were man magnets.

Barbara knew her feminine physical qualities but hid them. She was committed to a higher purpose than man hunting. She had as equally strong a drive for knowledge as Marty felt for the companionship of a male's penis. Barbara lived in a small one-bedroom apartment close to Main Street so she could walk to work, as she thought commuting wasted time.

Her daily routine was to wake early and work out for an hour in the apartment's gym. Father told her often the importance of keeping the body lithe, swift, and strong like the spirits of their paternal ancestors who came to Earth from far away in the heavens and walked from the far north to the Great Plains and points further south.

At work, Barbara immersed herself in learning all she could about the investment business. She read all of Susan's books about securities laws and regulations, the Harold Blumenthal series about the Securities Acts of 1933 and the Distribution Act of 1934, and his treatise on the Investment Company Act of 1940. When she went home at night, she read some more. She read books such as *The House of Morgan, The House of Rothschild, The Creature from Jekyll Island,* Taleb's *Black Swan* books, academic textbooks on economics, statistics, accounting, money and banking, financial institutions, finance, investments, and speculative markets and the use of derivatives.

Barbara drove herself endlessly, her motivations coming from within.

She worked with the determination of a loving heart. As Chief's protégé, she was determined to use her father's wealth to help their people. All of them had great potential, but few cared about them enough to show them what they could accomplish in the world outside the reservation. Besides her father and a few elders, they received little guidance. Outsiders were reluctant, even fearful, to get involved with them. As a result of generations of societal segregation, they knew little of the outside world, and even less about the white man's money ways. Most in her generation hesitated to even begin learning about this strange world and there were few elders who knew anything about it, thus encouragement was lacking. There were unspoken barriers that implied they shouldn't bother trying. What white man or woman would feel comfortable having an Indian managing their money? The stereotypes would surly arise. "He'll take our money and get drunk with it!" was only one prejudicial thought she expected. "Stupid Indians," and "I'm not investing with a woman. They're too emotional" were others. She was the first of her father's tribe to attempt to master the investment business, determined to break down every barrier to entry.

To shatter stereotypes Barbara needed to learn, conceal her true intent, and bide her time. Years passed and she learned the white man's ways, lifting herself to the level of knowledge and competence needed to compete with the white man on his own playing field and earn a share of business. Barbara was so driven to help her people that she allowed herself only one small luxury and one brief indulgence from her quest.

Every Sunday, she made herself one cup of coffee; other than that, she drank only milk or water. After she made her coffee, she allowed herself the pleasure of watching one sporting event on her television. Other than this one afternoon,

Barbara never watched television except for evening financial news. Her father told her that television made the mind idle and diminished the mind's great powers. Whenever she was tempted to relax, she was returned to her focus by her vision. She would hear her father's words that her people were meant to be the Great Spirit's most happy and innocent people, that the Great Spirit could never fail them, that he loved them and would always show them the way. Father often told her to keep her heart open to the messages from the Spirit, and she did.

Barbara followed the way of the Great Spirit and cherished her father's words of wisdom and love. She visualized little Native girls running across the prairie, innocents dancing with the winds over the grasses, and she imagined a little Indian boy sitting on a river bank watching his father putting out seine nets to catch the great king salmon fishes. Who would help these innocents succeed in the white man's world if not her? Who could bring back the buffalo for them? Could there still be innocence for them? Could the two worlds mesh and find harmony? She was driven to do her part, her very best for them. She would buy up lands and return the buffalo and all the other animals. *I will provide monies for them to become educated so they may thrive in the white man's world. They will break the shackles of emptiness and alcohol and handouts. I will be their voice, their helping hand, and their servant for good. I will make the whites want to understand us.* She was driven by a devoted daughter's love for her parents and her people. That love was so deep it dwarfed all her other feelings and drove her relentlessly onward, except now she had this feeling for something she needed to fulfill herself. She needed a man in her life. Not just any man, but one particular man.

When Barbara watched her television, she always picked a sports program. She watched football, basketball, baseball, hockey, track meets, soccer matches, and she watched all of these sports, one event every Sunday, with a particular set of eyes. She watched only men's events to see how men behaved when they were winning and when they were losing. She wasn't into the strategy of the games as much as she was into the behaviors and emotions the men felt when they competed. She knew she didn't have much testosterone, but she needed to know how a man with testosterone behaved when he was winning and when he was losing.

Through sports she began to understand men. Men were, with all their pretenses and bravado stripped away, like little boys, obedient and fearful and loving of their mommies. They were like boys who needed to prove their worth to their mommies. They needed mommies' comforts when they were getting shellacked on the playing field. They knew how to cry and hurt and they knew how to throw tantrums, and they had their 'oh shit' moments as well as their jubilations, much like a Native boy has when he catches his first fish. She'd done her book learning and saw how an investment firm should run; now she had a sense of how to work on the same playing field as a man. She was ready to honor her father's dream for her, to multiply his sizeable wealth and use it to help the people. She just needed to wait for the right moment.

. . . .

David was warned and cowered by Barbara, but nevertheless he felt victorious for successfully fondling the upright Native girl. He left the reception area and returned to his office.

Bob turned from the commotion that happened between Barbara and David and went back to looking at a matrix of vacation schedules by times and personnel. But his mind was not focused upon the schedules, having been jolted from its equilibrium. He had difficulty retuning his thought to centerline, to its tasks at hand.

Bob's conscience had a quick talk with itself. *Did I just hear what I think I just heard? David just lightheartedly admitted he was terrible at paperwork and forgetful about it. Yes, I heard that. Did he proclaim this to an audience for a reason and follow it with a deliberate distraction? Was that innocent or purposeful? Barbara didn't think it was funny by the look she's giving him. David had pissed her off.* Bob had never seen that side of Barbara before. She had made David back down, maybe even scared him.

Bob's mind did a backflip. *Did David just give you notice in front of an audience that there's no written proof of your deal anywhere? Then it follows that he's forgotten about your deal. How are you going to prove you have a deal if something happens to him? Isn't it about time to commit the deal to writing? If he died tomorrow, you'd be standing there with your dick in your hand with no company of your own after you busted your ass to build the firm. It's time to jog his memory and put the words on paper.*

Later that day, over drinks at David's club, Bob offered him the opportunity to make a written record memorializing their deal.

"We have a deal, you and I, whereby I've changed my career to build the fund and whereby you'd leave me the shares of the advisor and the underwriter upon your death. You remember that deal, don't you?"

David frowned. His eyebrows lifted and his head moved backward upon its neck post in a trace of indignation as he answered. "Why yes, of course. I'm a man of my word. I keep my promises."

"It's more than just a promise. It's a deal we made with each other, don't you recall?"

"Yes, of course I do. We have a deal between us."

"That's good. Then you wouldn't mind putting our deal in writing. I'd like to see you put the deal in writing." Bob leveled a focused gaze upon David.

David's head went back farther, his eyebrows raised to accommodate his wide-opened eyes as his mouth gaped open and his jaw dropped. It was a marvelous performance of incredulity.

"You don't trust me!" he blurted out childishly, as if mortally wounded by this audacious attack upon his integrity. His expression turned to profound hurt and dismay. The deal dance had resumed.

"No, David! It's quite the contrary. As before, when we split money based upon our handshake, I have for the past year been out selling and raising money, based again upon our handshake. So obviously, I trust you. I don't need to prove to you that I trust you. It's just that if something were to happen to you, if you were to die, I'd like to know that it's something you've already taken care of. And I'd feel a lot better if you'd prove to me that you've taken care of it."

Both men knew this request was perfectly reasonable. Bob leveled a penetrating gaze upon David that did not waver. David mustered his best nonchalant look, complementing it with a smile and an exhaled laugh as he replied. "Of course, I'll get back to you."

And David did. About two weeks later, he popped into Bob's office with a grin that could swallow a Cheshire cat. In dramatic fashion, he held his index finger first to his lips, then wiggled the finger to motion to Bob that he wanted the younger man to come with him. He whispered, "Come with me. I've got something to show you."

The two partners left the building together, crossed Main, and entered the Tower Bank building. Inside, they descended a flight of marble stairs into the basement vault lobby. David signed them in and instructed a custodian to retrieve two giant-sized safe deposit boxes. They were ushered into a private room and the safe boxes were wheeled inside on a gurney. It was an impressive setting, none better if one intended to perpetrate a fraud. There at the head of a long oak table, David had Bob seated in one of the orange leather chairs.

After the custodian left, David looked around the room as if to be sure they were alone and no one was watching. Bob glanced about the room also, but more quickly. His eyes were watching David's. Where had he seen that wary look before? There was a cautious, apprehensive fear about that look, but from where was he remembering it?

Of course! David's look was the same apprehensive fear he'd seen in the eyes of the deer in the forest he'd followed as a child. They looked about in that very same way when they drank the sweet water from the moss-banked spring pool upon Milltown's Cedar Mountain. The deer needed to be sure they were safe. Apparently, David also needed to be sure he was safe, but from what? There were no predators in this bank vault, and David obviously was not a deer. Why the caution?

As David opened one of the boxes, Bob's curiosity about the other man's penchant for secrecy subsided. David was just eccentric, secretive by nature, so there was no point in raising an issue about his melodramatic behavior. After all, the man's life history was likely in those boxes, so who could expect him to be anything but cautious?

David fumbled around in one of the boxes for a time. "I'm trying to find something to show you. I've got all kinds of stuff in here, and I have a hard time keeping track of where I put things. I've got stock certificates, property deeds, gold coins, silver bars, two quart jars full of diamonds from some stuff Dad got involved in during the war, the big war."

The impression David gave that he possessed a largess so huge he couldn't keep track of it had the desired effect upon Bob. Of course David couldn't remember to do his paperwork or keep things straight! He was so wealthy he didn't seem able to recall all he had, or so Bob thought.

"Let's see," David continued. "Oh yes. Here it is!"

The cautious eyes had given way to bright confident gleams of triumph as David pulled an envelope from the pile of papers in the first box. He opened it and retrieved a watermarked sheet of paper, which he handed to Bob.

The paper contained a codicil to David's last will and testament. It provided that, as long as Bob continued to serve as an officer or director of either the advisory company or the underwriting company, upon David's death he would inherit all the common shares of both companies free of any estate or inheritance taxes. David had signed and dated the codicil and had his signature witnessed by four lawyers from UGGA's law firm, along with Susan.

The fact that David had previously pledged on Marvin's death bed that, as a condition of David inheriting Marvin's controlling shares of the advisory company, David would leave both companies upon his death to the State of Israel was never mentioned to Bob. The codicil did not address the prior bequest to Israel, and David concealed it from Bob by his silence.

Bob reflected upon all that passed between him and David. David did all that he asked. Bob felt at the same time overwhelmed and sheepish for pushing the older man to prove to him that their agreement was committed in writing.

"Thank you, David, for taking care of this. I appreciate it," was all Bob could say.

After showing Bob the codicil, David returned it to its envelope, put the envelope back in the bucket-sized safe deposit box from whence it came, and summoned the custodian to return the two boxes to their places in the vault wall. As they left the bank, David told Bob to return to the office alone as David had some business to take care of with an old friend who had an office a few blocks further up Main Street. "You run along and I'll be back later," he said as he gave Bob a few fatherly pats on the back.

As Bob crossed Main Street and entered the fund's office building, he turned to watch David walking up the other side of Main. Bob felt a sense of gratitude and privilege, a feeling of status he never felt before. *This must be how a prince feels...special.*

All the years he'd lived without a father, all the anguish of feeling somehow inferior to other men, was now lifted from his subconscious. He felt the casting off of the stigma boys and their fathers had heaped on him over many years.

Acceptance and equality Bob had always sought but never received was something he no longer needed. A nascent inferiority complex that made him feel unsure of himself was leaving him. It would take some getting used to. Dark fears that others with fathers knew things he didn't were being swept away by the light of confidence. He was freed from that niggling demon! As he rode up the elevator to his office, he closed his eyes and whispered, "Thank you, David."

While Bob rode up the elevator to his office, David crossed Main Street from east to west, from a block north of the fund's office building. David proceeded north two more blocks. When he thought enough time and distance had passed, he re-crossed Main Street from the west to the east and walked alone back to the bank building. He reentered the vault, summoning the custodian once again to retrieve his safe boxes and leave him with the boxes in the private viewing room. "I can't believe I forgot to pick up a stock certificate while I was just here," he lied.

It was of no consequence, a superfluous remark, since custodians are sworn to silence and not allowed in the viewing rooms with the vault's customers under any circumstances. Once alone in the viewing room, David removed the codicil he'd showed Bob and replaced it with a similar one that left Bob a half million dollars instead of the one that left Bob the companies. There was no fear in his eyes while he performed the switch. Thereafter he never spoke a word to Bob or gave any hint about the switch.

As David left the bank and crossed Main to return to his office, a curtain from an office window high above slowly closed. Barbara returned to her desk in the lobby. She had witnessed the entire sequence.

Neither man let on to anyone about their deal and to many in the office the closeness of the two men caused rumors to swirl, but there was nothing tangible ever observed. Barbara instinctively knew she'd witnessed something important. Reaching into her memory for the wisdom of her father, she closed her eyes and recalled David scurrying back to the bank after running his route up Main Street and back down again. What was it Chief often said?

"Every animal has a central tendency that can be observed. Every animal returns to the core centerline of its behavior, for that is the soul of the animal. That is what it is."

She kept her eyes closed and remembered when Chief took her on her very first hunt. It was pitch black in the middle of a moonless night. Chief drove his old station wagon to Ravine Road and parked facing the ravine. They got out quietly and Chief retrieved two .22 caliber rifles from the back of the station wagon. Each rifle had a flashlight taped to the bottom of its barrel. They crept forward to the edge of the ravine, the tribal garbage dump set across it. Chief whispered to her to be quiet and listen. At first she heard nothing, then faint noises of movement and items rolling down into the ravine. At that exact moment, Sparrow and her father turned on their flashlights.

Rats were everywhere. Some scurried off while others stood fixed in place, blinded by the light. Then Sparrow and Chief shot rats.

"This was good experience for you, Sparrow," Chief complimented at the time. "What did you learn?"

"I learned that rats eat in darkness," said Sparrow.

"And what else did you learn about rats?"

"Many of them run from the light, but some ignored the light until we started shooting. Then they all ran from us and hid away."

"That is good, Sparrow. A rat lives in darkness, in secrecy of night. When you shine light on the rat and you attack it, the rat will scurry for his hiding place. That is the central tendency of the rat. Rat feed on the humans' leftovers, and the rat eats the weak and the very young. They breed readily and reproduce more rats. The rats are predators, but they're also prey for cat, coyote, wolf, hawk, eagle, owl, and snake. They will all eat them. Rats are afraid of their predators, but unlike mice, rats are dangerous and will attack there is no escape route. Never attack a rat directly or corner it, for it will bite you. Rats carry disease. Catch them in the open when they least suspect any danger and attack them from a distance, as we did. This is the end of your first hunting lesson, Sparrow, the lesson of the rat."

Barbara's revelation came to her that night when she was home alone. David's behavior was like a rat's. He scurried like one returning to its nest of safety. He didn't go far from his nest, and he went there in secret when he thought no one saw him. Barbara could only puzzle the meaning of the sequence of events she saw that day. She remembered the words of her father, "You must never attack a rat directly or corner a rat. A rat will bite you." Barbara kept her own counsel and bided her time.

ECHO

As days passed, a nagging doubt gnawed at Bob. The exhilarating feeling of being the anointed special son of David slowly drifted back to Earth. Bob didn't want to let go of the feeling. Special was special, he told himself, ashamed for ever doubting David. After all, they'd split millions before on a handshake. Sure, David could be trusted, Bob reasoned. David invited him to his house practically every morning when Bob was in town, gave him many gifts, including a fancy car. They'd lunched together over a hundred times, and besides, David had no apparent heirs. He was childless. Maybe he couldn't have kids; Bob never asked. He could think of no reason why David wouldn't keep their agreement. Why couldn't he trust David to never change the codicil in the bank vault?

Then the voice of doubt reared up from the earth. It rose like vapor steams lifting into the sunlight on a warm Appalachian Mountain spring morning. The spirit of doubt rose on fresh buoyant air and displaced the cool confidence of Bob's descending exhilaration. From the musings of his languid semi-conscious thought, his mother's voice came through in her insistent embittered certainty. The refrain of her incessant assertions echoed her deeply held belief, imprinting again upon him that which was instilled in him as a young boy, and in her, and likewise her ancestors before her. Estella's admonitions echoed in his mind whenever he thought of her.

"Bob, don't be a fool. You can never trust a Jew. They are sons of bitches. They'll always find some way to break a deal, to cheat you. They never deal in good faith, never. They always mislead you with a false impression. It's passed on to them as children. It's in their blood. It's who they are. They never care about the other person or how they hurt them. They have no honor. Cheating a gentile is honor to them. Their loyalties are like quicksilver, ever changing. Always remember, a Jew sucked the life out of your dear father!'"

Perhaps the greatest irony of her rants was that she concealed from her son his real parentage out of her protective instincts. Bob recalled more of his mother's old prejudices.

"Tell me the answer to this. Why did the Germans hate the Jews? It was just Hitler's propaganda you always say, but who ran the banks that impoverished the German people? Who gave them the impossible credit terms? Who tried to starve them? Who were the bankers who pushed Wilson to go into the Great War? Who were the bankers who were going to lose a fortune on loans to Britain and France if America didn't enter that war? Who were the bankers who pushed the impossible reparations on the German people after that war? Jews will forgive another Jew's debts but they will never forgive a gentile's. When they fight a gentile over money, they will fight to destroy the gentile: his credit, his employment, his family, his reputation, everything he has. They don't care. What did the fish merchant give us after he worked your father to death? Nothing! We got nothing from him, just a condolence card.

"You were a two-year-old baby. I had to work in a hosiery mill making silk stockings for rich women in New York. My fingers were filled with needle punctures from the machines. They weren't safe, but the Jews who ran the place didn't care. When I punctured a finger and bled on a stocking, I got fined for ruining the merchandise. I worked twelve-hour days and got twenty minutes for lunch. I had to raise my hand to get permission to go to the bathroom. Then I had to come to Florence's and get you and take you home and take care of you.

I had no rest. I lived years with no rest. They were cruel bastards, Bob. You always say we can't blame them, that it's just how it was, the best they could do, the best we could get. Times were bad, yes they were, but they didn't have to be cruel. They see us gentiles, as goyim, animals to use and throw away. Don't ever forget that.

"Two girls, their parents made them work there in that hell hole their family needed money so badly. One day on their lunch break, those two sisters went up to the roof of that ten-story building and jumped off together holding hands. They died. Next day they were replaced. The work didn't stop for even five minutes to remember them."

Bob remembered Mother sometimes cried when she talked about the silk mill. Often her story about poor Patty echoed in his mind. As Mother told it she was a pretty girl, a beauty. She cried a lot and was always unhappy because her parents made her work. They lived near the river in a small house near the tracks. It happened after midnight on a cold winter's night. It was in the damp air that numbs your ears and makes your nose run and makes you shiver all over. That's the kind of night it was when Patty did herself in.

She told Estella the day before that she was never going to come to work in the silk mill again, and her parents were never going to beat her again for refusing to go to work. That night Patty stood in a flimsy nightgown, nothing else—not even shoes, poor thing. Right in front of an oncoming coal train she stood. They found pieces of her broken body scattered over half a mile, but back at the silk mill they never stopped the work, not for a moment of silent prayer, nothing.

"We were lower than the animals, lower than the ground-hogs and the possums, and the Jews who ran that place never showed us they cared one wit that we lived like dirt. Remember that." His mother's words haunted him.

"I know the Jews, my son. Some day you will know them like I've known them. I see their ways. Some of them play the will game with their shiksas. They'll make an innocent girl into a sex slave and a house slave by promising her she'll get this or that in the will—a house, a fortune, whatever. Then they die. She gets nothing and she is ruined. No man will take her anymore. She's older, used goods. The Jew gives all to his own children, never to his shiksa. He'll even give to his divorced Jew wife before he gives to his shiksa who gave him her life of service and even her love. It's the eternal game Jews play. You give to them first, they give to you later, but they never do their part. Remember, the fish merchant never gave us even a discount after all your dad did for that man. So just stop telling me that you can do business with all these wonderful Jews you know. Times are different now, you say. You just wait. When you can see the end of your life like I can see mine now, then you just look back and see if you feel like you do now, or if you feel like I do now. One of us is right and one of us is wrong."

What is the mind if not the playground for controversy's wrestling matches with conjecture? When not on task, the mind idles away its protein fuels in bursts of reason or fits of fantasy. It flits about as a finch in a nest-building frenzy as it pulls in this fact or that and fits one fact into place or removes it after that fact is secured in its place, because the removed fact doesn't fit with its other constructs any more than the finch's newly brought construction prizes of horsehairs or ribbons. Yet the mind must at last rest, as the finch too does rest, when all pieces seem fitted together as best the gray matter can meld the jumbled scattered facts it knows or thinks it knows into a sensible, reasoned cohesion. The finch lays an egg in its constructed masterpiece, whereas the mind reposes within its construct of reason and logic a course of action or non-action as the case befits. Revealing the laid egg and revealing the mind's construct carries risks of a lost effort, but to meet the task of birth of chick or birth of action set into motion by the mind, the risks must both be taken or the mind's venture, like the finch's egg, will be stillborn.

Bob's mind wrestled with his mother's assertions. He hoped the struggle would resolve itself some way, yet it did not. Estella's life was hard; there was no doubt of that. Bob remembered her sitting in the big living room chair and crying softly in the evenings, the trips the two of them took with the bushel baskets to walk along the tracks where the coal trains passed, how they picked up fallen lumps of anthracite and trudged along until their baskets were half full and heavy, and how they kept the tiny house warm in the winter with those lumps of coal. Bob remembered how he saved up to buy a fishing reel from the Sears and Roebuck catalogue and how he used that reel to cast for sunfish perch and bass at the Cedar Dam below the house. How he proudly brought them to mother for scaling after he first gutted them, and how those tiny spiny scaly fish were many times their meal.

Estella cried for joy when the first Social Security check came to her for Bob's welfare. It was eight dollars a month and he was a ten-year-old. It wasn't much, but it meant the world to them back then. She had beaten and whipped him but also nurtured him, bought him his first bicycle and his ice skates and his baseball glove. There was a special bond formed between this single mother and her only child. She raised him to be tough, like his real father. Despite the beatings Bob received, he came to know his mother always meant well by him and loved him as no one else ever could. Mothers, the good ones, love their kids like that.

Now his mother was telling him through her voice from long ago that he was a fool to trust a Jew, but David was a Jew who'd always kept his word to him, who made Bob feel special. David filled the aching void Bob had often felt since his childhood. It was something he never outgrew. He couldn't do that, but now it didn't matter; the void was now filled. This was a business partner who split over four million dollars on a handshake. Then, as asked, David left him the companies in writing.

Was mother an anti-Semite? Yes, she was. Does that mean that I must be an anti-Semite? Was my own experience the same as mother's? How can I possibly justify trusting her counsel? Would that be any way to regard a partner? Shouldn't I break free of Mother's mold? Am I engaging in madness to even give this matter any thought?

Bob needed to make peace with himself. He'd already switched career paths, and he was making good progress building UGGA's assets. *If I go back to David and ask for a copy of the codicil, having seen it, would he cease trusting me? Would he think I'm going to just sit around and wait for him to die? Would David think the firm would never grow? Would his pride be hurt and our special relationship destroyed?* These thoughts churned in his mind and gave him a restless night. He awoke believing he'd wrestled an angel.

Despite his mental quandaries, Bob believed in logic and the scientific method of reasoning. Things happened for a reason. State the facts as you knew them and the truth tests out. Theorems could be postulated and they'd hold up to scrutiny or they would collapse. If such and such were true, then did not such and such have to also be true or not be true? The facts would lead to truth.

If David were sincere, why not make a contract? But he was sincere about splitting major money with a handshake. Why would David not leave him the companies? He had no children. The cold business logic of pushing further for a definitive contract might only serve to harm the close confidential relationship he had with David. The man was given to bizarre behaviors at times, but he was fun to be around. They laughed easily together about almost everything and everyone. What purpose would it serve to put pressure on their friendship or on their father-son relationship?

Yet, aside from his mother's admonitions, there was that one personal observation Bob made about David's behavior that didn't find a logical fitting place. He was vexed by what he saw while watching David's eyes in the bank vault. It was a look that spanned hundreds of generations. It was instinctive, impossible to conceal.

Bob couldn't let go of the thought that David, for that brief fleeting instant, showed fear in his eyes that someone was watching him, that someone might see him showing the codicil to Bob. That had to be the reason for the look. It was the only thing that fit. Why?

Bob's mind conjured up some dark scenarios. *Did David want no witnesses? Could that be for my own protection somehow? That seems too remote to contemplate. Animals that show fear like that show it for their own safety, not some fawn or cub hidden in the brush nurtured on mother's milk. Newborns do not drink water. Has David done this before? That seems highly doubtful. There would be talk and likely litigation. Maybe David was fearful someone else would see the quart jars of diamonds. There are several possibilities to ponder.*

Bob's mind returned again and again to those eyes, that clear flicker of terrified fear. He needed to checkmate his own fears, put his dilemma in a mouse jar, and find peace of mind without trampling upon David's feelings. He assured himself he was thinking soundly.

OLD MAC

Old Mac was counsel for the corporate underwritings Bob did the prior year. Mac also happened to be the attorney David used for some of his personal matters. In the course of working together on the due diligence investigations of the respective securities' issuers, Bob and Mac became amicable toward each other, sharing a number of lunches and beers together. Mac made good money on that business. When Bob called Mac to take him to lunch, for no other stated reason than they hadn't seen each other for a while, he readily accepted.

At lunch the two relived past times and congratulated each other on their successes. Then Bob asked Mac for advice on a personal matter. He relayed to Mac the bank vault scene and described the codicil David had showed him, complete with four witnesses' signatures.

"He showed you that?" Mac was taken aback. His bushy white eyebrows normally overhung his piercing blue eyes like cliff outcrops over two caves, with two sparkling blue sapphires set within. But now the cliffs lifted as his hands went to the rear of his wizened head. Mac began a thoughtful, time-buying, head-scratching effort. The eyebrows returned to their normal position, except his forehead was in a frown and his eyes squinted.

"Well yes. Our agreement is that I change my career, work to build the companies. When David dies, he leaves the operating companies to me. That's the deal, but David didn't give me a copy of the codicil. He returned it to its envelope and put the envelope back into the safe deposit box. I keep wondering if I should ask him for a copy, but my dilemma is that he'll take that as a sign of mistrust, and you know we've split serious money before on a handshake."

"Yeah, I know all about that. I've talked to him before about using contracts, but that's just how he is. It's an old-school sort of thing with him. You know, the best deal is a handshake between two honest men." Mac's hands lifted as he shrugged.

"That's not what they teach in law school, but there's a lot they don't teach in law school."

"So this is just his way?"

"It is for all the years I've known him."

Mac wore his poker face now and maintained strict silence about preparing the second codicil that made no mention of leaving the companies to Bob. His stomach churned, but he dared not show it. Playing games with a will codicil is something Marvin would never do. Listening to Bob describe the names of the signatories, which included four of the partners in Mac's law firm, greatly concerned him. It was only a draft that he'd given David to review and comment on, not a final witnessed codicil. There had been no such signing of signatures. He would have seen that in the firm's records, which he maintained as firm general counsel. This was a serious matter. Behind the poker face was a conscience that waxed angry. *David has possibly forged the signatures of four of my partners. If I bring this up to him, we could lose the UGGA account which is a big chunk of our business. Plus, I have no proof that what Bob is saying is true.* While he retained his silence, his mind was spinning for a solution to his dilemma. *How can I be ethical to my client and remain without conflict? I can't let my firm get caught up in abetting a fraud if that's what's going on here. I think I see a way to help Bob.*

Mac was at heart one of the world's few good guys. That was why he became a lawyer in the first place; he didn't like to see anybody getting screwed. He was an outlier among lawyers and rejected out of hand the notion that layering was just a game of separating clients from their money. He was a throwback to the morals of a hundred years before.

"So we're talking about this why?"

Mac sought to draw Bob out, as all good lawyers do, but even knowing what Bob was telling him, he could never know the whole story of the codicil because David never told Mac about his pledge to Marvin. David's normal practice was to never allow any one person to see the entire picture about anything. No lawyer ever knew the complete picture of his dealings. That was, for him, an essential business principle.

"Well, that codicil is all that evidences our agreement. I don't want to work for my whole career and find out it's been misplaced, accidentally destroyed, accidentally superseded, or that some bank was torn down or a bank vault somehow burned. You see my dilemma?"

"I hear you. I'm in an awkward position here. I am his lawyer. I drafted that codicil he showed you. I can't be conflicted, you know that, so don't ask me to intercede in this matter on your behalf."

Mac leaned back in his chair, his head bobbing up and down. The gray matter in that old skull was as fresh and imaginative as a twelve-year-old boy's. Mac's eyes smiled with their mirthful Irish twinkle before he flashed a friendly grin.

"David said you have a deal, so you have a deal. That's all you need to know, Bob."

"I can place trust in your assertion?" Bob was stretching an old friendship.

"Tell you what, Bob. You pick up lunch as my payment for my advice to you just now as my personal client. That's a deal we have with each other, and your copy of the lunch bill is your proof we met and I advised you. Now you can trust my advice. You have a deal with David."

Bob knew Mac's heart, and all his burdens of doubt lifted. He believed he could trust David, even though Mac stated that he could trust Mac's advice. If Bob's emotions weren't clouding his thinking, he would have noted that Mac never said he could trust David. Bob's reasoning was that if Mac thought he should not put his trust in David, wouldn't he have told him to go back to David and insist on a copy of the codicil? But he didn't. Bob lay to rest Estella's warnings that arose like Appalachian mists and slipped through the back doors of his mind.

Once again Bob set out with great enthusiasm to build the UGGA fund.

KNOW-HOW

Time rolled along. Bob covered the nation in his travels, finding small broker-dealer firms and persuading them to carry the fund. He also shook the tree branches of the larger national firms wherever he could talk his way in the door. Occasionally he found a sales representative with an independent maverick streak who would sell a fund even if it wasn't on the big firm's approved list. Bob's little fund could never pay those big firms enough reciprocal commission trade kickbacks to get any shelf space, but every once in a while there was a rep who would stay after hours, after the sales meetings, to listen to his pitch. Even though the branch managers threw up their standard barriers to block his contact with the branch's salesmen, he made it around those barriers often enough.

He took in pizzas and put notices on the salesmen's cars to meet at a local spot to get free pizza and hear a great story. Some attended his meetings, and some sold the fund to clients. He was building a giant snowball and it was picking up momentum as it rolled downhill, gathering adherents. He gave free tickets to a movie to receptionists to tell him which sales rep would be receptive and productive. Often enough, the front receptionist would set up a private meeting with him and the rep. If the effort resulted in sales, she received more movie tickets. It all took a lot of hard work. Thousands of flights, over a hundred cities visited, many of them several times. Many pairs of good wingtips were worn out and many white shirts replaced.

In addition to the initial contact and sales job, there was the task of maintaining data on each sales rep: what they liked and didn't, their politics, religion, married or not, what the spouse was involved with, kid's names and data on what the kids were doing. Whatever glimpse into the personal or prejudice was revealed, Bob made it his business to keep a record of it. Thus, whenever a salesman called the fund with a question, Bob picked up the phone with notes in hand. The rep was always made to feel like a valuable personal friend joined with Bob in the never-ending mission to bring good investment management to the world's ignorant unwashed masses.

Top sales reps were flown into Plaintown for sales meetings. Many were entertained in Vail, Aspen, or Estes Park at the world-famous Stanley Hotel. The previously declining fund was still small by industry standards, but it became a growing presence in the marketplace.

The fund attracted a cult following, created by differential sales literature which contrasted a fully managed fund with a family of fund funds, where there really was no overall asset management responsibility because each investor was expected to move their money into the right mutual fund at the right time. There was no one who could be held responsible if somehow that movement at the right time never happened.

In effect, the sales effort sharply differentiated the fund from its competition and sales reps who understood how to sell the differentiation were well compensated up front with a healthy commission. Having no hidden fees was a strong product sales feature. The fund became, in many respects, the actualization of the story every child knows of *The Little Engine That Could*.

Through relentless hard work and continued good performance, results piggybacked upon the halcyon years when the fund was stuffed with gold stocks, the fund grew from a puny dot on the landscape twelve million in asset-sized fund to a respectable midsized billion dollars in asset-sized fund. The worth of the operating companies grew from less than a quarter million dollars, including furniture and pencils in inventory, to a healthy thirty million.

Everybody in the firm heard the music of success. The whole office staff went on lavish junkets to seaside resorts and Las Vegas. Paychecks fattened, offices were upgraded from early vintage dirtbag to lavish French provisional. The company garage boasted ten new cars. Every good news item that came in was celebrated with another office party, complete with entertainment, and better than the previous party.

Bob continued taking plane rides and pounding pavements for sales. The fund was approaching two billion dollars in assets. The businesses made over five million dollars annually, but growth now slowed.

Performance actually nose-dived into the bottom ten percent ranking of all growth funds in existence, and there were now about ten times more growth funds in existence than when Bob first started selling. There was a second problem that impeded growth. The business model of one fully managed fund was losing market share to the multiple funds or family of funds business models. Salesmen saw themselves more in control of clients and the clients' monies when they had the power to move the clients' monies around. If a fully managed fund underperforms what another broker is doing with client monies by moving monies from fund to fund, then the credibility of the fully managed fund's ability to manage becomes suspect.

Bob entered David's office. "We're losing the battle for market share. Our credibility is in question because many of your stock picks haven't worked out. I think it's time we revisit our past decision to not have multiple funds. If we keep the trajectory our assets are on, we'll slip back to under a hundred million in assets."

David was well aware of his performance. In actuality he was trying to underperform all competitive benchmarks. He entertained the thought that if he woefully underperformed the average fund, Bob could get discouraged and quit to go elsewhere. After all, Bob had developed good industry contacts and could likely find himself a great position with a larger fund group. If that were to happen, he could simply destroy the replacement codicil, leave Bob nothing, and give the companies to Israel when he passed away or sell them and keep the money for himself. No one would ever be the wiser. As an alternative, David considered just selling the companies, living off the proceeds, and giving the remainder of his estate to Israel. That would sort of satisfy the promise he'd made to Marvin and the various rabbis who knew about the promise, especially the one who kept a copy of David's pledge to Marvin in his temple's safe.

Bob gave David hints about getting his performance up, but David was at the point in his life where he just wanted to live in peace with his animals in his barnyard. Instead of being candid with Bob and making a breakup deal, he decided it was time to put Bob to the ultimate test of his loyalty as a son of sorts and as a salesman. Besides, Bob was a gentile and David felt no duty to give him any relief from his part of the deal, even though David never intended to honor his own part of the bargain. He came up with a diversionary ruse to keep Bob fully engaged in selling.

"I see your sales are declining. I know performance hasn't been red-hot lately, but a great salesman finds a way to overcome every obstacle and keep sales moving forward, despite temporary setbacks. I know you're working hard. I know you're on the road two weeks out of three, but I've analyzed your sales results and I see a way for you to increase sales above where they are, despite the current performance."

"I'm all ears."

"Well, sit down." After Bob was comfortable in one of the swivel chairs, David looked up at his ceiling and brought his hand up to his chin, scratching it in thought before he spoke. "When I looked at the names of the salesmen who sell the fund, I noticed something in particular that jumped out at me. There's not a single Cohen or Stein or Gold or Schwartz or Unger or any other Jewish name among them."

"We have some Jewish salesmen. There's Sampson, Silver, Melon, and a Roth among those names."

"But proportionally you have maybe five percent Jews selling the fund and ninety-five percent gentiles. There's a subtlety you should know. There's no such thing as a Jewish salesman any more than there's a Catholic or a Muslim salesman. A salesman who is a Jew is a Jew who is a salesman. Jewish refers to a tradition, like a Jewish tradition, not a person."

"Sorry. I didn't mean to offend."

"Forget it. You're not offending. But it just goes to show that you don't understand the Jewish religion. No doubt you say things, do things, by accident without knowing or thinking about what you're doing when you're in front of a sales group and you're turning off the Jews."

"How can you be so sure of that?"

"Numbers don't lie. Half the people in the financial world are Jews. Here I am, a known Jew with a gentile salesman who I treat like a son, and I only see him getting about five percent of his sales from Jews."

"Well, can you give me some pointers? Should I take lox and bagels to my sales meetings? Or how about if I take matzo ball soup?"

"Don't be a wiseass. This is serious. We're missing sales you should be picking up. It's in the numbers."

"Okay. I see it. But what is there to do about it?"

"It's like this. All things being equal, if a Jew salesman likes our fund about the same as another fund, but the other fund has a Jew wholesaler out selling that fund, the Jew sales rep is going to give his sales to the Jew wholesaler's fund. That's just how it is."

"You need to tell me why that is."

"It's because of our persecution complex. We've had the living shit kicked out of us since the pharaoh in Egypt made slaves out of us, since the Spaniards had their inquisition that murdered us, the Russians had their pogroms that killed us and displaced us, the Nazis committed genocide, the Romans committed genocide, the Latin Americans came to our homes and made us disappear. We've got a victim complex. Can you blame us?

"When a Jew salesman sees another Jew selling something, he thinks maybe that Jew had a relative who got killed off way back when along with a relative of his, so there's a natural empathy those two Jews will have for each other. That's what you must overcome. Everybody already has sales relationships. Women understand that to bag a guy they need to break the guy's existing relationship with another woman, right? Sales are the same way. You need to first undo the existing relationship. Now can you see the uphill fight you have? How does a guy like you, whose ancestors probably killed the Jew's ancestors, break a relationship the Jew already has with another Jew?"

"It seems impossible when you put it that way. I feel terribly sorry, as a gentile, for what happened to all the Jews, especially from the Nazi era. Understand, I was only born in the month the war ended. I was a baby who couldn't even talk, much less kill anybody. I don't see how a Jew could think I'm responsible for what happened."

"You're not seeing it. They do hold you responsible because they think that you think about them the way your parents and ancestors thought about their parents and ancestors. They are actually terrified of you, partly resentful of you, partly angry and vindictive toward you, and partly jealous of you."

"I don't get the jealous part. Jews in America tend to do pretty well."

"Jealous because you don't have to worry about some anti-Semitic asshole killing you because you're a Jew. My God! You really don't see these things, do you? You just think everybody in America is equal and sees everybody else as equal too!"

"No, actually I don't. I have my half-orphan complex. I've talked to you about it the year we first met. I used to have issues with that, still do to some extent, but the way you treat me, like a father would a son, has helped me with that quite a bit. You figured out what made me tick. Now I feel like I'm special. I've never felt special before. I didn't mean to focus this on me. I know there are people who don't feel they're equal to everybody else."

"You're right. Your problem is how to break that Jew-to-Jew relationship. How are you going to get into that Jew's head and get him to sell for you?"

"Being a Jew, I'm sure you have the answer. What am I not doing?"

"It's like this. In order to gain the trust of a Jew, you need to be able to empathize with other Jews. You must be able to think like a Jew. In certain circumstances, you need to act like a Jew and behave as a Jew would behave. In order to think and act like a Jew, you need to know all about Jews. You need to know the history, the religion, the customs, the holidays, and the subtle differences between the Ashkenazi Jew and the Sephardic Jew. In order to think as a Jew, you need to become a Jew."

"What's the difference between an American Ashkenazi and an American Sephardic Jew?"

"The Sephardic are allowed to put peanut butter on their matzo, but the Ashkenazi aren't allowed to put peanut butter on their matzo."

"Ha! Wait a minute." Bob's mind caught up to what just passed into his ears. "Did you just say that to get Jews to sell the fund I'd have to become a Jew? Change my religion?"

"If you're serious about building this company, yes. You committed to giving it a hundred percent. In order to pick up the sales you're leaving on the table, you're going to have to be a Jew. That's the only way you'll relate to the Jews. You can still act like a gentile around salesmen who are gentiles, but around Jews you must be another Jew."

"But I don't look like a Jew. I have blue eyes and blond hair. I'm a lot taller than most Jews. My bone structure, my body frame is much bigger. Most Jews will know I'm not a Jew."

"All those are reasons why they will sell for you. Most Jews wished they had your looks and your body. They'll sell for you out of identity empathy. The women Jewesses will go crazy selling for you. To them you'll be like eye candy. They always give their sales to the cutest guy, as long as he's a Jew."

"Okay. Where do I sign up to be a Jew?"

"It's not that easy. It's not like buying a candy bar or a movie ticket. You need to study with a rabbi and learn the religion. After you learn the religion, when the rabbi says you are ready, then you get a circumcision and a mikveh ritual bath. Then you get a certificate that says you're a Jew. There's a lot to it. The study can take many years, and getting a rabbi to teach you can be difficult."

"Why difficult? I would think that after the Holocaust the rabbis would be trying to recruit and rebuild."

"No, quite the contrary. Rabbis are terrified that if they recruit people they will be seen as proselytizers. Other religions hate to lose market share, and the rabbis don't want to give other religions any reason whatsoever to be upset with Jews. They've been through enough shit with the Inquisition, the pogroms, the Holocaust, and those who disappear. They say, 'Enough, already.'"

"I'll think about it," said Bob, which was his polite way of saying he wasn't ready to consider David's suggestion.

After another year of grueling road work, Bob was ready to trade places with Sisyphus. Every new sale was offset by redemption money leaving. It was a losing uphill battle. Salesmen he'd cultivated switched allegiances to other fund groups. Brokerage firms staffed mutual fund departments to keep their reps selling the family of funds concept or see their commissions docked. Brokerage policies were obstacles to managed funds competing with national distribution networks. Bob felt demoralized. He wondered if David deliberately selected stocks that were more likely to go down than up. He sold based upon his own prognostications instead of the fund's results.

Selling past performance is infinitely easier than selling forecasts. Great past results are irrefutable proof that your management style works. Futuristic-based sales pitches are problematic. If a salesman agrees with the idea, he'll just as likely use it somewhere else or just go buy the stock that seems to be the core of the strategy. If he disagrees, there will be no sales at all. While no one can dispute a successful record, it's easy to disagree about the future. It's nigh impossible to sell on the basis that although the past five years were terrible, the next five will be wonderful. Sales representatives find it hard explaining to a client that they recommended a subpar performer if subsequent years also return subpar results. They fear being in that position and avoid the risk. When a multiple product salesman has one fund performing poorly, he simply trots out another fund and sells that one. Bob implored David to consider a change.

"You need to perform better or we're going to bleed assets. Do something! Get different newsletters, change your thinking on the markets, or merge the fund into a smaller one with a better track record. Use their track record and I'll sell that. I don't care what we do, but we need to make something happen. This is urgent. Everything I've built is in danger of coming undone."

David, ever quick to turn the tables, retorted, "You're never going to build the right kind of relationships if you're selling performance. You need to sell the salesmen on the basis of their relationship with you. Performance selling puts the clients first. A good salesman doesn't give a fuck about his clients. A salesman's relationship with you is the sale you want."

"I've got hundreds of relationships, but they'll never stick if the performance doesn't turn around. Even the best salesman can't persuade a client that a piece of shit is a candy bar!" Bob's frustrations boiled over.

"Nonsense, and don't be disrespectful." David snorted. "You have the wrong kind of relationships."

"Listen for once. These guys have been incredibly loyal to us and we're letting them down. What kind of relationship are we giving back?"

"You need the right kind of relationships. I keep telling you that. You don't have the right kind of relationships."

"What kind of relationship is that?"

"Jewish relationships are what you need, the kind that will stick with you through thick and thin. We've all, through our ancestors, been through the Holocaust together, the Inquisition, pogroms—" David was waving his arms wildly above his head like a mad man trying to fend off demons when Bob interrupted.

"David, stop. Just stop! You did not go through the Holocaust or the Inquisition or any pogrom. You are American born. Your 'feel sorry for me' song because you're playing your Jew card will not sell UGGA fund shares."

"Aha, that's where you're wrong! It resonates in the soul of every Jew. It sells."

"So you believe that, if I go to the Jewish firms and tell them I feel their pain from the Holocaust, they'll begin to sell our shares? You can't be serious! I can't see how that will get us anywhere!"

"I can."

"How?"

"It will work if you become a Jew yourself. I'm sure of it. They'll identify with you because they'll see that you identify with them."

"We've been here before, David. I don't even look like a Jew. I have the blue eyes and blond hair, remember? I look more like a Nazi than a Jew." Bob was incredulous, but David was serious.

"Doesn't matter. I've seen some tall blue-eyed, blond-haired Jews in shul. It's the words, the Hebrew, the Yiddish, not the looks that the Jew picks up on. Trust me on this. Let me go over it again so even you can understand it. Half the people in the securities business are Jews. In order to relate to Jews, to get along with them, you must become a Jew yourself."

JOINING THE TRIBE

"This is America. It's a secular world now. Tribalism is history, David. The world has gone modern, secular, and global. You can't be serious. You expect me to change my religion?" Bob thought David was being illogical.

"The world is only secular on the surface. Down deep inside your soul, and down deep inside the soul of every Jew, there's an unbreakable tribal bond. You may have had nothing to do with the Holocaust, since you were born in the last month of the war, but in truth you had everything to do with it. You lived and a Jew's baby died in those years. No Jew will ever forget that their cousins and brothers and sisters not yet born are not here because you are here. Your ancestors killed our ancestors. What do you think the words 'Never forget' and 'Never again' mean anyway?" David made the illogical sound plausible.

"Jesus Christ, you're serious about this. You really are serious!" Bob was shocked, but he believed what he was hearing.

"Yes, I'm serious, and don't give me any more of that Jesus Christ shit. That's just gentile code for it was okay to slaughter Jews by the millions because we killed Jesus somehow. Maybe if you can believe stuff that was written about Jesus two hundred years after he died then it's okay to talk about him, but I don't like hearing his name. To us Jews, it's just the okay to kill us again. I hate to hear those words. Most Jews who know their history know what those words really mean and it terrifies them, so please do not ever utter them in my presence again."

David was waving his hands in front of his face as if to ward off a swarm of bees.

"I am very sorry. I had no idea the impact of words I've used every day since I was a child."

David sensing vulnerability, decided it was time to drive his point home.

"You say you want to have a big asset management company. You say you're willing to do what it takes. I'm telling you the Jews' sales will stick because the relationship will stick. It's the tribe, man. It's the tribe! It's that old-fashioned religion, that old tribal relationship. It's more solid than any country club membership. Those country club types just play at acting important. They all have their heads up their asses. They can't see what's inside a heart like a Jew can. It's great to be a Jew. There's nothing quite like it. It's the greatest country club in the world. The gentile clubs don't even have a purpose, just about members screwing other members. Just trust me on this. You want to be a Jew, and you need to be a Jew. You're going to love being a Jew."

"All right, so how do I get started?" Bob was frustrated enough to try anything. He was about to undergo a religious metamorphosis from a pedestrian gentile caterpillar into either a heavenly butterfly or a neurotic moth, he wasn't sure which. *What the heck! Sales are in the dumpster anyway. If it might help sales, I'll try anything!*

"First you've got to overcome the rejections. You've got to convince a rabbi you're serious about this. He's going to turn you away three times, reject you. If you come back a fourth time, maybe he'll accept you, if conditions are right."

"This sounds like the cock crowing three times when Peter rejects Christ. I wonder if that Bible story comes from the rabbis' three rejections."

"Who knows? I don't know jack about Christianity. Religion is just mumbo jumbo anyway. You just have to get past it. It's kind of like running a gauntlet. You can do this if you put your mind to it! You can become a Jew!"

"You said conditions. What conditions?"

"Oh that. I was referring to your kids if and when you have some. See, the rabbi doesn't really give a shit about you, but he's going to want to see that you're enough of a Jew to want your kids to be Jews too. He's going to want to believe kids of yours will get a good religious education, and a Jewish religious education is the very best a kid can get. The rabbis hammer the crap out of the kids. They got to learn all the Bible stories and what they mean. They learn all about right and wrong, how God guides a good person's life. The rabbi wants to hear sometime in his preliminary talks with you that he has a shot at teaching your future kids the Jewish ways, so they'll grow up to be good human beings, mensch material. Rabbis are about saving humanity from its base dark side and helping people love life and love God and being a force for good in the world. He's going to want a shot at that."

"David, I have no kids."

"Well, you might someday if that Indian minx drags you into her teepee."

"You're giving me ideas, David," Bob pretended to jest. David pretended not to hear.

"You'll have to study like you're back in school again. It's not easy. It can take years of nights of study. You've got to learn the Hebrew language, the holidays, the rituals, the services. The rabbi, your teacher, will want to see you are taking it seriously."

"How long must I study?"

"Until your rabbi says you are ready, not before. It could be three years, could be ten, and could be never. It's up to the rabbi. He's not going to turn you loose on his congregation until he's satisfied he can present you as a bona fide Jew. It's an extremely serious process. I could never do it myself, to be honest, but we Jews who are born to it get in easier. We just have to go to Bible school and get our Bar Mitzvah. You'll have to learn all the mitzvahs."

"What are mitzvahs? Some kind of matzo?"

"Mitzvahs are the rules. There're six hundred and nineteen of them. They cover everything you should and should not do in life, from not killing to not walking behind a woman who's not your wife because her ass might tempt you, to looking into a stream when a woman crosses because the reflection of her pussy on the water might give you a hard-on and tempt you to fuck her, to licking up your wife's pussy before you screw her so she's got an easy slippery time getting your dick into her. If you follow the mitzvahs, you'll find life is just better."

"Do the Muslims have mitzvahs too?"

"I have no idea. I don't know much about them except they love being pissed off and they want to kill everybody. They're angry and miserable if they can't hate somebody. They like to shoot guns into the air and beat their women. Maybe that's required in their religion. That's all I know about them."

"So Jews and Muslims aren't similar, but both are from the Middle East?"

"Right. The two main differences are that Jews like life and Muslims seem obsessed with death. The other big difference is they ended up camping over the oil and we Jews ended up camped on the major trade route, the Levant. That's why we also have that third kind of Jew besides the Ashkenazis and the Sephardics. We have the Tel Aviv Jew."

"What kind of Jew is that?"

"The Tel Aviv Jew is the Jew who likes to do a quick trade and then move on to the next. They make good stock traders and deal guys, always looking to do a trade or put a deal together. They make the world go around but they have no integrity beyond the transaction, kind of like agency brokers compared to advisors. There's no care about a relationship or ongoing business with them. They don't care about peanut butter on matzo either. They live on pastrami.

"Thanks, this really helps a lot."

"You're welcome. Any time you have a question about how to be a Jew, just ask. But remember to always just do as I say, never as I do. I'm not what you'd call a model Jew."

"Okay, after I've finished all the studies and I'm rabbi ready, then what?"

"Then you get to have your service."

"Like a prayer service?"

"Sort of. You get to do some praying, and then you get your mikveh bath. That's a ritual bath. Then the molke comes. He's the special rabbi."

"What does he do?"

"He circumcises you. He takes this special knife and—"

"What!" Bob interrupted, alarmed. "I've already had that done when I was a baby. I'm not going to let some guy carve my dick. I'm an adult. This is crazy!"

"Not to worry. He's good at it. He's a prick expert. He just makes a clean pass at it, kind of sticks the knife into your dick and draws blood. It's ritual, that's all. His knife never slips. He's never sliced off a dick yet."

"You're sure?"

"Yeah, I'm sure. You'll get to keep your dick."

After trying three rabbis who sent them away telling them they were crazy, David and Bob found one liberal rabbi who, after three rejections, agreed to work with Bob. After eight years of study, he became a Jew.

TRACKING DAVID

True to her father's advice, Barbara set out to track the human animals that worked at UGGA. For animals, it was enough to listen to the elders talk about the tendencies of each, to hear and remember their stories, as was the custom of oral tradition that served her people for thousands of years. For human animals, the ones who left their tracks on papers, she needed more than memory of who was where and when, who said what and when, who talked about whom, what routines were followed and not followed, what protocols were observed, what information was freely available or guarded, and how the information was guarded. Thus Barbara began keeping a notebook of all these things. Her notebook had journal entries to record the times of observations and was further divided into sections for reference and cross-reference. There were sections dedicated to each employee and each firm contact, vendors, service agents, regulators, attorneys, accountants, and each salesman who sold fund shares. Her notebook blossomed into a miniature library of several volumes. She tracked every conceivable detail, convinced that through her diligence patterns would reveal themselves in her cross-referencing system.

And they did. For example, Barbara noticed that shortly after a visit from executives of a brokerage firm that sold the fund's shares, commission trades were placed with that brokerage firm. Oddly, but not coincidental, the dollar retention of the broker for the trades, after clearing firm costs, was always two percent of that brokerage firm's fund sales. Apparently David was paying an additional two percent for fund sales out of fund assets because these brokerages charged substantially more than execution costs of most firms and they had no research departments. Barbara calculated the fund payments in excess commission charges resulted in the brokerages receiving an additional forty percent compensation above the posted prospectus rate. She surmised David skirted regulations requiring full disclosure of transaction costs, and disclosure of allowable fund expenses.

Her tracking revealed David was a creature of habit. Every Friday he stopped in bookkeeping with a black briefcase before he left the office. He returned to bookkeeping every Monday with the same briefcase before he went to his own office. Prior to her tracking regimen, she assumed David just stopped into bookkeeping to check on account balances or sales, but upon giving the matter greater thought, Barbara noticed he never carried that briefcase any other times. He transported something in that black briefcase that he did not trust to leave unattended at the firm over weekends.

Chief told her the only way to understand the animal was to actually watch the animal. She mustered her courage and invented a reason to barge into bookkeeping while David was there on a Friday, after he entered with his briefcase. She timed David's stay in bookkeeping for three successive Fridays and calculated that the four-minute mark was the exact halfway point of his visit. The next Friday she made her move.

"Debbie," Barbara addressed the head bookkeeper as she flung open the door to the area. "Could I trouble you to please pull the files you have for tax payments for occupational taxes?"

David's back was to the door, but he was in the midst of receiving from Debbie Wasserman a large brass key ring containing a single brass key. Debbie sat in the back corner and the transfer of the key was not apparent to any of the other bookkeepers. Barbara was the only one who witnessed it. David turned to face Barbara, an alarmed look on his face. It was obvious he and Debbie were caught in the midst of an activity no one was supposed to see. David quickly regained his composure.

"Do you need it right now?" Debbie seemed annoyed. "What do you need it for, anyway?" Her add-on was a tell of sorts; bookkeeping had no business asking why an administrator wanted anything. It was plain to Barbara there was something going on between the pair, and Debbie was annoyed at the intrusion. Barbara, equally quick, was ready for this contingency.

"We donated some old chairs to Goodwill, and I want to revise our occupational tax report and get us a refund. Big bucks, Debbie! I think we can save thirty dollars a year." Barbara smiled her most Ms. Efficiency smile and 'fuck you for asking' look at the skeptical bookkeeper.

"Good thinking, Barbara," David chimed in, now smiling and believing the intruder. After all, what Barbara said was all true and it was part of her job. No harm in saving thirty dollars a year. That's what the office efficiency expert was supposed to do. David turned to Debbie, his back to Barbara, and gave her a nearly indiscernible head shake and dismissive smirk, indicating Barbara was nothing to be concerned about.

David and Debbie didn't know it, but an expert tracker was hot on their trail. The sight of the key ring transfer told Barbara there was a secret between these two that no one else in the company was privy to. It was time to know her animals better. It was time to go sleuthing.

On a hunch, on a Sunday, Barbara went to David's temple. She went inside, told the custodian she was doing some research, and was directed to the temple's vast library. She signed in under a fictitious name and was not required to show identification. She browsed about the shelves and stacks, picked up a book on Jewish humor, sat down in a chair where she could see the librarian, and waited. Sure enough, after about a half hour the old woman got up and headed for the restroom.

Barbara quickly went to her desk and went through the open drawers. She found what she was looking for, the temple's membership directory. Jews, unlike Christians, must belong to a temple and pay dues to be allowed to attend High Holy Days services. The membership directory showed who was a member. Barbara thumbed the pages until she came to Debbie Wasserman. Bingo! Her suspicions were confirmed. David and Debbie went to the same temple. Likely, they trusted each other to keep secrets.

Her tracking became a cat and mouse game. Barbara needed to find out why there was a brass key, where David kept it, and why Debbie handed it to him. More sleuthing was required. She'd need to work nights and weekends. Fortunately, she and Mrs. Rodriguez were trusted employees, so she had keys to open the main doors to the offices. On a Friday evening before a long weekend, she left the office like all the others but then returned two hours later. No one was there.

She went to Susan's office and unlocked it. In a desk drawer were the keys to all other offices. Taking the keys, she went to the bookkeepers' offices and unlocked them. Heading to Debbie's desk, she opened her top drawer. There was the brass key! But didn't she see David take the key with him? She looked around the office. There was a small fireproof steel file cabinet bolted to the concrete floor next to all the other file cabinets. It had two brass key holes fitted to securely lock it. It was just like a bank safe deposit box. She took Debbie's key and tested it. It fit one of the locks, but not the other. David's key had to fit the other lock. But he had that key.

Weeks passed while Barbara observed David's pockets. He kept his office keys in the right pocket and his car and house keys in the left. She saw him take office keys from his right pocket and hold them in his hand on two separate occasions; both times the brass key ring and its solo key were there, separate from all the others. Barbara carefully noted the times and movements of David and Muscle Boy. Office gossip was that Muscle Boy was sometimes summoned to David's office in the afternoons and once there, David locked the door and the two of them made disgusting male mating sounds, especially David who groaned loudly shortly before Muscle Boy left. Before he summoned Muscle Boy, David always, without exception, spent considerable time in the men's bathroom. Barbara waited to make her move.

From the office internal phone system, Barbara and Mrs. Rodriguez could tell who was on their phones. Muscle Boy's phone was almost never in use. When, on a Friday afternoon, David's phone light was on and Muscle Boy's also went on, Barbara's radar went on as well. Sure enough, shortly after the romantic men hung up, David walked past the front office to the men's room. Barbara excused herself and left her office, telling Mrs. Rodriguez she had to get something from Susan's office. Instead she went to David's, unlocked it, let herself in, relocked the door from the inside, and hid herself behind the window drapes.

It didn't take long for her tracking to bear fruit. She soon saw bare male asses. David was the first to enter, Muscle Boy arriving shortly after. Barbara peered from behind the curtain as the two men embraced and kissed each other passionately. Then, as if she'd scripted the scene herself, both men took their pants off and hung them behind the door. David went to the low bench and lied down while Muscle Boy began sucking his cock. David's head was hung over the end of the low bench furthest from the door. His eyes, when not closed, were facing the opposite wall and ceiling. Muscle Boy was kneeling with his ass to the door, looking down on David's cock. He was sucking in an up and down motion with his head. *Just like a common whore giving a blow job,* thought Barbara. It was time for her to make her move.

With both men engrossed in David's oral sex treatment, Barbara stealthily slipped from behind the curtain drape and tiptoed barefoot to David's left pants pocket. She removed the brass key ring and key and pressed the key into a warm wax mold. Silently she slipped everything back into David's pocket. She let herself out and locked the office door from the outside and put her shoes on. *In the old days I might have been a good horse thief.*

Getting a wax imprint of Debbie's companion key was simple fare. When all employees were gone, she let herself into bookkeeping, went to Debbie's desk, and made an imprint of the key. With the two imprints, she went to a locksmith in another town and had duplicate keys made. Now she was ready to learn what the curious David animal kept so tightly guarded from the world.

FINDING RUBLINA

Some mothers cannot suckle their infants because they simply cannot produce milk. Other mothers cannot suckle their babies because the rigors of career and travel place such extraordinary demands upon them that the logistics of the effort overwhelm them and create an unfair burden on the newborn. When a baby cries to suckle, it can't be told to wait a few hours until mommy's jet lands and she arrives home on the shuttle. A few women will not suckle their babies because they cannot stand the fact that the baby exists. They wish the kid had not been born. They hate the little bastard. Even apart from all these misgiving women was Eloweiss.

She was in a daze after birthing David. When the nurses asked if she was ready to hold her new baby, she said, "No." When Marvin asked if she'd like to have his bassinette wheeled into her hospital room so she could be with him, she said, "No." As far as she was concerned, she'd done her part and that was the end of it. She gave birth, which was demanded of her by her husband and her family. She'd consented to that. She'd copulated with Marvin, as miserable an experience as it was, until finally a doctor pronounced her pregnant. She promised no more.

Eloweiss saw little David as her adversary while he was still in her womb. He caused her to outgrow her wardrobe, morning sickness, to miss out on social engagements, to reduce her alcohol consumption, and to go to bed early. She was missing parties. She wasn't getting her fair share of caviar and foie gras. The only chances she had to pinch shrimp cocktails were when she was invited to a goy's party and no rabbi would see her eating a shellfish. Now she was being forced to live under a microscope while friends and relatives came to see her offspring. After David was born, Eloweiss's first priority was to find him a nanny, put him on artificial formula, and stay away from him as much as possible.

So it was. David grew up with an artificial mother and artificial nourishment for food and love. Marvin loved him all right, but Marvin loved the business and Susan more. David received short attentions from his father and less than nothing from his mother. Eloweiss made no bones about it when the topic of David arose between her and Marvin. She hated the kid. With every year that passed Eloweiss hated David more than the year before. He was a lazy, shifty, lying, thieving, devious homosexual and a worthless misfit, she declared to Marvin. Neither parent could understand their prodigy, nor why he behaved as he did.

After Marvin's death, when David had more of a say in his own business, he decided to psychologically compensate himself for the lack of his mother's love. He determined he should not be denied what other men had in any aspect of life, regardless of how late he would partake of its blessing. He placed a call to his good friend Eddie Wilkes, the firm's accountant.

"Eddie," David began, "I need your help finding a suitable personal assistant. I'm thinking her role will be, for corporate appearances and compensation purposes if you understand what I mean, Corporate Secretary to the UGGA. I don't want just any woman for this position. She doesn't have to be particularly intelligent. She doesn't have to be particularly beautiful either. Mainly, Eddie, she has to be very flexible, if you follow my meaning, and she has to have a certain appearance. The appearance aspect is extremely important for this particular role, if you follow what I'm saying."

"David, I'm always ready to help you, as I was your father. Tell me exactly what sort of appearance you're looking for." Eddie expected David to describe a hot-bodied type, ready to fuck for money. The answer from David took him aback.

"Well, you remember my mother, Eloweiss, don't you, Eddie?"

"Yes, of course, David."

"I can provide you with pictures of her when she was in her twenties and thirties if you like."

"David, that won't be necessary. Mrs. Wilkes and I were good friends with your father and mother. I have many pictures of the four of us together. Is the woman you're looking for supposed to resemble your mother?'

"Yes."

"May I be so bold as to ask why?"

"No, Eddie. That's none of your business. And about your pictures, Eddie. Do you have one of mother's sitting profiles, one with her big tits busting out of her blouse?"

"Well, no, nothing exactly like that."

"That's okay, Eddie. I'll have a copy of that picture made and I'll get it over to you."

"So what will I be looking for, David, a pair of tits or a face like your mother's?"

"Both, Eddie, as best you can find a match."

"Got it. But David, if it comes down to one with a closer face and one with a closer set of tits, which would you prefer?"

"I'll likely hire the girl with the biggest tits."

"And how about her religion? Must she be Jewess, or can she be a goy?"

"I don't give a shit about her religion."

With those instructions and a photograph copy of Eloweiss's profile which emphasized her mountainous tits,

Eddie went to work. He placed advertisements in the local newspapers for an executive secretary with vague descriptions of needed skills, such as:

"Must be comfortable in an executive setting, have flexible attitudes and work hours, and be willing to cooperate to accomplish demanding tasks. Relocation expenses will be paid."

He also contacted three personnel agencies and offered a thirty-percent commission based upon the successful woman's first years' salary if she was referred by their firm. There was no mention of typing or dictation skill requirements, no need for references, and no need for a work history. The employer was willing to pay 25% above the going rate for top-notch executive secretaries for the chosen applicant. Thus began a nationwide search for a perfectly matching set of tits.

Thousands of applications poured into Eddie Wilkes's office. He narrowed the field to three thousand by applying age discrimination methods. No woman over thirty-five and none under the age of twenty-nine passed the first hurdle. The second screen was marital status. Only single women and divorcees were allowed, and the field narrowed to twelve hundred applicants. Eddie set up a pre-screening whereby the final twelve hundred were personally interviewed by a junior man on his staff. Women traveled at their own expense from as far as a thousand miles away to get to the preliminary interview. Each was given some simple questions on a sheet of paper to fill out, questions like adding up a column of six numbers and answering who the president of the country was. It was a simple but necessary test to get a look at the applicants. Women the junior man assessed to have breasts smaller than size 38 EE were thanked for their interest and excused.

Eddie's junior man screened the prospects down to twenty women who had 'the right looks.' Eddie would choose the final three. Each of the twenty came to his office. He asked them to walk across the room and bring him a glass of water, then sit sideways in a chair. By their facial resemblance to Eloweiss in her prime, their body carriage, posture, and breast sizes, Eddie ranked the three most likely to meet David's approval and referred them to him for their final interview.

The first woman had an elderly mother afflicted with Parkinson's at home. While she declared that her mother's needs were amply cared for by caregivers, David suspected potential conflicts for his time requirements. He told her he'd get back to her.

The second woman sat across from David in his office and deliberately adjusted her skirt in a manner which plainly presented him with a beaver shot. Obviously, this woman was a player and an astute opportunist. David asked her a test question, mixed in with some routine ones about getting along in a team environment. "What would you do if you saw a male employee physically abusing one of the female staff members?"

"Like doing what?"

"Like raping her."

The woman's answer was reflexive. "Why, I'd tell you about it right away, sir."

"And if I weren't here, what would you do?"

"Well, I'd wait until you returned." David liked what he was hearing.

"But if I were away on hunting trips and not scheduled to be in touch with the office for another four weeks, then what would you do?"

"Well, sir, I think I'd go to the next person in charge and report him."

"You're the next person in charge. What will you do?"

The woman became flustered. After a moment, she asked, "Do I have the power to dismiss this man?"

"No."

After another moment, the woman said, "Well, I'd report this criminal act to the police."

Again, David thanked her for her time and thoughtful answers and told her he'd get back to her.

The third woman showed up in a disheveled state. Her blouse wasn't tucked in properly, her makeup was sloppily applied with lipstick smudged upon her cheek, she smacked bubble gum with her mouth open, and tendrils of her hair were adrift from their plastic retainers and dangling over her face. She had the annoying habit of brushing her hair away from her eyes. Even her brassier appeared to have been improperly arranged. It looked as if one breast were strangely positioned higher on her chest than the other. But the most egregious thing about this slovenly lassie was that she reeked of alcohol. Either she just came from an unusual happenstance where alcohol was flowing freely and she had no sense of self-restraint, or she was a drunkard. David's interest was piqued. She was the spitting image of his mother.

"And by what name are you called, miss?"

"Well, my formal name is Rublina, but people who get to know me call me Ruby."

Her words were slurred, and she had a goofy sort of smile that pronounced she didn't care about anything in the world. Her teeth were okay, not great. Dental work could make her mouth perfect. She was cogent somehow that this David fellow had some unfulfilled personal need and she was one of the finalists considered to fill it. She figured she needed the money, so she'd just play along with whatever this bizarre-looking duck of a man wanted. Her life was a moment-by-moment existence. David sized her up as a woman with no self-esteem, no morals, no sense of hygiene, and dead broke with no plans and no clue.

"Do you know why you're here?" David asked.

"You tell me, Daddy O," replied the interviewee, chewing her wad of bubble gum like a cow chewing cud.

This lush was bold enough to remind him he was old enough to be her father. She wasn't easily intimidated. "Well,

I'm looking for a personal assistant. Someone I can train to do some very personal work for me."

"Well, I can be as personal and as assisting as you want, Mr....?"

"David. Call me David, please."

"Well, David, as long as you're paying the big bucks, I'll be glad to do anything you want. You can fuck me every day if that's what turns you on."

"I said I wanted to train you. I didn't say I wanted to fuck you."

"Okay. Jesus Christ, don't get so sensitive. I'm imminently trainable, David. You train me to do it, whatever it is, and I'll do it. Okay?"

"Do you have any children or other dependents?"

"Yes, one. I have a son who lives in my apartment with me."

"How old is your son?"

"He's seventeen, David."

"Can you still manage him?"

"Oh, sure. He'll do whatever I tell him to do. He won't get in the way of any training you have planned for me."

Maybe it was this inebriated woman's intuition, or maybe she was just an easy squeeze for any man; regardless, she did the unexpected. She stood up, walked around behind David's desk, and wrapped her arms around his neck. She pulled his head up to her size 40 EE breasts and rubbed them against his face before kissing him smack on the lips. She was not the typical job applicant. "Pops, I could fall in love with you, if you let me. I'm ready for training," she declared.

David was taken aback by the woman's bold advance. He pulled his head away from her. "Kissing won't be necessary, Rublina. That's not part of the job description." As David said these words to her, he trembled slightly before her powers. She very much reminded him of Eloweiss. He was awed by Rublina's breasts.

She was hired two days later. She came to the office in dungarees and a halter top. All the staff members noted the oversized tits and there was some speculation Rublina had implants, but based upon comments from several women about the way they jiggled, it was concluded she hefted original equipment.

As a condition of employment, Rublina was required to sign a non-disclosure agreement with respect to any conversations or happenings or meetings of any kind which took place in David's office. She agreed that if she violated this non-disclosure she would immediately be liable and owing all sums paid to her from the date of employment. She was also required to purchase a home in the tiny suburb of Rondel Hills. The down payment was put up by David and Rublina signed a note to refund the down payment if she were terminated for any reason, for cause or otherwise. She was also required to sign a note to him for the mortgage amount owning on the house, and he made the monthly payments. This arrangement made her ask the first sensible question of her employment.

"David, honey babe, why are we signing all these papers?"

"For tax reasons," he replied.

Rublina was given a spacious corner office and an assistant who did all her work for her. Her days consisted of showing up for work when she pleased, usually drunk, polishing her nails, and reading fashion magazines. Her blissful routine was short-lived.

David called her into his office on the first day of her third week and informed her that her drinking was to stop. He also told her that she needed to take better care of her breasts because cancer was a heightened risk for women with large breasts. He gave her a list of required foods to eat and had delivered to her home three hundred pounds of raw oats. She was instructed to adhere to her new diet and eat massive helpings of oats for optimal breast health. After a month of her new diet, her breasts would be 'checked' to see if she complied with his requirement for healthier eating.

A month elapsed and Rublina was summoned to David's office. A private nurse was there dressed in street clothes. The nurse held a breast suction apparatus which attached to an electric pump. *This looks like something freaky is going on here. What are these two about to do to me?* Then she remembered the part about the job description, the training requirement, the notes she'd signed. This funny-looking little man owned her. *Well, how bad could it get? After all he doesn't want to fuck me.* She looked at David and smiled.

"Hi ya, honey babes. What would you like me to do here?"

"Rublina, I'd like you to meet Ms. Sinclair. She'll be your monitor for your health project. I'll leave while Ms. Sinclair conducts her first examination." With that introduction, David left his office.

Rublina sized up Ms. Sinclair. *She's a skinny athletic health nut type. Maybe I'm on a health program to make me look more like her. No way! Ms. Nursey has no tits and no ass.*

"Please sit on the sofa, Rublina." Ms. Sinclair was all formality and professionalism.

"Okay, hon, whatever you say." Rublina was obliging.

"Very good, now remove your blouse and bra please."

Rublina complied. "Is this a full exam, or are you just checking my tits?" she asked. *This place is fucking weird. I do absolutely nothing and get paid for it. Now this prim beanpole nurse is going to play with my tits? Bring it!*

Once Rublina was naked to the waist, Nurse Sinclair attached two suction cups to her nipples.

"Hey, tell me what's going on here. I've never had this kind of examination before." There was alarm in Rublina's voice as she began wondering just what she'd signed up for.

"These are suctions, dear. They won't hurt you. They'll just exert some sucking pulls on your nipples."

"Why in the hell do you want to have a machine sucking my nipples?"

"Oh, didn't you know, dear? They will stimulate your breasts as if an infant child is suckling you. I'm simply showing you how the machine works so you'll know how to use it. Mr. Sustack wants your breasts to be in perfect health, and the best way to ensure that is to have you suckled by the machine several times a day, just like an infant would suckle you. There's also an identical machine, all assembled, being delivered to your home this afternoon. You are to suckle the machine every four hours, day and night, until your breasts produce milk."

"Wait. This is crazy! Don't you know I'm not even pregnant? I haven't been pregnant for seventeen years!"

"So you were young when you had your last child. How old were you?"

"I was fifteen. His father left me and took off for California with some surfer chick. He was a worthless bastard, that one. But he sure was good-looking and he sure could fuck. We fucked all night long. The crazy thing is I still miss him."

"Yes, that does seem crazy, but it's your life. Obviously you live in the moment and don't think things through very well."

"What do you mean by that, huh?"

"Oh, nothing, forget it. I'm just here to show you how to use the equipment and to make sure it's in good working order."

"I thought David said this was my first examination. When's my second one, and what are you examining exactly?"

"Your milk production, dearie. Your next exam will be in a month, then every two weeks until I know you have good flow."

"What in the fuck? Why do I need good milk flow?" Rublina didn't relish the idea of becoming a breast-feeder to some machine.

"Didn't Mr. Sustack tell you, dearie? You're being conditioned to breast-feed him. Mr. Sustack needs your human breast milk."

"Jesus H. Christ! Motherfucking, and hell no! I am not going to let that old man drink milk out of my tits. This is fucking crazy!"

"Now, now, dearie, it's not as bad as you think. It actually feels good to be suckled, and you'll be doing a great human kindness and getting very well paid for it. At night, when Mr. Sustack can't be with you to suckle, you'll just have to put the machine on for a few minutes to quickly drain you. You'll actually start to enjoy it."

"You're nuts! This whole idea is nuts! I won't do it! Get away from me, you fucking pervert." Rublina was becoming hostile.

"Oh, dear, Mr. Sustack told me this might happen. He said I should remind you of the terms of your employment and your financial obligations to him. If you'd rather go back to your old insect-infested apartment, that can be quickly arranged. However, Mr. Sustack will garnish your future wages wherever you find employment until your debts to him are fully discharged. He figures with the loss on a quick sale of your house, you'll owe him about a hundred thousand or more and you'll be working for what amounts to minimum wages for the next ten years or longer. It's just a friendly reminder, dearie. Now, shall we act like sensible adults?"

"You fucking bitch. You're in on this with him, aren't you?"

"Well, I don't do private duty work for free, now do I? You don't expect to be paid to do nothing, do you? This is America and the free enterprise system, after all, dearie. Now be a good girl and settle yourself and let me put these cups on your nipples."

With her role in better focus, Rublina relented. The cups were placed in massage mode, which meant they gently pulled her nipples and alternatively pushed hard against them, all in the effort to stimulate milk production.

Rublina sat back on the sofa and let the machine do its work. "Jesus H. Christ! If anybody knew this guy ran a money management firm with real money in it, they wouldn't believe it. No fucking way! This whole place is full of weird shit and I've only been here three weeks."

"And always remember, dearie, you are contracted to silence. One word of anything that goes on here and you will be the sorriest girl in Plaintown."

"You know him, don't you?"

"Cousins, dearie, just cousins through marriages, but yes, we're cousins. Everything is in the family, even our little quirks and foibles. Just enjoy yourself. You'll be doing a human kindness. There's no shame in kindness. And by the way, dearie, these are for you." Ms. Sinclair handed Rublina a cardboard box sealed with packaging tape.

"What's this for?" Rublina had trepidations about any gifts from this nurse from the dark side.

"These are your supplies. They will last you one month, and then you'll get refills. The small cans contain nutritional supplements you must take daily. The capsules in the jar are to enhance your hormone production so you'll lactate more easily. The balm is for soothing your teats after they've been suckled, and the rubber-coated clamps are for your nipples. You are to wear the clamps in the evening and daily when you are not in the office. They ensure the nipples remain in a heightened state of stimulation so you'll lactate more freely."

"So I'm Mr. Sustack's human milk cow now, complete with my animal feed and instructions." Rublina held back her tears.

"Relax, dearie. Look at it this way. You only need to work for two twenty-minute periods five days a week and you'll be highly paid. Isn't that what you were looking for when you answered the advertisement?"

Rublina didn't respond. She was bewildered. She was agreeing to be a sex slave of a different sort than she ever imagined and she began an effort to rationalize her victimhood status. Obviously the outlet for some psychological disorder that held David in its grip, she tried to tell herself she was somehow helping another human being, but her rationalization couldn't overcome her innate fear for her future. She sat back and closed her eyes, her mind drifting. She tried to imagine the machine was her infant son of seventeen years ago, but there was a dark undercurrent to her apprehension. *What have I gotten myself into?*

EAGLES AND INSECTS

Sometimes certain stocks and certain markets are like fires. They start out with a spark that smolders in tinder; then emboldened fledgling flames lift up and lick dry kindling, which ignite with the vigor of fresh drafts of air. Kindling's heat forces the dormant logs to finally yield and burn with a sustained flame. Fires draw in more fuel, and stronger air gusts sucked into the fires fan their flames to before unimagined heights. Finally the finite fuel exhausts and the flames die into coals that glow, which in turn return to smoldering embers and die out into exhausted coldness and powdery ash that simply blows away, leaving nothing.

Initial investors may find success and their enthusiasm from the growth of some initial spot of money's growth licks their greed palate and kindles the urge to invest more. Once they invest more, they move the air some by talking about their investment to friends and family, or even their broker. As the initial group feels vindicated by price appreciation, the venture gains more participants, like crows to a feast. The fresh fuels of monies propel the value of the venture to heights previously unimagined, yet awed and rationalized. And finally the money fuel exhausts until the venture returns to earthly valuations, unless the inevitable unknowns or competitors arrive to reduce the venture's worth to nothingness, and all that is left are worthless stock certificates suitable for framing.

The mutual fund industry, itself a major investor in companies of all sorts, was in its initial transmogrification when

Bob first began marketing the UGGA Universal Global Growth Fund. At the time he made his first sales call, there were some two hundred competitors nationwide sponsoring some three hundred different funds. The industry morphed from a monthly investment repository for small-saver investor types to a repository for cannibalized monies from the upstart term life insurance industry's 'buy term, invest the difference' sales assault on whole life insurance policies. The original fund companies were pleasant gentlemen competitors sharing a growing but definable limited marketplace. But then the Fed took the financial markets into steadily rising valuations with extremely accommodative monetary policies.

Why Greenspan's Fed did what it did is not anything anyone will ever know, but attempts to reason Fed policies that would change the world as America knew it may be worth pondering, not for the captains of industry or the Chinese industrialist owners of slave labor shops which benefitted so greatly from the monetary largess, but by Americans who were screwed out of their jobs by it all. Perhaps the Fed received marching orders from the Bank for International Settlements. Perhaps the BIS felt pressure from industrialists to denude America's unionized workforce of its bargaining power by making credit so available for American consumers to buy ascendant China's newly favored nation status factories' outputs. Thereby, with the blessings of bribed Washington politicos who welcomed China into the World Trade Order with open arms, America's overpaid unionized labor force got screwed through the wall.

It was a fabulous time to be an investor. Company labor costs evaporated when payrolls of twenty-dollar-an-hour American labor were replaced with fifty-cent-per-hour Chinese labor. Sales were upbeat as America's consumption army gobbled up lower-priced Asian goods and telephone service centers sprang up in India. Stocks rose. Flames of greed fueled from investors' kindling reached the board rooms of the mutual fund industry. The board members, those staid wizened cigar smokers, rubbed the sleep from their eyes and ordered up fresh pots of coffee. Cobwebs were wiped off the planning boards. There was money to be made. It was time for change.

Somebody in some fund boardroom came up with a brilliant idea. The proffered reasoning went something like this: "If we only take in money with our one fund, when this Fed lunacy ends, people will just take their money back out of that fund and stick their money into a bank account. We have no idea when this will happen, so let's have a companion money market fund to go along with our regular fund and let the investors try to manage their money themselves by moving it into our money market fund. That way, we don't actually have to manage for big market changes by raising cash in the regular fund and trying to redeploy it, but we do keep a management fee coming in from that investor no matter whether the investor thinks the market is going to go up or down! Hell, the cross flows between the funds will probably largely net out anyway because some of the people will always think the market is going up and some will always think it's going down!"

That man—it was still an old boys' industry then, so that genius had to be a man—received a cigar, a champagne toast from his fellow board members, and many pats on the back. The industry no longer had to attempt to manage money like the old days, no longer had to worry about earning their fees. All it had to do was package investment fund products under any sort of cockamamie marketing scheme and have the sales force pitch the theme de jure to a receptive public that was beginning to bring their monetary fuel to a growing fund industry. The industry grew its fund product offerings into small capitalization, large capitalization, old people funds, young people funds, funds for dummies, for geniuses, for warmongers, for bunny huggers, for communists who wanted to be capitalists, for capitalists who pretended to be communists. All in all, some nine thousand funds proliferated since that genius birthed that first thought in that fund boardroom, but the industry still only had its original two hundred sponsoring companies, give or take a dozen or so. Oligopolies are like that, a small number of players all doing essentially the same thing at essentially the same price. The regulators were lobbied and bribed to keep the competition stymied and the public blindfolded, and the profits were carved up amongst the 'in' crowd.

The product-selling game changed along with the industry's structure. No longer did it matter as much how well money was managed within a particular portfolio for the overall well-being of the fund complex. What mattered was how well the sponsoring underwriters could package and sell particular funds at particular times in particular markets. Deceptive sales practices were walked past the Securities and Exchange Commission, which is heavily influenced by the Investment Company Institute, the industry's lobbying arm. Nonsensical adds like, "Some large percentage number of our funds beat some benchmark average," were allowed to be aired without disclosing that, as a percentage of total assets in the fund group, the beat number was a meaningless comparison. But for the great unwashed, the ads worked and the money poured in. The public believed there were brains there, when the group put out a dozen different funds with different strategies, closed and killed the doggy performers and merged their assets into one of their other funds. Other practices allowed were to show off a red-hot record for a start-up fund and then bullshit investors without making honest disclosures. Sales literature claimed only the owners of the fund sponsoring company had invested there until now, and it had a million-dollar investment requirement. Plus, until now it was only available if you were a New Jersey resident. But now, you schmucks could own it too because it's now magically available in all fifty states and the minimum investment has been dropped to—gasp—only a hundred dollars. What is never disclosed to the schmucks is that this same fund sponsor had similarly incubated ten other funds, but those others all had dog-shit records. The duds were killed and were never marketed because they would show how stupid the fund managers really were.

It's one thing to offer a competing product concept in an open marketplace, but when distribution channels get kickbacks to block competing ideas from being presented to the end customer, the effect upon a company which depends upon sales for its lifeblood is no different than an automobile engine that depends upon the electrical current from the alternator reaching down the wire harness to the end-point spark plugs when the wire harness is removed. The spark can't reach the combustible cylinder because the wires to its end point are blocked off. The engine ceases to run.

The man in the competitor boardroom who had the brilliant idea to proliferate funds reaped marketing success. The ability of salesmen to control clients' monies by moving their assets from fund to fund within a family of funds had tremendous appeal to broker-dealer distributors of funds, especially since these fund families gave continuous sales commissions to the dealers and their sales reps for keeping the clients' assets captive in a given fund family. It was a concept called the 12B-1 fee, poorly understood and opaque to clients but paid to distributing firms based upon assets the dealer kept with the fund group. Aggregated over many sales representatives and clients it was big money, and when a firm's sales representative quit the firm, the funds' residual commissions still flowed to the distributing dealer.

The competitors moved up their game. With market share momentum behind them and legions of wholesalers distributing fund products, they made a bold move that affected the distribution channels for mutual funds. They ripped out the wire harnesses single funds needed to get their message to spark in the minds of retail sales representatives. The age of financial planning was born!

"There are changes happening in the mutual fund market-place," Bob beseeched David. "More outfits are offering this family of funds concept with switch privileges to money market funds. Investors can switch between all sorts of funds depending upon how they feel about the markets. They are introducing bond funds, junk bond funds, country funds, specialty funds, hot area funds, topical funds. You name it and they're marketing it."

"Yeah, so what?" David seemed distant. "Why are you bringing this up?"

"I'm bringing this up because we're up against it. There's already a battle for shelf space in the big brokerage firms and in the regional firms. To get shelf space, the big fund groups are pouring tons of commissions onto these dealers' trading desks and we're getting moved down shelf and off shelf. Big dealers are also bringing out proprietary product funds. Between the reciprocal kickback commissions for sales headwinds and house products, we're getting marginalized with our fully managed fund concept. And that's not all. Recently I've been to branches where the branch manager will not even allow me into the office to talk to the sales reps. I've been told in a couple of places that the firm doesn't want me mixing up their reps' heads. They've got them trained to sell a certain way, the family of funds way, and they don't want the client to have a choice because they want to keep those residual 12B-1 commissions. They've been told by their top management that our sale will make their brokers think too much. They're afraid they'll lose sales if their brokers start to think, so we're now banned from the shelf in some places."

"Well, the big firms never sold much anyway. They've always programmed their reps to sell proprietary garbage, so what's new here?" David seemed nonplussed by Bob's anxiety over the distribution landscape. His time on earth was growing shorter and his thoughts had turned more toward retirement.

"The point is even insurance firms are buying this concept. They're becoming financial planning firms using multiple fund products. They're building their sales pitches around it. The public is getting accustomed to hearing this sales genre and its becoming mainstream financial lexicon. If we don't make changes in the corporate business model, we risk getting marginalized." Bob's anxiety was palpable.

David erupted in an uncharacteristic display of anger, like a latent volcano that unexpectedly blew the top off its mountain. "I don't give one flying fuck what these financial planning firms are doing," he began, like a roar from an angry lion. If a financial planner had been present, David would have punched him in the nose. His teeth clenched as he snarled. "These financial planners are the insects of the investment world. None of them know jack shit about how to analyze a company or understand their asses about the markets. They're just retreaded insurance salesmen, ass-kissers and dog walkers.

"Their fucked-up business models are based upon the false assumptions that the Fed will always be there to inflate markets for them so their phony financial plans will never be found out and there will never be another serious downturn, never again another depression. They're a lot like retail real estate brokers. They show Mr. and Mrs. Dumb Shit some beautiful retirement brochures with pretty photographs of idiots sitting on a beach hugging each other. It's all a lot of infantile idiotic, pie-in-the-sky, wet dreams horse shit! All these fucking financial planning maggots will ever succeed in doing is destroying the entire capital base of a once great nation."

"I'm just telling you we're getting our ass kicked in the marketplace for sales. I'm telling you it's something you need to seriously consider."

"Just one minute." David wasn't finished erupting. "I want you to think this one through." He pounded his fist onto his desk and held it there, pinning down the desk by his force of will. "What happens to a money manager in one of these la-di-da fund groups, huh? What happens to this growth fund manager? He's supposed to get growth, right? Let's say there's a market break, a flash crash, some hedge fund or bank or government throws up someplace. Let's say an odd Black Swan event happens. A big bank fails somewhere in the derivative laden world. You get a big sigma event, three to ten standard deviations from the norms. The multi-sigma events repeat themselves. This isn't supposed to happen! But it's going to happen. Not once every five hundred million years like the programmers' guaranteed, but once every five seconds. Every five fucking seconds! There's a financial earthquake. A tsunami crash crushes stock and bond prices. The hungry bear escapes his cage. People panic. They always panic because the idiots never knew what they owned in the first place. Their fund manager stayed on the momentum wave all the way up to the top of the market before it crashed, because if his performance numbers fell behind some goofy stock market index he'd get fired by the marketing guys who run the casino.

"Investors demand to switch to the money market fund. Suddenly the genius portfolio manager with the red-hot track record, the one the financial planner touted to sell his plan, his pie-in-the-sky 'dream plan,' suddenly—and I mean real suddenly, man—gets a phone call. Is this the call from his hot trophy wife asking him if he'd like pork chops for dinner? Hell fucking no!" David screamed and pounded his fist again and again on his desk.

"It's the phone call every one of these prima donnas dreads. Suddenly he realizes he's no genius at all, just a poster boy for financial plan sales, because the wave he rode was the one that worked at the time. He's a momentum junkie, and the momentum stopped taking him up! He's like the guy at the craps table trying not to roll snake eyes, but the marketing guys make him keep rolling! 'The phone call is from the fund services desk,' his secretary tells him.

"'Oh my God,' he screams. He browns his pants! It's craps! Game is over! Fund services got their calls from their dealers' margin clerks. The cashiers want their cash, baby. They want cash and they want it now! It's good-bye pretty beach pictures for all the gullible schmucks! Now they're just trying to save their asses so they can afford bologna sandwiches.

"Hell, they always knew in their heart of hearts, in those tiny corners of their tiny minds, that the whole sale, the whole financial plan, was all bullshit anyway, but hey! It made the wife happy and it gave the poor bastard a few years peace! He never believed in the investment. It never made sense. There was no one responsible for management of the investment, but he went along with it because it stroked his wife's security button and she stopped nagging him. The whole sale was just insurance run in reverse for the benefit of the insurance salesmen, so those insects could sell something. Instead of backing up the hearse to the kitchen table and telling the wife her poor bastard is going to die, so let's make him get insurance to cover your ugly ass. instead they tell her the poor bastard is going to live, so let's take some of his money and put it in a plan for you. It all assumes there's no such thing as a market, or the need to understand risks. It's an implied guarantee of eight percent per year, just like insurance is guaranteed to pay at death, but it's complete bullshit!

"So now we have the prima donna getting his cash call. What can he do? The time for showing pretty marketing pictures is *over!*" David was shouting even louder.

"It's time to sell something. What to do? *What?* He's got to sell right now, not ten minutes from now. The markets are falling and they are falling fast, baby. We're going downhill on a toboggan ride, but this ride doesn't stop on a nice level valley floor. No, baby. *Oh no!* This toboggan ride goes right off the cliff and everybody's money dies! Investors' dreams die because their money dies! Whee! It was fun while it lasted, but now we can't get off! But we gotta get off! Momma wants her cash, and she wants it *right now!*

"What can the prima donna do? He can only do what he must do. He can only sell those stocks that are liquid enough to have any market at all. Nothing else is trading. The dealers are ducking bids. Some firms put up order gates. The high frequency traders and the house account trades beat Momma to the exit doors. Momma can't get her money out of the corral!

"Momma's fucked, big time! But she isn't on the beach getting fucked. Oh no! She's getting fucked while making bologna sandwiches. The cash calls keep coming. Momma wants her ass saved now! Get the lady her cash! 'Oh my God!' she screams to her husband. 'Get our money back!' He calls his planner. The planner's secretary puts him on hold. There're other calls ahead of his. 'What's wrong with that fucking asshole?' screams Momma's husband. 'The market's going down!' She's screaming in one ear and he's hearing telephone elevator music in the other.

"Poppa wishes he could be off at a bar someplace, or at a hunting lodge, but he can't get away from his wife or the fucking phone with its fucking elevator music. He's trapped. Their money is trapped. Prima donna gets more calls. He sells his most liquid stocks and gets half what they were selling for yesterday. Other prima donnas are getting their cash calls too.

Now what? The market is going down more. Dealers will not bid for anything, so the prima donna goes off board to Instinet or Third market. He's got to take three cents on the dollar for stocks that were a beach house dream yesterday! The beach house just got sold for three cents! Three fucking cents!

"'What about the bank?' screams Momma Ruth. 'We still have our money in the bank, right?'

"'I don't know!' yells Poppa Bill. 'On TV, they're showing lines of people outside of the banks.'

"'That's just someplace in Europe, isn't it?' screams Ruth.

"'No. It's here!' yells Bill. 'There's Mrs. Keegan standing in line. She's waving her fist in the air and screaming something.'

"'What's she saying?'

"'I don't know. It sounds like, "fucking bastards this" or "dirty cocksuckers," some things like that.'

"'Are you sure it's her. That's not like her. Are you sure? How do you *know* it's *her*?' Bill and Ruth start shouting from their distress. Calm rational thought is long gone.

"'It's her, I tell you!' insists Bill. 'I'm sure of it. I'd recognize her anywhere. I used to fuck her!'

"'*What!* Ruth reaches for something to throw at her bone-headed husband. It could be a shoe or a lamp; it doesn't matter at this point. Ruth gets a momentary grip and holds off throwing her shoe. Money matters concern her right now. She'll deal with her husband later.

"'But what about our financial plan,' Ruth screams. 'Didn't that nice man tell us there was this plan we were in? Didn't he tell us he would rebalance our assets, our funds, whatever, so we couldn't get hurt in a downturn? I know I heard him say that. They were advertising that on the TV! All we had to do was follow what he said and we'd have the house on the beach! We'd have money for the grandkids, remember? We'd be secure! We *are* going to be secure, aren't we?' The look of panic spreads across Ruth's face. 'Bill, remember he showed us a copy of that speech Alan Greenspan made where he said America would invent everything in technology, the economy would grow and grow, and the rest of the world would do all the work? We're safe, aren't we, Bill? Bill. Answer me! We're safe, aren't we? Bill, tell me we're going to be safe! The rest of the world was supposed to do all the work and all we had to do was invest in this stuff and sit on the beach and drink mai tais. He told us we'd make eight percent per year and we had these nice colored pictures on a pie chart and we had that picture of the cottage on the beach and—'

"'Shut the fuck up, Ruth. We were nuts to listen to that huckster. How in the hell is he going to get us eight percent per year when interest at the banks is zero? Huh? I knew it was all bullshit when I heard it. The Chinese People's Liberation Army hacked into all our tech companies and stole all their source codes. Everything our companies can do the Chinese can do cheaper, plus they fucked our companies with their spyware and viruses. All that shit he sold us was a pipe dream. All this shit we own is worth less than dirt. I knew that cute fart didn't know shit from cannolis, but you were all gaga over the fucking plan, and I suspended common sense and—'

"'But he said we needed to follow the plan. He said he'd adjust the plan....'

"Bill doesn't answer, just looks at Ruth like she's stupid as a stump. He walks to the hall closet.

"'Where are you going, Bill?' Ruth takes a deep breath. She's alarmed.

"'I'm going out!'

"'What are you doing, Bill? You have your shotgun! Where are you going with your shotgun?'

"'I'm going to see that silver-tongued cocksucker who sold us this shit!' he yells, holding up some glossy brochures. 'That dickhead sold us a box full of dog shit and convinced us it was candy bars. I'm done, Ruth."

"'Bill, stop! *Stop!* What are you going to do with your shotgun?' His wife is sobbing hysterically.

"'Ruth, you stay out of this! We are not going to follow some idiotic plan like a robot running off a cliff with a herd of other robot lemmings! We're done with soaking up the bullshit!' Bill opens the closet, looking for his coat.

"'Bill, you answer me! Why the shotgun?' Ruth screams.

"'Because the rules ain't fair, Ruth. The rules are just there so big guys can screw us little guys.'

"'Oh my God, don't do something foolish. Bill, don't! You're all I have, Bill. Come back here. Don't!'

"'Never mind, Ruth. It's time to handle things my way!' Bill shouts as he puts his coat on and leaves through the garage door.

"'Don't go, Bill! You'll get into trouble. Don't go,' Ruth pleads, but it's too late. Bill no longer gives a shit about getting into trouble.

"He tears out of the driveway in the family sedan and Ruth sits on the floor and cries to herself. 'Oh my God! What's going to happen to us? Oh my God. No, dear God, no. Please tell me this isn't happening. Somebody tell me this is just a bad dream. I want to wake up now.' Ruth's cries turn to whimpers. She pulls her hair out, and then she holds her face in her hands. It is happening, and she knows it.

"This is what happens when it's all over, when cats start sleeping with dogs, when dreams and fantasies die, when families fly apart and men must eat their pasta off the grass on the front lawn. This is when women throw frying pans at their men and men kick their dogs and throw their beer cans at the TV. This is when grown men have to stop watching the NFL and go around begging for odd jobs to get money to eat. This is when America has to dine at the banquet of bad consequences, when we of the later generations get to eat the shit stick meal, when we suffer the consequences of the folly of Wilson putting a privately owned Federal Reserve Bank in private control of our economy and an Internal Revenue Service to feed the monster blob.

"This is the beginning of a depression. This is what it's like when nobody has any money. The banks close their doors, the ATM machines say they are out of order, the grocery stores have no food, and the credit card doesn't swipe at the gas pump. This is when Bill can't get beer, dog food, or gas. This is when people stop trusting fiat dollars and their elected government. This is when all the worthless retired teachers who dummied down innocent kids for a living and those useless union goons lose their pensions, which they never should have had in the first place except they voted like a block for the progressives who promised them a cushy ride and a free lunch for their votes. This is when people buy gold and silver if they can get still it. This is when morality creeps back into society and people learn to love one another and be good friends and neighbors again. This is when money leaves and religion returns. It's 'come to Jesus' time!

"That's just the beginning of the 'Hell for Dummies' times. Bill and Ruth have a beautiful, intelligent, well-educated daughter with a nice high-paying office or professional job. She's a nurse or project manager or corporate secretary, and she's engaged to another professional, a nice young lawyer or stockbroker or marketing brand manager. Suddenly the dollars they earn aren't enough to buy groceries. The dollar was mathematically worthless for years before, but it took a market break for dummy Americans to lose their confidence in it. The young hopefuls leave their jobs to get work in the mine fields digging for gold to sell on the black market. Their hands grow calluses, they get ruptured back discs, but they must dig dirt to buy groceries.

"It doesn't get better for them. The pits where they crack rock have mosquitoes. Mercury fumes from cyanide reduction stoves eat into their nervous systems. He shakes, then contracts malaria and can't work. She becomes a camp whore to make money, hoping to keep their dreams alive. Things get worse, never better. He succumbs. As death draws near, she asks him, 'What happened to us?' He tells her, 'We believed the socialist lies. We voted for the liar who the complicit media failed to vet, who the irresponsible political party that nominated the bastard demigod refused to vet. We voted for the Trojan Horse because we thought the country had such riches we could take a chance on being nice, good-hearted, stupid people, and we voted for our own destruction.'

"She buries him and it gets worse. She contracts syphilis. She loses her looks, teeth, hair, nervous system, and womb. She lives a miserable painful life and dies a painful death. Hope and change turn into hell and death. The Grim Reaper collects his final payment from the believers in stupidity. Bill, Ruth, and their daughter pay a horrible price for voting for the delusional ideological dreams of a deceitful liar's father. But hey, they just went along with the crowd! They're not responsible for their decisions! Who thinks about the importance of being smart with your vote, anyway? They were only drinking the same kumbaya Kool-Aid everyone else was drinking. The crowd can't be flat-ass dead wrong, can it?

"Well, I've got news for all the Bills and Ruths and their daughters and prospective sons-in-law. Not only will all this happen, but it will happen quickly. America doesn't have the luxury of being stupid any longer. The country must get back to honest money and get there quickly. Real wealth, gold and silver, must come out of the ground. That's the only wealth the Chinese can't steal or hack. But now there's a problem called the uphill battle. The elites, the one-percenters, stole the American citizens' gold from Fort Knox and the New York Fed. It was leased out to them for worthless paper dollars and it's gone. If it wasn't gone, they'd let independent auditors audit it. The one-percenters made the administrative rules that made the leases legal. The ninety-nines weren't allowed to vote on it. The one-percenters took the gold offshore, so good luck catching them and recovering it. You got swindled! You let rats into your granary! That's not entirely your fault. Your elected Congress was too complacent to demand an audit of the Fed and the gold. Your great-great-grandparents and every generation since them drank the socialist dream and voted for easy times in their own times too. They never dreamed their progeny would end up in this mess. Maybe they didn't think about it or even care if they did. Who knows? They're dead.

"The insects don't comprehend what's about to happen. The insects' clients don't believe it will ever happen to them. They just want to watch *Dancing with the Stars* and the NFL. They refuse to think. It's easier to dream! When their toboggan goes off that cliff of a phony propped-up market, they'll just want to sue. Problem with that is so will everybody else and there won't be anything left for anyone to get. When a debt bubble collapses, money gets vaporized. Even maggot asshole-eating lawyers will be washing cars and dogs for a living! All this hell will happen because the American dream goes off the cliff in the markets. And whatever happens in the stock market, the bond market will be just as bad, except for the yield hogs in the high-yield products. Those hogs will get skinned and gutted. There won't be anything left. The bear will eat them.

"Mark my words. The day is coming when the whole financial planning concept will get exposed by Mr. Market! Mr. Market knows bullshit when he smells it. He invites everybody onto the meadow with his fancy brochures and coaxes all the dummies to play and dream. Mr. Market sniffs the air and smells the time is right. Everybody is fully invested in his market of stocks, bonds, and real estate. Everybody is dreaming on the meadow. Then Mr. Market opens the door to a huge cage. It holds a surprise for all the dreamers playing on the meadow. The cage door opens, Mr. Bear comes out, and he's hungry.

"Mr. Market lets Mr. Bear out of his cage, and Mr. Bear goes into the meadow and eats all the dummies. Mr. Bear guts them and eats them while they're still living. It's painful when Mr. Bear shows up. He doesn't give a shit about the house on the beach, doesn't care about the glossy brochures, doesn't care if the wife screams. Mr. Bear just wants to eat. He's a voracious eater and he eats fast. He doesn't stop eating until he eats everybody's dreams. People lose everything they ever had to Mr. Bear. *Everything!* Grown men cry. Women scream. Then everybody gets mad. They've got to blame somebody! When the crowds come with their pitchforks, tar, and feathers, they don't stop with the one-percent elites who set the stage for this unholy mess. They come for the insects too. People get pissed off when they lose everything. They'll feed the insects to their dogs. You'll see."

"Your point is well taken, but the planners will say that an exchange in their fund to a money market fund is no different than the redemption of shares in a single fund."

"There's a huge difference. It has to do with how the fund is sold in the first place. If the customer is told that the manager will manage long term and the customer should just go to sleep for twenty or thirty years, most of them will just do that. The fund won't get cannibalized to raise cash to send to the money market fund. Investors who sell some fund in a family of funds in a panic were sold on the idea that the customer and the insects would move the money around. The insect sold Mr. and Mrs. Bambi in the headlights the notion that there was this wide array of pigeonholes each with a fund in it. Maybe even several arrays of multiple families of funds were shown to them. The insect whips out his computer, sticks in some numbers, and voilà! They have a plan!

"The computer says you've got to make eight percent a year! Well, here's a fund that made eight percent a year. Let's buy it and our problem is solved! Wasn't that easy? We didn't even have to think! Thanks for the commissions.

"Some time goes by and the eight percent isn't there. Maybe it's six percent or maybe it's a loss, or maybe it's ten percent. But we need to track eight percent. If the Bambis are running shy of eight, the insect finds a fund that did ten, and thanks for the commission. If they are doing ten, the insect says rebalance to something that did six to even things out, and thanks for the commission.

"Now the insect has burrowed into their skin. He gets a percent for seeing who's above eight and who's below eight. He's always getting a commission. He's performing a valuable service, he tells the Bambis, and they agree. What the Bambis never understand through the entire experience is that nobody is actually managing their money. Their money is just like rounded-up cattle in a corral, the corral being the Standard and Poor's top five hundred companies by market value of their stocks. The Bambis think they are in some big cap funds, some mid-cap funds, some this and that funds, but they are all just in the corral with all the other Bambis. But it's all a marketing con job. All the insects have all the Bambis trapped in the Bambi corral. All the Bambis own the same stocks, just packaged in different ways.

"The problem comes when Mr. Market lets Mr. Bear into the corral. That's called a bloodbath followed by a stampede. The herd panics and their money and their dreams get trampled. This is not money management. This is national insanity. The money market fund that Bambi was supposed to be able to switch his stock and bond funds into and get money to live off has closed its gates. He can't get money from it to live. It's kind of like Yom Kippur. If you don't repent before the rabbi puts the Torah away and closes the gates of the Holy of Holies on you, you're totally screwed. Markets freeze up. Bambi can't get out of the funds he's in and the insect won't return phone calls. His mutual funds will only give him fractional shares, for which he can't find a decent dealer bid, and the commission costs eat him alive anyway when the market finally opens. He gets pennies on the dollar for his fractional shares of stocks that were once his dream beach house."

"So I gather from your comments that we are not changing." Bob had the look of a man who knew he was destined to market poor performance, a losing hand of cards.

"That's right. We are not changing." David was matter-of-fact. Bob's lesson time was over. "Look, you are a great salesman, one of the greatest ever. The tide will turn for you some day. It always does. Forget the insects that control people with their shell game. Just find those reps and clients who want honest, good old-fashioned money management. That's enough. Just go out there and do it and don't look back. You keep building on the sales side as best you can, and I'll keep building here in the office, here at home. We're a great team."

David called Bob late one night, following that exchange. "I have a terrific idea that will definitely boost your sales. I want to prove something to you. Come over in the morning and bring with you, in your car, all of your suits that have any brown or tan in them. Also, bring all your brown socks, brown belts, brown ties, and brown shoes."

"Why? What's the idea?"

"You'll see. Just bring everything brown that you have."

The next day, Bob arrived with his car filled with all things brown. David helped Bob take all his brown clothes, shoes, belts, and ties to the far northwest corner of the barnyard. After they placed everything on the ground, David poured gasoline on the pile and set it ablaze.

"What are you doing? Those are perfectly good suits. A lot of those suits were nearly new." Bob was flabbergasted.

"I'm making a complete Jew out of you so you'll get more sales," shouted David above the roaring flames.

"How does this make me a complete Jew? You're burning half my wardrobe. You're just wasting money." Bob was appalled at the waste of perfectly good clothing and David's audacity, but he said nothing more.

"Come here away from the flames and I'll explain it to you." David motioned to Bob to move away from the bonfire and come to the opposite corner of the barnyard. As they watched the flames, David turned to his protégé to dispense his wisdom.

"You need to understand the way a Jew thinks. You see, Bob, the color brown makes a Jew remember the Holocaust because of Hitler and his Brown Shirt thugs. So when a Jew sees brown, he wants to get away from that color, and he resents the person wearing it."

"But the Holocaust was over sixty years ago. People alive today didn't live through that, except for a few survivors. Besides, I didn't have anything to do with it, so why would a Jew hold wearing brown against me?"

"It's not personal to you, but it *is* personal to them. It's the memory that clings, and it will cling for generations. The Jew sees you wearing brown and he thinks your grandfather or some relative of yours may have killed his grandfather or some relative of his. That's unacceptable to him and he can't forgive you."

"But I didn't do anything, and brown looks good on me. It matches my hair and skin color."

"Exactly, that's the problem. You already have a disadvantage with your hair and skin color. Maybe you should dye your hair black. And you should wear all blue suits."

"But you told me before that my appearance was going to help me get sales just like it is. You said my blond hair and ruddy skin was eye candy for female Jew stockbrokers."

"Yeah, I did say that, but that doesn't matter because the Jew girl brokers can't sell jack shit compared to the Jew male brokers. Women just think with their pussies anyway. Forget the women and concentrate on the men. You'll get more sales. There are some other things you need to change as well. Get rid of that German car you have and get a Cadillac."

"What's wrong with car model I drive?"

"It's made in Germany. The same company that manufactured your car used Jews as slave labor during World War Two. They made the German army's trucks and the slaves were used to build the concentration camps. No respectable Jew drives a German-made car."

"But my sales come from out of town. I drive American Japanese rental cars when I'm out of town."

"Doesn't matter. Some salesmen come here to be entertained. They'll see you have that German car and they'll tell other salesmen you're not Jewish enough. Word gets around."

"Aren't you getting paranoid here? No one who works in a German car factory today had anything to do with World War Two."

"Oh yes, they did! They had parents and grandparents who worked for that car company. It's in the car's culture. Cars have ancestry, just like people."

"Cars don't have culture, just motors and wheels. You're in a private war with ghosts of the past. It's time to live and let live."

"Don't argue with me. Get rid of that fucking German car. Now wait a minute. I have to do something before we leave here." David opened his fly and walked close to the smoldering remnants of the fire. Then he urinated upon the embers, sending up a column of wretched smoke stench.

"Did you have to do that?" Bob was appalled.

"Yeah, I had to do that. I had to give those fucking Germans some payback for the Holocaust. And you needed to have it impressed upon your doubting mind that some of us have deeply rooted hatred for what happened in Nazi Germany. You need to know that there are those among us who will never forget it."

"And does that mean you'll never forgive it either? Have you ever considered that maybe the entire tribe is suffering from some kind of collective Post Traumatic Stress Disorder from the temple sackings in Jerusalem, the Russian pogroms, and the Holocaust? It seems like a never-ending cycle. Can't you break out of it?" Bob was uneasy with the depth of David's revenge feelings.

"No, I don't want to break out of it. I can forgive those who had no part in it, those who came after the criminals, but it is hard for me to be forgiving when I smell the air and it tastes of anti-Semitism. I'll never break out of it. How can I when I know there are people who want to kill me?" David looked at Bob as if he were peering into his soul. *I'll wait to see Bob's reaction to my comments about the Holocaust. What will he say or do? My experience with many gentiles, or even Reformed Jews, is that they'll tell me I'm being overly sensitive, or they'll tell me that the Holocaust was a long time ago and I need to forget it and move on. That means they feel like I'm just manipulating them and they really don't give a shit about Jews getting murdered. I'll see if I elicited sympathy from Bob or if he reacts as if he thinks I'm just manipulating him.*

"I am terribly sorry, David. I didn't understand how deep these feelings were and how they'll continue into perpetuity. I will always be respectful and try to do better."

Later that day, Bob got rid of his German car and bought a Cadillac. David was pleased. He gave Bob a passing grade on his latest test.

Bob again went forth to slay the dragon of poor performance, wearing only blue suits, black shoes, and non-brown ties, but he refused to dye his hair black. He no longer wasted time trying to catch insect sales representatives; he cultivated only the salesman at the top of the food chain, the eagles of the business. Fund sales drew even with redemptions and, like a stabilized submarine, the company avoided sinking below its crush depth. That's when the asset base declines, fixed administrative costs engulf generated returns, and the ratio of expenses to assets skyrocketed.

Once again David succeeded in wringing out all the effort possible from his leading sales marketer. Just as he encouraged Marty to be a highly accomplished whore, he encouraged Bob to be the most effective salesman possible. David congratulated himself on his ability as a manager to extract the fullest measure of talent from key executives. While he molded the home office to his image, Bob resumed flying across the country and pounding the pavement.

There was renewed confidence in Bob's effort. He discovered something within himself that was not there before he became a Jew: he had greater self-confidence and deeper insights into human nature. He studied Torah with the interpretations of Rabbis Plaut and Rashi. He attended services in his reformed temple. He discovered a beautiful, enchanting, soulful religion with endless nuances and a religious people immersed in unique oneness with God. The services were joyous, adoring, and baleful with emotional mysterious outpourings. In time, what began as an academic challenge became uplifting discovery, awakening within him a sense of privilege, wonder, and peace of soul. His confidence was restored.

Bob improved to sales superman. He cast away pedestrian tactics of befriending, patronizing, and playing mind games to overcome objections. He changed his approach to direct and forceful, demanding sales and leading his sales network like a courageous general leading troops into battle. His credo became 'Competence, Confidence, Courage, and Conviction triumph over Fear, Ignorance, and Superstition.' He demanded results. Salesmen received inspiration and marching orders, quotas, challenges to top their prior heights. Bob went to firms demanding time with their sales forces. He was respected, believed, and a one-man force to be reckoned with.

Sales poured in. Growth resumed. The loyal network flowed money, despite lackluster investment results. Sales from Jew salesmen leaped from five percent to fifty-five percent. The focus on eagles paid off.

David complimented the improved sales during a lunch meeting. When Bob attributed the improvement to his heightened self-assurance, David seized upon the opening. "I'm glad you attribute your improved results to what you learned about yourself when you became a Jew. I'd like to suggest you could realize even further improvement if you went to an Orthodox rabbi and trained to join an Orthodox congregation. It would likely require another year or two of study, but now that you've passed the first hurdle of becoming a Reformed Jew, the next hurdle should be a lot easier for you."

"But I already get sales from Orthodox Jews and Conservative Jews. I like the people in my congregation. I don't see why I need to do this."

"Try to see it this way. Some Orthodox Jews don't see Reformed Jews as genuine Jews, so they won't accept you as an honest-with-God Jew. You'll never get business from them. Dad got a lot of business from them for the individually managed advisory business. Dad belonged to Reformed, Conservative, and Orthodox congregations. He joined them all."

"Well, that was great for him, but I can't help but wonder if he really knew where his heart was. He also had a gentile shiksa," Bob said, referring to Susan.

"Let's just say that Marvin was a widely loved man of the whole community who had ecumenical leanings."

"Maybe in the future, David, but I'm all over the country right now. With performance down, I need to hustle to keep us growing. I have a lot of balls in the air." Bob needed to lighten the subject. "By the way, do you know how to tell if a Jew is Reformed or Orthodox?'

"No. How?"

"Well, you go to the King David Hotel in Jerusalem on Shabbat Saturday. You stand in the elevator. Another Jew gets in the elevator with you and pushes the button to go to his floor. He's a Reformed. He did unnecessary work on Shabbat. More get in. They ask the Reformed to push a button for their floor for them. They won't do any work on Shabbat. They are Orthodox. Now what do the Orthodox do when they want to leave their floor to go down to the lobby? Do they push the down button, or do they wait for a Reformed to happen along and push it for them, thereby risking that they will miss services? And what do they do if there are no Reformed Jews on their floor, or none going down to the lobby for the next three hours? Do they break a mitzvah so they won't miss services, thus breaking another mitzvah, a Ten Commandments mitzvah to honor the Sabbath?"

"I don't know. What's the point?"

"The point is, and this I learned from a Reformed rabbi I respect, that there are differences without distinction and there are differences that exist for the sole purpose of having a distinction."

"Okay," David relented with a chuckle. "If you think you're Jew enough, then that's all that matters. I suppose we'll just leave it at that. After all, you're a Jew to all but a few." With a distant stare, he put the bottom of his necktie in his mouth, held it in his teeth, and looked through Bob to some place far away.

COFFEE

It was time. Barbara stoically endured a year of disgust and heartache knowing the office slut was on the road with the man she wanted for herself. She told herself Marty was only eye candy for salesmen with hot pricks and no brains. She endured a greater heartache and humiliation knowing that Bob still pined over Marty, as if he'd go back to the whore like a welcoming puppy after she'd tramped off with another man. Bob's heartsick behavior told Barbara he liked Marty's bed scene, and that he loved her. She realized Bob needed his love redirected to her. Barbara accepted her place. She wasn't married to Bob—yet. In her culture, it was perfectly acceptable for a young brave to buck some squaws before he married one of them and had children. There were no promises of betrothal between them. But she knew he'd loved and wanted her before, and she never stopped wanting him.

The time wasn't right then. Chief told her to let some time pass. She followed his counsel and gave it time. She didn't understand things then, but she did now. She wasn't ready then, but now she was. She woke up that morning and suddenly everything was clear. Nothing was the same anymore. She was ready for love, she had the cards she needed to play, and she was ready and willing to make a life with Bob. Now she needed to prepare him for her.

When Bob was in his office, Barbara walked in and sat on his desk. Without saying a word, she propped herself up on her arm and leaned her whole body across his desk, right on top of all his sales reports. Her long dark hair draped her face and flowed over everything. She moistened her lips and smiled with both mouth and eyes.

Bob was dazzled. He was an awakened red-blooded male who wanted to dive into her eyes and her body. She was more alluring than Marty ever was. Her move was overt, not subtle, yet she kept her mystique. She was special, all right. Any man would jump at the chance to be with her. Her move suggested intimacy in the future, but she still stayed slightly out of reach.

"It's time for you and me to start having coffee together," she said as she lifted her other hand and rubbed her finger slowly under Bob's lower lip. With her bold move and that one sentence, she took charge of their relationship.

Bob's blood pressure shot up. He felt like a little boy seeing a naked woman for the first time.

Barbara noticed the rising red shade of his skin. The magic between them never left. She intended to play Bob like a hooked trophy fish, make him beg her to stop the tease and slip into her net without resistance. She promised herself she would always be good to him. Bob agreed to a coffee date the coming Saturday.

"Tell me something, Bob. How many sales kits do you normally leave at a brokerage branch after you've made your visit?" Barbara asked over coffee.

"Ten or twenty, why?"

"Not a thousand or five thousand?"

"No way! No office carries anywhere near that much product inventory, even if you combine all the different products they carry."

"And where do you place your printing orders?" Barbara questioned further.

"We use Star Printing. Why the questions?"

"Have you ever heard of Monument Printing?"

"No, why the questions?"

"Well, according to some records I've seen, you order supplies from Monument and you leave five hundred to five thousand sales kits behind you wherever you go."

"That's crazy. What are you talking about?"

"Not crazy. Fact. And you don't pay Monument one dollar for each sales kit. You pay them five dollars."

"Come on, Barbara. You're off the wall with this. What's going on?"

Barbara opened her handbag and produced an invoice with Bob's name and signature on it. It showed Monument Printing supplying one hundred thousand sales kits to the UGGA distribution company at the cost of five dollars each, for a total invoice of five hundred thousand dollars. She also produced a marketing invoice from the distribution company to the fund for five hundred thousand dollars for printing expenses.

"There must be a mistake!" Bob cried in shock. "I've never heard of this outfit, never dealt with them. I never signed any invoices from them."

"Really, Bob? Are you sure?"

"Of course, I'm sure."

"Okay. Well let's go pay them a visit and see if we can straighten this out, shall we?" Barbara had gone to Monument Printing's location days before, but she wanted Bob to see their operation himself.

"Let's go right now."

Bob was clearly upset and wanted to get to the bottom of this. The two drove to a small town on the outskirts of Plaintown and went to the address of Monument Printing. They got out of the car and stood on the address marker on the road. It was a vacant lot.

"Did you know this was a vacant lot before we got here?" Bob was asking the questions now.

"I did."

"So what's going on? What do you know about this?"

"First, I must tell you there is danger associated with knowing about this. I don't believe you had anything to do with it. You're not that devious. I know you and I've worked closely with you. You were always completely honest."

"And I still am. What's going on?"

"Before I tell you, I want you to know I have copies of everything away from UGGA's offices in a safe place. And you can't breathe a word of this to anybody, not David, not any single person. No one must know."

"Agreed, now don't torture me. What's going on?"

"First things first, buster. What happened with you and Marty on your road trips?" Barb stood with her arms akimbo. She was defiant and wore the look of a woman insulted.

"That's pretty personal, Barb." Bob tried to scramble for an exit but found none.

Barb mounted a frontal assault. "You can tell me. I expect to hear the worst. I'm a woman, didn't you know?"

"Yeah, I know. You're a woman, all right. You're a woman who didn't want me." Bob tried to play on Barb's sympathies, but he found nothing there. Not many women were sympathetic to a man's dalliances with a rival.

"I never said I didn't want you, Big Stupid Horse! I said you needed to wait," Barb blurted out her feelings. She almost cried she was so hurt.

"What did you call me just now?"

"Never mind. My father and I have Indian names for everybody." Barb pouted and turned away from him. "I'm surprised you stayed with her as long as you did. That tunnel of hers was drill-bored and re-bored many times, Big Stupid Horse. I'm surprised you could feel the side walls. That tunnel was so well-lubricated at least I can assume you didn't get any rust on your prick? So much meat moved through that tunnel, I guess I can also assume no moss grew on your prick either, huh?" She looked angry. For an instant, Bob thought she was about to bite him.

"So that's it. You and daddy Chief think I'm stupid, that I'm just too stupid for you. That's why you put us on hold. That's why you're reluctant about tell me anything." Bob spoke as if he were a hurt little boy talking to a coy little girl.

"You're not stupid in all things, Bob. But when it comes to women you are very, very stupid. When it comes to understanding people, you need a little help." Barbara hinted there was more to be revealed than a woman's scorn. And she was direct.

"What are you talking about? Plain English, no tribal riddles, please."

"For starters, you need to learn there's a huge difference between loving and fucking," Barb shouted again. Obviously the woman had pain in her heart.

"Excuse me!" Bob's eyes told Barbara he was insulted. His feelings were now where she wanted them. Now maybe Big Horse was ready to learn.

"Bob, when a female dog fucks a dozen other dogs, do you think the dogs fall in love? Do you think the bitch falls in love? Or do you think maybe the bitch just has the urge to fuck?" Barb was still shouting even though Bob was only two feet away. She was skillfully playing the role of the woman scorned and hurt, even though it was she who had put Bob on a shelf in the first place.

"Are you saying Marty is just like a bitch in heat?" Bob tried to retaliate, with no success.

"As a matter of fact, that's exactly what I'm saying, you Big Stupid Horse asshole. Marty was fucking forty different salesmen in the year before you took her on the road with you. How in the hell could any sane man fall in love with something like that?"

Barbara was still shouting, Bob noted. He hated when women did that.

"You can't be serious." His eyes widened and his jaw dropped at Barb's bombshell.

"I am serious. I don't say things I can't prove." Barb pursed her lips and leveled a gaze at Bob, nodding slightly. That meant she had the goods to back up what she was saying. She didn't blink and she wasn't backing down. For a minute it looked like she might cry.

"Tell me what's going on," Bob pleaded. Suddenly it occurred to him that a woman could feel pretty badly if she lost her man to a common indiscriminate whore. *What was I thinking? Oh shit, I wasn't thinking. She's right! I was just fucking. Oh my God, what have I done?*

"First you tell me how I can be sure I can trust you."

Bob suddenly swept Barbara into his arms and kissed her. She struggled and tried to push him away, but he didn't stop. Her resistance faded and, after pounding his back with her fists, she relented, returning his kisses and hugging him close.

"I love you, you crazy girl. Don't you know that? I loved you years ago and I've never stopped. I just thought you were off-limits or on reservation or I wasn't allowed on the reservation or I didn't know what your world—"

Barb cut him off with a kiss. His telling her he loved her was what she'd longed to hear for years, and he'd finally admitted it. She knew he loved her. She knew she'd tortured him with her denials. Her kiss turned deep and they held it for a long moment while their bodies pressed against each other. They'd both been waiting for this moment and now it was finally here. They could feel it. They were, from that moment on, inseparable. "Now you're finally making sense, Big Horse. I suppose I will trust you now." Barbara had made her point and now she wanted all games between them to stop.

"You can trust me. I swear by all the buffalo on the plains and all the elk in the forests."

"Well, now you're really talking big, Strong Horse."

"Is that what you and Chief call me?"

"Yes, Bob. You are Big Strong Horse and sometimes Big Stupid Horse. You have interchangeable names. Consider it a big honor."

Barbara twirled in a circle with outstretched arms. She dived, swooped, and twirled her body, like a bird she pranced to an imaginary drum beat. She tucked her chin close to her chest and to the side, smiling a winsome coquettish invitation at Bob as she danced. Her hair flew freely from her head and caught the sun. She was a dazzling jewel, a human ornament of radiant happiness. She whooped and laughed a good belly laugh. Bob stared at her, now her bewitched, captivated man. Barbara was the enchantress and she charmed him in her expressive childlike way like no other woman could.

She walked back into his arms. As she crushed her body to his, Barbara promised herself no other woman would ever know her man. She would never let him out of her arms again.

"So why are we standing in front of a vacant lot?" Bob begged to be clued in.

"Here's what I know so far. Not a breath of this to anyone, especially David. It's dangerous to let him know we know anything. Very, very dangerous!" Barbara brought her index finger to her lips and nodded, emphasizing the need for secrecy.

"My lips are sealed," Bob vowed.

"There exists a separate set of files for the company, separate records of expenses. Your trips with Marty were paid for by Monument Printing. We're standing in front of their corporate headquarters, this vacant lot. It looks like you ordered a half-million dollars' worth of printing supplies to pay for a year-long fling with that woman all over the country, from

Hawaii to Maine to California, to Assateague and Shenandoah and New Orleans, New York, and on and on. There isn't a party you didn't go to, and what's worse, it looks like you embezzled money from the fund through fictitious printing bills to pay for a year of nonstop whoring with Marty. Now Marty's gone. Guess who this all points to, Bob? We have theft from a regulated investment company entity, the disappearance of a company officer, your name on all this phony printing from a company that doesn't exist. What will you say when the authorities start asking questions about all this?"

"I didn't do any of this stuff. Honest."

"But you were fucking Marty, weren't you?"

"Yes."

"Tell me, could you even feel her side walls, Big Stupid Horse? It must have been like putting your stick in a bowl of oatmeal, huh, Horse? I bet she was so stretched out you could clap your hands in there, couldn't you, Big Horse?" Sparrow baited him. The woman within her couldn't resist taking one last demeaning shot at her departed rival.

"Jesus Christ, Barbara. It was sex. Marty's life is built around sex. Is a man supposed to say no?"

"Well, I always knew you were honest. At least I hope she taught you a few things. I don't want to let some Big Horse into my bed who doesn't know what he's doing." Barbara was letting Bob know she was accepting him with all his previous baggage.

"You have to believe me, Barb. I had nothing to do with the phony invoices or the printing company setup."

"I already know that, Big Horse."

"How?"

"You cannot know that yet, Big Horse. Too dangerous for you to know. But rest easy. I know you had nothing to do with it, because I know who orchestrated the whole charade."

"You do?"

"Of course I do. I also figured out who the forged signatures. Little Sparrow flits around the office, unseen and unheard, Big Horse. I have more work to do to fit all the pieces together and solve this puzzle, but just give me more time. I'll be in touch. But I do not want you to worry. If they try to frame you for this, I can disprove it. For now, you just play along as though you know nothing. Do you understand me?"

"Yes, but tell me, are you in any danger yourself, Barb?" Bob's concern for her warmed her heart. He was a good man.

"Not so much unless some people get very foolish. Chief looks over Sparrow. Chief has powerful medicine. He's very dangerous to anyone who tries to harm Sparrow."

"But he's up in Montana, on a reservation."

"Trust me on this one, Bob. My father has people who work for him, who take care of what he calls 'the details.' One of Chief's men is never far from me. I don't worry. Don't you worry."

Bob was astounded by what Barbara knew and how fearless she was.

"You're telling me you have a protector, a bodyguard?"

Barbara pulled out a green plastic square from her purse. There was a red button in the center of it and it had two tiny blinking lights on one side. It was obviously a tracking device of some sort. "If I push this button, an armed man who understands his business will appear within one minute."

"You're kidding. How do you know that?"

"When both lights blink, he's within a minute. When only one light blinks, he's within two minutes. When no light blinks, it will take more than two minutes. If the light doesn't blink for a long time, like five minutes, Chief will be upset with my protection and he will be replaced. The light always blinks. He's no more than two minutes away."

"This is amazing. I've never seen something like this." Bob was astounded.

"You've never met a man like Chief. He is very protective of Sparrow."

"Will I get in trouble for kissing you just now?"

"No, Silly Horse. But you will get in trouble if you lose interest."

"I'm interested. I'm very interested."

"Sparrow knows, Horse, but Horse must still wait."

"How long?"

"Not too long, but not real soon either. Chief says we must allow time to play its magic."

"Jesus Christ. I'd never guessed any of this was real."

"It's real, Horse. And Horse?"

"Yes, Sparrow?"

"Don't swear, Horse. It belittles you and I am religious. It hurts my ears."

"Okay, Sparrow. No more swearing."

SPARKY OR THE BLATHERFLAMEER

The personnel requirements for the sales, marketing, and portfolio portion of the firm grew while the administrative requirements of the business remained constant. David felt an irresistible urge to exercise his growing power. He was free of Marvin's control. Susan's role in the firm was as important, but it remained fixed in administration while David's empire was expanding. He began sowing his oats.

The impish, devilish pranks and bad deeds David was repressed from doing as a child, bubbled up from his wellspring of parental hatreds. He wished he were a totalitarian dictator of subjugated people, but he had no military to command. He was only a businessman. To slake his sociopathic lusts, he used his money to wreak havoc upon employees, shareholders, and hapless innocents who became indebted to him. He made people squirm under his powers and tortured their lives and finances, much as he'd bedeviled insects as a child.

He ensnared the less fortunate who miscalculated or underestimated him. As the silent, stealthy frog of financial liquidity, he baited the unwary with his money; then, when the time was right, he shot out his unfurled tongue and stuck it fast to his unwary prey. The flies he'd once tortured by pulling wings from their bodies were replaced by human victims now. Contracts they signed were strictly enforced with no extensions or forbearance. His delinquency notices arrived unexpectedly at the most inopportune times, when his prey had no chance of escape. He never negotiated easier terms and gave no quarter. The white-collar monster was unshackled from his father's restraints. He expanded his reach slowly, first for control of the office, then outward to society at large.

David had rising cash flows which he put to use, not by hiring more sales muscle in the field but by creating a home office environment more to his liking. Three people were hired in rapid succession. Rublina was the first as a backup for Susan, in case she decided to resign or if she were to become ill. Susan resisted this hire saying she felt perfectly wonderful and intended to work at least another fifteen years. This woman's cost allocation came from David's sales and marketing revenues, so Susan eventually had to accept the incursion onto her turf.

After twelve months on the job, Rublina fell facedown in the office hallway, stone-drunk and comatose. She frequently ran to the ladies' room and barfed into a toilet during her morning hours in the office. It was painfully obvious to everyone on the staff that the poor woman would never come close to the grasp of administrative matters that Susan or Barbara possessed. Her IQ simply wasn't there, her desire to learn anything about the business was completely absent, and her work ethic was nonexistent. It was a mystery to many why Rublina was ever hired because the woman was completely dysfunctional and reeked of alcohol, but David told all doubters that he saw great potential in her and counseled them to be patient. Since Rublina was often so drunk she couldn't keep her head up off her desk, David hired a second woman as an assistant for her.

The assistant's name was Judith. She was in all respects a corporate workhorse type. She could follow the instructions in various manuals, dutifully kept the flow of reports to the regulators moving upstream to Barbara and Susan, and she quickly mastered everything about running Rublina's office. She propped up the office drunk.

The third female hire and the last of the new hires was Donna. She had a beanpole figure with straight brown hair and glasses. Her glasses practically covered her entire upper face and her vision was so poor that her lenses were well over a half-inch thick to bend light rays into a reasonably discernable image. The woman could have qualified for Social Security disability on the basis that she was legally blind and unable to drive, but she had a husband at home who she couldn't stand. The man only drank beer and watched football, so she preferred to be out of the house and working. She asked several employees if they'd like to earn extra money to help her kill her husband, but no one offered to help her. Rumor had it that Donna was some distant relative of David's and that she coordinated mysterious murder-for-hire business relationships for him.

Donna's office functions were two-fold. She was to assist Judith, Rublina's assistant, whenever Judith needed help in compiling a report. Her second duty was to keep track of Bob. She maintained a secret log of Bob's daily whereabouts, and whenever he was in Plaintown. She kept a second log of the people who visited him in his office, how long they stayed, and, if she could possibly hear by listening at the door, what his conversations were about. David hired Donna because he was paranoid that Bob would possibly succumb to the siren calls of a recruiter and leave the firm someday, or that Bob would unravel David's fraud.

After a year passed, Mrs. Rodriguez made a comment to Barbara that set in motion winds of change at UGGA. Neither woman brooked acceptance of another employee suffering abuse, unless of course the employee willingly agreed to it. Rublina stoked their curiosity. Initially, the woman appeared to be gaining health. The office grapevine said she was on a special diet and initially gained strength under David's personal interest in her well-being, but Mrs. Rodriguez never bought into that speculation. It was too shallow, too much not David. He never nurtured anyone. There was always an ulterior motive to every kindness he showed anyone. Mrs. Rodriguez's suspicions gained plausibility when Rublina began falling down drunk in the mornings. Often there were shouting matches between her and David behind the locked doors of his office.

One day, as Rublina walked past the front office on the way to David's office, Mrs. Rodriguez said to Barbara, "There goes the 10:00 a.m. express delivery."

"What do you mean?" Barbara had noticed the routine trip as well but decided to play coy, a trait she learned from Chief.

"She goes by every morning at ten. I'm sure you noticed. But look very closely at her breasts."

"Okay, I'm looking. What is there to see? She has breasts. We all have breasts."

"Remember how they looked."

About twenty minutes later, Rublina walked past the front office on her way back to her own office. Mrs. Rodriguez glanced at Barbara. "Look at them again," she said. "Do you notice the difference?"

"Yes, they are much smaller now, not so swollen."

"I'm happy to know it's not just my old eyes deceiving me," said Mrs. Rodriguez. "I've seen her come back sometimes with stains on her blouse where her nipples wetted through her brassiere."

Barbara hadn't paid attention to Rublina's breast size before that. She'd never born a child like Mrs. Rodriguez had, so she never thought to make the observation. Suddenly the thought dawned on Barbara, the same thought the old Mexican woman first had several months earlier.

"She's going to David's office every morning for twenty minutes to breast-feed him! Is that possible?"

"It's routine. Also, she goes at 2:00 p.m., right when the market closes. You can set your watch by her."

"That explains the mystery of her employment," said Barbara.

"You don't know the rest of it. You are too young to know what his mother looked like, but I remember Eloweiss Sustack well. Rublina is her body double when Eloweiss was in her early thirties, when David was an infant." Mrs. Rodriguez nodded, affirming her own revelation to Barbara.

"What does it mean?"

"It means David is a very sick man. It means he's using this woman to try to recapture his infanthood. He's trying to buy love from this flop that he never got from his mother. It means he hates his life and this world so much he thinks it owes him a second chance at whatever he believes he missed. I don't understand all of it. I am a simple woman, but I know there's something about that woman, about her looks and her tits. I believe there's something very unhealthy going on here. I think David pretends she's his mother."

"Isn't that kind of sweet, in a perverse sort of way?"

"No, not sweet. You don't understand. David hated his mother. I mean he hated her really and deeply, and all his life he wanted to hurt her, punish her. When she was dying, he delayed paying her nursing help. They retaliated, but not against him, against his mother. They left her to piss the bed and lay in it for days before they changed her out. He liked to see his mother suffer with bedsores. He even, according to one of the nurses I spoke to once, mixed in placebos with her medications. She had terrible Parkinson's at the end and she constantly screamed in agony, especially without her medications being right. The nurses told David and he went to the house to see her."

"To help her?"

"No, he went there to laugh at her!" Mrs. Rodriguez raised her voice above a whisper. "That's how much he hated her."

Barbara's jaw dropped. That helped explain everything.

"So that means at some point David will likely hurt Rublina, possibly very badly?"

"I am afraid so. I am afraid for that woman and her son." Mrs. Rodriguez stared into empty space and slowly shook her head. "This will not end well."

In time, David had Rublina under his complete dominance. When he was bored with his dalliances with his boy-toy employees, Muscle Boy and Man Child, he demanded that she service him with blow jobs. As a chronic alcoholic in desperate need of a paycheck, she complied. He plied her with alcohol, then complained that her milk was unsatisfactory. Her hair was dyed bright red and her face was always heavily made up with bright red lipstick and black eye shadow with black lash extensions, all as David demanded. She looked sexy in black webbed lace stockings and a tight black bodice that lifted her ample breasts upward and outward as if they were being served as a dessert dish. David insisted that she keep that attire in her office closet and wear it when he requested her presence in his office. When in her 'skin outfit,' Rublina looked like a Las Vegas Keno girl who was doubling as a prostitute.

David had no respect for Rublina and had no intention of ever helping the poor woman rehabilitate herself. Instead, he did the opposite. He kept her amply supplied with bottles of Boothby's gin, Jack Daniels sour mash bourbon, and Grey Goose Vodka, her favorite spirits. Rublina had no willpower and was in no position to resist David's demands.

David and Rublina's relationship went beyond the office. He often went to her home with alcohol, proceeding to get her totally inebriated. Then, while she was passed out, he would bugger her eighteen-year-old son. David threatened the lad with firing his mother if he ever said anything, and he threatened

Rublina with firing her if she ever tried to stop him. David rationalized his behavior by thinking that, with a mother such as this young man had, he had little chance to make his way in the world, so the destroyer of his poor trapped soul might as well be none other than himself. David relished the sadistic pleasure of knowing he was victimizing both mother and son simultaneously, pitting them against each other's well-being with his threat of retaliation if either broke their silence.

There were days when the tormented woman locked herself in her office and sobbed quietly for hours until she was exhausted. This went on for several weeks until finally her cries of mental anguish piqued another woman's conscience.

Barbara could no longer bear the sufferings of this pathetic human being, even if it meant she could lose her own position. She approached Bob and told him all she knew and related her conversations with Mrs. Rodriguez about Rublina's misfortunes.

As fate would have it, David's secret nursing fetish was revealed unexpectedly. An examiner from Financial Regulatory Authority, or FINRA, appeared at UGGA offices unannounced, investigating an allegation of fund dividend payment errors. Susan was out of the office, so he asked to see her assistant. Barbara was out of the office. He then asked to see any administrative officer of the firm. No one could locate David and he didn't answer his intercom. Bob inquired to Mrs. Rodriguez where David and Rublina were. Mrs. Rodriguez motioned toward David's office without saying a word. Bob took Barbara's master office key and went to David's office.

What he saw when he opened the door shocked him to his core. There was David suckling like an infant on Rublina's massive left tit. Bob needed to say something.

"David, there's a regulator here and no one to respond to him. You need to go to the front office."

"Tell him to wait in the conference room. Can't you see I'm busy?"

"David, this is serious. He knows you're in the office. He wants to see an administrative officer."

"Well, you're an officer. Take care of it."

"This is an inquiry about our dividend. It's administration, not sales. You need to get to the front office!" Bob was emphatic.

"Fuck him. I'm busy. He's just a fucking regulator. Tell him to wait."

"Not doing that, David. Up you go." With that, Bob yanked David off Rublina's tit. Milk was still squirting out of her as Bob stood David on his feet and shoved him out the door of his office.

"I'll deal with you about this later," snarled David as he adjusted his tie.

"You bet you will," Bob shot back.

Rublina was on her feet with a towel wrapped around her upper chest.

"Go home and get yourself cleaned up. Stay sober and don't come back to the office until you are called. And clean out your desk of all your personal items." Bob waited until she left David's office.

"Does this mean my life is over?" asked the droopy-eyed alcoholic.

"No. It means it's beginning. Now get out of here."

With the commands from a strong male voice, Rublina stumbled down the hall bare-breasted, cleaned out her desk, and left for the day.

There can arise a time in the affairs of fathers and sons when their relationship turns. In the case of the faux father and son duo, David and Bob, that time came. It arose because of the complaints Bob heard from the office staff about Rublina, and from what he personally observed. He provoked the confrontation in David's office, not waiting for David to bring it up when it suited his timetable.

"She needs to be let go," Bob demanded when David returned after promising the regulator he'd look into the firm's computer glitch. "It doesn't matter why you hired her, or what you think she can become here. Remember, this is going to be my company and I don't want some sloppy drunk demoralizing the place. She's worthless. She can't stay awake. She stinks. I told her to go home and stay home. She's out of here. I insist!"

"Oh, you insist, do you? I run this office. You get sales. This is none of your business, so stay out of it." David was adamantly opposed to relinquishing Rublina. She was his reincarnated mother image, a perfect victim for him to torture, with her son thrown in as a bonus.

"I'm not staying out of it. She's out."

"Or you'll do what?" David was visibly angry. No one talked to him that way and got away with it.

"Or I'll break your nose, that's what." Bob wasn't backing down.

David was shocked, realizing his protégé meant it. "Look, we can disagree on something small like this. You don't need to go to general quarters over it. Give me a little time to work something out."

"No, David. I'm doing this for your own good. This is going to get you and the firm in trouble. It stops now. I mean it. I love you as a father, but that will not save your nose. She goes, or you will never recognize your nose again."

"Give me one week to find a place for her."

"Okay. One week, not a day more."

"Agreed," David said, but he seethed with anger inside and deeply resented being pushed around by the younger man, even though he knew Bob was the one who was thinking clearly about Rublina. Within the week, Bob had Rublina in counseling and going to Alcoholics Anonymous, and he signed her up with a temporary help agency. David never did anything to help the woman during that week he said he needed. He was just trying to buy time to think of a way to keep her, but his scheme failed. Eventually the woman married a good man who worked construction and was blessed to discover a normal life. David harbored a deep-seated grudge about Bob's intervention, but pretended to forget about it.

His next foray into anomalous mischief was to decorate the corporate offices with animal heads. He enjoyed going to game farm ranches in Texas where the hunt was more of a relaxing excursion than an actual hunt in the wild. By using the heads he harvested for office decor, his accountant certified they were a legitimate income tax write-off. The animals were in tip-top shape and their habitat range was fenced in so they couldn't run off when the hunters came to shoot them.

With their luxurious quarters and fabulous food, David would sometimes go off for a week to one of these exotic ranches. During the daylight hours, after a hearty breakfast, he would be driven by his hunt guide to where a prime animal was located. There were wonderful selections from North America, Asia, and, of course, Africa. Every animal imaginable was available to be shot for the right price. Once located, the guide would pull up close to the animal, stop the vehicle, mount David's rifle upon hand-carried sandbags to steady the weapon's sights upon the animal, and then bring David to his rifle to pull the trigger. The guide did all the work of gutting and cleaning the animal, harvesting the meat if it was an ungulate, and capping the animal's head for mounting by a taxidermist. Predator cats got full body mounts, except for an adult male lion, which was capped to resemble the animal with its front legs and extended claws leaping through a wall as if in a charge. Its wide-open mouth with four-inch canines eager to bite was fearsome, shocking visitors who saw it for the first time.

With the animal heads, David created the image he coveted. He portrayed himself to employees and guests as the fearless, world-traveled big game hunter. He told guests and prospective investors he hunted stocks with the same ferocity that he hunted animals. The boast had mixed results. Some couldn't find the exit door fast enough but for others, their confidence in David soared, confirming in his mind that the world was populated with idiots.

Things didn't always go smoothly in the home office. One incident occurred on the day the two-man committee team finally approved a sketch of a new corporate logo. Muscle Boy and Man Child had worked on the logo for the better part of four months. They were anxious and very proud to unveil their work.

This day was special. They'd finally thought of something. It was a sketch of a globe with wings on it, meant to signify that UGGA was flying. Muscle Boy went to the reception area and asked Barbara to come see their creation. He was brimming with pride as he ushered her into his office. Man Child stood by, anxiously awaiting her approval. Four months of work had resulted in a circle with two little wings on it. Barbara looked at it for a long moment before her hand went up to her mouth and she broke into hysterical laughter.

"It looks like a piece of flying M&M's candy! It took you idiots four months to draw a picture of an M&M! You're both lunatics!" Barbara couldn't stand up from laughing so hard. She walked out of the office in fits of laughter, which were soon joined by the other employees. The two men were devastated.

What do numbskulls do when their egos are shattered by howling women? The two-man committee took their design to Man Child's office and stared at their spurned design. For two full hours they stared at the design without moving or speaking. Occasional office laughter from the females still erupted, but it was finally dying down. Finally, the males' tempers flared.

Blame was passed back and forth; then punches flew and they shoved each other's bodies around. Above the desk where they'd labored for months to create the flying M&M was mounted David's biggest and heaviest trophy. It was the male lion's head complemented with outstretched paws and claws, complete with open jaws displaying its four-inch canines.

Unable to contain his swelling rage, Muscle Boy blew his top. He let out a scream. "Fucking cunts!" he roared a few times, followed by a shout of "Fucking idiot!" Then he shoved Man Child into the wall, the force of his push reverberating throughout the room. The impact broke the wall and knocked the lion's head off its mounting, which landed squarely upon Man Child's head. It was head upon head, and neither had a brain.

Man Child was stunned and traumatized, the lion mount having almost knocked him out. Now it sat atop the flying M&M design, twelve inches from his face, and stared at him with its huge brown glass eyes. He was face-to-face with those terrifying teeth. His heart leaped to his throat as he screamed in absolute horror. The fight-or-flight response triggered his hypothalamus and primitive instincts overwhelmed the simple man. Instinct suddenly dominated all of Man Child's cognitive reasoning.

Gripped by terror, his teeny mind completely lost control of his actions. He ran screaming into the hallway, terrified in flight from an imaginary raging lion about to bite his head off.

As fate would have it, David was in the hallway that very moment, walking in the opposite direction toward the very space the females cynically dubbed 'Corporate Logo Headquarters.' Man Child ran right over him, screaming at the top of his lungs in abject terror, breaking David's glasses and knocking the wind out of him.

"You idiot," David groaned. "What's the matter with you?"

"It t-tried to k-kill me," stammered Man Child, pointing with a trembling hand toward Corporate Logo Headquarters. He honestly believed the lion had resurrected somehow, his simple mind unable to grasp that he'd been bumped on his noggin by a deader head than his own. Eventually, the two men picked themselves up from the floor, regained their composure and pretenses, put their romantic feelings above their upsets, and sorted things out. The traumatized man was given three weeks paid leave to help him calm down. David bought a new pair of glasses.

The card-fed computer was another cause for crisis every time dividend and capital gains calculations needed to be made. One hot August afternoon, the internal system that supplied cooling waters to the air conditioner in old Sparky's room sprang a big leak. Man Child, the beast's attendant, was in the lunch room eating a sandwich and reading a comic book when the disaster struck. Not every woman on staff called the BlatherFlameer 'Old Sparky.' The newer ladies to the firm never saw it spark, but they did see it punch and shred cards, so BlatherFlameer was dually named 'Old Punch and Shred' and 'Old Sparky.'

Man Child had Old Sparky running the annual capital gain and dividend computation unattended when the leak sprang. Without water, the air conditioner failed and the electro-mechanical beast quickly overheated. Soon Sparky was chopping the shareholder record cards into multiple pieces and spitting them up into the air. The record cards were shooting everywhere and then landing on the floor—or rather in the lake, as the floor was quickly covered in six inches of water. Then the big electrical fire happened. The computer began sparking and smoking. Before the fire alarm sounded and anyone noticed things were amiss, a torrent of water streamed down the hall into other offices and poured through the ceiling of offices on the floor below. Some water managed to find its way into the elevators and caused them to short-circuit, trapping passengers in the cars between floors and shutting down the office building. Sparks, smoke, fire, and water were shooting out of the computer room when the fire department arrived. Main Street was cordoned off and traffic rerouted around one block of the downtown.

All employees from all offices in the building were evacuated onto Main Street by order of the Plaintown Fire Department. Man Child stood crying next to Muscle Boy, who was also in tears. Both were afraid the firm would be closed indefinitely by order of Plaintown Fire Department. Where else could they go? What could they do? Rublina, still in her final week of paid employment, went to the nearest bar to avoid answering questions. Susan, Barbara, and Mrs. Rodriguez all sat on the sidewalk with their backs against the building across the street, reading paperback novels and newspapers while waiting for the all clear signal. David pleaded with the fire chief for forbearance, saying that it was all an unforeseeable mechanical failure and that it would be repaired by a competent air conditioning technician.

After order was restored and the elevators were working again, the task arose to figure out how much money needed to be paid out to each shareholder. David ordered an all-hands effort to tape the shredded and waterlogged computer cards back together. For the next three days, the entire staff was on their hands and knees on the floor, trying to match the torn soggy cards. When the effort concluded, everyone realized they had no clue as to who should get what. Some cards were torn while others were crumpled and warped, but still close to resembling something the machine could process. Some cards were reduced to shreds of soggy confetti. But hey, they could tell the Securities and Exchange Commission that they'd tried their best if anybody complained. Everyone just hoped no shareholder would do a personal calculation of their dividend and capital gains from their statement records and match it to what they were actually paid. David decided the distribution checks should go out based on pure guesswork as the optimal solution. If somebody complained, he instructed administration to tell the shareholder that their payment got mixed up with someone else's, that it was the bank's fault, and that they'd get it straightened out.

After every account was paid something, the firm's bank checking account for distribution payments still held eight hundred and forty-six thousand dollars. The balance should have been zero. If the shareholder servicing agent bank noticed this discrepancy, the firm risked a regulatory inquiry. Something needed to be done quickly.

David had Rublina issue a corporate resolution declaring a long-time loyalty dividend to shareholders who had been with the fund since the day of inception. This would be only one shareholder, David's mother Eloweiss, whose assets were held in trust with David as her sole beneficiary and sole trustee. Rublina signed a letter of resolution for the corporate records whereby she indemnified the trust account for any finding of wrongdoing. After all, she was still an officer and she had her errors and omissions insurance coverage for two more days. David ended up pocketing an extra eight hundred and forty-six thousand dollars. As a result of the fire and flood, the excess funds were reposed to his benefit.

The damage was repaired. There was some staff discussion and a recommendation to replace the old BlatherFlameer with a new computer called a PC, or personal computer, which did more, took up little space, required no elaborate cooling system, and required no cards to be punched. Bob told David the world was passing the firm by with the new technology of digital personal computers.

"We need to get rid of that thing. We could save office space, eliminate one employee, reduce our liability. It's only a matter of time until Old Sparky sparks and floods again. What's wrong with modernizing?"

"I'll tell you what's wrong with modernizing. First, the new technology isn't proven."

Bob interrupted. "The new computers don't catch fire and flood buildings. What more proof do you need?"

"Don't get smart about this. There's one very good reason to keep this machine."

"What could possibly be the reason?"

"It hasn't killed anyone!"

"What?"

"Those new computers are made by the successor company to the ones that had the old punch card machines in Hitler's Germany. Those punch cards categorized everyone so Hitler knew who was a Jew and who was a goy. He used the data on the punch card to hunt down German Jews and deport them to Poland and on to Auschwitz!"

"David, listen to yourself. These machines didn't do anything wrong. It was their misuse that caused the deportations."

"That doesn't matter! We have a lot of old wealthy Jews as clients. If they came in here and saw one of those new machines, they'd remember the Holocaust and take their money elsewhere."

"Where is elsewhere, David? Every elsewhere already has new computers. Where would they go and not see a new computer? David, this Holocaust thing is affecting your business judgment. These old clients you talk about already have the new computers in their offices and homes. I know. I've seen them. We need a new computer."

"We're not getting a new computer and that's final! I will not even consider it until they start making the new computers bigger. Bigger is better! That's always been true and it will always be true, everyone knows that. End of discussion. If I see a new computer in here, I will personally shoot it. No new computer!" David was beet red. His authority and reasoning was just challenged and he was like a bull seeing a red flag waving before his face.

Bob turned away and went to his office, throwing his hands in the air. There was no point in advancing a disagreement from an argument to a fist fight.

David vetoed the staff's recommendation to replace Sparky. It was already paid for, he declared, and a valuable employee was trained to run it perfectly. It was integral to the firm's record-keeping procedures, he explained. It would be like shooting a loyal old friend.

And indeed, the old BlatherFlameer was a great old friend to David, one that occasionally stole large sums on his behalf and paid him handsomely.

THE KEY AND THE BLADE

Sparrow waited until the Friday before a three-day Labor Day weekend. Everyone left the office for the last summertime break. Aspens were turning golden and beginning to shimmer in the late summer's breezes. The big game animals, the bighorns, the elk, the Dall sheep, and the deer were all sizing others of their kind for the upcoming rut. Many of the office staff planned to make a weekend pilgrimage to the mountains for the animals and fall colors. David was making a big game jaunt to a Texas game farm to harvest a prime ibex, all the staff women planned to be away, and the office boys left earlier that morning to do whatever it was they did.

Sparrow assured Mrs. Rodriguez she'd lock up before she went home, but wanted to read some new regulatory releases before she surrendered to a mini vacation. There was nothing suspicious about Barb's declaration; she was the notorious office workaholic. As employees filed out the door, she kept count until she was satisfied everyone was gone. Then, to be doubly sure, she went through every office in case she'd missed someone. Finally she was satisfied she was alone in the office with all the keys necessary to read the secret files in Debbie's file room.

She went to the woman's desk where she'd seen the brass key. It was there, right where she'd seen it that day weeks before. Barbara took the key and the copy key she had made from the wax imprint of David's. Together she inserted the two keys into the file cabinet and turned the odd, specially made lock. One key turned clockwise, the other counterclockwise. The cabinet opened, exposing a set of files that contained the secrets of the firm. Barbara's eyes widened as she read. Then she made copies.

One of the files contained the most peculiar invoices. They were for insect supplies. David routinely purchased tarantulas; emperor scorpions in shades of black, blue, and green; cockroaches; palmetto bugs; worms; beetles; grasshoppers; silverfish; ants; fleas; lice; and centipedes. After she'd copied all David's files, Barbara called Chief. The situation was ideal. David was away, his wife was away to Europe with her girlfriend, and there was no one at his house.

Chief sent Guido 'The Blade' Checini to help his daughter the next night, Saturday. There was no time to waste. Blade and Sparrow walked to the perimeter of David's property at dusk and waited in some shrubs until dark. Blade observed for a good hour to see if any shadows passed between the closed drapes and the inside lights. There were no signs of life except barnyard geese and possibly an inside dog.

Blade had been a cat burglar in his previous line of work, and his skills came in handy. He brought along three pounds of raw sirloin for any dog, complete with a sleeping pill powder rubbed into the meat. The two made their way to the house, staying low to the ground while approaching from the side opposite the ponds where the geese nested for the night. Blade had a master key ring, and one of them worked on a side entrance.

A friendly mutt of a dog came to the door and barked. Blade anticipated this and fed the dog the three pounds of sleep beef. Once inside, Blade quickly figured out the home had a sealed-off area and he searched for the secret way to open it. On a bookshelf, behind a Torah book, was a latch. He pulled it and the bookcase released from its wall fastener, opening to a secret room. It was pitch-black except for a small green glow that showed through the floor crack of a side door off to the right of the bookcase entrance. Sparrow sensed the smell immediately, the same one David had when he'd groped her. There was the pungency of decaying flesh and rancid ketones. The formaldehyde smell failed to completely mask the putrid scent; rather it mingled with it. They went inside and found a light switch.

Sparrow began taking pictures with her 35mm camera. There was an altar, complete with a gas-fueled Jenn Air industrial burner stove. Beyond the altar was a small recess with doors that latched. A small electric ten-watt light blinked over the doors. Blade opened the doors, revealing original Torah scrolls from a Polish temple that was destroyed during the Holocaust. They were probably hundreds of years old, complete with velvet covers in reds and blues and adorned with elaborate silver. Apparently the temple's rabbi or cantor escaped Europe with the scrolls. Possibly they were a gift to Marvin from one of the religious leaders in Poland or Germany that he'd rescued from the Holocaust, and they were now owned by David.

Sparrow looked closely at the gas grill. It appeared that some skin was burned fast to it in one corner and not completely scraped off. It was.... Sparrow gasped. Could this be human skin? It was only a small fragment, but was too smooth and thing to be pig, cow, or chicken.

Off to the right of the altar was another larger recess into an underground wall. It had a louvered partition door separating it from the main room. A soft green luminescence glowed from under the floor jam. Sparrow sensed the smells came from behind the door. She moved forward with some trepidation, for this was not some ordinary closet light escaping. When she opened the louvered door to peer inside, a brighter green florescent light went on automatically, soft and ethereal. Her face was slapped by a sudden rush of humidity, her hair and body steeped in a languid soup of clouds and green light. Then the stench overwhelmed her. This was David's chamber of death.

Rotted flesh and trace formaldehyde smells forced her to cover her nose and mouth to try to stave off the overpowering stench. As Sparrow's eyes dilated to adjust for the semi-darkness, she noticed random movements on the wall in front of her. With her light-gathering peripheral vision, she detected movement on the side walls also. As the objects came into focus, she stepped back in horror and gasped, Blade steadying her. All around them were glass-partitioned walls with insects of many species.

There were cockroaches, palmetto bugs, worms, centipedes, and spiders. Blade shined his flashlight into the glass cages. Insects of all sorts were feeding upon rotting flesh. In some of the glass cases were remnants of human hands and feet, along with multiple other parts and bones, all being methodically and meticulously stripped of all flesh. And there were three decomposing human heads with ants crawling into and out of the eye sockets, mouths, and ear cavities, obviously feasting upon whatever tissues remained within the cranium that they had not already eaten. Bold swaths of hair and scalp were missing from the grisly specimens, and swarms of silverfish tugged furiously at the hair roots seeking their meals. Ants did their work and silverfish did theirs, neither species interfering with the other in a nod to professional courtesy.

One head was smaller than the others, likely a woman's. Sparrow recognized enough of it to believe it was Marty's. In another separate compartment, there was a formaldehyde-filled jar containing a fetus of about three months' gestation. Suddenly the rush of realization weakened Sparrow's knees. The fetus was Marty's. No wonder she had such a happy peaceful sheen on her face the last few times Sparrow saw her. She was going to be married and have a child. Sparrow vowed to keep all this to herself and never tell anyone, not even Bob. Revelation of the fetus could only cause more pain and sorrow for him and Susan. No one would ever know about the murder of this unfortunate creation.

The green room was beyond anything Sparrow could have ever imagined. It made a powerful lasting impression, like seeing Niagara Falls up close for the first time, only the wonderment she felt was the opposite of majesty. It was a look into the opposite of that, the unfathomable darkness of a deranged human soul. Sparrow was shocked as she grasped the enormity of the insect room and the depravity of its evil genius creator. She only had a glimpse of the middle phase of David's body disposal operation. She did not see that she was in the midst of an ingeniously evil organic processing plant where rendered flesh was fed to the barnyard pigs; bones, cleaned by the insects, were removed and pulverized in David's wood chipper to fine granules and powder then returned to the soil as nutritional supplements for the rose beds; and insects that were injured or expired were fed to the guinea hens and other insects. But, what she did see was horrifying.

On the front wall were multi-partitioned glass cubicles containing individual quarters for tarantulas and various sizes of scorpions, including the large emperor scorpions. All compartments were connected by small glass tubes with glass doors that could block or allow travel by the ants between compartments. Apparently they were the ultimate cleanup crew for this hellish construction. Each compartment also had a shoot that opened from the bottom to allow the scorpions and tarantulas to make their way down to a miniature arena. In the arena were the assorted detritus remains of grasshoppers, crickets, cockroaches, beetles, caterpillars, and leg parts of tarantulas and scorpions. David undoubtedly came there to watch gladiatorial combats between the scorpions and the tarantulas, and likely fights between members of the same species.

Apparently the spiders and scorpions also dined there on the lesser insects. There were little tabs of paper taped to the compartments of some of the residents. Upon closer inspection, they had numbers on them, ranging from one to three. David ranked his gladiators and, presumably, the insects that lost their ranking in combat or got crippled were sacrificed as feed for the stronger combatants.

Sparrow took pictures of all that she saw, then she and Blade slipped away into the night. She was shaken by what she'd witnessed and documented. It required many gulps of fresh outdoor air to rid the scent memory of David's dungeon of death from her lungs. Stunned and sobered, Barbara and Blade drove away from David's as she realized the urgency of her task. The warden of this insect penitentiary must surely self-identify as one of these lowly creatures. David had to be without soul or feeling for others, devoid of any moral compass, dedicated to ruthless victimizing, devouring his prey without any sense of humanity or remorse. David was anything but a normal caring, feeling human. He was a calculating sadistic killer. She shuddered at the thought of seeing him each day and needing to wait, as Chief had counseled her.

At her own apartment, Barbara reconfigured her copies from Debbie's secret files into categorical duplicate files of her own. Into the insect file, Barbara added the developed photos of the decomposing body parts with their ant and silverfish scrubbers, and the cockroaches, centipedes, flea and lice swarms, beetles, spiders, scorpions, and other assorted insects she'd photographed. These wretched lowly animals and their lives and deaths were apparently David's preferred amusement. File by file, Barbara assembled a composite of the president of UGGA.

The second file, a rather large one, was a record of David's drug dealings. There were records of supplies costs for lighting and electricity and seedlings for growing marijuana plants in the basements of several employees in the firm's accounting department, including Debbie Wasserman. Apparently, Judith had recently joined the drug ring. There were records of cash transaction ledgers of monies owed to a Mexican drug cartel's local operator for supplies of cocaine and heroin delivered and cash owed. Both David and the local drug contact counter-signed each invoice.

This was not some word-of-mouth, dependent upon whom you know and trust street operation with people always looking over each other's shoulders. It was a 'higher up the drug food chain' business model, and it was conducted in gentlemanly, businesslike fashion. No guns, no hookers, no second-guessing and double-dealing were apparent. It looked like a long-standing arrangement where both parties needed the other. David received huge amounts of cash, which he laundered by making cash deposits on real estate investments and loan sharking deals. He was repaid with legitimate checks from buyers of real estate from his growing property inventory and from checks received from his loan paybacks. Running a mutual fund deflected any suspicion that anything nefarious was going on.

The third file was mundane record of people whom David loaned monies to, and copies of their promissory notes and evidence of their collateral. It contained first and second mortgages, along with promises of personal property collateral put-up, complete with photographs of the collateral, such as guns, jewels, and even three thoroughbred horses. David also kept a loan-to-value sheet on each borrower's sub file. Barbara noted he never went below collateral values that were twenty percent greater than his loan amount, even if the borrower needed to put up, in one case, a written guarantee of his dental office furniture, chair, and gold supply for tooth fillings.

The fourth file was a record of rents received on houses that were used by human traffickers to house underage girls from Central America, Mexico, Cambodia, and Thailand. David owned seven such houses in Plaintown and two in Springs. Each produced rents of ten to fifteen times normal market value. David made sure that the operators who leased the houses from him were never bothered by the authorities, the local police and judges receiving routine monies from him disguised as donations to various causes, or outright cash payments. Business was very good, and police and judges were welcome complimentary guests. Their visits were compensated by the house operator and deducted from David's rents.

The fifth file was an eye-popper. It was a Xeroxed copy of Marvin's last will and testament. Here was proof that Marvin's bequest to David was conditional upon David leaving the companies to Israel upon his death. The provision to keep Susan as the owner of the servicing company was also there, including the perpetual right for her company to administer all the regulatory and accounting functions. Clearly David was stuck with Susan.

The most chilling file was the sixth. It contained a list of rival drug gang members and prostitutes who were murdered. Apparently, girls who got out of line at the syndicate-operated brothels were executed and their bodies brought to David's for disposal. Each murder victim had a page with a photograph of the body along with a photograph of Donna, Judith's assistant, handing a wax-sealed envelope to an unknown man dressed in a hoodie and baggy clothes. The man receiving the envelope wore a mask. On each sheet there was an odd-shaped notation mark, apparently made by the same hand.

A money transfer took place and the mark signified that the person on David's end saw the cash placed in the envelope and sealed. David's role was to facilitate the payment to the killers and keep them anonymous; he arranged the hits and took in the money. Part of his compensation was earned by disposing of the bodies in his 'barnyard to insects processing plant.' Those contracting David's services had no way of knowing who did the job. Those doing the job had no way of knowing who hired them. It was impossible to tell if the hoodie man was the actual killer or if there was another step where the hoodie man turned the money over to the final provider of the service. The prices of the hits ranged from ten thousand to twenty thousand dollars each. Barbara was astounded at the genius of the arrangement and the cheapness of life in Plaintown.

A seventh file held records of regular cash payments made by various businessmen, along with photographs of them in compromising positions with women or other men in one or another of the seven high-rent houses David leased to friendly operators. It was small money per businessman extorted, only three-to-five hundred per month, but significant money, ranging from ten thousand to twenty thousand dollars per month per house. Barbara recognized some of the men photographed. They were substantial businessmen, and the cash payments for sex were pocket change for them. Apparently David didn't want to be an obnoxious taker; his extortions were not so large that his victims would retaliate and make trouble for him, but when cumulated, they added up. There was also a record of Bob, photographs of him and Rita at some bar. Obviously David wanted evidence that Bob was with some bar whore, completely unsuitable demeanor for an executive of UGGA.

Barbara created her own eighth file, which contained her developed photos of David's private altar, his holy storage compartment and Torah scrolls, and the green room with its insects and spiders and death offerings. Then she called Chief. The following weekend, she went to the airport with her files and boarded a private jet.

OLD GRAVEL THROAT

Redemptions, that predictable leakage from a fund's asset base by investors needing cash money, erupted into a crisis. Some brokers encouraged their clients who needed money to take it from the UGGA Universal Growth Fund. There was no trailing commission paid to brokers for keeping the money there, so it was a natural fund to target for client cash needs. David reviewed the fund's redemption reports daily. Each report contained the name of the client, the amount of money withdrawn, the amount of money remaining, the name of the salesman who'd sold the fund shares to the client, and the name of the salesman's brokerage firm.

Each shareholder redeeming shares for cash received a phone call from an elderly gentleman in fund shareholder services. The caller had a distinctive, authoritative, gravelly voice. The voice first told the shareholder he was taking a survey and asked why the shareholder needed the money. If the shareholder replied it was to remodel a house or a kitchen, or put an addition onto a house, the voice reacted with a gasp. Then the voice cleared its throat and told the shareholder that what he or she was about to do was a crazy idea; that people just weren't doing that any longer; that if the shareholder would wait a couple of years the costs of materials and labor would drop significantly and they'd be able to do the remodel cheaper, based on a top secret report the fund had, and based upon the fund's in-house economic survey. Of course, UGGA had no secret report and did no in-house economic surveys, but often as not, this approach worked. The investor changed his mind and the redemption request was canceled. The fund kept the money and the fees it earned on the money, often for many years thereafter.

If the redemption request was for a medical procedure such as triple bypass surgery or a double mastectomy for breast cancer, the gravelly voice would sound suddenly engaged and interested.

"Oh my God!" the voice would shout in alarm. "I'm glad I called you. I almost didn't call, but I see you've been a loyal shareholder to us for a long time." Any investor who'd been with the fund for more than six months qualified for the 'long time' pitch. "We really care about our long-term investors. Before you do anything, we have a firm expert on our staff who is very knowledgeable in your particular medical area. She's very familiar with your type of illness and she can do a lot for you. If you'll just hold the line a minute, I'll put her on the line. Her name is Jean." The phone was then handed to Debbie, who sat next to Old Gravel Throat for redemption calls.

"Hi there, this is Jean," she chimed. "Old Bill told me all about your condition and you can rest assured you have nothing to worry about. We know all about these no-good scamming doctors. They just want to carve you up so they can take all your money. Listen, we have a staff medical doctor who will read your medical reports for free. He'll talk to you about the procedure your doctor is recommending. Then he'll check out your doctor's complaint history on our secret in-house criminal complaint database and he'll get back to you. So just call your doctor and your hospital right now and tell them you need to put off the procedure for another six months to think it over. Don't tell them you're having us check them out. We don't want them to get suspicious. We like to hit them when they least expect it."

In about half these cases, the investor cancels the redemption. They send their medical records to the fund where they are placed in a drawer until the next time the shareholder calls, asking why he or she hasn't yet heard from the fund's staff specialist doctor. The investor is told that the review takes time because it has to do with his doctor. After a few more weeks when the investor calls a third time, he's told the staff doctor will likely get back to him within a week. Then, just at the one-week mark, the investor gets a call from Man Child, the mail clerk.

"Hello there. This is Dr. Johnson on the staff here. I've looked at your case carefully and checked out your doctor as well. Our opinion here is that you can wait at least five more years before you have that procedure and it will actually be more successful if you decide to wait. The problem will be better defined and there's a good chance it will simply go away by itself. I am sending your records back to you." About half these people die during the five-year wait period. Some survive as long as ten years with their untreated conditions, but UGGA got to keep their money.

Yet a third type of redemption is one caused by a salesman who is moving monies from the fund to some other product. The redemption reports will show a pattern of this that is easily discernable. For these situations, David makes a call to the salesman directly.

"Hi there, I've noticed you're pulling money out of the UGGA General Universal Growth Fund. How come?" Pause, listening. "Oh I see, you're doing this on the basis of short-term performance after you sold it as a long-term investment," or, "Oh, it's something more to the client's needs, huh? Well, listen up, you no-good slime. We keep records on these shareholders and on you. They are our shareholders and they are documented for long-term growth, and growth is what we give them here at UGGA General Universal."

There usually follows a long pause where the broker vents his frustration.

"What's that you say? Five years of bad performance is long-term enough? You listen to me and stop talking back. You're just a no-good little shithead and I'm a portfolio manager, see? I know what long term is and you don't. Here at UGGA, long term is twenty years, nothing less. You just sold the fund to churn it later to get another commission, didn't you? Don't mouth off to me, you little bastard. I'm going to ruin your life if you try pulling this shit one more time.

"Now you pay attention, slime ball. We've got friends at the Securities and Exchange Commission and in your state regulator's office. We're watching your activity and we're getting ready to turn you in. I'm giving you just this one chance, and then I'm going to tear your wretched hide off and destroy your miserable fucked-up little life. You call those shareholders of ours and you make them put that money back. They get thirty days where they can do that without paying another commission to you. You do that and you also put one additional shareholder with us and I'll leave you alone. If you don't do it, I'm going to get you busted out of the industry for churning your clients. You're just a no-good dirty filthy little cocksucker. I've dealt with creeps like you before. I'll get you busted down so badly you'll be selling used cars and sweeping floors. We at UGGA have an extremely high standard of ethics. The regulators all know that, and when they hear from us about your activities you'll get fucked right up the ass. Can you hear me, buddy?"

David shouts into the phone. "One week, you little prick! One week!" Then he slams the phone down. About half of all stockbrokers buckled under this intimidation tactic. Their sales redemptions stopped and some even sent the fund a new shareholder as a peace offering. David had a knack for being creative and thinking outside the box, an uncanny ability to find a way to blame someone or something else on a condition, to lay the solution to his problem into the lap of an innocent third party.

He was largely successful at staunching the outflows for home improvements, medical expenses, and the like, but one area of perpetual vexation was the shareholder group that actually sought to live off their investments. These people typically withdrew a fixed amount of money each month. This was somewhat predictable because the sales literature showed that one could do this on a reasonable basis and likely still have assets available to hopefully grow over the years.

Still, it was an outflow, like a slow bleed, and it annoyed David to no end. Finally he hit upon a plan to staunch this particular drain on the fund's assets. When shareholders turned seventy, and every year thereafter, they got a happy birthday call from fund shareholder services. During the call, a discreet inquiry was made as to the health of the shareholder and his spouse. If the call turned up an indication of failing health, a second follow-up call was made by Old Gravel Throat. If he determined that it was likely there would be a death in the next three years, he would make a constructive suggestion to the shareholder.

They were told the big secret, that a great way to provide for their beneficiaries would be to first stop their monthly withdrawal and place all their assets in a trust for the beneficiaries, then run up a bunch of credit card bills, getting more and more cards until the shareholder had twenty or thirty of the darn things. Then, when the shareholder died, just stiff the credit card company. If they didn't die when their cards were maxed out and the debt service was eating all their Social Security money, then the fund would recommend a lawyer who would settle the debt for ten cents on the dollar.

This 'plug the leaks' program worked very well with almost a ninety-percent success ratio. People naturally hated banks and credit card companies. It was the phony money crowd trying to get their hooks into people, and most people were all too willing to fight back if someone would just show them how they could get even with the bankers. After 'plug the leaks' was implemented, monthly outflows dropped by sixty percent.

Shareholders died, but their money didn't have to die with them. Often enough a dead shareholder estate administrator omitted or neglected to discover all the decedent's assets, including mutual fund shares. The funds, however, always knew about a shareholder death because the fund's annual and semi-annual reports were returned to the fund by the post office as undeliverable. A scan of the obituaries confirmed the investor's death. By law, decedent assets were to be placed into state unclaimed asset accounts. David made a practice of dragging his feet on that regulatory requirement; in fact, it was just one of those things he never got around to doing. No doubt if an estate administrator or a state regulator ever traced missing estate funds to the fund, they would have been promptly remitted; however, that never happened. Dead person's monies were held in David's mother's trust account for him as the beneficiary in what turned out to be the permanent disposition of dead shareholder's former assets.

People calling UGGA to solve their investment account problems were directed to a special help line. These calls ran the gamut of lost checks, mistakes on purchase or redemption orders, changes in account registrations, beneficiary declarations, lost statements, lost tax reports, questions about portfolio holdings, proxy voting instructions, timing of the next distribution of income and capital gains, and shareholder meeting dates. These calls were mostly from people who were too lazy to read instructions sent to them, too sloppy to keep track of paperwork already sent to them, and too screwed up to remember who their family members were. David devised a system to handle all these requests with maximum efficiency, thereby saving fifty thousand man hours of duplicitous UGGA staff work each year.

Through black market purchases, David obtained bootlegged software that replicated the automated telephone answering systems of the Wyoming Department of Wildlife, the Internal Revenue Service, a major oil and gas company, a major mutual fund organization that operated forty different mutual funds, and the Environmental Advocacy Agency. He had a software engineer splice these phone systems into the UGGA phone system. In Man Child's office, an electronic status board was installed. It looked like five inverted Christmas trees with descending rows of lights which tracked the progression of up to five simultaneous callers.

When a shareholder called for shareholder services, the receptionist determined from her checklist of call inquiries if it was a call that David classified as a time-waster. The receptionist immediately transferred those calls to Old Gravel Throat. He listened courteously to the caller and then assured them that UGGA had a department specifically set up to deal with that particular problem. It didn't matter what the problem was; each shareholder received the same courteous understanding voice of Old Gravel Throat. Then he would say, "Madam, let me transfer you to the right people right away."

The call was transferred into the UGGA telephone answering system. In Man Child's office, the top left light on one of the inverted Christmas trees lit up, letting him know there was a caller in the phone system. The caller heard a voice telling her it would take fifteen to thirty minutes for the next available representative because of heavy call volumes. She could leave her number and someone would call her back—but no one ever called those people back—or she could wait.

After thirty minutes, another voice came on and said, "Your call is now being redirected. Please continue to hold." Then a voice would come on and say, "You have reached the Wyoming

Department of Wildlife. Push pound for Spanish. To report a poaching, press one. To apply for an elk license, press two. A moose license, press three. A bighorn sheep license, press four. A bear license, press five. For small game and bird licenses, press seven-seven. Please stay on the line for the next available agent. In the Tetons, the temperature is three degrees above zero in Jackson and twenty below on the mountaintops. Winds are gusting between thirty and fifty miles per hour. In the Powder River Basin, it's twelve above zero. Please continue to hold.

"If you want to hear elevator music while you wait, press one. If you want to hear the sounds of a moose in rut, press two. If you want to hear a cougar killing a deer, press three. For shotguns blasting geese out of the sky, press four. For coyotes tearing a rabbit apart, press five. For wolves howling at the moon, press six. If you think you have reached this recording in error, press the pound key."

The caller would press the pound key and get sent to the next telephone answering system, which was the one for the IRS. The recording would say, "All of our agents are busy serving other customers. Your wait time will be seventy-five minutes. Please stay on the line so you do not lose your place. Your wait time is now seventy-four minutes. Did you hear about our new tip-off program? You can get ten percent of the money we beat out of your friends if you turn them in to us for auditing. If you want to help crack down on these despicable tax cheats, press two. If you want to ask one of our agents about our witness protection program, press three. Only use this option if you are turning in drug dealers who steal more than one million dollars; otherwise, press four and continue holding. If you are calling about a tax refund, we will switch your call to our super service call center in the lovely country of Myanmar, where we have people who can't speak English standing by to help you. You'll need to have handy your Myanmar-to-English dictionary to assist with our prompt service. If you think you've reached this number in error, press the star key on your touch pad or scream an obscenity into your phone. Our agents will understand that. If you are using an obsolete phone, hang up and start over."

For those intrepid souls who made it to the next level a voice answered with "Congratulations, you have reached Bigger Than Ever Oil Company, or BTEOC. If you are calling to report an offshore oil spill, press one. An onshore oil spill, press two. If you are calling because some caribou got his antlers stuck in one of our drill platforms, press three. If a platform blew up and is spewing valuable crude into the ocean, press four. If you are calling to get permission to dynamite the ocean floor with a seismic shot, press five. If you are trying to report refinery explosions, press six. If you are an environmentalist or a representative of some environmental group, please press the pound key followed by the letters SAND, as in pound sand. If you are a First Nations representative and you want a better deal from us, we'll connect you to our used mobile home rental subsidiary. We'll also give you a ten percent off coupon for your next tank of gas. If you believe you reached this recording in error, press all the keys on your keypad simultaneously."

Those callers were sent to the major mutual fund company's phone software. The voice answered and said, "Hello, please tell us your social security number for verification purposes. Also give us your two credit card numbers with the biggest available credit lines so we can doubly check who you are. We can't be too careful. You know how it is! Thank you for that information. If you are calling about our Big Growth Fund, press one." If the caller pressed one, the voice came on again and said, "I'm sorry. We don't have a fund like that with you as a shareholder. Perhaps you want our bond fund? If so, press two." If the caller pressed two, the voice came back on and said, "I'm sorry. You must be calling the wrong place. We don't even have a bond fund." Then the voice gave the caller a raspberry over the phone and said, "If you believe you made this call in error, press six-nine followed by the pound key."

After being directed to the environmental software, a voice came on and said, 'Thank you for calling Bunny Huggers Screw Big Oil, or BHSBO. If you're part of our special study group that enters data on how many times a day a fruit fly fucks, please press one. If you're part of our hundred-billion-dollar study about how to relocate six minnow fish in Little Dipshit Creek, press two. If you're part of the polar exploration group that went to the North Pole to study global warming but got stuck in the ice a thousand miles south of the pole, press three. If you're from a university that's on our kickback program for falsified scientific studies, press four. If you are involved in our new Kill the Eagles Program and would like to volunteer to run around on the ground dressed like a chicken, we can relocate you and your family to one of our wind farms. If that interests you, press five. If you believe you've reached this number in error, please stay on the line and our next available agent will pick up in about fifteen minutes."

While the callers migrate their way through the phone maze, the lights on Man Child's inverted Christmas trees keep blinking. Only the most determined callers get through to the last light at the bottom of a given tree, and that caller got to speak to Man Child. After the light was steadily on for fifteen minutes, he turned away from watching gay porn and picked up the phone.

He answered with "Hello. If this is an emergency, hang up and dial 911. Otherwise, I'm Sergeant Doofus Botchitup. I'm ready to take down your homicide or kidnapping report. I must tell you that you are being recorded and by making this call you are automatically our prime suspect in this case. Now please give me your name, address, phone number, the name of the person murdered or kidnapped, and your whereabouts minute by minute for the last forty-eight hours. Be exact, madam. This information will go into your permanent criminal record file. Our crime lab will be in touch with you shortly. An officer will come to your home and pick you up, take you to the downtown station where you'll be fingerprinted, your blood will be drawn for DNA matching, your eyeballs will be retina scanned while fully dilated and you'll have a mug shot with front and side profile. Your eyes will get back to normal after about three hours."

At that point even those few who made it to the final light on the inverted tree hung up. A lot of paperwork was avoided using David's shareholder services telephone answering system.

FINS

There are those amongst humankind who possess what a psychologist would term a high emotional IQ. Their sensory faculties are fine-tuned to detect the slightest variances in a voice tone or facial expression when a narrative is proffered. They are razor-honed to note and retain the telltale giveaway that others signal when change interrupts their ordered world, like the spider they are, sitting in the center of their handiwork, called to action by the touch of the fly upon their sensory web. The slightest tilt of the eyebrow, dart-away of the eye, twitch or purse of the lips, or the expected reaction to a comment that was too long delayed to credibly be the honest reaction—these were but a few of the things David noticed about people. He'd knowingly honed his signal-gathering radars since childhood. A child often naturally did that to get the best of his parents, especially if the child knew his parents did not love him and wished he'd never been born.

After office hours over drinks one day, David asked Bob how things were for him in his after-hours life. Bob gave the predicted "all fine" response, except David wasn't buying it, as Bob gave a very slight, fleeting grimace prior to speaking. David knew it was time to make his move. Much like a spider is quick to follow its feeling vibrations to its prey in order to wrap a strand of silk over it and bind it to the web, David cast out a line to Bob, a chance to spend some time outside the four walls of his apartment and take a break from pounding the pavement.

"How would you like to get out for some fishing?"

Bob did fly fishing when he could and he presumed David wanted to walk riverbanks with him. "Sounds like fun. What day do you want to go?"

"Actually, I was thinking we could go for four or five days, really catch some great fish. I thought we'd go for salmon out of Astoria, Oregon. Would you be up for that?"

Bob was all for it and a week later, he and David were checked out of the office. Astoria, on the mouth of the Columbia, was renowned for its blackberries, raspberries, ice cream and bakery shops, and lovely harbor. Bears and cats liked the town as well. It was the logical choice for a salmon fishing outing.

David pointed out the monument column to John Jacob Astor, telling Bob everybody had the thing wrongly categorized. The column had a wraparound mural that detailed the history of the Astor family, but David remarked it was an excuse to build a big shaft to honor the first Astor because the guy was probably a big prick. Anyway, regardless of the reason they built the thing, the guy got a lot of Indians killed and had also killed lots of animals for their furs. That completed David's history lesson of Astoria.

Salmon fishing wasn't really fishing. There was no thought put into it whatsoever. There were no flies to tie, no hatch to work, no presentation skills were needed, and no line handling expertise was required, but it was challenging. In the summertime, the little salmon boats took in their lines from their piers at four in the morning and got underway.

In the great Pacific Northwest, four in the morning was not an ungodly hour like it was in latitudes farther south. The sun wasn't up yet, but the people and the daylight were sort of sleepily up. It was a misty, fishy-smelling time of morning. Occasional harbor noises of gulls squawking, seamen opening and closing deck hatches, and emptying buckets of herring into boat bait wells separated sleep time from fish time. It was that yawn widely time, that eerie haunting time where boats bobbed to the slow harbor wave action and some dame in an artist's beret sat on a stool with her easel and paints. Cats yawned, stretched, watched the scene and licked their chops in anticipation of fish gut piles and unused bait that would be thrown their way when the boats returned.

David and Bob went to their chartered boat, met its captain, got their raingear for the predictable Pacific morning rain showers, and took their seats. The skipper gave them their nautical briefing, which was basically to hold on tight after he moved the vessel out of the harbor and downriver, or head below so they didn't bounce off. He told the landlubbers he'd take the boat over the bar. In years past, many ships failed to navigate the ocean breakers that met the mouth of this mightiest of all Northwest rivers. It was where ships breached into the swells and succumbed to the wave action, which broke up their keels, battered their gunnels, and sank many of them. Men died. It was where the ocean collided with the river. It was the bar.

His mighty twin diesel engine six hundred horse-powered craft was unlikely to meet such a dastardly fate, the skipper assured them. They would use max power and slam head-on into the swells and the waves, thus avoiding the fates of hundreds of lesser crafts. The only drawback to the skipper's method of clearing the bar was that all on board would feel like they were riding a rodeo bull while inhaling copious fumes of diesel exhaust, so of course his passengers should expect to barf their guts out. The skipper's briefing was followed by a hearty "Har har" and an offer of some warmed-up coffee left over from the previous day's outing, or whiskey, the staple of every man of the sea. David and Bob declined the coffee and whiskey, already skittish enough about the bar crossing and not wanting to put more stress on their stomachs. Bob soon wondered why he'd volunteered for this torture. After leaving the harbor, the skipper took the brave little vessel into the Columbia and raced for the bar. In short order, they were at the place where the mouth of the Columbia met the North Pacific. Columbia's mighty flow meets Pacific's swells, producing a relentless wave chop. The force of all King Neptune's fury lifted up and plunged downward the puny shipyard creations of mortal men. The landlubbers clung to their little chartered craft as it alternatively pointed vertically skyward and then headlong downward into the roiling gray watery Hades. As if the pitching and the roll of the mad ride weren't enough, for nausea-inducing measure the skipper slammed his throttles full ahead to squeeze enough power from the twin diesels to punch his craft headlong into the onrushing swells. Onward, ever onward they went, into their cascading water ranks of death and hell. The engines screamed and belched suffocating billows of nauseous fumes. The ride, the fumes, and the churning caused both David and Bob to barf over the side while holding onto the rail. After what felt like an eternity in hell, the boat finally reached the open ocean. They'd found the perfect spot to catch salmon, according to the skipper.

There was a fourth man on the boat. His job was to rig the poles, bait the fish hooks with herring smelts, and gaff the hooked fish. David joked to this hapless deckhand when they boarded after the skipper introduced him. "So you're the guy who baits the hooks, huh? I guess that would make you the boat's Chief Masturbator!" He let out a snickering laugh. The young man was embarrassed, and no one else laughed.

Fishing for salmon meant sitting around drinking beer out of a can while the bait man rigged the hooks and threw the lines in the ocean. Fishing poles were placed in socket holders and the boat chugged along at about one or two knots. Pole lines grew taut and rod tips dipped when the fish were 'on.' The customer then picked up the bending pole and reeled in the hapless salmon that had swallowed the hook and doomed itself before it could swim upstream to spawn. Once alongside, the deckhand gaffed or netted the hapless fish and swung it aboard in a well-timed motion. The line and hook were ripped or cut away from the salmon's gullet and its traumatized corpse. With still-breathing gills and flapping tail it was thrown into the fish tank. Once the daily limit of fish was caught, the boat headed back to the harbor. Paying guests suffered a second mind-numbing buckaroo ride as the craft traversed the bar retuning. With breakfasts long gone, nothing but greenish-brown beer slime remained to barf up on the return trip.

Walking off the pier toward the quay wall, wobbly sea legs halting their locomotion, David put his hand on Bob's back. "How'd you like the fishing trip?"

Bob thought David's hand was intended as a gesture of pride and solidarity in accomplishment when they'd accomplished nothing except paying to get sick and kill four helpless fish. The fishing was nothing like the challenge of stream fishing. Bob reflected that David probably had no idea what it was like to actually go fishing for the sport of it. He noticed that David purposely let his hand linger longer than necessary for natural camaraderie.

Two more fishing trips followed, one for sturgeon and one for bass. For the big bottom-feeding sturgeons, the duo again went to Astoria on a different week and chartered a boat. That time they went on a smooth trip upriver and dropped anchor. It was a hot sunny day. Their skipper suggested they strip to their bathing suits while he rigged the poles and baited the hooks. Bob went below and changed into his baggy trunks and a tee shirt. When he came up on deck, he saw David sprawled out on a deck chair wearing only a Speedo. Bob avoided looking at David's body. Marty had it right when she told him that she thought it must be gross. A huge flabby gut spilled over his lower abdomen, the fat ooze stopping just above the strap pouch which appeared to hold two tiny walnuts. They were distinctly visible against the skintight fabric. Bob sat in the adjacent deck chair while David babbled about how he loved the outdoors and fresh air. They caught three sturgeons each and canned them at the local cannery like they did the salmon.

A third fishing trip was to a godforsaken bass lake in the middle of Mexico, to which they drove in a rented car over several hundred miles of potholed roads. They passed a half-dozen checkpoints manned by teenage boys dressed in soldiers' garb and armed with machine guns. At the lake they lodged in a compartmentalized prefabricated structure with thin walls between the bedrooms. The cook was a jovial Mexican gal, and for three days they ate bass for breakfast, lunch, and dinner, fishing the lake in guided canoes for more. They caught dozens of the scaly, spiny-finned things. From weed-infested haunts amongst standing dead trees and floating logs, the bass unleashed their angry slams against surface popper lures. Like lightning bolts launched from a watery underworld, these game fish shot to the surface to hit the lures and fight mightily. The wide-mouthed monsters were bold and unafraid of the blood sport they played.

On the last day, David's straw sombrero blew off his head when a powerful storm came up. He yelled to the guide to forget the hat and row for shore, but Bob countermanded David. Speaking Spanish, he took charge of matters, he and the guide rowing dangerously broadside to the wave chop and retrieving the hat.

Back on the beach, David was furious with Bob.

"You could have gotten me killed," he blurted out. "I ordered him to go to shore because I can't swim."

"No reason to get upset. The water wasn't that bad. Besides, if we'd gone over, I would have swum for both of us and brought you back."

"But if I had struggled and fought you off, like a drowning man does?"

"Not to worry. I'd have just knocked you out, put an arm under your neck, and paddled you back."

"You would have actually punched me?"

"You bet. I'd punch you right in your mouth to knock you out cold."

"You wouldn't feel regret that you hit me?"

"No, none. Would you rather drown?" Bob's hypothetical answer was given with a matter-of-fact chuckle without the slightest hint of emotion.

David ignored Bob's question. "But there are poisonous cottonmouth snakes out there. I'd be helpless."

"Yeah, but they are over nearer the shoreline and the trees where we were fishing, not in the middle of the lake where you lost your hat."

David stared at Bob, looking perplexed, but said nothing.

That night, through the wall that separated their beds, Bob awakened from the sound of David crying. He listened for a while, determining it wasn't the cry of a man in physical pain. There was no cursing paired with the sobs and no inhaled hissings like men give when they cut a toe or a finger. This was a sobbing cry, a low-grade whimpering, muffled, private kind of cry from a man losing a wrestling match with his inner turmoil. Bob puzzled over this episode and rationalized that David was so deeply afraid for his life that day that he had a near breakdown over the incident. He figured David would get over it and then rolled over and went back to sleep. Bob couldn't relate to the feelings that tormented David.

HOOVES

North of Plaintown, elevation increases to the Grand Plateau. It rises gradually, gaining about a thousand feet whereupon it reaches a place Colorado men go to become real men, a place called Wyoming.

David suggested to Bob that he should become a big game hunter like himself. Hunting sharpens the senses and wits, he declared, and there was no greater thrill than to track down an animal in the wild, although he'd never actually done it. What better way to get acquainted with big game hunting than to go together on an antelope hunt in neighboring Wyoming. Bob agreed that it sounded like a fun idea, a chance to go into the wilds of open-space Wyoming. To properly outfit Bob for the hunt, David presented him with the gifts of a 7mm magnum rifle and a brand-new Jeep Wagoneer.

David rented a large sleeper trailer that accommodated six for the two of them. They provisioned it with enough food for a full week in the field and plenty of beer and whiskey. David's plan was to take the antelope by surprise. He consulted with some ranchers who knew the area and wrote down detailed instructions; they would be in position at the first light of dawn. As soon as their rifle scopes could pick out some big bucks, they would whack the fleet-footed beasts before they even got out of bed. That was the plan, but the antelope were never consulted about it.

There was a special, secret place in Wyoming about half-way north of the Snowy Range, west of Horseshoe and the edge of the Yellowstone Plateau which rose further west. A huge wide-open bowl-shaped basin area existed there where the mountains begin to lift up from the plateau. It was inaccessible from the north or the west or the east because of the rugged terrain, except for antelope, cougar, wolf, or bear. It was where the deer and the antelope played.

The lowest place in the bowl had water, a stream flowing into a catch basin from a cool water spring a ways off to the west. Just east of the little basin lake was an elevated spot where an old buck pronghorn liked to lay at night with his herd of thirty other antelope. He was out of harm's way there, sheltered on three sides by rugged rising terrain. He could see for about ten miles to the south, the only viable approach for man, his most feared mortal adversary. He was a wily old goat, this herd-master pronghorn. He was all muscle and easily topped fifty miles per hour running flat-out over rock-strewn prairie, changing direction in sharp-angle turns at full speed by planting his hooves and whipping his body into a new heading.

Close beside him on his lookout perch were seven adoring does. Each doe alternately looked up from feeding, turned her head, and scanned the horizon. When awakened, his herd had sixty eyes constantly searching to the horizon as one unified body. The herd master had outsmarted dozens of hunters' attempts to kill him over the past seven years. He understood that hunters would never relent in their quest for his magnificent standout horns, but he remained determined to never have his head and horns mounted on a hunter's wall.

On that particular morning, the faint prairie breeze started up as it was want to do in pre-dawn Wyoming. The tips of the cheat grass began to bend slightly as they had for millions of such fall mornings on the vast expanse. It was how the prairie welcomed the sun. A flock of junkets whirred about in some brush around thirty yards below the herd buck. He could hear their feathered wings flutter as they prepared to get out of their evening quarters and flit and skip over the prairie floor searching for rising insects. Dawn's first light was still about a half hour away, so except for the junkets all should've been still, unless a cougar or bear was stealing its way toward his herd.

But there was something else that morning; it was far away and made an unnatural sound. His ears pointed toward the sound, taking it in and processed all it told him. Men were out there, coming in a motorized vehicle. Its motor was straining a bit and it clanked along more than most he'd heard before. It was noisy, but still too far away to bother a decision about what he should do about it. He let out a grunt. Twenty-seven females and two lesser bucks lifted their heads. All sixty eyes were on full alert.

Bob drove the Jeep that towed the trailer over a narrow, twisted dirt road which featured massive rock outcrops along the roadside. The hunters were running a half hour behind their planned schedule, as David had to dump out his intestines just as they were scheduled to start off. That took ten minutes and couldn't be postponed. The instructions had to be off, David had declared about an hour before. The rancher told them to turn left at the intersection, which they did, and then they were to go for fifty-seven miles and turn right. That's as definitive and explicit as a Wyoming rancher gets when he gives directions to somebody driving up from Plaintown to hunt antelope. At the fifty-six-and-a-half-mile mark, there was a right turn. David claimed that that road must have been the one the rancher meant, or else the odometer on the Jeep must be off a little, so they turned right.

After about a five-mile drive that meandered back eastward, they came upon a ranch house right where the road stopped. They got out of their Jeep and looked around for a road bypass around the ranch house, but the road didn't go further; it just dead-ended at that ranch house. The commotion woke up a dog that barked its head off. Then a rancher with a shotgun came out to greet them in his pajamas. After making their apologies and gathering renewed instructions, Bob and David got back on the road. They went another half mile and turned right, like they were told to do in the first place. With great difficulty and considerable cursing, they turned their rig about and made their way along the correct road.

David was miffed. "You'd think that rancher who gave me directions would have told me about the first turn just a half mile before."

"He probably thought you knew how to follow directions."

Silence ensued. David resented cynicism.

The road they found was different from the ranch road. It didn't have deep pickup truck ruts with grass growing in the middle hump. This road was graded two years or so before, but it was in many respects more miserable than the first. Looking ahead as far as their headlights would take them, a fine gray-white gritty dust rose. The early prairie breeze was behind them. As their Jeep and trailer crawled along, the breeze picked up their trail dust, lifted it to the window level of the vehicle, and swirled it into the beams of their headlights. Antelope along the trail for three miles in every direction saw the reflective sparkles of dust dancing in the headlight beams. They all knew hunters were here.

When David rented the trailer, he'd inspected it completely to make sure the interior quarters were clean and working properly to his satisfaction. The shower, toilet, and stove all worked fine. In order to climb up to enter and inspect the mobile hunt headquarters, a set of metal stairs had to be released from their holding latch. The salesman didn't notice, Bob didn't notice, and David forgot to secure the stairs when he finished his inspection. Because of their delay getting started, his hopes of slamming the herd buck at daybreak were slipping away. Although it would mean making more noise to go faster, he hoped the herd buck was a late snoozer and wouldn't notice.

As Bob picked up speed, the rig made a clamoring racket as the trailer bounced over the hard feldspar road rocks, careening from side to side as it dragged behind the Jeep. He drove fast to keep the choking road talcum out of the Jeep's passenger compartment. Neither hunter heard the trailer's steps fall down from their upright stowed position. They were fully extended in their down position when the fast-moving Jeep passed between two gigantic rock outcrops. With scant clearance on either side, the trailer didn't make it.

The rocks were fifty-ton boulders which didn't yield a smidgeon to the steps that protruded three feet from the trailer's side. The hunters heard a sickening, gut-wrenching sound as the steps caught the right rock wall, the Jeep lurching left as the forward momentum of the rig ripped a gaping opening in the side of the trailer. The gigantic rock can opener with its ragged jaws ripped the aftermost two-thirds of the trailer wide open and jerked its body sideways off the trailer frame. The rig twisted free from its hitch to the Jeep and rested diagonally across the road. It was a wounded metal beast lodged between the rocks. Their hunt was off to a terrible start.

Farther up the trail, at the basin, the herd buck stood up and peered in the direction of the clamoring and crashing, but he couldn't see around corners and the rig came to rest below his visible horizon. Nevertheless, he and the others arose, evacuated, and moved west about a mile before they began grazing. Antelope couldn't be too careful.

Bob and David decided to forgo hunting that first day and drove the Jeep back to a nearby town. Towns in much of Wyoming weren't very large, and this one was no exception. It had a gas station, a liquor, and a general store outpost for hunting and fishing supplies and licenses. When they pulled up to the general store, Bob and David noticed there was a German shepherd lying in front of the entrance door.

"I wonder if he'd bite us," David said.

"Don't know. I'll blow the horn and see if anybody comes out." After a horn blast, an older man, tall and sinewy of build and heavily bearded, shoved the door open and moved the dog out of the way.

"What you fellers want?"

Bob reckoned he was the owner of the place.

"We need a place to stay the night, and we need somebody to retrieve a damaged motor home trailer," said David. He went on to explain how the trailer got stuck in the rocks on the trail road to the basin.

The tall bearded man spit out some chew tobacco and began laughing. "You boys wouldn't be frem Colrado, wood ja?" It was obvious the station master—or mayor, or owner, or whatever he was—was sizing them up to see how much he could charge them. People from Colorado were likely to be easy pickings for overcharges.

David confessed the obvious; after all, the Jeep had Colorado plates. He agreed to an exorbitant, bordering on extortion, sum to have the trailer retrieved. The sinewy man revealed he was the owner of the general store, as well as the motel across the street. His wife ran the motel and he doubled as the go-to man with a bulldozer for emergencies such as rescuing Coloradans who got themselves into messes in Middle of Nowhere, Wyoming.

David rented a motel room for the duration of the hunt. He called the rental dealer in Plaintown and complained about the latch not holding the steps in place, threatened to sue the trailer maker and the dealer for faulty equipment and putting his life at risk, and told them he'd deal with them when he returned to Colorado. Meanwhile, he and Bob got the only remaining room in the motel that night; it was hunting season and the only time the motel was more than one-tenth occupied. Their great hunt would start tomorrow.

In their room with two twin beds, David shouted out loud, angry with himself. "We blew it. We weren't thinking. We should have thought it through first."

"What? Thought what through?"

"The accident and the trailer! We should have set fire to it and let the rental company collect the insurance instead of billing us for the accident."

"That'd be worse. That's arson. Those things get investigated by insurance companies. They don't just automatically pay. If they find arson, it's jail time. We're doing the right thing. Besides, there's insurance for the collision."

"Yeah, but we'll get stuck paying the deductible."

"Beats jail. Good night." Bob turned the lights out.

After a while David turned the lights back on. Bob was nearly asleep when he turned toward David's bed to see why he'd turned the lights on. There was David sitting naked on the edge of the bed, crying while stroking an erection and looking wistfully at Bob. Through sobs and teary eyes, David moaned in pitiful whimpers. When he saw Bob was awake, he began a baleful tale of woe.

"Nobody has ever loved me," he sobbed in a wretched display of self-abasement. "Nobody wants to hold me and kiss me because I'm so ugly, and I can't help it. I'm terribly overweight and I have awful body odor. I stink. I'm sure you've smelled me, haven't you?" Bob just shrugged as if to say 'so what.' David continued. "I can't urinate right. A lot of my urine comes out through my skin. That's why I stink so badly. I shower three times a day. I use colognes, but I still stink." He paused between his sobs, his eyes hopeful for sympathy.

"Well, why don't you see a doctor about it?" Bob was non-committal, eager to change the subject.

David continued stroking his penis.

"I hated my mother from the time I was a child. My father was always trying to get rid of me, trying to send me away. They left me millions but they never loved me, especially mother. I even heard her say that she wished I'd never been born. I've hated all women ever since I heard her say that."

"You hate all women?" Bob couldn't understand David or anyone hating women. He adored women, practically every one of them, even though his own mother was abusive and dictatorial toward him as a child.

"Yes, I hate all women. Over the years I've grown more and more distant from women and closer and closer to men. Oh, I've tried to be attracted to women, and some of them I've even been able to make love to, but it's impossibly hard for me."

Where David was trying to lead Bob with his pitiful suggestive words and behavior was unmistakable. All his suspicions about David came into focus. David's lingering hand on his back at the pier in Astoria, the trips away in and of themselves, the gift of the rifle and Jeep, the trip they were on now—all were his manipulations to try to get Bob to become his lover. It was never about a father and son relationship as David purported it to be, nor about a business partnership. It was all a grand pathetic manipulation played out over many years.

Bob rolled his head to the side, away from David, who persisted. "When we first started working together, I saw in you a man like my father, only something more. Dad was Dad, but he was also my partner and my best friend. I loved him, but he never loved me." Bob wasn't about to ask what more he could be to David than son, partner, and friend. Lover was the only base uncovered and Bob wasn't about to go there. He was as straight as a man could be.

"I thought you said your dad always pushed you away?" He pointed out David's inconsistency.

"Yes, he sent me away, but I still thought of Dad as my best friend. I loved him, but he didn't love me. When you and I met, I thought we could have the same relationship Dad and I had, only more. I thought I could be like a dad to you and a partner and a best friend, only more. I thought I could love you and you could also love me."

This was getting way too weird for Bob. He needed to disabuse David of any notion that they'd ever be lovers. His eyebrows went up to their full extent and his jaw dropped open as he stared at the ceiling.

"Look, David, I've got to be honest with you. You are a great guy. You are a great friend and a great partner, and you are like a dad to me. I've learned a great deal from you and we're making the business grow, but you need to forget about me loving you. You need to understand that I'm wired very differently than you are. I love women. I mean that I love them as an opposite sex love. I love holding them, kissing them, and fucking them. There's nothing about any man that even remotely interests me. I've been attracted to women sexually since I was a little kid, and I also like a lot of them as people I can be friends with. That works for me and I'm not going to be changing that. I'm sorry to tell you this, but I had no idea that's what you expected of me. I just can't be in love with you. I was in love with Marty, and I guess you could say I'm open to a woman's love again, but that's it for me. I've never been in love with a man and I never could be. I'm not a homosexual, and I don't want to become one either. You need to understand that about me and forget this notion of yours."

"Haven't you ever even considered trying it, just once? It can really be beautiful." David wasn't giving up easily.

"No. I've never tried it, I've never thought about trying it, I don't even want to think about trying it, and I really want to stop talking about it. Okay? Look, David, there are probably a lot of men out there who would like to be your lover. I'll bet even a few of them you have in the office right now would happily be your lover if you asked, don't you think?" Bob gave David a knowing look.

"They're not the same as you. They're not smart. They just get what they can from me. They use me." David's face was sad, the model of rejection.

"Well, that's something you need to work out with them. You always said you were going to handle the office, so I'm sure you can handle it if you set your mind to it. Now let's get some sleep and get out there tomorrow and whack us a couple antelope. That's what we came here for, wasn't it?"

With that, Bob turned over to go back to sleep, leaving David sitting there holding his penis and nursing hurt feelings.

The early fall sun beat down hot and harsh on Wyoming's high prairies. There was a light wind the next day, a little stronger than the previous day's. It would be only a few more days before a brisk steady wind would suck out the residual scant moisture that clung to the soil after the hot dry summer. Those last vestiges of wetness were rising skyward into the high Wyoming blue and becoming wisps of cirrus that would race away to Nebraska. The ground was already caked and blistered. Trails made by man and animal were rock-strewn dust paths on the omnipresent talcum gray grit. On some few mornings as this one, a hint of dew kissed the leaves of sage and clung to the shrubs' blue buds and dark grease-gray brambles. The antelope were pocketed in small herds close to what water they could find, with the finest animals commanding the best watering holes.

Morning came for the fearless hunters from Plaintown, but they figured there was no point getting an early start. It was more important to eat a hearty breakfast, as strength would be needed to steady their rifles and stamina demanded to dress their kills. They wolfed down bacon and eggs, letting their Jewish taboos about not eating pork take a holiday because of the dire necessity of the hunt. They ignored the Jewish aversion to hunting, so they figured they might as well capitulate to goyim food as well. They packed pancakes drowned in maple syrup and hash browns drenched in Tabasco into their tummies. To properly fortify themselves and screw up their manly courage to face the wild beasts of the plains, they each had two shots of whiskey before they headed out, telling themselves the local antelope were in for a heap of trouble.

Back on the gritty dust trail, passing the wrecked trailer, Bob's mood was upbeat and anticipatory. He tried to crack some antelope and jackalope jokes, but David's mood was dour and sullen as he rode shotgun while Bob drove. David barely spoke. He wasn't having fun and he determined, while bouncing and bumping along over the dusty trail road, that he wasn't going to let Bob have any fun either.

When they arrived below the little rise atop of which one could glance at the entire basin, the duo stepped out of the Jeep and climbed the hill. The sun had already risen enough to evaporate the dew. Images in the distance appeared through the binoculars to waver and shimmer in the midmorning heat. Through their binoculars, there appeared to be a herd of antelope off in the distance, gathered around a small lake at the lowest part of an immense topographical basin. The hunters reckoned their quarry was about five miles away. The antelope were gathered around a small lake at the lowest part of an immense topographical basin. There were jutted rocks on a steep hill behind them, and the hilly terrain reached down in a wide arc like a pair of arms reaching almost all the way across the basin. The hunters reckoned their quarry was about five miles away.

David spoke first. "I think we're in luck. It looks like we've got them trapped right there against those rocks. I know something about antelope. They like to run on the flat prairie, so they're not going to want to run up into those rocks. The only way they can get out of there is to come out onto the prairie, to run straight at us. So here's what we'll do. I'll drive while you chamber a round and roll your window down. Now don't let your rifle barrel be seen aimed out the window because they'll see the glint of the sun on the metal and they'll know we're after them. Keep the rifle in front of you with the butt end on the floor of the Jeep and the barrel pointed up to the roof. Got it?"

"Got it."

"Okay. We'll start off slowly toward them so they won't notice what we're doing. If they look at us, we'll stop for a minute before we drive forward some more. When we get close enough, I'll gun the car and we'll run straight at them. They'll have to come running straight at us to get out of there. When one runs by the side of the Jeep on your side, you shoot it."

Bob was visualizing a head-on cavalry charge between a Jeep going fifty miles per hour in one direction toward the antelope herd running fifty miles per hour in the opposite direction.

"Don't you think it might be hard to get a bead on one of them? We'll be bouncing all over the place, the antelope will be jumping and running, and our relative speed will be a hundred miles per hour."

"You can't obsess over details at a time like this. The antelope are right there in front of us. They're trapped! They can't get away. We may never get another chance like this in our lifetimes. Details have a way of working themselves out anyway. Maybe one of them will accidentally run into the Jeep and we won't even have to shoot it, or maybe one will break a leg near you and it'll be an easy shot. Just go with the program and get ready for a shot, okay?"

"Okay."

The old buck antelope knew it was hunting season again. The day before, he'd heard some shots in the distance and figured the hunters would soon be coming to his basin pond looking to take one or two of his herd. The rancher only allowed one or two hunters on his property each year. The old buck figured that out years back because there were always only one or two hunters. They always hunted together, or nearly together, so once he located them and understood their tactical plan, he easily outsmarted them. The hunters only killed one or two of his herd every fourth year. The old buck liked his odds.

This year started off curiously for the herd master buck. The day before, he'd heard a terrible racket of metal being ripped apart by rock. This was a tactic he'd never encountered before, so his senses were on high alert. He and his females could see the two hunters five miles away when they crawled up on the far hillside to peer at his herd with their binoculars. He'd seen hunters do that before. That usually meant they'd be sneaking around to the north or south, keeping themselves invisible by staying low to the ground and slipping between the rocks. He probably had a good two hours while the hunters stalked his herd. He would watch north and south for their telltale signs.

Some sparrows or a magpie would flush up unnaturally, or he'd catch a glimpse of the shiny orange vests they wore. Maybe a ground squirrel would be disturbed and it would scamper up on a rock and bark at them, or it could be a prairie dog. It didn't matter how quiet they were or how long they took; he would know exactly where they were, where they were headed, and how much longer he had before he moved the herd. He was an old hand at this game and was much smarter than the best of the hunters.

What the old buck saw next positively amazed him. There was a Jeep driving straight toward his herd. The buck knew the hunters never shot from their vehicles, so he wasn't quite sure what this Jeep was trying to do. Then it stopped. The buck looked carefully. It was about three miles way now, still out of rifle range. The buck looked for signs of the hunters. They were still in the Jeep, and no other hunters were near it. Then he saw a tiny reflection coming from inside the Jeep. The bolt of the rifle carried by the man in the passenger seat caught a glint of the sun's rays as the passenger moved it ever so slightly. The old buck realized they were going to illegally hunt his herd from their vehicle.

This required an innovative strategy. The buck sent his leading female off to the north with the herd. She led the others close to the rocks along the down slope. They knew enough to run straight up the rocks and over the top of the ridge if the Jeep came toward them.

The old buck devised a plan. If the animal had been a human chess player, he would have been a master. About a half mile due south of the basin pond ran an arroyo about twenty feet deep from its prairie level top to its bottom. The trail through the washout was strewn with rocks on its sides and floor, deposited there by centuries of flash floods from downpours. The rocks were foreboding silent sentinels that thwarted the arroyo's passage from all but the nimblest creatures. The old buck didn't like going in there, for he handicapped his greatest advantage by doing so—he could only see for a few feet ahead instead of for miles. But this was war between man and beast, and he was not one to play by conventional rules. Over the years he'd seen dust fly up near his hoofs from the whining rifle bullets. He'd heard the bullets zing past his head and watched their lethal effect upon his does and his offspring. He didn't know how to be angry or to hate, but he knew something about the men who did.

The arroyo was a topographical barrier between the basin pond and the open prairie, a feature the old buck used to his advantage when he needed it, as he did now. If the hunters were going to play dirty, so would he. He followed along behind the herd for a while, and when he was behind some field boulders he broke off and crawled on his belly with his head low until he was out onto the flat, unseen by the hunters. He slipped down into the arroyo, then ran along its bottom channel until he figured he'd be directly in front of the men. He heard their Jeep approaching, moving faster now because the hunters saw the herd moving. When he was certain they were less than a half mile from him, the old buck sprang into action. Up out of the arroyo he bounded, standing in the open. He was the most magnificent specimen on the prairie. Many a hunter coveted his rack and visualized his head upon their trophy room wall. He stood proudly in front of the Jeep a mere half mile distant, but beyond the left front driver's side. The passenger shooter had no shot.

"There's a real big one!" screamed David. "It looks like we've got the herd buck. Let's get that one!" He turned the Jeep toward the old buck and floored the accelerator. The buck just stood there, frozen as if he didn't know what to do. At about four hundred yards, the buck took off running in a sprint toward the east, running parallel to the top of the arroyo. In the space of two seconds, the buck went from standing still to a fifty-mile-an-hour blur of white, brown and gray. David turned right, giving chase at full speed. The buck slowed slightly, allowing the Jeep to close some. "He's slowing down. He's confused!" shouted David. "Get ready for your shot." The buck let the Jeep come still closer.

The Jeep was now going fifty miles per hour on open prairie, bouncing over rocks and clumps of cheat grass, crushing sagebrush as it flew over the ground. At a perfectly timed moment, divined by the gods of antelopes, and in their innate genius to use relative movement to their advantage, the old buck turned again slightly. It was the antelope move to go down in the history of all antelope moves. It was the move that grown men marveled over as they drank their whiskey by their campfires and extoled the genius of this magnificent fleet-footed creature that outran the wind.

The old buck veered right, a quick jaunt to the south, now running hard, flat-out toward the open area. There was a blur of brown and white muscles flexing full power, propelling flying hoofs to stretch over open prairie. First the outreaching front hoofs touched earth; then, just as the front hooves touched down, the muscular rump gathered up the back legs underneath the buck's chest and thrust them back in a bounding, graceful motion, propelling the buck forward. The buck's dodge move succeeded. David careened the Jeep toward the antelope but before he could ascertain the landscape, it was too late. The Jeep was headed straight toward a blackish-purple rock outcrop on an otherwise open plain. Rocks grew on Wyoming's prairie surface like dandelions grew on suburban lawns, and there were several dead ahead.

"Stop! Rocks! Turn!" screamed Bob, but it was all too late. Maybe David could have turned the wheel and avoided the rocks. Maybe he was just too slow, or maybe he just didn't care. The Jeep hit those rocks going fifty miles per hour. There was a sickening sound of metal crashing and grinding on rock as sparks flew from the basalts and granite in the hardened, unmovable jumble. The body of the Jeep tried valiantly to rush onward without its undercarriage as the vehicle engaged the unmovable mass of unyielding, unsympathetic rock. The Jeep's axles, transmission, drive shaft, oil pan, and assorted parts accessory to the engine were all left behind on the rocks. The frame welds snapped and the body shuddered as it ground itself into the dirt. Then came the ominous hissing sounds, followed by the flames. The fuel tank ruptured and the Jeep was burning. The two hunters scrambled from their wreck and ran for their lives.

The vehicle didn't explode, just burned quietly. Jeeps are made to serve the stupidest hunters in the world, to the very end of the vehicles' lives, even while they are going up in flames. That's why hunters swear by them.

Once he heard the Jeep hit the rocks, the old buck slipped back down into the arroyo. He ran along its bottom, back in the direction from which he'd first entered the formation. He knew to stay invisible to hunters between his appearances. He trotted out on the far bank about a mile and a half away, when he knew he was out of their rifle range, and then turned back to peruse his handiwork. Two men stood off about twenty yards from a flaming wreck. They were staring at the wreck and no longer paying attention to him.

No one could say for sure what that old buck was thinking about that day. Was the whole Jeep chase something he'd planned? Did he know the outcome before he entered the arroyo in the first place, or did he improvise as the chase moved along? The two hunters finally turned and looked at him from afar. Across the divide of distance, species, and evolution, the two antagonists stared at each other for a moment to memorialize their encounter. The old buck turned away from them and loped off to join his females. The hunters could only wonder what that old goat was capable of as they watched him slip away.

"Let's go back to town and get somebody to come out here to clean up this mess," David said. "I'll give you some money to make up for the Jeep. I just didn't see the rocks in time," he fibbed.

Bob kept his mouth shut about David's driving, but he was seething inside. The hunt didn't need to be the fiasco it'd turned out to be. He couldn't help but wonder if David, when the opportunity was there, decided to punish him for not being a homosexual. If that were true, there was a side of David's personality he was seeing for the first time, and it was chilling. Barbara had given him fair warning. The man could be a monster, a duplicitous schemer, and a vengeful bully child in a man's body when he couldn't have his way with other people.

Bob was relieved to be on the ground with his life back under his own control. It felt good to walk. As they walked along on the sun-parched prairie, their plodding steps stirring the alkaline gray grit powder, Bob wondered if his entire relationship with David was based upon an elaborate trap by a terribly desperate and lonely man who was in a deep human need for a homosexual companion, a steady love interest who had a brain.

Was Bob just the mark in some elaborate sick game? Were the fishing trips all a pretense to bait a relationship? Did David deliberately fail to secure the stairs? David knew there were rock walls on the trail; he'd mentioned it on the drive up from Plaintown. The only significant difference between the trailer and the motel room was the motel had running water. The trailer had limited water. David needed frequent showers. Could it possibly be that David went to all this trouble just to make a pathetic advance on him? *The mind can go into paranoia at times. It must be doing that now.* There was no way David could have known the motel would have one room available, unless he'd reserved it in advance. That would be confidential between David and the motel owner.

Bob willed his mind to climb off its hamster wheel. Regardless of David's personal turmoil, they had their agreement and Bob was performing his part. The agreement was separate from the personal, and David would never break a deal. Despite his personal difficulty, the man was honorable. Their mutual loyalty to each other and the firm was very strong. Besides, after working for the firm for eight years and taking a terrible drop in income, Bob could see his best choice of action was to keep his part of their deal and see it through to the end, until David died.

He felt sorry for David and wanted to be a good friend to him, but he just couldn't become a homosexual. He wasn't wired that way, and the thought of behaving against his natural heterosexual attraction to women repulsed him. As he and David walked past the wrecked trailer wedged between the rock boulders, two doe antelope stood off about a hundred yards from the trail. They alternated, first one standing there chewing its mouthful while watching the hunters as the other one grazed on cheat grass and sage and then switching.

The four antelope eyes weren't the only ones that tracked the movements of the hunters. The excitement of the hunt and the Jeep crash caught the attention of a fully matured male half-breed lobo. His yellow eyes watched the old buck's movements and the antics of the hunters with the thought that he would learn some lessons for his hunts. He attentively watched every detail of the old buck's movements before his olfactory senses told him this hunt offered more than he saw.

David did not shower that morning. Amid the scents of digesting bacon and whiskey, the huge canine detected something different. Coyotes and wolves can smell opportunity from miles away; only one molecule in a million needs to touch their scent receptors. The lobo detected a hint of internal decay. His nose informed him the older human was in the early stages of internal organ distress. David's renal functions were declining and, if left untreated, he would succumb as urine failed to process and gradually poison him. This condition was unbeknownst to David, but the lobo knew.

When an animal's organs begin to fail, its body tries to rid itself of poisonous wastes by secretions through the pores of its skin. The lobo instinctively knew if he tracked the smell of this afflicted animal long enough its scent would eventually lead him to its carcass. When the two hunters drove back to Plaintown in their rented car, they kept the windows down to enjoy the rushing breeze of the cool high plains air. Many miles behind them, following patiently and occasionally stopping to scent the air, trotted the huge lobo.

PEACHY

David wasn't about to give up on Bob. Marvin taught him, if he taught him anything, that to be successful in any endeavor he needed to be persistent. Marvin succeeded in building the UGGA's advisory business by cultivating the opinion leaders of all Plaintown's temples. Marvin succeeded in cultivating the Plaintown's union pension plan business by being persistent, going to their meetings, championing their causes, coaching them on political initiatives to gain greater influence in the city, and ultimately sharing Susan with their leadership. His mantra was "The recipe for success in anything is to do whatever it takes." His parental mentoring was the guiding principal for David, in business and in life.

For a time, David rationalized Bob's rejection. *He's just immature or from such an uncultivated childhood that he simply doesn't know the pleasures of homosexuality exist. Likely in his childhood he never had a single homosexual encounter. Likely he's never even known anyone who is a homosexual. No wonder he rejects my advances. He didn't experiment in childhood like I did with Hirsh. He only knows the pleasures of women. The poor man doesn't know what he's missing.* Of course! That had to be the reason for Bob's rebuff. He just didn't have any idea how great it was to suck another man's cock or to have a penis thrusting into his ass. The solution was, as Marvin always said it was, to be patient and persistent.

David decided to nudge Bob's perspective by degrees. If he would make himself appear to look more like a woman, perhaps the transition to homosexuality would be more palatable for Bob. No matter how idiotic this idea might seem to a heterosexual male, to David the idea struck as a spark of genius. He decided to go 'girl' for Bob. Heedless of Bob's admitted attraction to the opposite sex, David endeavored to make himself more appealing to the younger man by appearing to be a woman. Never in this rush of inspired thought did he consider what he would look like as a pretend woman compared to the physical attractions of a Marty or a Barbara, both stunning femme fatales. Undaunted by logic or common sense, he reasoned he could persuade, persist, and prevail.

It was on a Friday afternoon, about two weeks after their foiled antelope hunt, that Bob got the call from David.

"Hello there. I thought we'd get together for drinks after work today. I have some ideas I'd like to discuss with you. How's your schedule?"

"My schedule's open. When do you want to go?"

"Actually, I thought instead of going to the club you could meet me in the Cowboy Hotel. I'd like you to come pick me up in the hotel barber shop, and then we could go to a place I like from there and in your car."

"Okay, fine by me. What time should I pick you up?"

"Let's say three o'clock. I should be finished by then."

Bob, ever the dutiful junior partner, arrived promptly at the Cowboy's barber shop at three. David was just getting into the barber chair, as his appointment started at three. As Bob opened an outdoor hunting magazine and began to read, David began his transformation. First, he instructed the barber to straighten his hair and then curl it on the ends, layering it along the sides so it fell softly away from his face. Then two women appeared, one a manicurist and the other a pedicurist. David placed his hands upon the arms of the massive barber chair's leather arms and put his feet on the expandable foot bench. The pedicurist removed his shoes and socks and washed his feet over a bucket filled with warm water. The manicurist washed his hands and rubbed his palms and fingers with her proprietary lotions. After his hands and feet were thoroughly cleansed, the women went to work sculpting David's nails.

He instructed the barber to put curlers in his hair and perm it so the curls he created would stay in place. The manicurist and pedicurist applied a peachy pink nail polish, near David's skin tone but a slight shade pinker. The women then applied a coat of clear shiny lacquer finish over all ten of his nails. Bob sat and observed David's makeover which took an entire hour in the chair. David looked approvingly in the barber's mirrors at the man's handiwork, then carefully examined each one of his toenails and fingernails. His three attendants stood by awaiting his approval.

"Nice job," David complimented them. "I feel like a whole new person. In fact, I believe you three experts have made me look better than a lot of women I've seen." He lavished them with double their normal tips, which was not his usual practice. After he got up from the barber chair, he put on his suit jacket. He was wearing a suit Bob hadn't seen before, a peach-colored linen and silk blend of unusual and stunning fabric, and obviously very expensive. It was a suit a man might wear to a summertime outdoor party to celebrate the running of the Preakness horse race at a social gala attended by gentlemen with their ladies attired in fancy hats and elegant dresses. Bob noticed David also wore a new pair of white spats. They closely resembled what a woman might wear for a formal occasion.

"Well, Bob, how do I look?" David asked, seeking approval.

Bob stared at his mentor, his lips clenched and his smile drawn back tightly. He bobbed his head up and down slightly, a motion that confirmed he knew David was really nuts. He summoned his best comportment to not burst into laughter or blurt out, "You look like an oversized, fucked-up duck!" Instead, with utmost discretion, Bob stated most soberly, "You look just fine, David. That suit becomes you." He couldn't bring himself to compliment David's hair or nails. That, Bob correctly intuited, could invite an unwanted advance.

"Great. Thank you for picking me up." David and Bob climbed into Bob's new Cadillac and David directed him to drive a few miles east of the downtown area to a special watering hole called The Others' Place. Once inside, Bob's eyes became accustomed to the dim lighting. David looked at him to gauge his reaction. Initially, Bob just stood poker-faced, taking in the scene. There were men everywhere and no women, at least none that David could see. There were men hugging and kissing other men, all dressed in an eclectic mix. Some wore normal business attire, likely lawyers and executives on the way home from work. There were construction workers showing off their muscular physiques, and then there were the flaming gays, those men who wore outrageous female dresses with bold prints, accessorized by belts and handbags and platform shoes. David's heart fluttered to see that everyone there was truly happy! Men were laughing together, singing together, kissing one another. David was very excited to be at The Others'.

Surely Bob can see how wonderful it is to be gay! How can he not? These men all love each other. This is true camaraderie at its very best, and taken to that wonderful place beyond camaraderie to the wonderful place of sexual intimacy. It's so beautiful to behold. It's breathtaking. Here's where I've met so many of my secret lovers. Surely Bob feels the magic of this place! David pointed out to Bob the dim-colored light bulbs in the elegant chandeliers, the lovely flocked wallpaper in purple and taupe velvets, and the sweet jazz music. Winston Marsalis, T.J. Booker, Louis Armstrong, Eric Clapton and so many other great ones played here. "This place is like heaven on earth," David proclaimed.

He was in his element and completely aroused. He reached for Bob's hand and held it closely in his own. Bob didn't pull away, not at first, but then, alas, rejection! Maybe there was still hope. He hadn't pulled his hand away initially, after all. Maybe he was in the mood, but then his upbringing reasserted itself. David reached for Bob's hand again. That time the younger man immediately pulled his hand away.

The duo sat at the bar and ordered drinks, a pink daiquiri for David and a scotch on the rocks for Bob. The drinks were apropos for the moods of mentor and mentored. They were like a married couple who'd suddenly realized they were completely incompatible. It was impossible to talk about the markets or the business in this place, so the two said practically nothing. David heard Bob mumble something about the music being good, but he knew by then that his junior was only trying to make small talk to assuage his bruised feelings. There was nothing to say.

After Bob drove David back to the garage where they kept their cars, he felt a tinge of sorrow for his friend. He felt the need to be brutally candid, whether David would be hurt by it or not.

"David," Bob started, and then paused.

"What?" David stood by Bob's car, still holding the passenger door open.

"David, I know what you're trying to do. I know you want me as your lover as well as everything else. I get it. I really get it. But you need to understand that I am not a homosexual person. I have never been a homosexual person and I will never be a homosexual person. That place we went to made me extremely uncomfortable. In all honesty, David, what you did today, the way you dressed yourself up to look more like a woman, your clothes, the way you took me into that place to pretend to those who saw us that we were somehow an item together... well, frankly, the entire experience made me feel like throwing up. Please understand that I'm not trying to hurt you, David. I know you are a very sensitive and loving person at heart, but I cannot be your lover. So I must ask you as sincerely as I can to please stop your advances toward me. I am your willing partner in business and your friend, but that is the limit for me. Can you acknowledge that and accept me as I am?"

David stood there staring at Bob, taking in all that he'd just heard, especially the part about vomit. His heart ached and his stomach churned. Never since he'd heard his mother tell his father that she wished he'd never been born had he felt so utterly unwanted and unloved. He hated himself and wished he was anyone or anything but David. He wanted to die.

Bob sensed an impasse and tried to reach out to David. "Can you at least say something?"

There followed a long silent moment while David just stood staring at Bob. Then he slammed the car door with such fury that the glass in the passenger window cracked. He turned his back on Bob and walked away without saying a word.

SNOW AND COFFEE

It was early spring or late winter; the seasons were blurred and hard to differentiate on the Colorado high plains. A huge upper atmospheric panhandle low parked itself for three days over the Texas and Oklahoma lands where native Kiowa, Comanche, and Apache once hunted buffalo and traveled from there to trade as far west as New Mexico's Taos Pueblo. Now the reservation Indians made rugs and jewelry and traded with tourists, but not on this day.

This winter storm was a monster. Storm warning and blizzard conditions caused impossible whiteout conditions for drivers from the panhandles to New Mexico and north to Colorado. Gulf of Mexico waters were spun aloft and hurled down upon Colorado's San Juan Range. Five feet of fresh powder blanketed Telluride and Silverton slopes, and the storm kept moving north and west. Snowfalls of three feet whipped by howling winds piled snowdrifts six to eight feet high along the Colorado Front Range. All roads into and out of Plaintown were closed. Drivers were stopped by beleaguered troopers of the highway patrol and ordered off the roads into motels or local churches and school gymnasiums. Conditions were life-threatening. As the storm whipped Colorado's Front Range, life shut down.

Cattlemen desperately tried to move their herds into shelters and barns, but this storm came too fast for many. Thousands of cattle and horses did their best to withstand the white fury, trying to get into low gullies and behind hills, anything to get out of the gale-force bitter winds. They turned their backs into the wind in order to breathe and see, but all their efforts were hopeless. Tens of thousands of cattle and horses died the day of the onslaught. Calves died next to their mothers, bulls lay buried in snow at the bottoms of ravines. The devastation was widespread. Animals and people unfortunate enough to be outdoors simply had no chance against nature's howling white fury.

The Front Range mountain forest animals fared better than their brethren on the prairie. Deer, elk, bighorns, and mountain sheep retreated to the western-facing slopes and hid down low in the pine forests. The mountains' immovable might broke the snow's onslaught and the bending howling pines tamed the fierce winds. The wild creatures slept huddled close together for warmth and lived while the domestic herds of the plains' cattlemen died.

For the city dwellers, the storm was a welcome holiday. Like the animals, people also stayed hunkered down as best they could. Children pressed faces to windows and watched the snowfall in wonderment from the safety of indoors. Adults occasionally stepped out into the fury to shovel driveways and walk briefly before retreating inside for warmth and hot chocolate, determined to resume their fight against the elements after some rest. As quickly as it blew in, the snowstorm left and moved east, passing as such storms usually do.

Road crews appeared with plows and gravel to make the main thoroughfares passable. The highway patrol tried frantically to rescue those caught for three days in the storm. Some survived, some did not. The towing companies licked their chops, grateful for several days of booming business. Private snowplow operators were paid small fortunes to ransom private roads. Way high up on the mountaintops, a mantle of white radiated with a crystal sparkling light. The snowpack deluge would last until late August, and then fresh snows from the west would start the snow cycle anew. Skiers rejoiced and thanked the snow gods. The thin ribbon of road, that highest continental U.S. road that crosses the continental divide, the one Coloradans call the Trail Ridge Road, was a road no longer. It was buried under eighty feet of snow. It would stay closed until late June or sometime in July when snowmelt reduced it to a ten-to-twenty-foot depth. Then giant plow machines would mount their attack against the endless wall of white.

Animals began to stir about. The cows and local buffalo that survived pushed their heavy heads and faces deep into the snow looking for meager stubs of grass. Ranchers would be days before they could get hay to these desperate creatures. To find grass was to live. For these cattle, life was a race against time. Here and there on the prairie, a mother cow stood over her dead calf half buried in snow and bawled her mournful bellow. It was the saddest sound, one a rancher hoped he'd never hear. No one could ever tell him, after hearing a cow in mourning, that these poor dumb animals had no feelings.

The sun came out as it always must. A brilliant blue sky and cold clean air greeted the citizenry. People inhaled to the fullest expanse of their chests, tasting the wonderful air deep in their lungs. Blood was reinvigorated with copious oxygen. There was a quieter level of voices now, a more respectful tone toward others, a feeling of sympathy for the rancher who lost everything. People, for a while, were more like people should be all the time, thanks to the white wonderment of nature.

In Plaintown, office workers were treated to a three-day vacation by order of the mayor. All unessential people needed to stay home until crews could clear the roads. Firemen and police were on high alerts at their stations for citizens in distress. People were good to each other and civic-minded like they should always be, compliments of Mother Nature.

The fun lovers, the human otters who made Colorado such a special place, took full advantage of the white bounty. There were people out on snow-covered city streets, but they weren't clomping miserably through the white stuff. They were on top of it and having fun. Snowshoes were bounding about with people's feet strapped on top of them, making mirthful tracks in snow. Cross-country skiers slipped along from homes to stores, to neighborhood watering holes and theaters. Coloradans can't be stopped by snow; it's what they live for. Children were free to go outside again, and they did what children do. There were snowmen to make, snow forts to build, sledding to do and, of course, snowball fights to enjoy.

Up higher in the Front Range towns, people dug out. Their first order of business was to shovel the weighty snows off their roofs, then their driveways. Once they had their Jeeps and Land Cruisers chained up, these people were good to go anywhere. They loved their little villages and lifestyles and chuckled with an underlying dismay at the dull lives of those who lived on the prairie, or 'out on the flat' as they called it. Bob had just gotten back from the store and was taking his snowshoes off when Barbara called.

"Do you love the snow, Big Horse?" she asked.

"Yes. Just in from my grocery run. How's Sparrow?"

"I'm good! Is today a good day for you to meet for coffee?" Barb knew it had to be since the offices were closed.

"Sure." Bob wanted her for more than coffee, but he took what she offered.

"I'd like to meet at an out-of-the-way place. We should talk. How about Old Pablo's?"

"I'll meet you in an hour."

At the coffee shop, Bob and Barb ordered lattes and settled into a quiet corner. Barb told Bob what she and Blade did the week before and what she saw. Bob didn't want to believe her at first.

"You've got to be putting me on. You're talking about murder, drugs, prostitution, loan sharking, a hidden altar, insects and spiders? All this and phony invoices too? Are you sure you're not delusional?" Bob shook his head as if he could shake off the truth.

"Not delusional. I saw these things with my own eyes. I took pictures of all the stuff in David's secret room. I'm telling you, Bob, the man is not in his right mind."

"You're talking about my best friend, Barbara. First you say there's a phony invoice problem, and okay, maybe David tries to keep taxes down, but now this? Why are you doing this?" Bob didn't want to believe her. He wasn't expecting this and he wasn't ready to hear it. Her assertions were an affront to his world view and his status as the fair-haired boy and son to inherit the throne. Bob was torn. The father he always wanted was being attacked by the woman he loved. There had to be some mistake.

"Because you're living in an illusion. You need to see the truth."

"But David has always kept his word to me, Barb. How can I turn against him?"

"You will not turn against him. He will turn against you." Barb was confident.

"How can you know that?" He wished what he was hearing wasn't true.

"I trust Chief. He knows animals and people very well. He's an expert tracker. Chief and I talked. I showed him what I told you I saw. He has everything, all the file copies. I flew to Montana to see him last weekend."

"Let me guess. He also told you to be patient." Bob was cynical.

"You have no place to make light of one who tries hard to help you. Chief is good. You must always show respect. Always! And yes, he says we must still be patient. Bob, you may be in danger. You must not let on in the slightest that you know anything." Barbara's face was stern. Her consternation with Bob's cavalier attitude flared.

"Okay, okay. I'm sorry. I apologize. But try to see things from my perspective. David is like a dad to me. We split serious money on a handshake. Now you want me to turn away from a man who's been like a father to me and a special friend? How can I be that kind of person?"

"That handshake was long ago, Bob, many years. You working on a verbal deal now or what? I have looked everywhere and found no evidence that you have anything other than a retail rep deal. But you're not a retail rep. You're wholesale. So what's your deal, Big Horse?" Barb sought to draw Bob out.

"I will inherit the operating companies when David dies. That's my deal."

"Whoa! Really, Big Horse? You have that in writing?"

"It's in writing." Bob's clipped answer didn't answer the question. Barbara caught the omission.

"Bob, may I ask where this writing is?"

"It's in a safe deposit box."

Everything suddenly came together for Barbara. The scene she'd witnessed from her office window years before suddenly made sense.

"Big Horse, is the writing in your safe deposit box or David's?"

"David's."

"Big Horse, did David show you this writing?"

"Yes." Bob described the bank vault scene to Barbara. Now everything finally made sense.

"So, Big Horse, you changed careers to build a company. You made a deal with David, he put the terms in a will codicil, and then he showed you the codicil. Is that right?"

"Yes."

"This is important, Big Horse. What did David say to you when you left the bank?"

"'See you later,' I guess. I can't remember."

"Yes, you can, Big Horse. Think. Did you and David come back to the office together?" Barbara wanted to shake Bob's memory.

"Yeah, we always come back together." Bob looked at her but she just stared at him, her head cocked and eyes squinted in disbelief. Her look jogged Bob's memory. "No, wait! I remember now. David told me he needed to go up the street to see an old friend about something. Yes, he did say that. I remember it clearly."

"Very good, Big Horse!" Barbara put her hands on his arms. "Now Sparrow must tell you something, but first you must promise to keep what I'm about to tell you to yourself. Promise me. It is very important for you to promise me."

"Okay, I promise I will keep to myself whatever it is you are about to tell me." Bob thought this was getting corny.

"Bob, dearest man I love. I hate to tell you this but it is truth you are about to hear. David did not go up the street to see an old friend that day. You came into the building. David walked one block up the street, crossed over to the other side of the street, walked another two blocks up the street, then crossed back to the bank side of the street and walked back into the bank. Sparrow watched the whole sequence from the window of the little room with the extra chairs and tables and lamps."

She looked deep into Bob's eyes. He looked wounded by what he heard.

"Are you sure?"

"I'm sure, Bob. That codicil you saw was probably destroyed that very same day you saw it."

"But you don't know why David went back to the bank."

"No, but the behavior fits."

"Fits what?" Bob's hackles were raised. He didn't want to believe the worst.

"Look, Bob. Marty thought she was special as well. David let her get away with whoring all over the country as long as she was useful to him. She also had her mother's protection while she was here. But where is Marty?"

"Who the hell knows?" Bob still had lingering emotional pain over losing Marty. He was not ready to believe theories or innuendos.

"Bob, you need to be smart here. Chief has theories about what happened to Marty and one of them is worst-case. She may be dead, Bob."

"Come on, Barb. Stop this. I know you didn't like her, but dead?"

"Think, Bob. Who decided to hold off on filing a missing person report?"

"Susan and David both did."

"Yes, but did you ever think that Susan wanted to save her daughter from embarrassment? That explains her decision, but what about David's? Why was he so nonchalant about one of his marketing stars going missing?" Barb raised her eyebrow.

Bob had an answer. "By then I was doing sales nationally. We'd changed our marketing strategy."

"Sure, but suppose you failed? And what about continuing help for the locals? That was Marty's area. Why wouldn't David want her back right away working on local sales?"

"But Barb, I was succeeding. Our sales were going up faster than ever before."

"You're right! That's what I could be missing, but that would give David even more reason to...."

"You're not suggesting what I think you are"

"It's one of Chief's theories, an active theory. It fits every-thing so far, except a body. I saw some human heads in the green room, partially decomposed with insects crawling all over them. He uses insects to dispose of his victims' bodies. One of those heads could have been Marty's. And that's not all, Big Horse. Chief and I did a little tracking work. David started a subsidiary under UGGA's holding company to do real estate investing. But it's just a front for money laundering.

"He has an exclusive deal with a Mexican drug gang. They arrange contract murders through David, and he keeps the hit men separate from the contractors. Marks are killed by long-distance sniper fire from high-velocity target rifles with silencers. A separate unit immediately picks up the dead bodies and takes them to the barnyard for processing. No body, no crime. Just people disappearing. Sound familiar, Big Horse? David is paid cash for the hits. The remains are fed to the barnyard animals and the insects. Insects that need disposal are fed to his guinea hens. It's an ingenious cycle. The real estate subsidiary also runs a string of whorehouses. Cash from prostitution and drugs is put in a lawyer's escrow account and used to buy dilapidated houses in dodgy neighborhoods. Man Child goes along with the lawyer to the closings dressed as a simple carpenter who's going to rehabilitate them.

"They get fixed up and the tops are popped. Then David brings in underage girls and boys from Cambodia, Thailand, and south of the border to do prostitution in those houses. They also sell drugs there, the hard, nasty stuff. Debbie keeps a secret set of separate books. I sent a copy of all these records to Chief. They run seven houses in the metro area and two houses in Springs. They make five million a year tax free. There's a file page in the murder file with girls' names, all Asian and Latino names with ages and house numbers next to the name. It's like a human inventory sheet of girls that went bad, got disposed of, and needed replacement. Girls who get out of line are murdered and processed in the barnyard, then fed to the animals and the insects. David sees these girls as parts in a machine. He doesn't see people as people. He's completely disassociated from human feelings. The operation gives a whole new meaning to the word 'insecticide.'

"Some of the money goes to bribe politicians and police to look the other way. They have four hundred johns on their list of regulars. The regulars even have credit accounts up to fifty thousand dollars. Then, if they don't pay up in cash, the Mexican drug guys do enforcement work. Many johns are prominent Plaintown politicians and businessmen. All the houses pay expenses in cash wherever possible. What must be paid by check, like real estate taxes, is paid by the UGGA subsidiary. It's a big operation, and it's growing so fast it will soon be bigger than UGGA's investment management business.

"And it's not just about making money. There's also a subsidiary within the real estate subsidiary that sells worthless junky consumer products. The come-on is that if the customer doesn't like the product, they can get their money refunded by sending it back. So people buy all sorts of junky products made in China and Vietnam. Then they don't want them. They try to send back their mechanical exercise machines and espresso machines and mail-order motor scooters. None of this stuff works. None of it! The hitch is they need to call the company to get an authorization number to send the crap back. When they call, they get put on hold for an hour and then the call disconnects. For David, this is all a great big yuk. He just loves screwing people. That's what juices his life."

"I can't believe I'm hearing this."

"David loves to pit people against each other. UGGA is like his personal amusement park. He has girls in the office fighting minor turf wars over stupid stuff all the time. He has different ones order different amounts of pencils and then sets them up to blame each other for which one of them made a ten-dollar mistake. He puts two different people in charge of the same thing and then makes sure the project fails so he can watch them blame each other and fight about it. He loves fights. He loves watching people fight.

"And Bob, as I told you, it extends to insects too. He loves to watch tarantulas and scorpions fight to the death. He loves watching spiders eat grasshoppers and crickets. He loves watching a scorpion paralyze a roach and eat it. I'm telling you the man is sick. He also loves to destroy young girls with his whorehouse rental business. He destroys children in the schools through his drug distribution business. He destroys employees' homes and marriages by loaning them money and then cutting their pay for some idiotic reason or another so they can't pay him back. He does the same sorts of dirty tricks to people he loans monies to outside the companies. He loves to destroy. He is a classic sociopath, a monster. He just hides it well behind this image of a benevolent man who runs UGGA. It's all bullshit, Big Horse. It's a disguise for what he really is. He's a destroyer of everything. He drains the work, the careers, and the lives out of everyone he comes into contact with. And people trust their money to this monster.

"Now Bob, what makes you believe a man like this wouldn't pit you and Marty against each other to see who would defeat the other? Can't you see it? Weren't the two of you fighting initially before you started screwing her?"

"Yes. We were at odds. She tried to block everything I tried to do at first, but she failed. I leapfrogged her blocks by going nationwide."

"Yes, and that worked. That showed David you were smarter than her. Don't you see it? He tested you both. He probably instructed her to give you a hard time to see what you were made of. She failed. You succeeded. He looked at the two of you as sort of gladiators. She lost, so she had to die. Don't you get it?"

"It's pretty crazy, Barb."

"Is it? What if the two of you got married? What if that kept you here in Plaintown and not on the road selling? Can't you see what a threat your marriage would be to sales growth? David whips you constantly for more sales. I see it. He wants to squeeze the life out of you. He's got you becoming a Jew for more sales. He's got you on the road and working you to near death. You're out in the rain and the snow. He's here playing with his homosexual boyfriends and laughing at you. Bob, listen to me. Chief and I talked about this. Chief is wise. He believes the father-son business David did with you was just a sales job to take advantage of you. It has caused you to make decisions to work like a dog for David, not out of logic but out of emotion. Chief thinks David made you into an emotional cripple."

"I'm an emotional cripple?"

"Yes, you are, Bob. Marty was emotionally crippled also. He used emotions to cripple both of you like he cripples insects by taking some of their legs off; then you, like the insects, are at his mercy and dependent upon him for your survival. He uses you as he pleases, then gets rid of you. But you are not to worry, Big Horse. Sparrow loves you, truly loves you, and Sparrow and Chief and the people will help you heal. We will, Big Mighty Horse I love. But you must see what has happened for yourself before you can heal."

Barb had Bob's attention at that point. He was being worked to near death by David. He remembered his mother's comments about how Gordy Goodman worked his father, Nevin, to death and then treated Estella no better than a stranger.

"Have you noticed, Big Horse, that when you now fly between cities you are routed to take as many flights as possible? Did you ever think that maybe David changed Judith's instructions to try to wear you out or possibly get you killed from all the takeoffs and landings? If you go to fifty cities in a year, you could normally do it on a hundred or a hundred and thirty flights, right? But Big Horse, you are taking four hundred flights. Doesn't that make you stop and think David is trying to destroy you?'

"Look, I admit it's hard, but I sleep all right on planes. I try to keep costs down."

"Does anybody else try to keep costs down? UGGA and its subsidiary are gushing money. David and his boyfriends are always off partying in some hotel or bathhouse. They go to Las Vegas to the shows. Do you?"

"Well, David's worked all his life and he deserves a—"

"Bullshit. David has fucked off all his pathetic sick life. You're allowing yourself to be manipulated by this creep because you lost your father and you have a blind spot. I feel sorry for you about that but you must break free from it. You can do this. David is excellent at spotting human weaknesses, and he has your number. You believe you are special to him. He's conned you into thinking that. He spotted your weakness right off. He's good at that. That's all he's good at. You are not special to him, Big Horse. He keeps a file for you also. He has you set up with phony invoices and even has a photograph of you kissing some woman named Rita in a seedy bar. You are like tissue paper. He intends to blow his snot mess onto you and throw you away. You need to understand that you cannot take the words and behaviors of a sociopath and juxtapose them into explainable terms as if they were merely quirky oddities emanating from a normal person. A sociopath like David is far removed from normal. He is vile. He is evil. He is, at his core being, a hateful inhuman monster. He is the devil who walks among us. If you don't come to grips with the character you are dealing with, he will find a way to destroy you because all he knows and understands is destruction. He has no capability for empathy or love or kindness or any other sort of normal human feelings toward others."

Bob recoiled with alarm at Barbara's description of David. He felt frightened and threatened. "Okay, so you think he killed Marty. You think he's going to kill me next. You think I should break my deal. Are you going to the police with this? What else?"

"Not the police. There's a better way to deal with this."

"How?"

"Leave this to me and Chief. You know nothing and you say nothing. Mark Sparrow's words. You just play along with David. But always be careful and remember he is extremely dangerous."

Bob did not tell Barbara about his conversation with Old Mac. He was again in midair now, just like when he'd tempted fate at the dam breast when he was a boy. Again he put his trust in the unknown. Would his skates come down and bite into the ice and save his life? Would Old Mac be honorable and be there when the chips were down to save his deal to inherit the companies? He could only close his eyes and hope then. He could only close his eyes and pray now. He looked at Barbara without the slightest hint of concern. If anything, he was fearless and brave.

"I'm not saying anything except be careful. Remember, you are simply being used like a piece of tissue paper. Just be careful!" She was emphatic. Bob knew she was serious. She cared about him, and she was taking a risk talking to him this way. "This is just one of Chief's theories," she continued. "Chief says we must both wait. If David has a card, he will play it because he must. Just be ready for it and do not be stupid, Big Horse. Chief and Sparrow are with you all the way on this. Chief's theory is that David is unlikely to kill you. Marty disappeared. If something happens to you or you also go missing, that would be too suspicious. Chief says to just be careful and wait. David will act like a rat that must come out of his hiding spot. He will make his move."

Bob looked out the window of the coffee shop. The white snow and cold outside contrasted sharply with the dark coffee and warmth inside. The world always offered choices, and he reckoned it was his privilege to make one rather soon.

MENTORING

It was time to find a new protégé. Bob's rebuke and rebuffs sobered David. There was never going to be a male-to-male romance between the two. Acceptance followed denial, but slowly and angrily. Loathing of self and despairing exasperation followed. Where had he gone so terribly wrong? Had he not given Bob everything? A career path with security, a showering of gifts and perks, a paid-for arrangement with the greatest sexpot whore in Colorado, the trips, the executive prestige, the cars, the lavish compensation, the extravagantly appointed office and secretarial help—all these things he'd given freely to Bob, and what little had he asked in return? A blow job now and then, a hug or two, some soft word of love for an older man who adored him. Was that too much to ask? Did Bob have to humiliate him so badly that he had to cry and beg for love?

The loathing and despair gave way slowly, and he began to find little faults here and there. A sales call forgotten, a stock analysis that seemed too hurried and inconsequential to the creator indicating there was something else besides the firm vying for attention. Then the pressures, the demands to do more sales calls per day, per week, to take more flights, to run faster. All these things revealed David's prima donna sales executive was a mere mortal, not a god. He had faults that showed under greater and greater pressure, like a quarterback feels when down three scores with six minutes to play. The more pressures applied, the more likely the man will make mistakes. A hurried throw, an incomplete pass; a forced throw, an interception. Another firm got the salesman away from us; a linebacker ran a pick in for a touchdown. The other team got the big sales. Not good enough. Never mind the defense. Let the other teams run up huge competitive advantages; can't be defense's fault. Must be sales aren't good enough. That's it! Imperfection causes the waters of patience to boil.

Time to groom a new quarterback, but frustration makes it tough. In his heart of hearts, David knew lousy performance, lousy defense, caused money to walk and made getting new sales muscle very difficult and expensive. Stuck, more frustration, boiling over furiously with it, David turned to an inner self looking for new direction and purpose. It would be hard to get rid of Bob. The business would suffer and backslide. *I must mentor a new protégé. But where will I find one? Who will he be? There's so much on my mind, so many things to keep track of. There's the business and there's the secret business. Who could succeed me? Who would want to think about all this? It's getting so maddening!*

"Dolly, I'm going to have a big fight night tonight. The new big blue scorpion will take on my number-two-ranked tarantula to see who gets a shot at the title. I won't be with you tonight, sweetheart. I'll be watching the fight with Andy, my new best friend."

Dolly just stood there chewing her grass.

That night, in the green room, David took down the fetus jar and placed it on the chair next to his. Then he opened the dividers between the tarantula and the scorpion. David and Andy had the best seats in the house. Now the two mortal enemies were in the same enlarged glass cage. Only one of the combatants could survive this encounter.

"Andy, I think it's time you and I had some serious discussions about your future," David began, addressing the fetus in the formaldehyde jar. "You see, you and I actually have a great deal in common. Nobody loves either of us. Mom and Dad didn't love me, and your mom and dad didn't love you either," he lied to his imaginary protégé.

The fetus in the formaldehyde jar said nothing. It was forever preserved and dead, but it didn't give David any back talk. It had a chance of succession.

"No, they did not love you, Andy. Don't try to tell me they did. I know they didn't. Your dad just loved your mom's pussy, not you. He didn't even know you were conceived, so he couldn't possibly love you. I'm never going to tell him either. You're too good for him. He will never know you were alive, so he can't possibly ever love you. And your mother, Andy. Your mother was more interested in getting fucked than what the effect of her whoring was going to have on you. She might have hurt you, Andy. You might have been born with a disease, or some penis might have dented your brain and you could have been born mentally disabled. So you see, Andy, I saved you by killing your mother and taking you from her.

"Now you belong to me. Now we can both share our feelings that our mom and dad didn't love us. But we do have each other, Andy. We'll always have each other. I'm going to tell you how the world works, and how to live and how to think about things, and I want you to pay close attention to everything I say. Remember, Andy, just do as I say. Always do as I say and never as I do."

Of course, Andy said nothing.

"Well, I'll tell you why I say that, Andy. It's because sometimes I can be a very bad boy and I can do terrible things to people. I don't want you to grow up to be like me that way. I want you to grow up to be a wonderful man. Maybe you'll become very wealthy or possibly even become a senator or the governor. You'll go far if you listen to me, Andy.

"People are the most important factor to be managed in business. Most executives look at people and categorize them by their talent areas, like mathematical aptitude for analysis, conversational abilities for salesmanship training, attention to details for bookkeeping, neatness for secretarial work, things like that. But that's the wrong way to think about people, Andy. The correct way is to categorize them into only two categories. There are smart people and there are stupid people. Smart people should never be hired in the first place because all they want to do is take advantage of you and squeeze you for money. They ask too many questions. They want to know what's going on all the time, and generally they are just a nuisance. What you want working for you at UGGA is stupid people. These are people you can make promises to and get them to work for a promise. They assume they are going to be treated fairly, so you can tell them just about anything and then screw them later after you've gotten the work out of them.

"Unfortunately, Andy, your mother and father come from the stupid crowd. Marty believed I'd give her the moon and she screwed her ass off for good old UGGA. But now she's gone. The beauty of her deal was that we have the assets she brought in and none of the residual costs. The men she fucked can't come to us and blackmail us or turn us in to the regulators because she's dead. You always need to think ahead, Andy. Pick dummies to work for you, promise them what they need to hear, and then get the work out of them before you screw them. But always be thinking about how to screw them in the end before you even hire them in the first place.

"Your dad still works for us, Andy, but it won't be for long. I have a plan to screw him also. I've had it for a long time. All I need to do is get him to sign a simple piece of paper and we'll be rid of him. Don't get upset with me, Andy. Remember, he never loved you in the first place. He was only interested in Marty's pussy.

"I'll be honest with you. There's one employee who presents an enigma to me. It's the Indian woman, Barbara. I'm not sure I figured her out correctly when we hired her. I thought she'd just be a dull person who did as she was told. I even researched her background before I hired her. It was sketchy. She lived on an Indian reservation, then went to college. There was no information about her parents, but how much could a couple Indians know about business? I researched Indian women who were beautiful, because she is very beautiful, and guess what? I found this article about beautiful Indian women and it had pictures of about twenty of the most beautiful ones in the country. They were scantily clad in bikinis and very sexy outfits. And there she was!

"Barbara posed for her photo in that article. So I thought, naturally enough, that someday she could work as a beautiful whore fucking her brains out for sales and making great money doing it, right alongside your mother. But that didn't interest her, Andy. Something about her job interviews really threw me. She said she wanted to start working not in sales but in clerical staff. She said she wanted to do all the menial jobs that no one else wanted to do. I didn't figure it at all. Here's this knockout beauty trying to work in the most inconspicuous job possible. Well, I figured she was trying to hide from a boyfriend or she felt guilty about being beautiful, so I told Susan I voted to hire her. All women are nuts anyway. It was Susan's call, but if I had strenuously objected she might not have hired her.

"Now I'm not so sure hiring her was a smart move. See, Andy, the Barbara woman always studies the business. She reads regulations, learns all sorts of things about how the firm works. She also studies investing. Why she does that, I'll never know. She doesn't make enough to invest. We barely pay her enough to live on. I think she knows more than she lets on, but she keeps quiet about it. She never asks for a pay raise. It's almost like she doesn't want money. Maybe she's afraid if she doesn't know everything, she'll get fired.

"I don't understand her. I felt her up one day not too long ago and she gave me a look like she was going to kill me. That's just weird, Andy. Most women kind of giggle when I feel them up. I think they all secretly like it but are afraid to admit it. But not Barbara. She was angry with me, like hostile angry! That's just part of my concern about her. She's also sweet on Bob, your dad. I can tell. They try to hide their interest, but I see how they look at each other. It's like they have a secret code or something. I just don't like it when I'm not sure I know what's going on. But you just watch how I handle this situation, Andy. I'm sure there will be a lesson in it for you. I'm going to make you into the best executive UGGA ever had. You're learning from the master. Just trust me and believe in me. Remember that I always have your best interests at heart. You have a brilliant future at UGGA.

"Look, Andy, the arachnid just parried the direct thrust from the scorpion. Now the tarantula has two legs pinning the scorpion's stinger. This is exciting stuff. The scorpion can't use his stinger. If the scorpion can't pivot around, the spider will soon find a chink in his armor and put its bite beak into the soft flesh."

The excitement of the delicate dance of death between the archrivals in the arena gave David an erection. In the presence of his protégé guest at ringside, he unzipped his trousers and began to masturbate. The heightened sensory pleasures of his childhood were still with him, just as they were when, years earlier, he'd discovered the joys of tearing wings from hapless flies.

And so began a series of conversations between David and his imaginary friend and protégé, the fetus in the formaldehyde. And the spiders and scorpions went on about their age-old rivalry, oblivious to David's mentoring of his fetus protégé, mindlessly tearing each other from limb to limb, with the winner killing and systematically devouring the loser. And the whole experience, the generosity and goodness of healthy male fellowship, the kindheartedness that comes from taking the time to help a fellow troubled soul, and the shared camaraderie of the thrills only the best of friends could experience together at ringside satisfied David's deeply seated need for love.

REYNARD THE RED

When Bob was a young child in Milltown, he spent a lot of time at his uncle's farm. Uncle Eddie understood people from his years running a pool hall. For relaxation, Eddie liked to observe animals and acquired a learned understanding of them over the years. Most animals found Eddie's favor. He even loved skunks and raccoons, regarded by most people as pests. The only animals he didn't care for were crows, ravens, and starlings. Eddie, thinking nature somehow erred by having blackbirds of any kind, nurtured a deep hatred toward them. Blackbirds killed young songbirds and the babies of squirrels and rabbits, all creatures that pleased him to watch, even though they ate his produce. Not a man content to allow nature to take her course, Eddie devised a trap for the pesky blackbirds.

The trap first involved the capture of a red fox. To catch the fox, Eddie built a chicken coup. It was a magnificent chicken coup, with a trapdoor in the floor with another floor below. In the coup, Eddie placed a few chickens and waited. Sure enough, in a few days a fox showed up. He was a big handsome red fox with beautiful full fur, and Eddie soon referred to him as Reynard. The fox enjoyed his evening chicken feasts so much that he got a bit too bold about raiding this unprotected chicken coup. Eddie had the door propped wide open for the fox. The prop was a simple clothesline prop stick with a notch carved into the top to hold the line up. One evening Eddie had the coup propped open for the fox and old

Reynard went inside for his meal of chicken. The prop was attached to a long line with Eddie waiting on the other end. He pulled the string, the door swung shut, and Reynard was caught.

Eddie made the fox his pet, as much as anyone can make a pet out of a fox. He fed the thing, brought it fresh water, and talked with it daily. He fed Reynard so well it was doubtful the animal would try to get away if given the chance. It had comfortable quarters under the coup, with a warm wooden floor and straw bedding up off the ground. Eddie and the fox developed a routine; one could say they had a friendship and an understanding.

Each day Eddie set out a trail of corn near the coup. Like he did for the fox, he held the door open with a clothes prop. The blackbirds ate the corn trail right up to and into Eddie's chicken coup. There were no longer any chickens; the coup was now the blackbird coup. When the coup filled with blackbirds, Eddie pulled the door prop out and captured the birds. He'd devised a floor trap that he opened by pulling on a second line, giving Reynard access to the upper floor. Each day Reynard ate five to ten blackbirds, then returned to his quarters on the lower floor. Reynard became a very fat fox. The other animals and songbirds approved of Eddie's arrangement with Reynard. Songbirds, squirrels, and rabbits multiplied profusely on the farm. Eddie was also a good shot with his 20-gauge shotgun, and Florence's table fare often featured squirrel or rabbit.

It so happened that Bob was selling in Roanoke, Virginia, when he saw a beautiful print of a red fox. It reminded him of his late uncle Eddie and his farm with the pet fox. Bob bought the print and took it with him to be framed. On the day he was going to take it to the framer's, he remembered the little plug of fox hair he'd found in David's barn. It would make for a nice touch, he thought, to have the gallery slip the plug of fox hair into the picture in the lower left corner of the frame, opposite the artist's signature.

Bob hung the framed print in his office. As many times as David was in the office, he never once looked closely at the fox print. David was, other than his sexual preferences, wired the same as most straight men, and men generally paid less attention to the details in a picture frame than women did. If something was out of place in a picture, many women would notice it right away, whereas most men were oblivious to the very existence of the picture itself, let alone the details within its frame.

Judith studied the picture closely and slowly the story behind the picture filtered out to the other women in the office. The picture on Bob's wall was different than the other office decor of animal heads, mountain scenes, and portraits of dead people. It even had an actual piece of the animal itself in the picture. There was speculation amongst the office staff that Bob shot the fox after he took its picture. He related the story of Eddie's fox to Judith, and how that memory attracted him to the picture. Somehow the office grapevine story became that the little hair plug was from Eddie's fox, and Bob shot his uncle's fox.

Barbara inspected the picture very closely and deciphered its telling clue. She'd seen many fox pelts on the reservation and this hair was not from a fox, nor a coyote. It was too fine, too silky. It was human hair.

She learned from Bob that he'd picked up the hair plug in David's barn. Her tracking skills told her that David had something to do with Marty's disappearance, and she believed the skin was likely Marty's. The head being cleaned in the ant and silverfish compartment was also probably hers. Likely David murdered Marty, but somehow the reddish-streaked portion of Marty's hair, escaped the insect room. And there it was!

Barbara craftily kept this information to herself. If there was to be retribution against David, it was not her rightful place to settle things. He could not be her kill, nor did she wish to reveal all she knew and suspected by turning the matter over to the police. David would merely lawyer up and prolong matters, and justice for Marty might never be served. Instead she went to Susan and told her about the wonderful picture in Bob's office. She made the point of telling Susan to look very carefully at the beautiful hair plug, urging the woman to ask herself if she'd ever seen hair as beautiful as what was attached to that plug. Then Barbara patiently waited and observed the movements of the human animals in the UGGA offices as nature took its course.

Eventually, Susan made a point of visiting with Bob while he was in his office. She admired his fox picture. It was beautiful artwork, she opined. She carefully inspected the hair plug, staring at it for a long time before she asked Bob why he'd kept the patch of hair from his uncle's fox.

"Oh, that's not from Uncle Eddie's fox. That was something I picked up in David's barn. Apparently a fox got in there and somehow it got torn from the fox's fur."

"It seems like a long patch of hair. Must've been a fox with pretty long hair." She again complemented the picture and left Bob's office.

The human senses constantly acquire data inputs. The acquired data finds a location to repose itself in the brain someplace, and there it waits and sleeps as if it has no importance in this world, was simply put there to be stored away for safekeeping. Sometimes a mind will repress what it sees for good reason. It was easier for Susan to believe Marty was alive somewhere than to objectively receive evidence to the contrary. Yet her subconscious knew something about that hair plug didn't fit that picture. It fit some other picture that was being concealed from her.

Months, even years, could pass and the data point slept undisturbed. But then one distant future day, another data point finds lodging in the noggin and thenceforth two dot points slumber, isolated and unaware of each other. Then a small miracle happens. Somewhere in the mind, usually when the mind's owner is in a relaxed, unhurried state, a spark of neural electricity leaps through the brain's synaptic nodes and neural pathways from one dot to the other. Miraculously, the sleeping dots awaken and become dancing partners, like former high school sweethearts tripping down memory lane together.

A spark fired in Susan's mind about a week after she saw the fox picture. It happened during a late Thursday afternoon as she leaned back in her office recliner, reminiscent and remorseful over her missing daughter. She was recalling the time she'd traveled to the East Coast to visit Marty during her junior year. That was the time Susan was shocked to learn the true nature of her daughter's heart. Marty was going to be the queen of the junior prom at the neighboring high school. All the schools' boys voted for her, and she was trying to decide which one should drive her back to her dorm after the evening's parties. Susan tried to alter her daughter's life course during that weekend, suggesting she join the Peace Corps.

"There are so many children in Africa who are starving to death. You could be a big help to humanity if you went there and worked with them in one of the villages. Help them learn how to raise crops and animals so the children won't starve." That was the gist of Susan's parental suggestion. That's when she heard the truth.

"Mother, don't be ridiculous. After you spent our whole life pushing me away from you so you could have your precious career, now you want me to join the Peace Corps? Puh-*lease*! There's no way I'd ever do that. Look at it this way. If we help them, they'll just breed more until the world is full of starving children. They'll overrun the rest of us. It's never going to be possible to save all of them, and by saving a few you don't make them stronger. You make them more dependent and weaken all of them. It's better to just let them starve and hope the survivors figure it out."

"You sound so heartless. I don't like hearing you talk that way."

"I'm just a realist, Mother, and I know who I am and where I want my life to go. Frankly, I care far more about which boys are next on my fuck calendar than I could ever care about some poor kids dying of starvation in Africa. I keep my priorities straight, Mother. I have no time for distractions."

Susan had gulped and swallowed hard when she'd heard Marty talk that way back then, and she gulped and swallowed now as she recalled that afternoon. It was not possible for Susan to ever stop loving her daughter. She'd been missing for almost a year, but the lumps in Susan's throat, her feelings of guilt from not being closer to Marty, had never left her. She remembered her daughter as the beautiful child she was, how curious and happy and full of life she was, and how Susan sometimes braided her hair into pigtails. That's when dot number one sent off its electrical charge to dance with dot number two.

The plug of fox hair in the frame played upon Susan's mind. Something about it didn't make sense. Hadn't she heard from David at one of the company parties held at his house a few years before that the coyotes were getting after his geese and had killed off all the foxes around his farm? If that were true, then how did a fox end up in his barn? A chill went straight down Susan's spine. That was the fateful moment when she suddenly realized nothing would ever be the same.

No one stayed late at UGGA Universal, at least not during the in-between times, those times between when regulatory report deadlines and filings must be met. Susan lingered that clandestine night, waited until all the at-will hires left, walked the halls to be doubly sure, then made one of her supersleuth corporate secretary moves, the kind that set her apart from the worker-bee time clock punchers. She slipped into Bob's office with her night tools, a paring knife, a screwdriver, and a small pair of cuticle scissors. In a few minutes, she'd removed the fox picture from its place on Bob's wall, removed the backing, and snipped a small sample of hair from the underside of the plug. She reassembled the picture and hanged it in its original position. Inspecting her work, she satisfied herself that no one would ever notice the missing hair sample.

Then she left.

NO

After a few months, Bob thought less and less about the antelope hunt and The Others' Place episode. Traveling, selling, keeping track of individual salespeople's requests and idiosyncrasies, and making hundreds of flights on time focused his mind on the present.

David looked more toward the future. Since the antelope hunt, he'd hired two additional male employees. Their employment duties were more of the same farcical nonsense sorts of jobs that his previous two hires performed.

The first hire, Lester, was a man David found greatly to his liking. The man was malleable, always agreeable to any suggestion David made, had no moral center, and was totally devoid of ethics. He had feminine mannerisms, but not their cleanliness or neatness. His shirt was often unbuttoned by three front buttons, his trousers were dirty, his fingernails were grimy, his hair was greasy, his teeth were yellow from smoking, and his halitosis was so vile that the ladies often gagged when they conversed with him. He often sought the camaraderie of the women in the office, but was shunned and went uninvited to any of their gatherings. His savior for companionship was David, who spent ever increasing after-hours times with Lester and soon gave him a prominent role in the firm. Lester was assigned to be the office observer, which was a nice way of describing someone hired to snoop on everyone else. The office women had a code name for Lester, calling him 'Slurp.'

The second hire, Charles, was given the official role to substitute. He was instructed to sit in the lunchroom each day, every day. His job was to eat lunch slowly, extending a normal lunch hour into an eight-hour food fest, and to always remain in the lunchroom to report directly to David any conspiratorial conversations that might take place. Officially, he was designated on regulatory reports as an assistant employee and carried on the fund's expenses. Although Charles knew absolutely nothing about the company or its various employee duties, reporting, and record-keeping requirements, David deemed him intelligent enough to learn the other employees' job functions by listening to them talking in the lunchroom.

Charles, or Chas, was the most obese employee UGGA ever hired, perhaps the most obese employee in all of Plaintown. Fat rolled off his face and chin, and his arms and legs. His stomach and backside were so huge he could not fit into a chair—which was a good thing, for if he were to ever sit upon a normal-sized chair with normal-sized legs, it was a near certainty that his weight would crush the chair and he would likely injure himself. Chas wore specially constructed trousers, made by stitching together two normally large trouser pairs and repositioning the zipper. He had a very fat face with huge lips and an ever-present smile. He was partially bald, although he was only in his late twenties, and combed what little hair he had forward over his dome so it looked as if there was some sort of splattered mural effort above his eyes. A special oversized sofa was constructed for him and placed in the lunchroom. The office girls soon had a nick name for Chas also, calling him 'Sub,' as in subpar. They pitied him for his obesity and openly speculated that his real job skill was giving the other men superlative blow jobs.

Susan's girls, led by Mrs. Rodriguez and Barbara, continued to do the work of the office. Now the ladies had plenty of male combinations to quip and laugh about. They devised a man pool, similar to males' football pools. Each woman picked a numbered ticket from a bowl which matched male combination pairings, as well as a jackpot number which represented the total number of verified male pairings that occurred the previous week. Each ticket cost one dollar. There was a winning prize for which number picked the most winning male combinations. There were rules to determine what the males were deemed to be doing based upon who arrived at work with whom, who stayed late with whom, who went to lunch with whom, who was seen behind closed doors with whom, and who brought gifts for whom. When one male was spotted rubbing his hand over the ass of another male, there was a bonus wild card noted in the female logbook. Those two males, if they appeared on the winning ticket, earned the ticket holder a double bonus, and all other women not holding the ass rub combo on their tickets had to pony up an additional twenty-five cents each to the winner. Each combination of male incidents had to be verified by two women, and each male combination pairing was given a point ranking for total jackpot points.

Pool ticket pairs included Sub Slurp, Man Muscle, Slurp Man, Muscle Slurp, Sub Man, Muscle Sub, Chas Man, Sub Chas, Slurp Chas, and Muscle Chas. Each ticket had three different pairings. As the weeks rolled by, the log entries lengthened and the pots were paid out. It was obvious that some pairings repeated more often than the others, and there developed a marketplace for certain pairings which sold at a premium. The women developed their own private exchange trading place. Suspicions grew amongst the males when one of the ladies would encourage a male to rub the ass of another in front of two other female witnesses, especially when the two would-be rubbers were likely to be a winning pair.

Barbara was especially keen on this plan. She soon had a standing premium pay offer for certain likely winning pairs and then, once she had her likely winning tickets, she would challenge her pony pairs, as she called them, to rub asses. After a time, the other women began to lose interest, as Barbara was winning far too much of their money. But it was all good fun while it lasted, except when a shareholder was present in the office. Watching grown men walking about rubbing each other's asses didn't sit well with some of the older investors and they pulled their money. David eventually caught on to the games being played and issued one of his edicts forbidding office betting. No edict was issued forbidding ass rubbing.

David's income waxed fat from the sales improvement, despite the added expenses of two additional office drones. Money had a major effect on his behavior. Although David already had a lot of money, his attitude and outlook on life were affected by whether his monies were increasing or decreasing. The addition of Bob to the firm resulted in a quadrupling of firm cash flows, and for David personally, a ten-fold leap in income. A swelling of his ego and sense of self-importance took place the more riches poured into his fold. Suddenly, the idea that he was a business genius overcame David. Every decision he made, he believed, turned into gold. He resented any challenge to his authority and believed himself invincible.

Bob was in Plaintown enough to notice that the office was a playpen for homosexual males and a source of friction for the women relegated to do the work. And he told David as much. He made clear his opinion that David's drones were a hindrance to getting work done; that they were an unnecessary, even if affordable, cost which should be eliminated; and that while David always exhorted Bob to do better, it was time for him to look into the mirror, for Bob asserted that David could do better as well.

David rebuffed Bob. The way the firm was structured made perfect sense to him. He never sought to be a large investment firm, just a comfortable one. He always had a hankering to meddle in the lives of others and watch their reactions to his meddling. He liked abusing people as much as he'd liked abusing insects as a child.

After Bob rejected David's advances, his adoration of the younger partner turned to contempt. He held all straight men, including his late father, in contempt, and he learned to disguise it very well. He regarded Bob's business acumen with contempt as well. He reasoned anyone gullible enough to trust him was merely a fool to take advantage of. As much as he tried to enlighten Bob about the joys of homosexuality, Bob remained impossibly rigid in his moral persuasions. He ascribed Bob's prudish morals to his Christian mother's influence. Estella and David met once on a visit the woman made to Plaintown. He'd instinctively hated her, although he masked his feelings well. He also correctly surmised that she instinctively hated him as well.

David chafed at his self-inflicted predicament with Bob. Deeply hurt by Bob's rejections and resentful of his junior's opinions about his manner of managing the office staff, David held the man's very persona in contempt. He tried to disguise his contemptuous feelings from Bob as best he could, but there was a change in his demeanor toward Bob. There was a chill that hung in the air between the two men, like a late fall day's penetrating coldness that will not warm away, even after the sun has risen high.

Bob was dismayed over David's decline into squalid behavior. Perhaps his father figure, his sniveling, sobbing mentor who begged him to become a homosexual lover, had finally found some men who acquiesced to sucking him off, body odors notwithstanding. Bob had no understanding of male homosexuality and never sought to delve into those behaviors. The notion of a gay father figure was hard for him to stomach at first. His initial feelings were that of revulsion of David and all his drones, but then, after it was clear that this was the life David was choosing for himself or the life he was born wired to live, Bob was able to compartmentalize the older man's personal sex life as a personal dimension of David that he would just simply ignore. And he did.

But Bob's appeasement with David, who no longer acted like a partner, who sought to change the fundamental nature of their relationship from business partnership and personal friendship to homosexual lover, was not enough to satisfy David. It is said that it's impossible to change the spots on a leopard. It's a saying worth heeding, for the leopard is masterful at camouflage and disguise. It is a stealthy animal that sneaks about in dark shadows, intent upon ambushing its prey. It always has the upper hand when it strikes, and it's the rare prey animal that escapes the leopard's attack and survives to live beyond it.

There comes a time when even the greatest fraud artists must reveal themselves, for to complete the fraud they must dispense with their part of the bargain they made with their intended victim. The art of fraud is, in essence, to cajole, coerce, or falsely promise an action or a deed to be performed later in return for the mark's earlier performance. Frauds can range from the simplest, such as promising a child a piece of candy in return for a quarter but then not delivering the candy, to the most heinous, such as telling Jews they are going to a resettlement camp only to pack them into a gas chamber instead.

David's fraud was a sordid, disgusting matter which took place over an eleven-year period. It resulted in a great diminution of Bob's career potentials and vast unjust enrichment for David. Based upon misplaced trust and false friendship, it was designed from the outset to be a knockoff of the will game that some men play with a mistress. The woman may perform favors for years or decades based upon the promise that the man will leave her well provisioned when he dies, only to discover afterward that she is left with nothing.

While Bob was on the road working his hardest to build long-term relationships for a business he was, by agreement and will, to inherit, David was secretly on the telephone having conference calls with potential buyers for the UGGA complex. Despite David's dismal, cellar-scraping investment results following the halcyon years enjoyed because of Bob's gold stock picks, Bob's dogged sales efforts resulted in substantial growth of assets under management, and the worth of the operating companies had grown from a quarter-million to over thirty million. David was no longer content with his million-dollar annual compensation. Now a paunchy aging man in his mid-sixties, his libido and interest in playing office games with his staff were both waning. He wanted to take the entire worth of the business for himself and leave Bob nothing.

The grip greed held on David's soul was selective and discerning. It was not a universal grip that held any group, tribe, or nation state's membership entirely within its grasp. The greed grip selected its wearers well. Slighted by his circumstances, hated and reviled by his mother from infancy, shunned and shunted away by his ambitious father, David learned to resent everyone he encountered who was handsome or beautiful, readily accepted, or loved by another soul. The nurturing and bonding that others drew strength from, that centered their character, simply wasn't there for him. He learned as a child that he was an object of derision and felt so rejected that he learned to loath himself. And he learned to mask his self-loathing very well.

He learned to be the jovial friend, the shoulder to lean upon for those he barely knew. He wormed his way, using his bubbly obsequious wife as the entryway, into the homes of the socially prominent. Then, when confidence was gained and the hapless new friend needed a loan to weather a rough spot, he was there with the cash, but at a price of a first deed of trust upon the friend's home. Just for tax reasons, nothing else he always assured his quarry. Once documents were signed, he surreptitiously moved heaven and earth to create obstacles which made it hard for his debtor to repay him. If the man was an accountant, he would learn the man's clients and seek out another accountant to underbid his debtor. Once the debtor's revenue stream was diminished and payment could not be timely met, David pounced. Collateral worth a million on a loan of one hundred thousand was seized. Litigation followed, and either an exorbitant settlement was extracted or the collateral fell into his hands.

Many employees mortgaged their homes to David, who was very liberal with advances and credit to them against their future salaries. Once he held their first deed, their employment mysteriously came into jeopardy. They were suddenly no longer performing up to par. Their pay was docked until they fell behind on their payments; then their emotional distress was deemed too disruptive to the firm and they were let go. Legal action followed and these employees lost their homes, unless they agreed to increase their incomes with a side business opportunity financed by David.

One fast friend owned a chain of liquor stores worth three million. David loaned the man three hundred thousand to help him past a tough divorce, but the stores were put up for collateral. Predictably, David took actions to impair his debtor's ability to repay him. Young teens were hired to defile the stores with spray paint and throw bricks through the windows. The disruptions mattered and had their desired effect, and David settled for one of the stores. A loan of three hundred thousand returned a million when the store was sold a few months later. David discovered that providing ready liquidity for those in dire straits was a way to make outrageous returns quickly. With the cash flow from the firm servicing his expanded bank credit lines, David became the go-to guy for cash. He was the proverbial cash rich, ever liquid, friendly but ugly frog that would throw out his tongue, snap up hapless flies, and swallow them whole. He was waxing fat on debtors as well as his swelling income from the firm.

If his father and mother were still alive, David's progression toward greed would not have surprised them. They knew their son. Others who met him after he'd reached adulthood would only see a bizarre jovial sort of fellow, a skilled artisan of financial combat who lurked in waiting for his prey. Compensation for self-loathing became his obsession. Projecting his loathing onto others, taking their spirit down to a level as low as his own, destroying his victims financially, became a source of immense joy for him. He saw life and its souls as players in a great game, all arrayed as opponents and victims-to-be. He believed in the adage that all was fair in love and war, especially financial war.

He engaged in financial combat outside the boundaries other participants in financial squabbles respect. His objectives were to never seek fair resolutions of disputes. Satisfaction for him was only realized by the destruction of the opponent. The feeling he craved to savor was the same feeling of power he'd felt as a child when tearing the wings off flies. David worked as hard off court as on court in his efforts to ravage an opponent. Wives, children, business associates of the opponent, organizations, charities, and worthy causes supported by his opponent were all fair game in his quest to demean and destroy. Libel, slander, destruction of property, threats against friends and supporters were all in play. He defined the rules in the games he played, not society and its norms, and most laughably not the courts. Those who did engage David in financial combat got to know him well. Not the jovial, helpful friend he pretended to be, nor the understanding and respected businessman his public relations efforts pretended him to be, but a vicious, greed-obsessed, vindictive malcontent who made his destructive presence felt.

It was to be an eventful Friday afternoon and weekend for Bob. He had plans to go to the mountains, but that was not fated to happen that weekend. David called and asked him to come into his office. When he entered, David stood facing him, not at all like the first time they met when David sat in his swivel throne chair with his back turned to his guest. The men were partners now, so there was more conviviality to this fateful meeting.

David was brimming with cheerfulness as he expressively motioned for Bob to sit in the middle guest chair in the semicircular array of audience chairs. He took a seat next to Bob in an audience chair, something Bob had never seen him do before.

"Here's an agreement I'd like you to sign," David began. "It's necessary to give us more flexibility in growing the firm. For a time, I'm going to remove you as an officer and director of the operating companies and have you focus on retail sales. I'm giving you a very lucrative contract. It even gives you the entire underwriting concession for your retail sales. If you work hard like you always do, I believe you'll make an even greater income than you're making now, especially since wholesaling is going slowly. You have a chance to make even more money this way, plus you can be home in Plaintown more."

Bob was shocked. Perhaps Marty felt the same sense of shock when David ambushed her with his lethal grip and ether-soaked rag. But in Bob's case, David made a tactical mistake. The leopard within him failed to plan a fatal ambush for Bob and instead decided upon a paper one.

"Well, let me read through it," Bob said. David shoved a pen in Bob's face.

"It's just a bunch of legal mumbo jumbo. I assure you that nothing in this changes things between you and me. It's lawyer stuff, just trust me. Go ahead and sign it."

"Just let me read for a minute."

As Bob read the proposed representative's contract, he noted the release language. It stated that there had never been any prior deals or agreements between them, that this agreement was their full and complete understanding.

"Wait a minute," he said. "There's a release in here. This would release you from our deal, the one I've relied upon to work all these past years building the fund, the deal I took at your urging and the one we made which took me on a whole different career path. By signing this, I'd be saying the sun never rose and the buffalo were never present on the plains. Remember the codicil you showed me in the bank vault? Have you lost your mind?"

"No, I haven't lost my mind. The lawyers just want uniformity for the regulators. We still have our deal. Nothing changes that. Just sign this damn thing and let's get this over with."

Bob leveled a skeptical gaze at David. "No."

"What do you mean, no?" David's jaw dropped. For an instant he thought he'd been caught flat-footed once again like when he was caught stealing cookie money from neighborhood housewives.

Bob detected a hint of apoplexy from his now former mentor and friend. There was before him a petulant child in a man's body, straining at his furthest boundaries of mental projection, insisting his will upon a subordinate junior, and being told no. It was simply unfathomable to David that his commands would be refused.

"I want to take it home with me and read it before I sign it, and then I'll get back to you." With that, Bob took the agreement with him and walked toward the door.

"When?" David demanded.

"When I decide to get back to you," Bob shot back. "That's when."

During the following week, Bob met with Solomon Slyman, an attorney who practiced civil litigation. Thus began a lawsuit that was to become one of the nation's defining legal cases on the elements of fraud, and in cases involving the use of the Statute of Wills as a defense against claims of fraud in the inducement. It was to be the beginning of a battle royal.

ASSUMPTIONS AND BARGAINS

Any rabbi worth his salt will tell his congregant to "never assume," properly admonished with an accompanying finger wag in front of the listener's nose. Never assume means what it says. Never assume you have all your bases covered in a deal. Never believe you know everything there is to know about something or someone, for to assume based upon what your experience tells you or upon what someone has passed along to you can be your undoing. Assuming falsely is born of hubris and overconfidence when those two tricksters are paired with underestimation. Never assume you know the outcome of a venture before you embark upon it. Another way of putting it is to say "never underestimate your adversary." The military has a succinct way of terming it: "All battle plans become obsolete as soon as the first shot is fired."

From the outset of Bob's Faustian bargain with David, David always assumed he could never be held to perform his own part of the deal. The assumptions he relied upon were multifaceted. First of importance among all his assumptions was the fact that the maker of a will or a codicil to a will has the freedom to change it. David's confidence in this assumption was ironclad, for he had independently of Old Mac consulted with one of Plaintown's most prestigious law firms. That firm's senior partner, whose practice was trusts and estates, assured David that a man had every right to change his will or a codicil to his will at any time and for any reason. Otherwise, he comforted David, testators could be cheated by those whom were promised an inheritance conditioned upon a performance not earned. David, as was his nature, never revealed to this lawyer that he had shown the codicil to Bob to cement their deal, or that he had made an even earlier pledge to Marvin to leave the businesses to Israel.

A second assumption was that Bob would never be able to produce a copy of the codicil at trial, should matters ever get that far. In the event the codicil ever ended up as evidence in a courtroom, based upon the Statute of Frauds, the only written evidence of a bargain between the pair would be a standard Registered Representatives contract because Bob did not possess an actual copy of the codicil. In that eventuality, the dispute forthcoming would devolve into a contest of who said what, and the rep contract would be determinate. No judge could instruct a jury otherwise.

The third assumption was that Bob would never be able to afford a protracted legal battle and, even if he could, the battle would leave him so depleted he'd have to settle for pennies on the dollar for his claims. David believed a basic axiom of America's legal system was that it was set up to ensure the rights of the defense, that the plaintiff had the burden to carry the case forward, and that burden could be made expensive. David had great faith in the ironclad principle that, in America, the rich could crush the poor.

David's fourth assumption was perhaps his most sinister. He counted upon the avarice and low morality of Bob's former secretary, Judith. Should a battle result from his unilaterally breaking his deal with Bob, he believed he could buy Judith's loyalty. By offering her money and introducing her to some unattached wealthy male friends of his, he believed he could bribe Judith, a woman he always regarded as a bitch who would do anything for money, including turning on her former boss. Thus David could rely on her to fabricate testimony. The possibilities for counterclaims dragging out litigation for years plus a poisonous witness to rebut Bob's case assured it would be a lengthy wrestle in a mud pit. Bob would break and settle cheap.

David held close within his heart his unshakeable fifth assumption that all men who strived for betterment of their personal circumstances were prone to suspend their morality until after they had seized the fruits of their desire. Judges' decisions, lawyers' commitment to their clients, witnesses who would swear upon a Bible to tell the truth, all who waltzed into and out of the courtrooms, and all who met in conferences before and after motions, pleadings, and decisions were mortal men with all their attendant weaknesses and foibles. David looked forward to litigation with confidence.

Bob had three assumptions of his own at the outset of the conflict. His first was that Old Mac would be true to his word, and that Mac was the personification of the soul sought by Diogenes in an otherwise grimy, slime-infested world. As a precaution that David might somehow lose or misplace the codicil, since he'd stated he was terrible at keeping track of paperwork, Bob had already apprised Mac of his situation in the hope Mac would retain a codicil copy in the event of David's memory lapse. Unbeknownst to Bob at the time, there was no memory lapse precipitating David's actions; rather they were consistent with the perpetration of a calculated, blatant fraud. Bob could now only trust that Old Mac was true to his character and would keep a copy of the codicil. It was a tenuous assumption yet to be proven true.

The nature of a fraud can go beyond the simple act of one party lying to another. Fraud can easily don the cloak of conspiracy by drawing in multiple actors at different times along the timeline of the fraud. People necessary to corroborate the fraud can often be bought by the fraud actor to bend the truth, testify falsely, create false records, conceal or lose important evidence, and so on. Bob could only hope that Old

Mac was an honorable man. Now that reposed hope caused him great anxiety.

Bob recalled a conversation he once had with another lawyer on the topic of legal ethics. The man had explained a lawyer's ethical dilemma by way of personal example. The lawyer's client had taken the lawyer to lunch. The bill was five hundred dollars because wines were involved. The client pulled out from his wallet five one-hundred-dollar bills for the tab and placed them on the table; then the client pulled out another hundred for a tip and rested that bill separate on the table. The client left first and the lawyer remained at the table. The lawyer picked up the hundred-dollar bill his client left for the tip and replaced it with a ten-dollar bill, but the lawyer noticed that the hundred was freshly printed and was actually two one-hundred-dollar bills stuck together. The lawyer pondered his ethical dilemma, which was whether or not to tell his partners about the second hundred. Bob shuddered at the thought that Mac might, like so many others, place his ethics in a dark locked closet.

Bob's second assumption was horribly flawed. He believed that David had probably succumbed to syphilis or some such malady. He could not fathom, despite David's changes in behavior toward him ever since he'd rejected the older man's homosexual advances, that David had befriended him at the outset of their relationship with the full intention of destroying his career and taking from him the fullest measures of his life's work and talents. At the outset of battle, it was inconceivable to Bob that his good best friend, his senior mentor, and self-proclaimed father figure had plotted against him all the while, over all the years, and was now figuratively thrusting a knife into his back. He actually felt a modicum of pity for his once best friend that David could fall prey to such inconceivably vile conduct.

That empathetic feeling that the defrauded has for the perpetrator of the fraud is the hallmark of a truly accomplished con artist, one that shows no empathy for his victim or remorse for his deed. In fact, the true fraudster feels he's entitled to screw others, as if it were his God-given right. Perhaps it was so, for God did create Satan as one of his angels, one God bantered with, tested Job with, and one God somehow must've believed was necessary to improve the human condition, through its endless trials and tribulations with evil personified.

Bob's third assumption was actually more of a presumption. Most secretaries stayed loyal to their bosses if the relationship was amicable, as Bob's was with Judith. Other themes, however, tended to encroach upon the weak of moral fiber. "Show me the money" seemed to have equal cache with loyalty and honesty in the bosoms of the greedy.

Solomon's initial complaint included a motion for a restraining order against the disputed companies and against David for the purposes of preserving evidence in discovery. The motion requested that files and records are retained and Bob not be dismissed from the firm. The judge assigned to the case was a bespectacled gray beard with a reputation for harsh maximum punishment when he decided criminal sentencings. A general flavor of disdain for attorneys spiced the judge's utterances, both from his courtroom bench and in his spartan chambers with its metal audience folding chairs.

White-haired, mean-spirited, and impatient, Judge Sandbone sat at his chamber's desk before eleven lawyers, named by defense counsel as all those known to the defendant and the firm's corporate secretary to have performed legal work of any kind for the defendant or the firm during the prior fifteen years. The day before, the judge had issued each of them a summons to appear in person in his chambers at 8:00 a.m. They now all sat before him, mystified and with some trepidation as he took his chair, opened his file, and read from the complaint.

"Any of you gentlemen recall preparing a codicil to a will for a David Sustack, leaving the advisory and underwriting companies of UGGA Universal to a man named Bob something or other?"

A silence ensued as the lawyers looked around the room at each other. At first it appeared there would be no response. Finally, from the middle of the second row of seats, after assuring himself that no one else would first raise their hand, Old Mac raised his.

"I believe I prepared such a document, Your Honor," Mac stated.

"Do you have it? Did you retain a copy?"

"It's been a number of years, Your Honor, but yes, I do believe I retained a copy of that codicil in my files."

"I hereby order you to produce that document to me forthwith. Bring it to me in my chambers here no later than one o'clock today. Let no one else see it or touch it before presentment to this court. Speak of this matter to no one."

"Yes, Your Honor," Old Mac replied.

"But, Your Honor, that document, if it's even authentic, hasn't been entered into evidence or attached to any affidavit," responded the attorney for David who was present.

"Never mind formalities. This is my own pre-discovery request from this bench. I want to see what kind of bullshit I'm going to be dealing with. Do you want to note any objection to that?" Sandbone's staccato voice was accompanied with a glare and a snarl at his irritator.

"No, sir."

"All right then, gentlemen. The rest of you are dismissed. Let's have you, you, and you back here at one o'clock," he said as he pointed to Solomon, Old Mac, and the lawyer for David. Bob's complaint survived the opposition's first efforts to kill it.

In one respect a lawsuit is somewhat like a track runner at the starting blocks. If the runner stumbles out of the blocks, likely his race will be lost at the outset. But if he has alacrity of mind and foot combined, if he anticipates exactly the instant of the firing of the starting gunshot, then he has the jump on his competitors and great odds to run a good race.

The second chance to kill the complaint came at the one o'clock hearing in chambers. There, Sandbone, after reading the draft of the codicil and noting that it matched identically the language in Bob's complaint, offered the defense a perfect escape hatch, a chance to make their opponent stumble at the start.

"This looks legitimate to me. I'm going to allow discovery to go forward and grant the motion to restrain during discovery, subject to counsel's request for bond."

This seemingly innocuous proposal from the judge was a flubbed opportunity by the defense. Solomon noted the defense counsel was caught flat-footed and had no number in mind, nor had he conferred with his client beforehand should this possibility of discovery and bond proposal arise.

Solomon, ever the fastest afoot, looked at the defense counsel and shrugged as if the request were a mere formality. Then he spoke. "Sure, Your Honor, we'll give the court a bond. How about fifty bucks?" He looked at the defense. "You got any problem with that?"

The defense counsel should have rightly said, "Hell no. Those companies are worth thirty million. I want a bond of ten million." But he said, "Okay," instead, obviously not realizing that the bond could be a barrier to discovery of a multi-million-dollar claim. Solomon was inwardly gleeful, for now he had free run of the books and records of his named defendant and his companies for several months with negligible cost. He quickly fished a Ulysses S. Grant from his wallet and handed it to Judge Sandbone.

"Done," said the judge as he snarled at the defendant's counsel, regarding him an incompetent idiot.

The staff legal team for the defense sat in the second row, sinking back into their chairs as a hush descended upon the judge's chambers. With swift strokes of legal genius, Solomon destroyed any chance the defense had to kill the case in infancy by filing a motion to dismiss, based upon the Statute of Wills, had a substantial bond been demanded. Discovery would have never drawn a breath. Now there would be records and depositions. Two law school students who clerked for the judge sat in the back row of his chambers office. One whispered to the other, "The plaintiff now has a copy of the codicil! Can you believe what we just saw? The plaintiff has a heartbeat and this case has legs!"

"Amazing how the defense blew it. Weirdest case I've seen yet. Should be fascinating." The second law clerk chuckled. The fight was on!

David's reaction to the production of the codicil was not what his lawyers expected. Far from showing any hint of anger at their bumbling, he was nonplussed and resolute. From the outset, he'd made it clear to his legal team that he viewed this litigation as a great opportunity to totally destroy a man whom he now regarded as a pretender to his throne. His orders were that no legal avenue of counterattack would go unexploited; no method to delay the proceedings and extract their toll on Bob's costs would be bypassed; no motion, no matter how questionable, ridiculous, or unreasonable would be omitted; and every attempt to destroy Bob's relationships would be made.

David ordered Bob's new upstart investment advisory firm attacked. All regulatory contacts that David's law firms had were to be engaged in constantly harassing Bob's new firm. There would be false complaints filed against him at the assorted securities' regulatory bodies. He would be investigated endlessly in an effort to drive him from the securities business, thus proving David's contention that he was not worthy to inherit the companies. David reveled in the anticipation of pitched battle against a weaker, poorly financed foe. It would be like tearing the wings off a fly all over again.

And so the battle went. Motions flew. Counterclaims were filed. Expenses mounted. Bob's personal assets dwindled rapidly. His bank account declined to a zero balance in less than two months, his pension plan assets lasting another two. He had two real properties which he sold cheaply for badly needed cash.

All the while, David kept up the off-court pressure. He bribed Judith to sign a false affidavit that Bob was a worthless whoremonger who had boasted to her that he suckered an old man into giving him his companies. She received a free condominium and season tickets for her beloved Denver Broncos.

She was soon to learn that she'd made her own Faustian bargain. David told her that in order to keep her job she was required to allow a drug dealer from Columbia to move into her home with her and the children. After a short period of time, Judith was sleeping with a criminal drug dealer who was firmly ensconced in her bed. She was required to make drug drops to local high schools where David's network of distributors supplied Colorado school children their heroin and cocaine. Meanwhile, marijuana plants were grown in her basement. Her marijuana distribution network soon was expanded to cocaine sales smuggled into Colorado from Columbia. The proceeds were turned over to David, the drug smugglers' financier.

Things looked dire for Bob. A counterclaim attack was launched against him. Competing mutual fund firms with multiple funds and a dozen or two dozen wholesalers, combined with multimillion-dollar television and print advertising budgets, and with multimillion commission payment kickbacks to broker-dealers for shelf space, were able to raise billions of dollars compared to Bob's mere hundreds of millions. By the logic of David's countercomplaint, Bob should have done as well as any competitor and he should owe David one hundred million in damages and lost profits.

The nefarious counterclaim was eventually dismissed, but it achieved its desired effect. Bob needed to pay legal expenses and experts to continue to bring his case forward and disprove the fallacies of the counterclaims. His resources were rapidly dwindling and he resorted to borrowing on credit cards to pay legal bills, food, and rent. He was beyond broke, reduced to selling personal items to keep himself and his case alive. The stamp collection he'd started as a Boy Scout and his coin collection were both sold. If he were a fly, he would've known his wings were torn off.

Every day and nights until 9:00 p.m. Bob made cold calls to retail client prospects to try to generate income. His avenues of employment in the traditional brokerage business were shut off. David had filed, as Bob's former employer, reports with the regulatory authorities that he was a dangerous and unstable person who had to be dismissed. Things were looking hopelessly bleak for him until, by some miracle, he happened to make a cold call to a former Catholic nun.

As luck—or divine intervention—would have it, this poor nun had a crippling terminal disease and had left her convent to rest at home. A good-hearted soul, she took in men who were afflicted with the AIDS virus as boarders for modest rents. When her phone rang that night, she was in the anguished throes of trying to decide what to do with the million dollars she'd just inherited from her late father. She knew nothing of finances or money management and actually held money in some disdain, but had prayed for guidance from Almighty God to put her inheritance to good use.

It was Bob on the line asking her if she might be in need of investment assistance. A person of faith, Nun Bertie was certain the call from Bob was divinely inspired. She listened to him for a while and then shouted toward the kitchen ceiling, as if to peer through all man-made structures and call out to the heavens, "Thank you, God, for answering my prayers. You have sent this man to me just as I was praying for your guidance." Returning to the phone, she said, "Young man, you come over here right away."

And with that, a great relationship was formed. Bob invested Bertie's monies well. She took in more AIDS sufferers and took out insurance policies on them as well. Bertie and Bob together combined their wits and wills to postpone death for as many sufferers as possible for as long as possible.

Bertie was not a soul who held back. Every person known to her—and she knew a great many people—soon came to her home to get acquainted with Bob. She declared that Bob was sent to her by God and that her prayers were answered in her darkest hour. As further proof that he was sent as a blessing, Bertie pointed out how much her cat, Tom, loved to rub against him.

Knowing that Bertie's good heart operated from divine guidance, friends of hers were soon calling Bob to help them with their investments as well. She had friends over for coffees to meet him. Tom became very attached to him at these get-togethers. Bob was allergic to Tom, but for the goodwill and the good business he overdosed on allergy pills and let Tom rub all over him while he sneezed and snorted into his handkerchief.

Perhaps miracles beget more miracles. There are things that happen in one's life that reach beyond human comprehension. Bob received an anonymous phone call one evening about Judith's new house guest and duty fuck-buddy. He was wanted in Australia on an arrest warrant as an accomplice to a homicide. Bob played sleuth, parking his car several blocks away and watching the house in the evenings. Only two nights into Bob's detective work, the drug dealer pulled his car in front of the garage and stopped briefly while the garage door opened. That was all Bob needed. He casually walked down the street, passing the garage just as the car pulled in and the door was closing. Unseen, Bob got the license plate and went to the police with what he knew. Two days later, a county sheriff came to Judith's, picked up the Columbian, and shipped him off to Australia to serve out a twenty-year prison sentence.

The next miracle came from Judith herself. Completely unexpected, she called Bob the evening before the case went to trial.

"I just called to tell you not to get your hopes up about your trial tomorrow. You are going to lose. The judge has been bought and paid for. I got that from the chief financial officer at UGGA. He's in on all of it and told me all about it. I can't do anything about what's happened to you in the past except to say I'm sorry. I did what I believed I had to do to survive for me and my kids. I don't expect you to understand and I know we can never be friends again after all that's happened, with the bitterness and all, but I want you to know that I'll try to do what little I can for you when I can. Just don't get upset with your lawyer when you lose tomorrow. You two will have lost before you walk into the courtroom."

Bob related that conversation to Solomon. "She's crazy," Sol declared. "The judge can't be bribed."

Bob pondered Sol's reaction. It made him feel uneasy.

The third miracle—or turn of fortune, whatever it was— came from Barbara.

"Bob, I called to talk. It's time. The fund is going nowhere without you. The salesmen aren't selling, the assets are dwindling. David is now calling dealers and offering to buy assets to manage temporarily to show that he can grow sales without you, but they aren't real sales. I hear him crowing that he's got you pounded into the ground and nearly destroyed, and it's making me sick to hear it. I just thought I'd call and see if you're ready for some help over there. It must be hard running a one-man band with no money and no help."

"Well, Barbara, it *is* hard, and I *could* use the help, but I can't afford to pay you."

"Never mind that. How much money are you managing, and how much do you need?"

"I could use about twelve million, and I'm about ten million short."

"Okay, well, when do you want me to start?"

"Barbara, I just told you I can't afford you."

"Yes, you can. I'll bring ten million with me."

"Barbara, we can't rip assets out of UGGA. I have a court order prohibiting that. My lawyer and the judge would both kill me. My case would be lost."

"Who said anything about taking from the fund? I'll bring some of my father's money with me. Chief has controlling interests in six casinos. He also owns three ranches, water rights in Montana and California, and overriding royalties on twelve gold mines and three hundred oil wells. I'm one rich Indian princess. I've just been waiting for the right situation to go into business on my own. Chief said I needed to give it time. It's time, Bob. It's time for us. What do you say we become equal partners?"

"You're putting me on."

"Nope. I'm Big Chief's only child, and Daddy likes to spoil his Little Sparrow. You want an Injun princess squaw for your very own? She comes with a heap of wampum, Big Horse, and she knows the securities business inside and out. And she can do many other things also. She's a good trade."

"And what's the trade?"

"I told you. You be an equal partner with this Injun girl. I own half, and you own half. I'll bring more to the trade too. We'll get an audience with tribal chiefs, some of whom have a big heap of wampum. Also, I heard some white men think Injun girls know how to make great whoopee. We might see about that, but the deal must come first."

"What makes you think I'm interested in whoopee at a time like this?" Bob teased her. He loved her and they both could feel it.

"All the girls in the office talk, and the grapevine leads back to me. I hear all. All the girls report white boy Bob looks long and hard at my backside while I walked away. You might as well have put up smoke signals, Big Horse. I heard you looked at my ass many times and took deep breaths after you looked. You're not very good at concealing your thoughts, white boy."

"Barbara, I want children and a woman with a home life, not all business."

"That's okay. I have ranches and horses and bows and arrows. Things work themselves out."

"You make everything sound like it's a business proposition."

"It is. Children will come in time. Big Horse is always in a rush. Chief says to give everything time. He's very wise. This Injun girl isn't stupid. Sparrow knows what a woman's role is, but this Injun girl also has a master's degree in business administration and all licenses for securities compliance. You could do worse, and you *did* do a lot worse, remember? Now it's time you try thinking with your big head instead of your little head. Deal or no deal?"

Bob only paused for a breath. "Deal, but from now on you call me Bob."

"Okay, Bob Big Horse. I'll be at your office tomorrow morning with the paperwork for my stock shares and my license transfers, and some checks to open some accounts."

"Checks from whom?"

"From Daddy. I cleared all this with him ahead of time."

"How did you know I'd go for this?"

"Because I'm Barbara, and I'm a woman. Women know things about men before men can figure out what the woman is even thinking. Trust me and you will never go wrong, Bob. Your decision was never in question; Daddy's was. He thought dealing with a white boy could end up getting me screwed, but he's okay with you now. I told him that you were my ticket out of David's pederast playpen, and that you were very ethical, not like some white men. I told him I've known you long enough to know you're the guy I want to work with and maybe even more someday. Anyway, I told him he could trust you. So we both trust you, Bob. You and I will need to go meet my father."

"Where and when? Don't tell me he lives in a teepee."

"No, silly, we have a huge ranch in Montana, but Father does keep a teepee out behind the house. He goes there to think sometimes and to meet with the other chiefs, like the chiefs did in the old days. We're not reservation Indians anymore, but we do belong to the Cane Breaks Cherokees and we are true to our roots and our people."

"How did Cherokees get from Georgia to Montana?"

"It's a story that might make you cry. I'll tell you about it, but this is not the time."

Within an hour, Bob's firm became Bob and Barbara's firm. Its assets instantly grew six-fold and Bob went from wondering where he was going to find money for food and rent to becoming a viable business. He woke that morning a lonely pauper, contemplating the surrender of his licenses and closing his business, possibly even running away to Alaska or South America and starting life over from scratch. He went to sleep that night with his mind leaping with future possibilities for the firm and anticipation of a life shared with his heartthrob Barbara. As he fell away into slumber, he visualized her braided hair swinging rhythmically back and forth across her mesmerizing backside while she walked before him the first day he met her. She was mysterious, smart, and savvy and had a beautifully innocent savageness about her. She had more of life's spirit within her than anyone he'd ever known, including Marty. Barbara was an enigmatic soul who was slowly absorbing his soul into her own. He could feel it happening. He noticed he didn't like being apart from her. He began dreaming and wondering what she really thought of him, not as a business partner but as a man.

Barbara made her call to Bob on a Friday and was at his office, unbeknownst to David, on Saturday morning, working on affecting her transfer of licenses and allegiances. Meanwhile, David sat on his veranda that Saturday morning looking at his rose garden. He had Dolly in his bedroom that morning in her position box. He had the highest regard for Dolly. She never complained nor asked for any payment, and their business matters settled quickly.

He smelled the sweet wafts of rose fragrance and reflected on his genius in pulling off a perfect murder, very pleased at the robust canes his bone-nourished rose plants produced.

David wondered how the authorities could have possibly gotten wind that his Columbian macho man was shacked up with Judith. He decided to cut her loose as soon as his litigation settled. He had all the lawyers and she had none. Still, her kids were just kids, and kids could talk. The more he thought about it, the luckier he felt that they had not been busted selling drugs. It was a stupid idea. Besides, if something happened to Judith or her kids, it could open up the possibility that he was linked to Marty's disappearance.

What was he thinking? For the first time in his life he doubted his own judgment. What made him so sure that her kids would actually want to be involved in his drug distribution business? Not all kids were like he'd been. He remembered how he hated his parents and how he rejoiced when he learned Marvin was dying.

Judith showed signs of wavering loyalty. Barbara left him to work for Bob. He always suspected the Indian girl wanted his top salesman. Was he going to be fighting Barbara too? He had too much on his plate at one time. As much as he admired Hitler's ruthlessness, when it came to battle tactics the man was an idiot. How smart was any man to get involved in multiple fights at the same time? David felt the world closing in on him.

As he sat on his veranda, his thoughts turned to torturing Bob slowly through the legal processes and how that goal could be accomplished at no cost to himself. David naturally hated lawyers. He didn't trust any of them, especially the ones who worked for him. He'd reasoned it all out years before—every lawyer, no matter which side he represented, was really only representing himself. Every law school student, he learned, took a class day where one of the professors, a part-time professor and a practicing lawyer, told the students that the legal profession was a business.

The first duty of every lawyer businessman was to make sure they were paid and paid well, regardless of what happened to their client. The client was just a venue for payment and the case was just a piece of business to milk to the maximum. As a lawyer, they were not supposed to be thinking about ethics. They were supposed to think about money. The ethics stuff was just for the movies and television for the dummies in the public who believed what they saw on *Perry Mason* reruns.

Ethics was only a framework that defined limits, so they mustn't get caught in ethics violations, but they were never to be driven by ethics. If all lawyers were driven by ethics, there would be no compensation incentive to ever become one in the first place.

With his reasoned understanding of lawyers' motives, David shaped a plan to take advantage of all the lawyers involved in the litigation, especially his own. He didn't buy into the lawyers' "mano a mano" mantra. It wasn't about man against man in a pitched court battle; that was a lot of lawyer bunk to sell the gullible public on hiring one of these slimy bastards in the first place. It was really a matter of mano a mano a mano, etc., for as many lawyers as there were, with David being the first and most important against all the other lawyer bastards.

As the first step in his plan, David sought out a lawyer who was an expert at convicting other lawyers of legal malpractice. He retained Mr. Green to advise him how he could set traps for all the lawyers in the case so he could have the greatest chance of either winning the case or, if he should lose or be forced to settle, make his own lawyers pay for the settlement due to the mistakes they made. Blaming others for his problems was always his backdoor escape from every jam he'd found himself in since he was a little boy.

In David's world view, he could not possibly lose this fight. A lawyer once told him he could change his will; that settled the matter as far as he was concerned. True to his sociopathic mindset, he believed himself entitled to do anything he wanted in any way he wanted to do it. Anything which caused him to lose or settle could only be due to the malpractice or negligence of his lawyers!

Mal Green kept his practice extremely confidential. David found him through non-legal channels by asking doctors whom they used to defend them in malpractice cases. Then he asked those lawyers whom they used to defend them in malpractice cases, and then he asked *those* lawyers who their best adversary was in a malpractice case. Eventually, through meticulous searching, the names of the slimes that ate other slimes distilled down to the man most feared by all other slimes.

By sliming around, David found a marriage made in heaven. He found Mal Green. Mal advised him to take notes immediately after every meeting he had with his lawyers, and to hold meetings with them in his offices where the room could be bugged whenever possible. The objective of hiring lawyers was not to win the case, although that would be a nice outcome, but to protract the litigation, make the opponent suffer as much as possible, and, regardless of the outcome, make his own lawyers pay for the settlement and forgive David's fees.

Everyone engaged in litigation learned things through depositions they never before imagined about other people. Bob learned in one deposition session when a former secretary, being asked why she resigned, stated that she liked working late sometimes but people ran around naked in the offices after hours and their cavorting about made it hard for her to concentrate.

Another revelation was that every other week or so, three armed men with Spanish accents, sunglasses, bald heads, and heavily tattooed arms, necks, and heads would show up shortly after closing carrying large shopping bags filled with cash. The bags were left in David's office for his vital role in the drug trade, the laundering of the money. After the counting of the cash, he and the three would walk to the elevators together while smoking large cigars. The men would, all three, kiss David on his cheeks and leave with one of them carrying a single legal-sized briefcase.

Depositions also revealed that several witnesses, supposedly friends who would testify for Bob, were away on extended cruises when their depositions were supposed to occur. They all had doctors' excuses that they needed to leave the high altitude of Colorado for their health for an extended and indefinite period of time. People Bob thought were reliable, honest friends were easily bought off. He reminded himself that the investment business was, after all, only about money.

David's defense team engaged in harassment tactics to do their level best to prevent Bob's new firm from gaining or retaining clients. They filed motions to discover whether he had stolen clients from the fund, which necessitated his new firm to obtain protective orders so clients' personal files would not be revealed, or that they not be barraged with slanderous or libelous commentary about Bob. The defense attacked his elderly mother, seeking to depose her to determine whether or not he had difficulties getting along with other children when he was a child, as if some comment could possibly be elicited from his aging and infirmed mother that could tenuously be linked to David's bogus claim that Bob was a dangerous and disruptive force in the office which necessitated his being let go. That nonsense was also quashed with a protective order.

Barbara also became the object of attacks after she left the fund. Her deposition was taken in an effort to find out if she and Bob had a romantic relationship which caused them to collude to sabotage the fund and steal its clients. That fishing expedition went nowhere, as Barbara had no such relationship while at the fund or any time up to and including the day of her deposition. Barbara was followed by David's private detective while her home was monitored with a wide antenna listening device.

Yes, she talked to Bob sometimes in the evenings, but it was all business. David's lawyers advised him that harassment charges against a woman in business might give them difficulties to defend, but he persisted. Barbara was tailed around the clock, every day of the week. The private detectives found nothing, but the surveillance continued.

One evening David's hired surveillance man, sitting in his car across the street from Barbara's home, had an encounter with undocumented aliens. They pulled their car alongside the private eye's. Three men got out armed with baseball bats and hammers. All windows and lights in the surveillance car were smashed, every panel of the car's body was dented, and its four tires were slashed. They dragged David's surveillance man from his car and beat him with their bats until his ribs were broken. Then, just as quickly as they appeared, the illegals drove away. The police interviewed Barbara about the incident, but she genuinely knew nothing about it.

The next day in their tiny office, Bob asked Barbara about the dustup.

"Chief has his ways. It would be like him to send somebody and not let me know about it. I never said a word to him about the surveillance guy, but Chief would know anyway. It's strange being his daughter. He is everywhere but unseen, like the wind. I told you before that he always watches over me. He's been like that since I was a little girl. I know this much for sure. If he was behind this—and I'm not saying it *was* him—the police will never catch him. He's too clever to be caught and he'd use some middle men. Those three guys will never be found either. Chief's very thorough. I'll bet either the surveillance stops or David has to pay two guys triple each what he was paying that one guy." Barbara's pride in her father was apparent in her voice.

"I wonder how David feels getting a taste of his own medicine. Maybe the dirty tricks and harassment he's been putting us through will stop now. Who were those guys? Do you know?" Bob was awed by Barbara's father, whom he'd yet to meet.

"I can't know. You need to know that. I'd be guessing." Barbara tried evasion.

"Indulge me, partner. Take a guess."

"Well, it works like this. Chief gets a cut of the casinos, right off the top. He splits with Jo Jo. Jo Jo's job is to take care of details. Jo Jo has Bobby, Phil, and Guido who do groundwork. When Chief needs a favor, he asks Jo Jo. When Jo Jo needs a favor, he asks Dad."

"Wait. Jo Jo, Bobby, Phil, Guido. Who are these people?"

"They're the 'get it done guys.' Jo Jo Paulo, Bobby Robbie, Phil Capobianco, and Guido 'Blade' Checini."

"Your family works with the mob?"

"Dad runs all legitimate businesses, and he prefers to work with people who have good business experience. Now you know all you need to know."

"So where do you and I fit into this?"

"We manage investments, passive investments. Dad happens to be a good client."

"Tell me about the money."

"It's all legitimate, from duly incorporated U.S.-domiciled businesses that pay their taxes, their employees, their license fees, their rents and utilities. They are totally clean, no criminal complaints, no union problems, and no political problems. Jo Jo keeps everything clean. Bad actors and bad girls aren't welcome. Legitimate independent operators can do business with Jo Jo if they're legal and pay rent. Now you know more than you need to know. No more questions. We are clean. Our firm is clean. We have lawyers who know the securities business and they checked us out, checked everything out. We are whistle clean. Sparrow is your good clean partner, the best friend you could ever have. No more questions."

Barbara guessed right. David's surveillance did stop. His lawyers told him they'd never get anything for the effort anyway and he'd just look vindictive to a jury if it came out that he was engaging in harassment tactics. He decided to redouble his legal efforts and cease the thug tactics, but for the first time in his life he felt he might be dealing with forces he didn't fully understand.

The legal case morphed into multiple cases against the defendant, David; and against the companies of the codicil; and against the service company. All actions went the slowest route possible and, all in all, David utilized the services of fifty-four different lawyers to defend himself and the companies. Years passed. Lawyers gave notice of their appearances and later requested permission to withdraw. David found reasons to change law firms several times, causing multiple delays. His strategy of grinding Bob to a pulp wasn't working. The litigation cost him a fortune. Bob's attorney was on a contingency arrangement, and the long hours and bitter fight took their toll on Sol.

Finally, after years of delay, David sat at the defendant's table in court listening to Bob testify about their relationship and their agreement to have Bob change careers in exchange for the companies upon David's death. He showed some audacity to the jurors, the judge, and Bob and his attorney.

Through the whole of Bob's testimony, David sat sprawled in his chair, his ass barely resting on the edge of the seat. He obnoxiously chewed gum, smacking it with his mouth open throughout Bob's testimony, and he frequently shoved his hand down into the front of his pants and adjusted his testicles in front of the entire courtroom. The judge asked David politely, twice, to please sit upright in his chair. He complied for a time and then reverted to his prostrated slouching position. The judge gave up trying to correct him.

When David took the stand, the questioning went along routinely until Bob's attorney made him recount his visit to the bank vault with Bob. Then David exploded, lashing out at Sol from the witness stand.

"Why are you picking on me about this crap? It's just my will. It's my fucking will, you fucking son of a bitch! I can change my will any time I want. That's the fucking law. You know that. You're a lawyer. You're just picking on me because I'm a Jew, aren't you? What's the matter with you? You're a Jew yourself, aren't you? Since when does one Jew go out of his way and try to shame another Jew, huh? Answer me! You say you're a Jew, but no Jew does this to another Jew! Fuck you, and fuck the horse you rode in here on! You're not going anywhere with this crap. I'll fight you until I'm dead if I have to, you asshole! You're not stealing my companies! You're just a slimy bastard trying to steal from a poor old man. You're trying to take away from me what I've worked all my life for. Fuck you. Fuck you. You're just dreck. You're going to end up eating your own shit on this case, buddy. Nobody fucks with me like this and gets away with it." David screamed like a man possessed by demons.

The judge was pounding his gavel from the moment he heard the first sentence and the jurors were appalled, but David would not be stopped. A true sociopath believes that he can do whatever he wishes and nobody has the right to deter him. David relished his moment in the limelight and he wasn't about to have anyone steal it, not even a judge. The judge recessed the court and called both attorneys and David into his chambers. The jurors were filing out when he admonished David. He held out his index finger, pointing it as if it were a pistol barrel right between David's eyes as he peered over its imaginary sights.

"I'm warning you for the last time. If there's another outburst from you in my courtroom, you will be held in contempt and incarcerated."

David shot back at the judge. "You'll regret that."

The judge had already agreed to dismiss the case for a payment to his favorite charity. Now he was confronted with outright contempt for his bench. He was stalemated by this devious sociopath. Would David actually go so far as to risk criminal bribery charges just to bring the same charges down upon a sitting judge? Sandbone had already surmised that David was an evil actor, but he doubted the man was stupid. Lowering himself to this scumbag was exactly what the narcissist wanted, to demonstrate that the whole show revolved around him, the principal actor. He swallowed hard and appealed to David's self-interest.

"Please, Mr. Sustack. Let's all just get through these proceedings here. I'm asking you politely to be reasonable. We must go through these formalities in good order, for the possibility is there that these proceedings will be appealed. Do you understand what I'm telling you?"

David understood the subtle message. The judge was telling him in a nice way that he was actually working for David, trying to earn his bribe, but if he didn't cooperate, the whole matter could be thrown out and David would end up in a different courtroom with a different judge and an uncertain outcome.

THE URINALS

When the actors had taken their respective positions, Judge Sandbone called the jury back. Bob, the plaintiff, took the stand. He gave testimony about the long-standing relationship he had with David, the money splitting on their handshake, the trips, the gifts, the countless lunches and dinners. Then Bob related the bank vault scene and described the codicil he was shown by David. His recitation was exactly as he'd stated it in his initial complaint, again in his deposition, and it matched exactly the copy produced by Old Mac.

David's testimony coincided almost exactly with Bob's. The trial was going smoothly until Bob's lawyer began a line of inquiry that David was not prepared to answer.

"When you inherited the companies from your father, was there any condition attached to your inheritance?"

"What do you mean, condition?" David answered, a little hesitant.

"Let me introduce plaintiff exhibit number forty-six. This is your father's, Mr. Marvin Sustack, last will and testament. I'll read to you the relevant part, David. It says that your father is gifting to you the ownership of the underwriting and the distribution companies that operate the UGGA Universal Growth Fund, and that as a condition of your inheriting these companies from your father, you pledged to him that upon your own death, you would leave these companies to the State of Israel. Am I reading your father's will correctly, David?"

"Yes, that is a correct reading."

"When you made that promise to your father, was it your intention to honor that promise?"

"Yes."

"Are you a devoted Jew, David?'

"Yes."

"Was your father a devoted Jew?"

"Yes."

"He was, wasn't he? In fact, he was a committed Zionist, wasn't he? He helped smuggle Jews out of Nazi Germany, isn't that true? He also gave large donations to Jewish causes throughout his lifetime, didn't he? He was also a major contributor to the American Israeli Political Action Committee, or AIPAC, and a devoted contributor to the Zionist political parties in Israel, isn't that true?

"Yes, it's all true. So what?"

"So what? Here's so what! He loved Israel more than he loved you, didn't he? He would never have given you those companies without that pledge you made to him on his deathbed. You needed those companies to make a living so you made that pledge, didn't you?"

"Objection, badgering!" shouted the defense counsel.

"I'll allow it," Sandbone shot back. He'd been bribed to dismiss the case at trial, but he was going to allow the plaintiff every chance to win on appeal.

David glared at Sandbone.

"I'll ask again," Sol said. "Did you need those companies? Did you intend to keep that pledge?"

"Yes, I intended to keep it."

"Okay. So now when it's years later, you have Bob in the bank vault showing him this codicil, promising him you'll leave him the companies if he'll work with you to build the companies. Did you intend to keep the pledge to your father when you showed the codicil to Bob? Did you intend to give the companies to Israel as you pledged to your father as a condition of inheriting those companies when you were showing the codicil to Bob?"

"Well, I was just showing it to him."

"That's all been established. The question is, when you were showing Bob the codicil, were you still intending to honor your pledge to your father and the State of Israel? It's a yes or no answer, David. Did you intend to honor your pledge to your father while you were showing Bob the codicil?"

"Yes. I have always tried to be a good son, and I intended to leave the companies to Israel when I died when I showed Bob the codicil."

"So, you were willing to let Bob change his career, work for much less money, make you and the companies worth millions, and then give millions of dollars in valuable companies to Israel and leave Bob with nothing. Is that what your intentions were?"

"Well, I thought I might give him something later on."

"Tell us about that."

"Well, I replaced the codicil with a new one that left him a half million dollars."

"When did you do that?"

"About a year before the lawsuit started."

"I see. About a year before the lawsuit started, the companies were worth about thirty million dollars. You took away thirty million dollars from Bob when you removed that codicil and left him a half million. Is that correct?"

"I can do anything I want with my will, you son of a bitch. You know a man can change his will."

"My question is, did you tell Bob that you replaced the codicil leaving him the companies with a new one that leaves him a half million?"

"No."

"Why not?"

"It's none of his business what I do with my will."

ROSEMARY LIGHTFOOT NESS BITNER

"Now, is the half-million codicil still in effect?"

"No. I destroyed that when he started this lawsuit. He's an ungrateful bastard."

"So now Bob gets nothing. The man worked the best years of his life based upon your promise. You were like a father to him. He lost his father when he was two. He was a half orphan and you took advantage of him. He believed in you based upon the underwriting deals you made with him, splitting four million dollars on a handshake. He even became a Jew based upon your schtuping—I'm sorry, for the jurors who are not Jews, based upon your pushing and coaxing—and now he gets nothing. Is that what you're about, David? Ruining a human life to enrich yourself and then give the money to Israel?"

"Objection, argumentative!" Defense counsel sounded sick and halfhearted that time.

"Sustained," said Sandbone, feeling sick to his stomach.

"No, I'll answer this," David shouted. "This is all a bunch of fucking bullshit. A man can change his will any time he wants to. That's the law. You're just trying to smear me and the State of Israel. You're all just a bunch of anti-Semites. I don't need to sit here and listen to this shit. And you!" David, his face beet red, pointed his finger at Sol. "You should get out of here and hang yourself. You are a fucking disgrace to your tribe, to Israel, to everything that is Jewish. You represent this filth, this gentile who pretends to be a Jew. You disgust me. I did nothing wrong. You have no right whatsoever to question what I did with my will, none whatsoever! I have no reason to even be here. Fuck all of you!"

That last outburst resulted in the courtroom being cleared. Judge Sandbone impaneled the jury while he considered the defense's motion to dismiss the case based upon the Statute of Wills, a codified law adopted into the Uniform Commercial Code as adopted by some thirty-six states. Simply stated, the law provided that the last will and testament was binding upon a deceased's estate, absent a writing presented to the contrary. Based upon the fact that David had not provided Bob with a copy of the codicil when they were in the bank vault, the defense motion argued that Bob could not rely upon the mere showing of it.

After the courtroom cleared, Bob and Sol were standing side-by-side in the men's room before two large five-foot-tall porcelain urinals. Sol was first to speak. "We're going to get our asses thrown out of here. The judge hates our guts. He's going to buy their dismissal argument."

"After all that? After the way David mouthed off? After you showed his intent was to keep his promise to Marvin?"

"None of that matters. The judge won't stick his neck out. He won't buck the statute, regardless of the testimony. He'll dismiss."

"Judith told me she heard from the fund's financial officer that the judge was bribed."

"You can't believe what a woman who worked for you says. Can you prove it?"

"Not yet. She said she'd give me the proof when she was ready to."

"Okay, I'll talk to her. We'll deal with it later."

When court reconvened, Judge Sandbone stated that, based on the evidence presented, Bob was an employee of a subsidiary company of a holding company and that the holding company and its owner were not responsible for the acts of an officer of a subsidiary company, even though the persons of the subsidiary and the holding company were the same. Therefore, the case turned on the Statute of Wills, the contract claims fell, and the fraud and unjust enrichment claims also fell. The case was dismissed.

Sol and Bob left the courtroom. Sol put his hand upon Bob's shoulder and said, "I want you to know that the Jewish people are not at all like David. He's a no-good filthy cocksucker who gives all of us Jews a bad name. Most Jews are good, honest people you can trust. This is a tragedy, what happened in your case and your life, and in the ruling we got here today. I will be appealing this. In fact, I have a hunch I'll be filing appeals for the next ten years, but I will stay with you all the way on this. The law is simple. It's designed to say you can't just go around screwing people. That's all we need."

THE SUPREMES

The case was appealed five times based upon arguments of law as to who was responsible for putting David and Bob together in a bank vault. Was it David, or was it one of the companies? Was Bob really working for David to enrich him and Israel, or was he working only for the companies, just to build the companies and not inherit them? Were the claims really just quantum meruit claims brought in another form by a disgruntled employee? Did the Statute of Wills actually apply here? Did Judge Sandbone err in his ruling to dismiss the case based upon his finding that, by not possessing a writing, Bob had not met the Statute? Could the statute be governing here when it was clearly shown in the evidence that the defendant had no intent to leave the companies to the plaintiff? Back and forth went the appeals, from appeals court to trial court. Legal precedents affecting all states that adopted the Statute of Wills as definitive were being decided.

At a second trial, ordered on remand from appeals court where the case was next tried against the companies, that case was also dismissed. David testified that the companies he owned had nothing to do with his personal decisions, and he was not acting as an officer or director of either company when he showed Bob the codicil. After eight years of wrangling in the appeals courts, the cases came down to one man, David, sitting in the witness chair saying in the first case that the companies made the deal with Bob, thus it was a simple quantum meruit case. But when the companies were tried in the second case, the party responsible for being in the bank vault was David personally—but he had the right to change his will. Sol argued this was a lot of nonsensical Kabuki theater. It was analogous to watching a clown pointing in opposite directions with both index fingers, shouting, "He did it!"

Meanwhile David was leading the life of luxury, trotting off to vacation spots all over the world and having full use of the companies and their cash flows, which Bob had grown by his own labors. David continued expanding his growing drug distribution business, poisoning the youth of Colorado and other states, and victimizing others with his loan shark business. Being a sleazy fraud was paying off very well for him.

In a tortured mind, still confused about the true nature of his relationship with David, Bob sometimes allowed himself to believe that his would-be dad was showing him through cruel example that many of the things he'd taught him were actually easily born out. Public officials could all be bought off, and that apparently included judges on the Colorado District Court level. Lawyers could be paid to do illegal things for you, such as bribing witnesses and psychologists to give false testimony. Illegal aliens were readily available if one just asked around a bit, and they could be employed to damage property or even commit murders.

David's personality always fascinated Bob. Like any Faustian, Bob was entranced by this bizarre, evil persona. And like many others who succumbed to fraud, he actually empathized with the character who did him a great wrong. Despite wrongful behaviors which Bob observed David doing while working together, he deluded himself into believing that somehow he was personally exempt from being on the receiving end of any of David's behaviors. Sol needed several sessions with Bob during which he told his client that he was just another patsy, just like everybody else who worked with David. Sol eventually got Bob to accept that the only father he ever had or would ever have was his dead one. His compassion for Bob went beyond the duties of the lawyer to his client. Like Arlene, the school nurse in Milltown, Sol's deep well of humanity likely saved Bob from living his life in undeserved purgatory.

Just when the case appeared to be reaching a final judicial interpretation of the Statute of Wills as related to a defense for fraud, a terrible thing happened to Bob's attorney. Bob got the news a week before the case was scheduled to be heard in the state supreme court—Sol had died of a massive heart attack in the middle of the night. Bob needed to obtain new counsel, and that whole process took another three months. Eventually, an attorney with a twenty-percent success rate agreed to represent him, subject to reduced compensation due to his outstanding legal bills owed to Sol's estate. The new lawyer's name was Benjamin Slipperman. His colleagues called him 'Slipup.' He was possibly the least imposing personal presence ever seen in a courtroom.

Standing a mere five feet tall and weighing over three hundred pounds, Ben carried with him a breast pocket full of cheap cigars and a string of three handkerchiefs, tied together in knots and hanging from his back pocket, dangling halfway to the ground. It was a bizarre sight to see and hear this living marshmallow of a man. One's first impression of Ben was that he was likely a child with a perpetual runny nose, who might still live with his mother. Only a mother could make a grown man carry three knotted handkerchiefs dangling from his back pocket that way. But wait! Ben still *did* live with his mother. He was fifty years old and had always lived with her. He sometimes laughed about his situation, saying that his mother, a New York Jewess, was highly selective about the women in his life and she hadn't found one as good as herself yet.

When Ben was before a judge, he coughed and wheezed a lot due to his chronic bronchitis. Undeterred by the prospect of an early death, he smoked at least three cigars daily. When he spoke, he annoyed every judge who ever endured his orations. His chronic postnasal drip caused a constant stream of snot to flow from his nostrils, and his sentences were interrupted in mid-phrase by the vacuum cleaner-like sound of Ben trying to snort up the snot stream from his dripping palate roof. These snorts were disgustingly followed by a forcible gulp as he swallowed his snot pile. That maneuver caused his Adam's apple to bulge noticeably, his face reddening. Some judges would place their hands over their eyes while this repulsive procedure was carried out; others would look off to the side. Jurors snickered or put their heads down into their reading while Ben cleared his nasal passages. In winter months, this interruption could take place every two or three minutes.

Ben, his colleagues said, was his own best reason for losing so many cases. For all he was lacking physically, he was capable mentally. He was not exceptional, far short of brilliant, but capable. His corpulence, his snot problems, and a frequent unlit cigar in his mouth were accented by a pair of glasses with lenses as thick as Coke bottle bottoms. He was the human rendition of a mole, but this was one mole that knew how to sniff out money.

As Ben researched cases far into the evenings, he came across an appeals court ruling from Wisconsin with facts involving a shiksa case, where a woman was denied recovery from an estate even though she had a napkin with a vague written promise of money after death for her lifelong services. He called the plaintiff's counsel.

After discussion and strategizing, the two lawyers petitioned the U.S. Supreme Court to hear Bob's case, represented by Ben, on a writ of certiorari. It was a daring legal maneuver, especially since no federal court had ever ruled on this issue. It was outside the Federal Rules of Civil Procedure, yet it did involve a Federal Statute that was adopted as law in thirty-seven states. It likely only had a one chance in a million of being heard, but Ben figured it was worth the shot. He had nothing to lose. And even if he lost the writ, the move would buy him more time to prepare for his appeals in Colorado. Time went by, first one month, then three months, then six months. Ben told Bob that the justices must've been scratching their heads over this one. The joined cases had national interest because the Statute of Wills was now defining and governing law in thirty-seven of the fifty states.

One day in late November, just before Thanksgiving, a courier opened the door to Ben's office. Behind a pile of files and paper was a smoking cigar with the dome of a bald head facing down on a massive oak desk.

"Mr. Slipperman, counsel for Bob Burke?" The courier was Army sergeant material the way he barked out a name.

"Yes," replied a sheepish voice, with its attached head not looking up.

"I bear a writ order from the United States Supreme Court, sir. I'll need your signature."

Ben hastily opened the packet, and there it was, just like that! The one-in-a-million shot was granted. Ben Slipperman, the mamma's boy with the runny nose, the fat kid all the other lawyers laughed at, was getting his shot at making legal history! His petition for writ was granted. The case that never had a chance to succeed from day one was going to be heard by the United States Supreme Court. Ben's cigar dropped to the floor. He stood to shake the courier's hand.

"Thank you, son," said the stunned and humbled attorney. Ben's faith in the judicial system was renewed after all his career losses and derisions. He was infused with the same idealism he once had when he was a kid entering law school.

On the day of Supreme Court oral arguments, Bob met Ben before the justices took their chairs. Ben showed Bob around the Supreme Court facilities. They were positively luxurious. Large soft leather chairs, a dining room, beautiful offices, thick carpeting, commanding views—the justices had it all.

Ben commented, "These guys know how to live. I have to believe it would be impossible to bribe any of them. Maybe that's why there are nine of them. If you try for a bribe, you first don't know which ones or how many will hear your case, and if you do try to bribe one, you could get the wrong one and end up in the slammer. It'd be too risky, even for David. I don't believe these guys buy slime for sale."

"Then you believe my first judge was bribed?"

"Not saying. Can't say what I can't prove," said Ben, but he had a smile that resembled a cat's that had just snagged a canary.

Bob took his seat in the back of the courtroom, joining Barbara. She pointed to David seated in the front row, slouched in his chair as was his normal signal of contempt for all judges and the entire legal process.

During arguments, the justices, all nine, were present. They wanted to understand why the Statute of Wills did not bar a claim to recovery since David had not given Bob a copy of the codicil when they were in the bank vault. David's attorney droned on about case precedent. There were no cases ever, anywhere in America's history or in the history of English Common Law, that permitted recovery of any claims of any kind whatsoever without the plaintiff establishing that he had in possession a copy of a writing to make a will, an actual will, or a codicil to an existing will. The law was unambiguous and clear.

Bob's counsel was trying to show that what David did was unconscionable conduct when the chief justice asked the fated question. It was a dagger that was touching at the very heart of Bob's case, and the entire room could feel the chief justice was poised to thrust his dagger into Ben's argument and destroy Bob's case.

"Your client had no writing. You obtained a copy of the writing through your discovery, but your client never had possession of a writing given to him by the defendant. There are numerous cases throughout judicial history where plaintiffs claim that they did thus and such based upon a will promise, but they never prevailed. I think some in some culture even call it the 'shiksa game,' but it goes on without any successful challenge. For over four hundred years, the law is clear."

The chief justice was almost shouting. He was visibly agitated. It was obvious he was angry at what David did, but he could see no way to open the door locked closed by the statute. Recovery odds for the plaintiff were zero.

He continued after a brief pause. "It's lamentable what happened to your client, Counsel, but that is not a matter of law. Now the English common law has even been chiseled into stone. We now have before this court the Statute of Wills. The law is abundantly clear, Counsel. You have no writing! How can you expect this court to render a decision other than one that is consistent with the statute?"

A long hush descended over the courtroom. Ben took off his glasses and set down his briefing book upon his lectern. He stepped away and stood directly before Chief Justice Renlow, who was poised upon the forward half of his chair staring fiercely at Ben. A certain charge of electricity flew between the two men. The small fat man tilted his head far back to look up at the chief justice seated high above him.

Chief Justice Renlow wanted so much to not have this case before him, yet he could see the injustice being done. He was clearly frustrated that he couldn't quite point his finger in the direction of a path to relief. All routes were blocked by the statute. He could see how a man's life and career got screwed. That wasn't supposed to happen in America. The chief justice knew that. That basic rooted belief that you can't use the law to screw people was his sustaining force for his entire life; he was almost insane with the conundrum posed by this case, and told his fellow justices so. They'd agreed to grant the writ by a six-to-three majority.

The most conservative justices wanted nothing to do with the case. Their position was to let the state legislatures deal with the issue, but they were outvoted. The idea of just letting people get screwed by the Statute of Wills defense until some legislatures decided to do something was a terrible injustice to those who were out there, the next ones to be screwed by this misuse of the law. A majority of the justices just couldn't stand the status quo. Now they had to figure out what was wrong with the law of the land that there could be such a shield for wrongdoing.

The chief justice was terribly frustrated. The idea of ruling to deny remand and upholding this sham misuse of the law to shield a fraud sickened him. He was all ears, waiting and wanting to be unburdened, but very skeptical. There before him was a man who was so short he could barely be seen from the bench.

Ben was clearly not a skilled orator, but David's lawyer was. He'd just summed up a very convincing argument that this matter must be left to the states and their legislatures to remedy, if they even decided remedy was desired. It was a balance between rights of giving on death versus those who could be harmed by a wrongful predator. The chief justice hoped this coughing, wheezing, cigar stench-soaked man could somehow make an argument if he didn't keel over from anxiety first.

Ben's attention wandered when he heard the question from the chief justice, who could tell this nervous little man was afraid to speak. There passed a fearful moment where all present thought the little lawyer might faint. Gently, Chief Justice Renlow repeated the question, his arms extended with his hands palms up.

"How can you expect us to render a decision that is inconsistent with the statute when your client had no writing?" He widely spread his fingers and raised his eyebrows as if he were a wide receiver waiting to receive a football pass. This was to be the defining moment. The whole case would fall or go forward based upon Ben's response.

There were about one hundred people in the gallery that day, including the press corps that followed Supreme Court cases. They all stopped taking notes and looked down from the gallery, all eyes focused on the perspiring, snorting little fat man. He needed to make his case at that moment or return to flyover country.

Ben spoke in what was to be his finest performance ever as an attorney. "I agree with everything you say, Your Honor. We have no writing, and based upon that simple fact our appeal should be denied." The judges and the spectators held their collective breaths.

Ben continued.

"Except for one thing, Your Honor, which is why you cannot rule to deny! When David was in the bank vault, it is his testimony, by his own words, that he intended that he would keep the pledge to his father, to leave the companies to Israel upon his own death, while at the same time he was showing the codicil to Bob. Therefore, his true intent could never have been to leave the companies to Bob. His true intention was in fact to defraud Bob, defraud him into giving up his career—his life, essentially—for a false promise in the inducement to gain his performance for all those years. David's intent could not have been anything other than to defraud. This court cannot find that the statute shields such unconscionable conduct! It simply cannot be a shield for fraud! The court *must* remand our cause with instructions, instructions directing the trial court to order a trial by jury. No other ruling could be just."

Ben wiped his eyes, choking back his emotions as he uttered his final soft-spoken words. "Petitioner rests." The phrase hung silently in the air, as if its absent echo continued resounding from the walls of the courtroom. The gallery spectators knew a magnificent oratorical performance when they heard one.

With his eloquent delivery, Ben Slipperman made legal history. The chief justice knew it when he heard it. His head went back as his eyes closed and his mouth gaped open. He slumped back in his chair. A second justice reacted as well, lifting up his hands above the bench as if to reflect he was having a 'eureka' moment. The chief justice now had his chance to render an opinion that would be cited in cases of fraud and fraudulent intent. His ruling would set judicial precedents down through the ages. He had just heard a precedent-setting case, a case that pushed aside the notion that the Statute of Wills was inviolate, that will makers could use that statute to defraud innocents by falsely promising an inheritance in the face of clear testimonial evidence that there was no such intent. He recognized he'd been given the means to rule such conduct could not be so.

Ben had laid out the groundwork of the matter clearly before his court. Of course! It was now all so clear to the court. The truth burst through decisively and suddenly, like it was wont to do in matters of convoluted logic that must be untangled. The chief justice knew from his old days as a judge's clerk that one always had to look to the testimony and the conduct of the parties. His frustration with this case was lifted from his shoulders. He'd opened his eyes, literally, as Ben had removed the legal scales from them just seconds before. He appreciated legal genius, and he knew he'd just heard it from the little fat man who hardly ever won a case.

Rarely before had Chief Justice Renlow shown any hint of his leanings. Lawyers who came before him referred to him as 'Old Poker Face.' Today was different.

"Thank you for that eloquent elucidation, Counsel, and thank you for highlighting that item of testimony at trial. In matters of law, this court ordinarily does not seek to rule based upon interpretation of testimony, but in this case the testimony divides the proofs of the claims of contract and contract to make a will shielded by the Statute and the claim of fraud, thus we shall consider it. We will retire to chambers now. You will have your opinion after we finish deliberation."

Bob was in shock. He knew something significant had just happened, but he wasn't sure he understood it. Tears streamed down his cheeks. A twelve-year legal ordeal had just passed a turning point. The justices were going to consider his case based upon testimony, something they just never did. But then again, they were the justices and they could do anything they wanted. He turned his head from side to side and looked far away, seeing his life telescoped before him into a moment he could only pray went well.

Barbara took his hand and squeezed it. "You just won your case, Big Horse"

Ben was more cautious and reserved, telling Bob later that he thought they did all right.

On his way out of the courtroom, David passed by Barbara and put his face up close to hers. Then he hissed and stuck out his tongue at her as if he were some sort of snake. She later recounted the incident to Bob. "I thought for a minute there I was looking into the eyes of an evil snake."

"You were." He no longer felt sympathy for David, the man's pitiful childhood stories, the mastoids in his ears, his body odor problems, his sexual hang-ups about women, his ugly appearance, his homosexual needs, his tortured and distorted views about the inferiorities of women and other cultures, his lack of respect for authority and social rules—any and all of it. He was finally free of the monstrous sociopath. The oral argument by Ben awakened Bob from a long nightmare. The real David was just a sleazy scumbag and closet criminal, a pustule on the ass of social normalcy, a disgrace to his Levite namesake and ancestral king. He was just a pathetic sham of a man who played the Jew card whenever it suited him to gain sympathy. He was quick to allege his actions were being challenged because he was discriminated against because of his religion, when in fact his religion had nothing whatsoever to do with the charges brought against him. Bob was free of David at last.

"Why do you think David did what he did?" Barbara wanted to understand what happened through Bob's eyes.

Bob started to explain his understanding of the factor that drove David to be the way he was as best he could. "Well, there is a certain subset of the tribe, those Jews who God created as an ingenious social invention. God saw the need for the goyim to be deceived into taking action they otherwise would not take. So in my case, he sent David as his agent to deceive me into building a firm that otherwise would never have been built. On a larger scale, he set up central banking to induce spending through the government to advance society faster than it otherwise would advance. You see, the goyim tend to take the bait of instant gratification and God knows that, so he sends his agents, the Lucifers, to issue the temptations to the goyim. The deal the Lucifers have with God is that they will tempt and promise and deceive, and God is okay with that because he wants to see if there will ever come a time when the human condition advances past the hatreds of the tribe against the goyim and the goyim against the tribe.

"Meanwhile, there are sordid interplays of false promises, reactions, and hatred, and the tribe turning inward in reaction to the hatreds like the Holocaust and the reaction being the founding of Israel. It's a cycle that is not unlike holding out candy to a child and then taking it away. The child and the goyim react and throw a temper tantrum—or a holocaust or pogrom, as the case may be. The parent—the tribe—hardens against the behavior it receives. The reaction of the tribe knits it closer together, but there are factions within the tribe that derive their power base by constantly reminding the members of their grievances. The goyim constantly hold suspicions about the tribe. There are some within each faction of tribe and goyim who seek to extract vengeance against the other, and they are championed by the power base factions. So the cycle goes on."

"But why do you believe God would create such a vicious dynamic?" Barbara sought a deeper understanding.

"To move humanity forward, I suppose, but also to see if humanity will ever become secular and rise above the cycle. It's not new. It's an interplay you can pick up by reading ancient scriptures, like in the Book of Judges. The tribe goes astray from God, fights off a potential destroyer, and then it goes back to God."

"But wouldn't rising above that dynamic eliminate the need for God? Could there be another reason?"

"Yes, possibly. I think the ultimate reason for it all is God creates the interplay for his amusement. It makes for great human drama. Everybody loves amusement, even God."

"But everyone has a choice to sign on to the cycle or not, right?"

"Yes. Everyone has free will. Everyone may make their own choice."

MISSING SHEEP

Mothers like to believe their daughters will turn out well and have good lives. No mother gives birth to a daughter and wishes upon her child that she'll grow up to become a prostitute or some kind of amoral nymphomaniac fuck-bunny, yet that's what happened to Susan's little Marty. Between the time she was Joseph's little girl, bouncing on his knee, laughing, running about in the yard with her pinwheels, her bubble-blowing soaps, her little dolls, and her little pets, and the time when she was suddenly gone into a time warp and returned to Plaintown, something went terribly wrong.

An older and wiser Susan sat alone in her office that afternoon, late into the day after the others had long gone home. *What went wrong? Why did Marty turn out to be the adult she turned out to be? How could I have contributed to Marty's life choices, and what's to be done about it now?*

Susan reminisced over her countless days and nights with Marvin, how she immersed herself in his world while relegating Marty to second place for her attentions. She told herself, unconvincingly, that she did the best she could to raise her daughter. Marty always had the best of everything—the best clothes, the best schools, nice cars, plenty of money. Susan was frustrated in those years past. It would have all been so perfect if only she could've had Marty with her in a family life with Marvin, but try as she might, she saw she couldn't become a Jewess and pry Marvin away from his wife.

Eloweiss would have none of it. That bitch would ruin the business and her own husband just to spite Susan and Marvin if it took that to keep him, so a tacitly understood stalemate took hold between the two women. Susan could have him, bed him, fuck him in the office, the rental house, in Susan's own house, and on their trips away, but she could not have him in Eloweiss's house, or on Friday nights, or on Saturday Bar Mitzvah days, or on High Holy Days. Maybe she should have just broken it off with Marvin. Maybe the money wasn't worth it. Susan hadn't birthed those thoughts while Marvin lived, but now that he was gone the remorse of losing Marty had her second-guessing her life choices. Guilt haunted her and gave her no peace.

Susan gazed at her suit jacket hanging behind her office door. She was deep in thought as her stare fixated upon the Monarch butterfly pin Marty gave her on her fiftieth birthday. Susan always wore the pin now, as a proud mother, regardless of the garment she wore. It was a striking piece of jewelry with golden orange mother of pearl wings, a line of deep red rubies making up the body of the pin, and ten white diamonds bordering the edges of each wingtip. The veins of its black wings were delicately hand-painted. When Marty first gifted the pin, Susan's reaction was to gasp. With the mother of pearl, rubies, and diamonds, the piece had surely cost a fortune. It was a large pin, a good four inches across, and clearly custom-made.

At first, Susan thought of the pin as merely a unique piece of spectacular jewelry, but the more she wore it, the more she wondered about her relationship with her daughter. Had Marty intended to make a subtle statement from daughter to mother with her gift? Was Marty trying to declare, in her muted painful way, that she could also earn big money by prostituting herself, just like her mother did?

Susan remembered when she'd visited Marty during that last year of boarding school. As Marty was getting dressed, Susan was shocked to notice a tattoo. Marty sported a red and blue butterfly tattoo low over her backside, and there was another noticeable orange-winged Monarch butterfly one on the inside of her uppermost thighs. Although Susan only had a fleeting look at the tattoo which surrounded Marty's vagina, she instantly realized it was her daughter's declaration of uninhibited sexuality. Perhaps Marty's message to her mother was simply that she had become just as good a whore as Susan, and the butterfly pin represented some sort of merit badge for her carnal leg-spreading achievements. Susan could now only wonder about Marty's feelings toward her and ponder these thoughts within her own heart. Whatever Marty's motive or message behind the gift, Susan now wore the butterfly with a deep sense of maternal love for its giver. Looking at the pin now, she felt the pain in Marty's soul.

Susan reflected on the previous time at the boarding school when Marty informed her in no uncertain terms that she intended to go through life putting her pleasures first. Perhaps she should have slapped her daughter, upbraided her and immediately taken her home to Colorado, but alas, how could she do that? Susan's moral authority failed her. How could she have any credibility with Marty, any moral high ground, when she had put her own desires first all her own life?

Later, when Marty worked as a prostitute out of the fund's offices, why didn't she try to put a stop to it? Could she have had any influence at that point with her grown daughter? Probably not, Susan reasoned at the time, and now she realized it was true. Marty would have just worked out of some other business. Only a mother can wonder about a daughter in such ways.

At least with Marty at the fund, Susan could know whom she was seeing based on the expense and sales reports. When

Carl's wife made the news with her suicide and the murder of her children, it saddened Susan but it didn't surprise her. Marty was capable of wreaking havoc in others' marriages, and her daughter never shied from confrontations with hostile wives. Susan only hoped some crazed wife wouldn't kill Marty or hire someone to do it for her. She told Marty to try to keep things on the light side and not to try to separate women from their husbands. She was never as brazen as her daughter. It was the only advice she could give at the time, but Marty paid her mother no heed.

Maybe Marty felt she had to one-up her mother. Maybe that's what sent Marty into the dark regions of malicious intents and her quest to wreck marriages. Maybe that's what the daughter saw in her mother. Maybe the daughter figured out that her mother's own behaviors drove Joseph to suicide, and the daughter wanted to prove to her mother that she could get someone to kill themselves over her behaviors as well. Those maddening thoughts came to Susan again and again until she was obsessed with them. Nothing she could do now could bring her Marty back, but perhaps she could finally be an honorable mother to her presumed-dead daughter. She could find out what happened to Marty and have some sense of honor and decency befitting her little girl, whom she loved so dearly and now so terribly missed.

What happened to Marty? That question dogged Susan every day and sleepless night for the past year and a half. Even with their relationship strains, Marty always called Susan on her birthday and on Mother's Day. She always sent a Christmas card, always called the week before to see if they could go together to the Mass of Saint Cecilia at Holy Spirit Church in downtown Plaintown. Despite her shortcomings as a mother, Susan knew her daughter loved her deeply, that she always wanted to be closer to her than Susan would allow when Marty was a child, and those thoughts left her heartbroken. Marty was gone now, to some faraway place with her Savior, not away on some fling as David wanted everyone to believe.

Susan had taken to prayers in these dark times, something she hadn't done in years. She often sat in her office and prayed her Rosary. Now she prayed fervently. They were deeply felt and sincerely spoken now, with a conviction the rote prayers she'd recited as a child never had. But then, she reflected, what did children really know about life? How could a child or a young woman know the pitfalls, the trials, the sufferings, the pains of life? She prayed that Marty, in her final moments, had found some measure of peace. Marty was gone for good, likely dead; Susan knew that with certainty, deep within her gut.

Now she sat waiting patiently for the silent blink under her desk, indicating the call on her private line, the line that no one knew she had. David was gone by now anyway. He left about an hour after the markets closed, at two o'clock Mountain time. John, her dutiful friend and trusted lover, told her the laboratory would call after five. They knew it was a delicate and confidential inquiry, and she was paying extra for the secrecy.

When the light blinked, she lifted the receiver from under her desk. "This is she."

"This is your report," said the caller.

"And where are you calling from?"

"It's a local landline call, from the Cow and Steer Hotel's Travel Agency."

"Verify the work order, please."

"It's from Lab Termanspeil, Neumuehlequai, Zurich, 8006. Order 3PLR34."

"Take it to the UPS box in the basement of the Western Bank building. At exactly six o'clock, drop the envelope with the report in it on the floor in front of the box and leave without looking back."

"Understood."

Susan waited inconspicuously around the corner of the bank's basement corridor at the appointed time. She heard the drop and waited until the messenger entered the elevator and the doors closed behind him. Picking up the report, she went straight home. She sat on her reading chair and held the envelope for a long moment before she opened it. Hopefully her suspicions would be proven wrong. The report looked very thorough, very official in appearance, the sort of thing one would expect a crime lab would provide for a homicide detective.

Her lips quivered as she read the analysis aloud. "Both of the hair samples were reviewed by microscopic spectrometry, which indicated they were from the same species: Human, Caucasian.

"The DNA comparison of the two samples revealed a match correlation of 99.9999 percent.

"Based upon microscopic spectrometry and DNA analysis, the two samples are from an identical source with probable certainty of 99.9999 percent."

Susan now knew what she'd dreaded acknowledging. The hair from the fox picture in Bob's office and Marty's hair sample she'd supplied from the cutting in her locket were identical. Marty had to have been in David's barn sometime between the time Bob last saw her and when he found the scalp cut with the hair attached. Susan's focus narrowed. How could Marty's scalp and hair have gotten into David's barn?

Susan was no fool. She was David's babysitter for years, when he was just a precocious child. She knew he was capable of wrongdoings to animals, especially insects, but was it a logical extension to believe he could have harmed Marty? Had he figured out that she was his half-sister? Would that have mattered to David if he *had* figured it out? Would he be that vindictive toward her and Marvin that he would destroy Marty, take her life somehow?

Susan suspected that David very well could commit murder. He was a devious little monster, always conniving, always slipping away and hiding from the truth, always doing bad things for no other discernable reason than because he could get away with doing them. He always tried to get people to pity him, and he then used their pity as a ruse to gain their confidence and take advantage of them. That was his predictable pattern. She remembered thinking when he was a child that he would be a strong competitor for Hitler if David had an army behind him, but fortunately he could only wreak his havoc in the corporate dictatorship Marvin set up for him. Susan now had a firm foundation upon which to base her suspicions. She knew she was likely dealing with a murderer, and David was both secretive and ruthless. She proceeded with caution.

Susan thought hard to recall those times she'd been at David's. She tried to remember everything she could about each visit. Details suddenly mattered. What was there to focus on? Where the cars were parked? How many people were at the parties? What did Marty do at the parties? Whom did she talk to? What food was served? It was all a blur. Susan needed to focus, but focus on what, exactly? She made herself a Gibson, sipped it slowly and tried to relax. She believed she was on the right track, but she needed to be sure. Heading to bed, she lay there, looking at the ceiling. Nothing came to her. It was like that for her, night after night, for the next vexatious week. How did just the red hair patch end up in David's barn?

The mind is a most peculiar companion. When it's given a problem to solve that has it stymied, it places the problem into storage, sealing it up into a mouse jar of sorts until it's prompted to recall the problem and resume its deliberations. It must have been a good ten days since Susan first pondered the question of how Marty's hair and scalp had found its way into the corner of David's barn. She couldn't rule foul play either out or in without a theory.

Thus was the straightjacketed state of Susan's mind when John, now her weekly dinner date, suggested they dine at the Ritz Chateau that Saturday evening, after a theater show. His wife had passed since the days when he controlled the union pension plan, so his dinner dates with Susan were the high point of his week. He showed his appreciation by always taking her to the finest dining rooms in the city. They'd finished cocktails, discussing the play, and ordering wine. Susan ordered flounder for her entrée. John often merely doubled her order, but that evening he chose lamb chops. As he closed the menu book, he remarked that the way they did lamb chops at the Chateau made for the best meal in Plaintown. When the entrées arrived, Susan had order envy; John's chops looked absolutely succulent. "Maybe I should have ordered the lamb chops as well! They look delicious."

The mouse jar opened and the mouse struggled to get out as Susan first stared at John's chops, then at his tie, then at the chops, then at her dinner partner's eyes. "John, give me a moment, won't you, dear? I need to think. Something just came to me."

John, affable as always, replied, "Sure, babe. Take your time," as he looked away at the tables around him and sipped his cabernet. All the while, Susan's mind was racing over observations she had made in years past. At David's parties, he sometimes served lamb chops or leg of mutton to his guests. She recalled one particular occasion about three years past when she had dropped off some filings that needed David's signature. He was going on one of his 'hunts,' but the government filing deadline was that afternoon.

After she got his signatures, she paused for a moment on the driveway next to the barnyard to count the sheep. She had no reason to do that other than idle curiosity before she drove downtown. There was the omnipresent Dolly, the black one. There were also seven white sheep—all females, she thought, except one white ram. It was in the fall, she was sure of it. Her filing deadline was September 30th, and David was going hunting for an ibex in Texas at one of those disgusting game farms.

The next spring, it would have been at David's party for the office staff on Memorial Day, at the end of May. There were lamb chops and leg of mutton served. She recalled—dimly now because she didn't want to think about where the meat came from at that time—that there were fewer sheep in the barnyard on that Memorial Day than there were the prior fall. Instead of the seven whites, there were only four female whites and the ram—and of course Dolly, the black sheep.

David received many compliments about the meat, but no one, including Susan, asked where it came from. She was the only staffer who made occasional trips to the house, at least that's what she believed back then, thus no other employee would have noticed that three sheep were missing, or so she now believed. Susan had assumed at the time of the Memorial Day party that David had sent them off to be sold or sent to a butcher. Now a nagging doubt overshadowed her prior assumption.

"You're very deep in thought and off to a faraway place, sweetheart." John gently brought Susan back to the dinner they were sharing.

"Sorry, dear. Just one of those moments where I thought I forgot to do something important at the office."

Her thoughts were indeed off in faraway places and times. She could tell white lies to John. He knew she did it often and he really didn't care. He had become like an old faithful dog, always there for her, always eager to please her. That night while she bedded him in her comfortable maiden position, she looked up at the ceiling and back into her past.

Her thoughts raced through time, through all the actors she knew on a time-traveled stage. There passed Marvin, her beloved; Joseph, her betrothed; Marty, her great failure and heartache; and David with his boy-toy harem playmates she'd tolerated these last few years while sitting in her office, smoking an occasional slim panatela cigar while staring at the portrait of Marvin and the butterfly pin Marty gave her, wondering how life could pass by so quickly.

CHAIN FALL

Susan came to the office that Monday with a sense of purpose she hadn't felt in years. The firm was drifting listlessly. David was embroiled in litigation, often away in conferences with his lawyers. Barbara had run off to join forces with Bob. The loss of the two of them took the wind from everyone's sails. They were the energy of the place. Everyone liked them, but David now told everyone to hate them; they were the enemy. They were traitors to David and to all other employees, he proclaimed. Susan chuckled silently to herself when she found out that Bob had won the U.S. Supreme Court decision.

David knew he'd lost that day long before the decision was handed down. He was in his office that afternoon, screaming at Susan's staff girls for failing to keep his desk cleaned off and his papers properly filed. He always had some difficulty with the men's room door because it had become warped from age. For decades David, and all other men who used the facility, simply gave the door a slight increase in force to open it, but not that day.

David kicked the door and continued kicking it. After repeated kicking, David finally succeeded in destroying the beautiful fruitwood-paneled door. He went to Mrs. Rodriguez and ordered her to call building maintenance and have the door properly repaired so it no longer stuck. He chastised her for not calling them years before.

"Make sure you tell them to shave that door down so it no longer warps in its frame. And tell them to search for identical replacement paneling," he barked.

David was just like the little boy she used to babysit, Susan noted. He was still trying to tear wings from helpless flies, still tearing legs from ants, always eager to inflict his miseries upon the helpless beings of this world. Some things and some people never changed.

But this David was more dangerous to people than the one she knew as a little boy. Marvin must have seen that evil quality in his son; otherwise, why would he have created an unofficial unaffiliated advisory board to watch over the firm, and David, after his death? Why had he structured the firm's service contracts to leave Susan to watch out for David, putting her in the position to try at all times to make sure he did the right things with the business after Marvin died? Why else had he made her a lifetime fixture at the firm after his death if it wasn't to make sure David stayed on track with the law and the regulators?

Susan understood his wishes now. She would always be true and obedient to him, even after his death. She owed the love of her life that much, and she forgave him for making her carry such an unsavory burden.

Muscle Boy was the likely suspect for Susan's inquiry, but she needed to be discreet about confirming her suspicions. He was seated at his drawing board, now in his third year of trying to create a new logo design, when she walked into his office unannounced. When she saw his latest logo rendition, which looked like a flying saucer being struck by lightning from above and below, she could barely keep a straight face.

"Good morning, Muscles," she began cheerfully, trying to dispel the natural antagonism he felt toward all women. "I'm in a bit of a jam and I don't know where else I could turn to for help. I'm going to be hosting a party for my women's executive club ladies and I wanted to serve a sumptuous dinner of lamb chops and leg of lamb. I remember that party at David's a few years back when lamb was served. I didn't want to trouble him with this, but maybe you could be kind enough to tell me which butcher shop he used to buy the meat from?"

She had the most imploring look of sincerity Muscle Boy had ever seen on a woman's face. Ordinarily he would have told Susan to stop bothering him because he was concentrating on getting his logo's lightning bolts properly angled, but seeing her sincerity, he allowed the female organization to pierce his force shield just this one time.

"Why, Ms. Maloney, David didn't use a butcher for that. I did it," he said proudly.

"You did it? What did you do, Muscles? Did you go fetch the meat?" Susan's query was most sincere.

"No." Muscle Boy was getting ruffled. "I butchered the sheep for the dinner." His reply intoned a measure of self-importance.

"Really!" Susan put her hand over her heart in amazement. "I had no idea you were such a tremendous talent, Muscles. I should have made good friends with you long ago! Tell me, where did you do the butchering?" Her eyes widened. She was on the trail of her missing daughter; she could sense it.

"Why, in the barn at David's farm." He was suddenly friendlier. Rarely did anyone ever pay him a compliment, even David.

"How could you do that? I hear they're pretty strong animals. How do you hold them down while you cut them up? How do they stand still for that?" Susan was wily and projected honest curiosity about his talents.

"Oh no, Ms. Maloney, I string them up and kill them kosher style. David showed me how the rabbis kill kosher. I don't do any blessing on them though. I just cut their throats and let them bleed out before I cut the guts out of them."

"Well, you must be very strong to do that. Hold them up with one hand while you slit their throats. You do amaze me, Muscles." Susan looked as if she were in awe of the cretin, but she was just playacting.

"No, ma'am. You don't understand. I grab their back legs and tie them up first. Then I lift them on the chain fall." Muscle Boy was eager to tell all.

"Really?" Susan was fascinated. "What's a chain fall?"

"It's a long chain on a block of double pulleys, ma'am. David keeps it in the barn, in his toolshed in the back corner. I hook it up to the big hook on the top rafter of the barn and hook the bottom hook to the rope that ties the sheep's back legs together. When I pull on the chain, it's easy to lift a sheep up in the air."

"Oh, I bet you're just saying that. You're very strong, aren't you?"

"No, ma'am, I'm not just saying that. Using that pulley, even a weak man like David, or even a child, could easily hoist up a fully grown Angus bull."

"You don't say. Have you ever seen David hoist anything with it?"

"Oh yes, ma'am. He's hoisted up a big sheep, a hundred-thirty pound one. He hoisted a big one before I got there."

"Well, I guess I won't be getting my chops there. I wouldn't want one of David's sheep to have to die for me. I think I'll just go to a butcher shop. Thank you, Muscles." As she started to leave, Susan turned back to her new information source. "Tell me. What on earth do you do with the parts of the sheep that can't be eaten after you butcher one of them?" Susan posed her afterthought as a mere natural curiosity.

"Well, first we sheer the sheep while she's hanging upside down. That way David doesn't waste any wool. He sells the wool to some lady who comes around every year, exchanging it for his knitted socks and scarves. But the gut piles David feeds to his pigs and the bones and skulls go through his wood chipper several times until they're just fine bone chips. He uses those to fertilize his vegetable garden and rose beds. He turns the chips into the ground mixed in with his compost from his compost pile."

"Well, I'll run along now, Muscles. Thank you for all that. Now I *know* I'll go to a butcher for my meat. I couldn't *bear* the thought of hurting one of those *darling* ewes. They are all *so, so cute.*" Susan acted the part of a squeamish little girl and turned away.

Muscle Boy returned to his logo quest, thinking that Susan was kind of okay for a woman, but overly girly.

Susan left his workshop and walked slowly back to her own office, trying hard not to throw up. The thought of her beloved Marty being butchered by David in his barn flooded her constitution with revulsion, remorse, and despondency. What had poor Marty felt while hanging there upside down? What thoughts, what terrible turmoil her poor innocent child must have suffered. What had her daughter ever done to deserve such a horrible ending? Sure, she'd busted up some marriages, but she'd never physically harmed anybody, had never raised a hand against anybody. Marriages that were too fragile to withstand a little whoring weren't worth being marriages in the first place, she silently opined.

And David! What about *David*? Why would he *do* such a thing? Had he discovered Marty was his half-sister? Was he doing her in as a favor to some broker's estranged wife? What on *Earth* could be David's reason?

When it rains, it pours! The answers began coming pitter-patter. David wanted Bob as a lover. Bob was David's property, at least in his mind. The stupid, arrogant little bastard! Bob was totally straight, never had a homosexual bone in his body and could never made into a gay person. Bob loved women. He loved her Marty. Marty got in David's way. She had to be murdered so David could have a chance with Bob. That suddenly explained the fishing trips, the antelope hunt, and it explained the destroyed Jeep. Bob had rejected David. He wouldn't be one of David's pathetic fuck-buddies.

Gay men were no different than straight men when it came to dealing with rejection. Some handled it well, some not well at all. Rejected in love, David took out his frustration first on the Jeep and then on Marty. David acted out behaviors like a child who couldn't have his way in a sandbox, taking his toys away. He took away what he had given Bob—the Jeep, the portfolio performance to help sales build the firm, the firm itself, and even Marty's life. The devious little prick probably destroyed that codicil the same day he showed it to Bob.

David's behavior was his revenge play to destroy Bob's life. If he couldn't have Bob, then Bob couldn't have a life without him. That had to be the operative theory. Everything suddenly fit! Susan noticed that David had stopped spending time with Bob, only playing with his 'gay boys for hire' now. Their commonality was they were all women-hating creeps David picked up off the street or at a gay club or bathhouses. He was a vengeful, lonely man who'd scraped the barrel bottom of gay male partnership choices. He hadn't changed one bit since childhood.

Yes! Now Susan understood why Barbara left after the lawsuit commenced. It was business for her, but even more. Barbara saw that, with Marty gone and Bob on his own, she finally had her chance to become his woman on her own terms. Susan knew her people well. She got distinct vibrations from Barbara whenever Bob was around, but Barbara was so discreet, so smooth at hiding her feelings, that she could never be certain.

If Marty had lived, Barbara would still be there, making Susan's life and chore load much easier than it was presently. Susan had long ago thought of Barbara as a second daughter.

She was brilliant, diligent, ethical, honest, and dependable. Susan missed her terribly and began thinking she needed to let Barbara know she fully supported her decision to join forces with Bob.

She gazed at her blazer hanging on the back of her door. The beautiful butterfly pin over its right pocket connected her to many fond memories.

ISRAEL'S SIDE

David sat in a conference room chair in his lawyer's office absorbed in his thoughts, reflecting, strategizing, contemplating the antics of his antagonist, planning and mentally rehearsing his own responses. Long gone were the times years before when the litigation commenced. Then he was flush with confidence that he would crush Bob and Sol. He'd hired the most reputable and most expensive law firms in the city. He'd trusted their advice. They had the plush offices, the deep blue and red carpeting, and the chrome and brass railings on their opulent staircases. They showed off their impressive quarters, their panoramic views from the Rockies all the way around to the east, seeing as far as Kansas no doubt.

Why shouldn't he have believed them? There was the Statute of Wills. He had the right to change his will. Repeatedly they'd assured him he was in the right, those money-thieving bastards! It was just a simple quantum meruit case. They were so sure of their position. They'd looked at hundreds of precedent cases and charged him plenty for all their work, the fucking pricks! He did tell them he wanted the most aggressive defense they could possibly mount, told them that settlement was not an option. He demanded a ferocious counterattack.

The lawyers he hired played off court all right. To buy time and delay, to move the goal posts on Bob so he wouldn't get any closer to relief, David changed his major law firm in charge of the case, not once or twice, but now for the fourth time. Each change bought him a good three months' time or more, but the cost was now running over three million invested in destroying Bob and he had not yet done it. Success eluded him. Bob would not break.

Try as he might, David was unable to crack the key to the success of Bob's firm. How could a no-name upstart without clients, staffed by a man embroiled in litigation, with no money and a quiet skinny Indian girl as partner and secretary, possibly survive in the competitive investment business? David tried twice to use a trumped-up excuse to get a court order that would allow him to see Bob's books and records. He couldn't prove there was a silent enemy of his hiding in the weeds, backing Bob and Bob's litigation. He had no evidence, he just suspected it. But twice Barbara filed for protective orders to block his demands for discovery and twice the courts granted her order. He was unable to find any dirt on Bob or Barbara or their business and he was going nowhere with that idea.

David kicked one of his dogs the night when the lawyer from his second law firm told him he needed to drop the idea of harassing Bob's firm. He was told if he persisted Bob could file harassment charges. David hated feeling stymied. He tried to find out about Barbara, her parentage, her family's wealth and connections. Susan told him she didn't know anything about her. That surprised David. Ordinarily Susan could rattle off all sorts of information about any of her staff girls, but she was strangely silent about Barbara. All he could pry out of her was that Barbara was extremely bright and very competent, a very diligent worker who never talked about herself or her background. She didn't smoke or drink, which made sense for an Indian, he figured. She knew all the corporate evolutions, understood the Investment Advisor's Act, the Investment Company Act, the Securities Act, the Securities Distribution act, and all the pertinent rules that were promulgated by the regulatory agencies under those acts. She was diligent at keeping up with changing regulations, and she was so savvy at reading requests for comments that she could actually anticipate regulatory changes before they were promulgated. That skill was a tremendous advantage for any firm to have.

He knew she was a trusted resource that Susan sorely missed, but why in the world had she left his firm to join Bob? She was paid extremely well, could take time off whenever she needed it. David couldn't imagine that Barbara saw Bob's firm as a once-in-a-lifetime opportunity. He had no idea that her family had money, political power, or staying power. All he knew was that her father lived on some Indian reservation, but that meant nothing to David. He imagined her father fishing and hunting, chanting while pounding on a drum, and weaving baskets or making silver jewelry, nothing more. As far as he was concerned, Indians were a worthless defeated people.

For David, it all boiled down to the personal. Either Barbara was holding a grudge against him for the time he shoved his hands into her blouse and squeezed her tits, or else Bob had been secretly fucking her all the time she was working at David's firm. But that would be impossible because Marty was fucking Bob, and she would draw so much energy from a man he couldn't possibly have the strength to fuck a second woman. David wondered if Barbara was fucking Bob now that she'd left the firm. He reasoned those probabilities unlikely because she was always so reserved and businesslike and Bob was always selling. Besides, Barbara was Indian and they tended to stick to their own kind.

The question that vexed David remained. Why had Barbara left the firm? His paranoia landed on anti-Semitism. It either had to be that Barbara secretly hated him because of his playful tit-squeezing incident or because she just hated Jews. David whittled the reason down to his belief that Barbara must hate all Jews. After all, he reasoned, all women secretly loved to have their tits squeezed. It had to be the Jewish thing, or the prim, studious Indian just wanted to get Bob into her teepee. He couldn't quite put all the pieces together and eventually gave up trying, chalking up Barbara's decision to just another case of a woman thinking with her pussy instead of her brains. Nothing else made sense to David, who couldn't comprehend anyone being repulsed by unethical personal conduct.

The very thought of Bob made David scream. He forbade any of the office staff from speaking his name. All letterhead with Bob's name had been destroyed long ago. If anyone on staff heard Bob's name spoken, the speaker was to be reported immediately to David and that offense was grounds for dismissal. He personally destroyed all the furniture in Bob's office, which David had paid handsomely to obtain from the finest furniture store in Plaintown, and the pieces were sent to a storage locker to which only he had access. Bob's former office was locked and yellow crime scene tape was strung in dramatic fashion across the door in a forbidden oversized X. To propagandize his position, David instructed that all visitors be told Bob's former office was still an active crime scene, although the space had long been stripped of its contents and this was strictly a civil matter. It was David's way of rewriting history; to generate a false rumor by misleading a hapless visitor; of demanding that the staff, if not the courts and the real world beyond UGGA, see things his way.

Despite his endless stream of venom, David still was haunted by his thoughts of Bob. Why had Bob rejected him after all he'd done for the younger man? What could he possibly see in a woman that David couldn't provide? If he had to have a woman, why couldn't he also allow David into his love life as a male companion? He'd offered Bob friendship, love, wealth, status, and all the benefits of his wisdom, yet Bob still rejected him.

David's heart ached from his alienation from Bob. He worked to replace the ache with relentless fury and his quest for vengeance. Here was a man who now knew Judaism better than

David. Bob was in many respects the perfect son. David had coached him to always see a fight through to the end, to take over companies, wage proxy fights, gain control of corporate boards, all of it. Now he was fighting David like the Jews of Masada fought the Romans. It was a fight to the death, or at least a fight to the demise of one or the other's corporations.

David remembered telling Bob that all good Jews loved a good fight, especially when it was against another Jew. Now his protégé was taking David's lessons all too literally. Ben had told David's latest lawyer that Bob would rather fight until hell froze over and even fight him after death on the ice than ever settle with him. Bob now regarded David as a no-good son of a bitch; Ben passed along that tidbit in no uncertain terms. There was no way David was going to pass this off as a simple misunderstanding. He was appalled. Bob had taken on some of the same tenacious determination that David taught him and that David saw in his own father, Marvin. He'd had a horrible nightmare the night before he heard how much Bob now hated him. He dreamed that Bob and Marvin were talking about him. His dead father, whom Bob never met, and Bob, David's protégé, were talking about David as their common enemy,

"He's always been a sissy," said Marvin to Bob. "I did what I could for him. But now, here you are. You're more of a son to me than he ever was."

Bob said to Marvin, "I always had to look through him to see you. All this time I knew him I secretly laughed at him. He was never the man you were." The two men who haunted David's nightmares embraced as father and son might, while they closed a door on David who was sitting in a chair in an adjoining room watching them.

It was a horrible dream and he sat upright in his sleep, in a cold sweat in the dark, and spoke out to the ghost of his father.

"Dad? Dad, are you there? Can you hear me, Dad? Why is this happening to me, Dad? Why didn't you love me, Dad?

Why didn't Mother love me? Why doesn't anyone love me? What should I do, Dad? Whose side are you on, Dad? Whose side are you on?"

Then David had a vision of Marvin in his talus at temple. His father was joyfully singing the Shema. Marvin's voice was speaking for hearts of the People of the Book. He spoke to Bob, and David overheard him say, "Israel is all you need to know and believe in. I and the good souls of Israel will deal with this wherever it goes. I will stay in touch with you. You will never be alone. You and Barbara go on building your business and enjoy your lives."

David poured sweat as his body chilled and shivered. He heard his father's voice leaping out of the Torah. It roared at him and held him down by his throat. He wrestled with the voice and tried to shake it away. Then he awakened, screaming and trembling as the dawn broke. He'd betrayed Father and Israel. Father always told him to earn money legally and send money to Israel. David disgraced his father and Israel by making money illegally and keeping it all for himself. Marvin's ghost had found him out and had shaken David to his core.

His wife ran into his bedroom and asked if he was ill. He sent her back to her room and just lay there for hours wondering whose side Marvin was on in this fight. He stared at the ceiling. What was happening to him? Then David heard his father's voice speak again. It rang in his ears and in his mind as if it were a bolt of lightning shot from the blue sky. "You are a disgrace to me and to Israel. You have earned all that will befall you." It was suddenly clear to David: Marvin was on the side of Israel and no one else. He trembled in fear that a harsh judgment would be rendered against him. Marvin's voice spoke for good, for the People of the Book.

PARTNER BEN

As David looked out the window of his latest lawyer's office, he watched two birds splashing in a fountain birdbath. Long passed were the glory days of the case, the grandiose meetings with five or six lawyers and their secretaries all at a big conference table looking out over the city to the Rockies, strategizing on how to destroy Bob's case and his life, with David paying them a collective ten thousand dollars per hour to do little more than chew the fat. It seemed so important then, so intriguing. Now it all came to naught. The lawyers made a fortune off him, those filthy pricks.

All that seemed important now was to get this messy affair finished and behind him so he could play a little in his twilight years, like those two happy birds in the fountain. But it wasn't finished yet. David reminded himself that he needed to be tough. He dared not show the slightest sign of weakness. Like the period of the Judges, he needed to be the personification of Israel's strength renewed. He needed to sweep the Golan, the Gaza, and Samaria and retake Jericho, engage and destroy the Canaanites, Sidonians, Hivites, and all the evil worshipers of Baal, all the evil forces that were encroaching upon the sacred land given to his people by God. David promised himself he would atone for letting his guard down, for failing to be strong in his generation like Marvin was in his time. He would fight his way back into the good graces of the tribe. He was older now and wiser, beaten in the courts but unbowed.

Mal, David's secret weapon against the legal community, had dutifully tracked the practices of all the lawyers in the case. He had meticulously observed all the proceedings, recorded them secretly, and made notes of who was in the courtrooms at each appearance before a judge. He had gathered enough malpractice dirt on two of the firms to make a valid case that they had harmed David to the tune of several million dollars. Even though David had been the instigator of the dirty tricks strategies and even though he had paid them double their customary fees to execute the bribes, Mal made sure David was buffered by one or two intermediaries in each instance so he could be exonerated of criminal wrongdoing. Mal made sure David was in the clear and his former attorneys were on the hook.

Mal also ran exhaustive checks on Ben. Every team operating in opposition to another team or teams has to have a weakness. David reasoned if neither Bob nor Barbara was the chink in the plaintiff's armor, then perhaps the weak link would be Bob's attorney, Ben. Mal's reports convinced David his hunch was on target. Ben had no money. His mother was ailing, Ben himself was ailing, and he had a sister whom he also supported. Diabetes ran in the family and they had no insurance, but all three needed regular dialysis treatments. Ben would owe money to Sol for the prior work done, and that debt made it imperative that he not lose at trial. Trial was a risk Ben couldn't take any more than David could. Ben had to know that David could possibly find a way to bribe a judge again or a couple of jurors and that, even with the U.S. Supreme Court behind him, Ben could still lose. David reasoned there had to be a settlement that separated Ben from his client.

After cordialities, the lawyers got down to talking about money. Ben made his first mistake. He spoke first, indicating he wanted to settle the matter in the first place. David saw the weakness and felt confident of Mal's assessment. Ben threw out the first offer.

David scoffed. "Your case is still a quantum meruit case. I could have easily hired a man to do what Bob did for one-tenth what you're asking, and I'm sure a jury will see it that way."

"Not true," Ben fired back. "You and I both know you acquired Bob's services by fraud. Even the Supreme Court saw it that way. Read the remand instructions back from the Court of Appeals. And I will tell you this. The longer this matter drags out, the more valuable the case becomes. You can hire new counsel all you want, but the clock is running against you, not us. Damages are compounding. You have other exposures also. No one in the world would want to invest with you knowing what they're going to find out about you when this goes to trial. Assets will flee.

"Israel also has some exposure here. Did you ever think of that? What were you thinking when you took him in the bank vault? You were just going to take advantage of a half orphan, screw his life and career to the wall and run away with everything. Israel wasn't going to get a dime either, isn't that true? You were just going to have a big playtime with all the money, weren't you? You were trying to sell the companies while Bob was out there working his ass off. How do you like what I'm saying? How do you think a jury will like it?"

"You assume too much, sir. You could lose. I have a witness who says Bob had a plot to take over the companies."

"You're talking about that blubbering Judith, the one you and your lawyer bribed for a condo and a pickup truck to commit perjury. Go ahead and put her on the stand in district court. Put her up where I can get some decent cross on her instead of your cheap-shot 'I feel threatened' horse shit restraining order. A jury will see right through that. She cried her eyes out under a gentle soft cross, and she made a record that proved she had no idea what she was talking about. She'll come off like a bought-and-paid-for nincompoop and you know it. I can't wait to tear into her with a hard cross. I'll end up nailing you for witness tampering and perjury.

"Why did she call Bob asking for some money before she agreed to commit perjury for you? Two weeks before! How do you explain the interval? She was never afraid of Bob! She called me after the stunt, called me eight times bawling her eyes out. 'Tell Bob I'm sorry,' she said to me, all eight times. You put her up and you're getting perjury and libel on top of everything else. All you end up with is nothing. Put her up, I dare you. All you're going to prove is that you are a slimy off-court player and a bribing bastard.

"He had a plot to take over your companies, you say. Hah! You mean the companies that you already gave him in the bank vault. Don't be ridiculous. He can't take away something that you already gave him. You're fucking ridiculous. You're through, David."

"Gentlemen, lets back up a minute. We're not here to try the case. We're here to see if there's a way we can both put this tedious nightmare behind us," said David's mouthpiece.

"Frankly, Ben," David chimed in as if on cue, beginning his well-rehearsed lines, "I've heard great things about your work over the years." Actually, the opposite was true. He knew that Ben usually lost cases. "You were absolutely brilliant when you were in front of the Supreme Court." Flattery always opened a door. David needed to make a friend of this newcomer lawyer and enlist him in a common cause.

"You know, if I'd had decent lawyers to start with, the case would never have gone this far. The advice I kept getting from them was to fight Bob every step of the way, fight him with everything I had. They should have advised me to settle at the outset, but they didn't." David proffered a half-truth. He'd wanted to destroy Bob. His attorneys only told him they could provide a vigorous defense. "Anyway, I apologize that things got so out of hand. Tell me something that I don't understand though. Why on earth did you agree to take on this gentile in a fight against Israel?" David reflected upon his tilt toward graciousness. Flattery from a fox will get a crow to drop his meal from a high branch into the mouth of the cunning fox. It was an old European fable, and David worked it well.

"You know, I'm so impressed with your work, I'd like you to do some legal work for me after we settle this mess." David was on a roll. "The way I see it is like this. Here you are, risking your practice and reputation in the Jewish community by helping this gentile. Why not take a sure settlement, get paid for all you've done and all Sol did, and then I'll let you have some easy work and I'll pay you some more. Doesn't that make more sense than rolling the dice?"

"David, it's not about fighting against Israel. Do you see Israel named as a defendant? It's a fight of Bob against you, David, against the wrong you've caused my client, the wrong to his career, to his new business, all the harassments, all the vindictiveness. What made you decide to take off on Bob like you did?"

"Well, I just didn't want to see him stealing something that was going to belong to Israel. We're both Jews. I'm sure you can understand my feelings."

"Bob's a Jew as well, David. You even witnessed his conversion. Let's just keep money as the issue here."

"He's not a Jew! He's just a Reformed, a wannabe Jew. Reformed Jews aren't real Jews! They are just fuckups! I offered to help him get an Orthodox rabbi and he didn't want to take me up on it. He didn't want to be a real Jew!"

"What if he had, David? Would you then have pushed him to become Hasidic? Where would it all stop, David? You just wanted to make him into your boy-toy, didn't you? You wanted a fuck-buddy, something besides that black sheep of yours, didn't you? What's the matter? The sheep won't talk to you?

Not intimate enough? And he rejected you, didn't he? That's really what all this is about, isn't it?"

"He's not a Jew!" David shouted. "Reformed Jews aren't real Jews!"

"He's as much a Jew as you or me or any other Jew. Stop the fucking nonsense. He knows Torah, Tanakh, the services, the Holidays, the mitzvahs, all of it. He knows it as well as you and me, probably even more so. We're here to talk money, David. I can't bring him back to you. It's over. Whatever fantasy you had about him, it's over. It's just about money now."

Five thousand years before men penned the Declaration of Independence, which gave birth to a republic founded upon secular principles, God's words were forever etched in the minds of Jews. God's words as spoken to Abraham were decidedly non-secular and excluded those who were not of blood issue.

"It can't be just about money. It's about Judaism also. If Bob is really a Jew, he should know I could never leave him Dad's companies, my companies, Israel's companies."

"How can you say that? When you made the deal with him, he was a gentile. You concealed from him your pledge to Marvin that you would leave the companies to Israel upon your death. Then, after you took away the codicil you showed him in the bank vault, you were telling salesmen in Bob's presence that Bob would inherit the companies. You knew that wasn't true, but you repeated it to several different salesmen at different times so they'd keep selling fund shares. So you've got fraud written all over you, plus violations of the Securities Distribution Act. How could Bob know any of this?"

"Well, he knows now, yet he keeps after me in court. And he became a Jew, so he says, so you say, so some stupid Reformed rabbis say. Well then, he should know the meaning of the story of Abraham!"

"Excuse me. I must be missing something. The deal you made was made under twentieth-century secular laws. It was not made under Torah laws five thousand years ago."

"He testified he's a Jew! He isn't stupid. He knows when God and Abraham made their berit, their covenant between the cut-up animals, that God told Abraham that his own issue shall be his heir."

"That was about Ishmael and Isaac. Later Abraham and Sarah had Isaac. Sarah and Isaac pushed out Hagar and Ishmael because their blood wasn't pure Hebrew. Don't try to rationalize what you did to my client by playing the Jew card. It's not going to fly. You made a secular deal. You made a covenant deal, one man to another under secular law, and you broke the fucking deal, David. It's clear. You live in the United States of America, not in the land of Ur or the land of Canaan. Besides, Abraham pimped his wife to the pharaoh for food stamps, so maybe Moses's bloodlines didn't have pure Hebrew blood either. I don't think you're using a great example to invoke sanctimonious purity and integrity in your dealings. If anybody should be trusted to give those companies to Israel, it should be Bob. Your intent was to sell them and go spend the money. You have no honor, David."

"God also told Abraham that his descendants would people many lands and inherit great wealth. Your client is not a descendent of Abraham. I did not cut a covenant deal with Bob. We did not cut the animals and agree over their bodies and their blood. A deal that is not a covenant deal is no deal at all. What I did with Bob was to enhance the gift my father left me to give to Israel. That was the only agreement that mattered. Goyim think their laws matter. That's not my problem. Only a covenant, a bris, matters. When we were in the bank vault, Bob was a gentile. Your own words acknowledge that. That makes his deal a secular goy deal, not a covenant deal. I merely made use of a fool, but I made no deal."

"Cut out the bullshit. Wahhabi Muslims use that thinking to justify taking from those who are outside of Islam. This is tribal thinking you're spewing, but we now live in a secular world. God said a lot of stuff to a lot of people and you can use scripture to rationalize anything, but we live under secular laws. Learn the story of Ruth."

"I know it."

"Well, Bob fits that scripture story."

"The Ruth story is bullshit. Reformed rabbis use it to justify conversions." David wasn't about to let Ben make him feel empathy for Bob.

"Don't get so righteous, David. Your roots are Khazarian, not Ashkenazi. Your tribe was forced to choose a religion so they'd stop thieving or the Turks were going to kill them. You're not from the blood of Abraham either. You're no different from Bob." Ben liked to keep topics in sharp focus. He wasn't about to let David mix logic.

"My parents, their parents, belonged to a temple. Bob's mother is not a Jewess," David shouted like a hurt child. He scrambled to change the reference frame of his argument from where he'd started to one which had a timeline that more suited his rebuttal.

"Let's get down to business. The time for bullshitting about three-thousand-year-old Tanakh passages is over. Do we deal or go to trial? I assure you, every day that passes this case becomes more valuable, not less. It's just about money." Ben was getting tired of religious philosophy.

"No! It's not just about money!" David was still shouting, his face strained to beet red. "It's about my dad, Marvin, and the promise I made to him. Marvin was a Zionist, you surely know that."

"I know that."

"And I'm a Zionist too. I just had a weak moment, that's all. I made a mistake when I made my deal with Bob. Can't a man make a mistake just once in his life? Can't you see your way to help me get past a simple mistake? I'm an old man. I shouldn't have to suffer so much. My heart isn't good. My kidneys aren't right. I have gout. My prostate needs to come out. All this is stressful and it's hurting my health. It's not human to put me through this. Let's say we work something out where this all didn't happen and nobody knows about it. We should be able to come up with something workable. You and Mal are smart lawyers. Come up with something reasonable."

"Reasonable means the Jewish community can't know about your deal."

"Then you know these companies must go to Israel, especially now. Why did Sol and you ever take the case? No one needed to know what happened here. The secular laws of the United States are irrelevant in this matter! When it comes to Israel, it's the laws of Torah that matter, nothing else. The mitzvahs matter, nothing else. There are no other laws, only God's law. Nowhere in the mitzvahs does it say that you must honor your promises to a gentile. Goyim are beneath us! Fuck them, use them, and piss on their pathetic lives. It doesn't matter what we do to them. They don't matter. Their laws don't matter, and their lives don't matter. Their country doesn't matter. God is all that matters."

Ben wasn't buying into David's rationalizations. "David, you need a reality check. You are about to face a jury of your peers and they believe that their laws matter a great deal. Trust me, they will relish the chance to skewer a fat Jew who broke a deal. You are fucked, David. Stop kidding yourself. This isn't about God or mitzvahs. It isn't even about you giving the companies to Israel. You broke that deal. You might as well go piss on your father's grave. You've made an inconceivable mess, David. Money is the only thing that can fix it now. It's about money. You fucked up, fella."

"All right, since it's about money, what about you, Ben? What about your money? I can't believe your practice is going gangbusters. Be honest."

"It's not about me, David. It's about my client and, by the way, he's pushing me to get a trial date set. Once I do that, there will be no settlement."

"Listen, we're all trying to get to the same place here. We both want out of this case. You want your money, you need the money, and you want to move on."

Ben was suddenly paying attention. David struck a nerve. By the hourly rate Sol put into the case, Ben was out a fortune in fees he owed Sol and he couldn't pay unless he won or settled. He looked at David and said nothing.

David sensed he'd finally driven a wedge into Ben's wall. Now he needed to take control of the meeting.

"Look, I don't begrudge you making a good living, Ben, but I don't want to enrich a man for more than he was worth to me. I'm willing to put some serious money on the table for you, but you need to be a reasonable man. And we can't go putting a stain on Israel."

"Tell me what you're offering."

"It's like this. I can sell my old lawyers up the river and deliver them to you on a silver platter. They did malpractice. I can prove it. My lawyer here can show you the stuff I have on them. I hired a malpractice expert to check over everything they did. There are many millions there. You agree to settle this case for what I'm offering, nothing more, and I'll let you represent me afterward against my former lawyers, or you can just blackmail them and pocket the money yourself. Bob can have his costs back, nothing more. You'll make more than your cut of a win at trial and you take no risk."

"That's unethical. I can't do that." Ben bristled at the thought of betraying his client.

David shouted, spittle flying, "What do you mean, unethical? You're a fucking lawyer! All you cocksuckers are unethical. Look at it this way, Ben. If you don't take my deal and you go forward, you could win, but you'll still lose. I already have all my assets in offshore trusts and you'll never find a dime of any of it. I'll have my money moved to new jurisdictions every six months. I don't care what it costs. Also, I've bribed a judge and a witness before and nothing stopped me. I'll just do it again! I can't believe you've been a lawyer all these years and still haven't figured out that the legal system isn't about making things right. The legal system is about helping rich guys screw little guys while you lawyers and judges get paid to make the crooked farce look honest. Bob is never going to see one dime above what I'm offering. I understand you need to get him some money to walk a deal past a judge, but that's all he's going to get."

"You can't do this. What you're offering for stealing a man's life work is too little."

"Too little, you say. I've spent three and a half million and burned through fifty-four lawyers fighting you and Sol, you fucking morons. You are broke. Sol died broke. Everything he made as a lawyer he lost in the markets. He was a fucking idiot stock player. You want to help somebody, Ben? Help his widow. She's a charity case. She could use some gleanings. You don't have much either, Ben. I've checked. You and your wife are down to your last two hundred thousand. You haven't taken home money for years. I bet your wife loves being broke.

"Let me tell you about too little. If you go forward to trial, I'll gladly spend another three million objecting, appealing, switching lawyers, filing frivolous motions you'll need to respond to. I'll run you into the ground, bankrupt you. I know this game better than you do. The big guy keeps spending the little guy into the ground until the little guy drops dead. I kind of like this game the more I play it. It reminds me of when I was a kid. I stepped on caterpillars and watched their guts squirt out. Then I scraped my shoes on the sidewalk and smeared their guts all over the place. I felt great fucking up those little caterpillars. That's what I'll do to you guys if you go forward, squash you like caterpillars. You will lose. I will destroy you and you will get nothing."

David made it clear to Ben that the nuanced factor in making his offer was the amount of money he needed to pay out of pocket to get the case past a judge. Anything above that he would not pay. He'd rather go to a scorched-earth strategy where Ben would get nothing even though David's business would be tarred and possibly ruined, but David would keep the monies he had amassed through his nefarious dealings over the years.

"Stop it. Bob's a human being. He has lost his career and half his professional life because of you. For the sake of decency, think about what you've done."

"I don't give a shit." David slammed that door shut. Morality had no bank account.

Ben tried a different approach to soften David's resolve. "Let me ask you something, David. Why weren't you honest with Bob from the start? Why didn't you just say, 'I made this promise to my father to leave these companies to Israel and I intend to keep it, so after ten years of great experience you'll have to go somewhere else'? Why couldn't you just make an up-front deal?"

"My testimony and his testimony covered it. He was going to leave to go to Texas and take the Indian girl with him. He was going to abandon me after all I did for him. How else could I keep him?"

"David, that's just business. People move around. You don't own people."

"It was more than business. He was like a son to me. I loved him. I treated him well. He was just going to take the

Indian and leave me. What do you expect? I gave him a terrific opportunity to make good money."

"He made less than he was making before your phony deal, but let's not belabor that. We have experts for that. What I want to know is why you didn't settle this right away when your codicil was discovered. Why did you fight through five appeals courts? Surely you had to know you'd eventually lose. And why did you put crime scene tape over his office door after discovery was completed? Why did you personally destroy his desk with a hatchet after they left? And why did you forbid the employees from ever speaking his name? I guess he got to you, huh? I mean, if you were going to give the companies to Israel, why would you care so much and why destroy company property? Why did you take this so hard?"

"I didn't like feeling betrayed, that's all. I got a little upset with him." David looked away. He did that sometimes when he was caught off guard about not telling the truth.

"I don't believe you, David. If you cared about Israel, you would have prevented all this adverse publicity. It reflects terribly on Jews everywhere. You can't sugarcoat what you did. People who find out about this will think we all do business this way. No, David, I believe you were taking calls from business brokers because you didn't have any intention of keeping your pledge to your father. You didn't have any intention of leaving the companies to Israel. You acted more like a jilted lover. You got emotional, didn't you?

"You were going to sell the companies. You were going to steal from Marvin, steal from Bob, and steal from Israel, weren't you? All your father's friends who put money into UGGA thinking they were helping Israel were going to be betrayed as well, weren't they? You're no different than a little kid stealing from a cookie jar, isn't that true?"

"I owned the companies. What I did with them was my business!" David was animated, shouting once again. "Fuck

Bob! Fuck his Indian girlfriend! Fuck Marvin! And fuck Israel! All my life it was 'Marvin this, Marvin that. Look how handsome Marvin is. Isn't Marvin so smart? Doesn't Marvin do so much for the community? If you have a problem, see Marvin! Marvin! Marvin! Marvin!' How much of Marvin's shit is his son supposed to swallow? Everything was for his shiksa, everything was for Israel. Then I'm supposed to choke that down and also give the business to a goy? What about me? Was I too ugly to be loved? Fuck all of you. I don't give a shit what the community thinks of me. Fuck them and their money. They made money in UGGA. They got no damages. They can't sue. Those companies are mine. Mine!"

David was shaken. He leaned forward into Ben's face. "They are not going to Israel. I don't give a shit about Israel! All my life, everything Dad did was for Israel. Well, I don't even give a shit if the Muslims get Israel. I have no heirs. I don't need a place to escape to. I don't need Israel. It's no skin off my nose!"

"So you lied in your testimony that you intended to keep your promise to your father!" Ben sat back and responded calmly. "You never intended to leave the companies to Israel. Do you see what I can do to you on the witness stand? Even if we had an all-Jew jury, they'd all side with Bob after hearing what you just said." He stared at David, as if he were seeing the defendant for the first time. Never had he known a Jew to say he didn't care about Israel. Never did he know a man who didn't care about his own soul.

"Fuck off. If you go to trial with this, you may ruin me with the community, but I'll ruin you too. The difference is I don't give a shit." David glared at Ben. He looked like a trapped, angry rat, but he wasn't about to compromise.

"Side deals give us all a bad name. This flies in the face of assimilation. Think about the consequences." Ben sounded the trumpet of reason. "This is where anti-Semitism gets its credibility. This is shame." His eyes were heavy with sadness that this choice was being forced upon him. "I'm making a last-ditch appeal to your loyalty to the community, to the tribe."

"Fuck shame. I don't give a shit about shame." David remembered all the angst he'd suffered as a child because his mother never loved him. "Where was Mother's shame for the way she shunned me? Where was Dad's shame when I didn't see him for months at a time? He never spent time with me. Where's the shame in that? I feel no guilt. I owe no shame to anyone," David said matter-of-factly. His emotions were back under control.

"You need help. Your mind is off, thinking this way. Everybody needs somebody. A moment ago you were pleading for me to help you out of your mistake. Now you say you don't care about Israel. Which is it? Who am I talking to?" Ben tried to pry a crowbar into David's inconsistency.

"Cut the crap. You're a fucking lunatic." David was a big donor to many Jewish causes and no lawyer was going to threaten his standing in the community. "You hear me now!" he shouted in Ben's face. "This is only business and money we're talking about. If you go forward, I'll let the American Israeli Political Action Committee, all the synagogues, and all the other Jewish charities and their contacts know you're the one who's fucking Israel over. I'll take out full-page ads in the Jerusalem Post. I'll piss all over you. Every rabbi within a hundred miles of here will get a letter from me. You'll never get one more fucking dime of business. You'll never see another client in Plaintown. You'll be hurt so badly you'll wish you'd had a post driver pounding sand up your ass instead of what I'll do to you. You'll find out what happens when you turn your back on your own. You'll be known all over the country as the lawyer who gave Israel a bad rap. That goy may have what I'm offering and not one more dime for him. You may have a fabulous extra compensation for yourself as my collection agent for my injuries from legal malpractice, or you can run lifetime blackmails on those cocksuckers. It's your choice."

"Your malpractice money. Do you mean the malpractice that you directed and paid for, that malpractice?" Ben wasn't about to let David's slight of tongue slip by him just because it was blended with threats and insults.

"Don't get your back up. They were goy firms. They were stupid. They deserve the fucking you'll give them. You can have all of the malpractice money. I wash my hands of it. It comes to more than you'd likely win for your share of a contingency at trial, which you'd never collect from me anyway. I'll show you our proof against our other lawyers, our billing records, my agreement with them to bribe the judge, the payments to the judge's wife's charity, the canceled checks from the witness bribes, all of it, everything we have. They'll be easy takedowns for you. I'll draw a memo of understanding between us, and you can have all the collection money, all of it. They are easy proofs and the goy firm will want to settle with you. I'm giving you easy money right now! Bob can make it up later. He's younger than we are. This way, we both keep our good standing with the tribe, and you don't screw Israel. That's my final offer, Ben."

Ben just stared at David. He felt like throwing up his lunch. Finally he spoke. "It's not enough money."

Mal spoke up after Ben's remark threatened to collapse the negotiations. "Gentlemen, gentlemen, let's not lose our focus here. We're getting close. I've listened to you both. I can seal a deal between you, find a way out for everybody.

"David, you want to have and enjoy the companies. You don't want to lose your standing in the community. You don't want to bring shame to Israel. We all agree to that. Ben, you need money. Bob needs money. Israel needs to stay unblemished from this shameful fiasco. We all agree to those principles. Here's the solution. David and Ben draw up an agreement giving Bob his costs back plus something for his borrowings to stay alive while he fought this battle. Not much money, just enough to walk it past a judge who holds his nose so he can't smell how unfair this deal is to Bob.

"Ben, you force the pittance settlement on him. Shove it down his throat. Threaten to quit, threaten to put a lien on the case files, tell him you'll sue him for nonpayment of fees. Do whatever you need to do to get rid of this goy.

"David, you pay the settlement you offered Bob. Give Ben the dirt on the firms and fuck them, but you also make a new will. In your new will, you leave the companies and all your personal wealth, except enough to provide for your wife, to Ben. After you die, Ben inherits your assets. The assets stay with the tribe.

"You give a copy of this new will to Ben so no one needs to go through this litigation again after you die. Ben, you now have a huge incentive to get yourself healthy and stop smoking those stinking cigars so you can outlive David who is twenty years older than you. I'll put a borrow provision in the will. You can borrow money on a will instrument like that. Ben, you can stop living on a starvation diet. Then you join a gym and take off seventy pounds so you can fuck your wife again.

"Bob continues to starve with his Indian lover, but like you said, Ben, he still has half a life. So you stop feeling sorry for him. This will be our secret Khazarian side deal, a beautiful deal to end all side deals, and it will be our only real deal. Secular law can just go fuck itself. We abide by our covenant deal here. There's Abraham, there's God, and there's us. That's it! Goyim secular law is cut out—fuck all of them! No one knows about our side deal outside of us three.

"Ben, you pledge to David that, upon your death, these companies go to Israel. You cannot sell them nor will them to any other person or entity. After David dies you can take profit distributions from them. This way, David's pledge to Marvin is kept whole. David can be buried in Mount of Olives when he dies. Israel gets everything Marvin Sustack promised her, only she gets it a little later. Israel lives on."

"So the only one who gets screwed is the guy who built up the business. That is shame." Ben had to poke Mal and David with one last insult.

"Shut up, Ben. That is our deal." Mal placed his hands in front of his face, and then he cut his hands away as if he were Abraham cutting animals in half in his covenant with God, or like Moses parting the Red Sea. Mal stared at Ben with a matter-of-fact look that said he knew there was no other way and understood everyone else also realized there was no other way. Then Mal gave the same stare to David. He meant his words to be the final say on this matter.

Ben thought for a long moment. *I am selling my soul and my honor, but I have my mother and sister to care for and I am very sick myself. It's getting hard to hide that fact. The old saying that a bird in hand is worth more than two in a bush is finding resonance in my mind. David does have a valid point. I do need ongoing business from the Jewish community. How far has this profession come from the English solicitors who were not allowed to sue clients who would not pay? The legal community was about service to the people and civic harmony back then. Oh God, why do I feel so dirty? Some things will never change. The tribe of Israel will last into perpetuity. The sun will rise and set. The oceans will rise and fall with the pulls of the moon, and life will go on. And everyone involved in this sordid mess will carry their deeds with them into the Book of Life. May God hold his nose when he reads about our deeds.*

"Have your counsel draw a memorandum of agreement. Also give me copies of all your evidence of malpractice. I may decide to pursue those lawyers separately, after all this is settled. I can threaten them with exposure for payment. After all, they were goy firms, so who gives a shit about them. I'll sign for your evidence under confidence to you, of course." Ben felt he'd done all he could.

"Of course," said David, smiling like the happy frog that just swallowed a fly as he extended his hand to Ben, thinking at the same time that nothing solved a sticky problem better and faster than a bribe to a lawyer willing to commit malpractice.

Ben took David's hand, thinking at the same time he was sealing a deal with the scum of the earth, but a very profitable deal. Mal placed his hands above and below their clasped hands.

David and Ben both spoke the tribe's covenantal promise words. "Mazul um Bruchah." Their word was their bond. Mal was their witness. Their side deal, the real deal, was now sealed.

Ben, now David's partner, would go on to force a shabby settlement down Bob's throat. He lied to Bob, telling him this was only a necessary step toward getting a larger settlement from David's earlier law firm, a much bigger settlement for bribery of a listed witness, libel, ex-parte communications with a judge, and bribery of a judge. He also promised Bob that there would come a reopening of the case they were about to settle once the wrongdoing was exposed after David died. None of this was true, of course, but Ben reasoned that, with time, witnesses would die or move away from Plaintown, the barrier of latches would bar a reopening of this historic case based upon legal malpractice; and quite possibly he himself would also be dead and the companies would be safely in the hands of Israel.

Ben threatened to resign as Bob's attorney unless he settled, to place a lien on the case for all his and Sol's hours of work, and said he would refuse to release Bob's case files to another attorney. Bob's funds to put experts on the stand again were another consideration for his case, and Ben shut that down by stating he'd not allow third-party involvement in the case files. He'd not allow Bob to get help from Barbara, Bob's new partner in business. He'd go to the judge and request to withdraw from representation, stating that Bob refused to cooperate. Ben told Bob he was not allowed to make any inquiries to sell off a portion of the case or to seek financing for another round of expert testimony before a jury. By these unethical tactics and a false promise of future litigation once Ben uncovered the wrongdoings of David's previous lawyers, which he had no intention of pursuing, Ben forced Bob to settle.

Ben concealed the true terms of the settlement from the court. He omitted the side deal he'd made with David and then submitted the false settlement terms to the court. The judge ordered the case closed and Ben became a wealthy man at the expense of betraying his client. *David had a point. Mitzvahs matter. Countries and their laws and legal systems will come and go, but the tribe will endure as it always has. Secular law doesn't really matter, even though I make my living practicing it. It's all just a game anyway. Let the goyim believe in it. Let them believe in Lady Justice and her stupid blindfold. It's all just bullshit to preserve social order and to make a good living representing the fools who are stupid enough to sue each other. And maybe I was wrong about the Reformed Jews. Maybe they really aren't much different than gentiles.*

That last thought was too philosophical, too theological for Ben to contemplate. He didn't dwell on it. *Anyway, having a lot of money in my own pocket is a good thing. Yes, having money in this narcissistic world is a very good thing.*

It was perhaps too much to expect a man to go beyond his moral limitations, especially if that man was a lawyer. For years after the case settled, Ben would visit Bob, pretending to be a trusted friend, and misleading him to believe that, upon David's death, there would be evidence brought forward that would open a fresh case against David's previous law firms, when in fact Ben himself had long since personally collected on that opportunity. Ben mentally calculated that his malpractice potentially exposed him to sixty to a hundred and twenty million dollars of liability, but he figured the millions he got up front were worth taking the risk.

Being the deceitful scumbag that he'd become, Ben made sure that any wrongdoing he committed, any breach of professional ethics, would likely not survive a latches defense, thus Bob could be time barred if he figured out what happened and tried to bring a case. People did die, witnesses did move away, the truth did get shoved under the rug, Israel prospered, and the pathetic human goy beast continued their toiling blindfolded to the ways of the world, unjustly enriching the more powerful and corrupt among the populace. And life went on. The only risk to Israel and the community was that somehow word would get out about what happened and public sympathy for Israel would suffer, but the sympathetic media, the rabbis, and the political machinery would easily bury this sordid episode. Anyway, it would be someone else's worry, not Ben's.

Besides, Ben rationalized, the case in chief was so voluminous, so complex and intertwined, that even a determined ethical lawyer would blanch at the idea of taking on a malpractice case against him. Especially if the lawyer was from Plaintown where every lawyer knew every other, and gentlemen of the bar didn't normally sue each other out of professional courtesy. Ben stayed friendly with his client long after he'd screwed him.

Ben hoped no evidence would ever turn up to trip him up, and the statute of limitations on malpractice would run out before Bob became the wiser. Ben reasoned it was unlikely there would ever be charges brought against him or David's earlier lawyers for suborning perjury, malpractice, the ongoing bribes paid to conceal perjury, or the circumvention of justice, whatever that was. Ben stopped smoking cigars and got himself healthy.

Ben and Bob saw each other every quarter for twenty years under Ben's guise that, when David died, they'd come into possession of bribery evidence that would allow a reopening of the case. Ben promised Bob the case would be worth sixty to one hundred million dollars with the libel component.

At long last, after David's death, Bob asked when they'd have the evidence to proceed against David's former attorneys. It was the moment of truth. Ben confessed that he'd worked for David years before, collecting a handsome sum of millions on a side deal concealed from Bob and that he'd "cleaned up some loose ends for David."

"Forget about suing his old lawyers," Ben said. "People have died and moved away. Too much time has gone by. Forget about suing me too. All the money I got from David I lost in the stock market. I am without much means."

Bob asked but one question of his shadow friend and betrayer. "When you had the settlement discussions with David and Mal, why wasn't I included?"

"You are a Reformed Jew. David and Mal and I are Conservative Jews, closer to the ways of the Orthodox traditions. David and Mal would not allow your attendance. It was two against one."

"You mean three against one, so you could work your side deal to screw me, don't you?" Bob's question was met by Ben's stare into the floor. He could not hold Bob's eyes. "Get away from me. Shame on you. You are without ethics or morals. You are a disgusting scumbag. Never call me again."

As Ben left the table, Bob was alone with his thoughts.

Those who rail most against anti-Semitic sentiment are Semites who refuse to assimilate into a secular society, try as they might or pretend to believe they can. When all cards are laid bare on the table, it is the law of the tribe that prevails. Until there is no theology, or until secular notions of inclusive society are abandoned, those who believe in universal honorable conduct amongst fellow humans were delusional fools. It was a noble goal but an unobtainable one. The Torah asks whether God should spare a sinful city to save the life of one righteous person. The converse might be should an entire tribe be blamed for the misdeeds of a few unethical dirtbags?

Bob contemplated over a second iced tea before he left the table. *If goodwill amongst people is nurtured by thousands of good deeds, then this fragile tower of goodwill must be cherished for there is great goodness in it, despite my individual pain. It is a cut into the soul of goodness, yes, but it is not a fatal cut. I must learn from this and move on with life. I must not succumb to clichés such as 'do not trust a person from such or such a tribe or profession or that.' Accept that wrong often goes unaddressed, like Aaron needed to accept that his sons were killed by a holy flame and God never allowed him to know why. Let those who choose to live like scum live that way. Continue to love God and move on. Be thankful for your blessings and be a good partner for Barbara. She needs you.*

COMPLAINING TO ANDY

After his side deal with Ben, David felt the need to share his learned lessons with his protégé. After he locked up the barn and went into the main house, he went to his secret green room to spend time with Andy. He had a problem in the arena with the tarantula. In the battle with the scorpion, the giant spider lost three of its legs. It was useless as a combatant for future fights and it needed to be disposed of. David took Andy down from his shelf and positioned the fetus so its head was turned toward the arena case. He flipped a switch on the wall behind him and a low-frequency humming sound filled the room.

Once situated, Andy and David watched the disposal crew do their work. David opened some glass dividers that linked connecting corridors of red army ants to the gladiator case. It didn't take long for the hungry ants to get the scent of the injured spider. Soon a few advance scouts entered the case and attacked immediately, biting the tarantula's remaining legs. As the ants bit the hairy spider legs, the humming sound intensified in volume. David's sound system was uniquely adapted to receive frequency vibrations from the spider and the various insects that were engaged in mortal combat in the gladiator chamber.

As the ants carried a prize leg back to the ant colony, they were passed by swarms of their pheromone-sensing comrades headed to the feast. Soon the doomed spider was covered with ants. It writhed in agony, and the pitch of the humming sound increased noticeably. David quietly watched the animal began its death throes while sipping whiskey on ice. Andy sat there ready for his mentoring lesson. By now David's UGGA firm was in shambles. The stresses of his litigation had aged him terribly and his reasoning powers were failing him. He was approaching the borderline of dementia and his abnormal sociopathy spiraled further downward into full blown psychopathy. He was now reduced to being the coach and mentor to a fetus floating in a formaldehyde filled jar.

"Andy, today I concluded some messy business. I want it to be a lesson to you. Lawyers can't be trusted one bit. When I first went to see a law firm about defending myself against Bob, I asked them what the entire process would cost me. They told me there wouldn't be an entire process. They told me this whole thing would die on preliminary motions. It would go away in three months, six tops, they said. As for the money, they told me it wouldn't cost much. Their best guess was it would only take ten or twenty grand, thirty tops. Well, here we are, Andy. It's been a twelve-year fight. It cost me over three million dollars, and I still had to write checks to Bob.

"I know Bob was your father, Andy. I need you to know that I loved him too, but he betrayed me terribly. After all I did for him, the status, the office, the secretaries, the cars. He even got to screw your mother, Andy. She was the best whore I had in the firm. All I ever asked in return was that he love me and become an Orthodox Jew. But he wouldn't suck me off or even let me suck him off. He refused to compromise. He wasn't a good friend. Don't make the same mistake I did. Make sure the people you surround yourself with are honest and honorable, like me. When you grow up, get good treatment before you give a favor. The same goes for lawyers. Make sure they show you up front what they can do before you give those pricks a dime.

"Lawyers are deceitful, Andy. They work together to suck you into their process. They con you into believing it will be quick and dirty and over, but in truth the whole time they are supposedly working with you, they're actually working with the lawyers on the other side to keep you in the process, to drag it out, to prolong it, to milk it for all they can. The truth is, Andy, no lawyer gives a fuck about his client. That's just some bullshit public image they try to sell people. Their only concern is where the money is in each case, and then they conspire to carve up the money like a turkey feast.

"Andy, here's my advice to you. Never sue and never get sued. Always try to make a deal first without lawyers involved at all. That way you and the other party can both save a lot of time and expense. If I'd paid Bob a million or two right off, we'd both have been better off. Instead, he got less and I paid more than what we could have worked out. The five appeals court decisions that the lawyers wasted my money on, I can't get back. That was three million dollars, Andy. I paid six hundred thousand for each appeal so these idiots could waste my money yammering at each other. I paid thousands just to have these pricks read e-mails they sent to each other. What were the e-mails about? Where's the best whorehouse? What? I'll let you look at the bills when you get older, Andy. You won't believe what I got charged for!

"They charged for research hours! How do you know if they researched for five hundred hours or a half hour? How can you know if they already knew the things they were supposedly researching? They spent hours conferring with opposing counsel, but they don't say what they talked about. I bet they talked about weather, sports, and the best places to get pussy and then charged me for it. I think all lawyers are Democrats, Andy. They belong to the Trial Lawyers Association, which is a communist organization designed to get everybody to sue everyone else to fuck up the economy and make these cocksuckers rich. They're all parasites, Andy, just like the lice and the silverfish. They pick the bones clean off the corpses of their litigation victims.

"Make a lawyer give you an audited financial statement before you ever hire one, Andy. If you don't, you'll run into a situation where the lawyer is overextended with his bank lines and he'll just run fees on you like crazy. You can't trust them, I'm telling you. Pay attention when I give you great advice, Andy. Look at their references, their revenues, and the kinds of cases they worked. Get a list of their last twenty clients and see for yourself if they had a conflict. I'm telling you, Andy, do not trust any of them.

"Someday I'll get control of the American government, Andy. When I grow our money big enough I'll do that. I'll do it for you, Andy. The whole government is for sale, and when I have enough to buy it, the first thing I'm going to do is replace all the lawyers with baboons that throw paper and banana peelings at each other. Things couldn't be worse than they are now." David took another sip of whiskey and turned his attention from his protégé back to the glass arena.

"Oh look, Andy! The ants are starting to tear another leg off the spider! Can you hear the spider screaming, Andy?" The pitch in the humming ceased. Now the speakers of the ultrasensitive sound system gave out a strange hissing sound with intermittent spikes or screeches, much like a chalk scratch upon a blackboard. "This is great fun, isn't it? Just stick with me, Andy. You are the perfect friend I always wanted. We'll go far together.

"Now understand this, Andy. I enjoy a good fight, so I'd do it all over again. It was worth all that money just to torture Bob. I thought I got him close to suicide a couple of times, but he didn't do it. So Andy, here's a case of do as I say but not as I do. Take this lesson to heart and don't forget it. You'll be a fine executive someday, Andy. All you need to do is remember all I've told you." David sipped more whiskey.

"Women are the cause of all the problems in the world, Andy. You need to understand this. That Susan woman got to Dad, and her daughter got to Bob and spoiled my chances to make him my lover. Now that damn Indian woman Barbara has gotten to Bob and he's gone forever. But I've got the best of Bob right here in you, Andy. Back in the good old days, women never had the kind of power they have today. Back in good old ancient Greece, every man was a homosexual. That proves a man can become gay if he works at it. The Greeks kept women in their proper place. They just used them for housework and breeding purposes. Then something went horribly wrong with the world and we became the bad guys.

"Women caused that change, Andy. They are dangerous. They lay traps of inducements to draw you in close to them. Once you become vulnerable, they spring their trap. They make you think you love them instead of a man. It all started when they figured out how to make their pussies smell better. A pussy has a natural advantage over a mouth or an asshole, Andy. If you can get past the pussy's smell it slides smoothly over your shaft. But don't mistake that good feeling for love. Only we men know what love is. No one deeply loves you the way I do, Andy.

"I did my best to even the score. I wish I could have rescued you from your mother's womb before I gutted her. You would have been there beside me watching my good deeds. Booboo, one of the goats, had his hoofs on Marty's body. He was trying to eat her blood-soaked hair and I had to push him away. Then I took revenge for all sons who had mothers who rejected us. I struck a courageous blow against their wretched hateful sex, Andy. I wanted to do it all that afternoon while I looked at it, but I held back and let Marty reveal all her wicked ways. Finally I had the courage to do what I almost succeeded to do to little Betty Trout. I bit Marty's pussy! I finally did it! And do you know what, Andy? It didn't taste all that great. I don't know why some men get so excited about kissing a pussy. I just don't understand it.

"Just know this, Andy. You can always trust me. I have your best interests at heart. My genius knows how the world works. I also have experience dealing with all sorts of filthy creepy people. With your good looks and youth, Andy, together we'll build a huge organization. I'll think the great thoughts. I'll come up with brilliant ideas. You'll do the leg work and fly all over the country to carry out my ideas. You'll meet top salesmen, top businessmen, wealthy movie stars, pension plan executives, you name it. People will love you, Andy. You'll have the finest suits, the best shoes and cars. People will hang on your every word. We'll go far together. We'll conquer the entire world!"

Andy, the fetus in the formaldehyde jar, sat silent and motionless facing the glass gladiator arena. And the ants carried off the second whole leg of the tarantula. Others began to dig the meat out of its abdomen as David continued with Andy's lesson.

"Oh Andy, look at the ants. I love it when they tear apart a spider. It's so thrilling I can't help myself. Can you see the agony of the spider, Andy? See how it moves its remaining legs wildly about. It's helpless to combat the ants eating its flesh. Look how tormented that spider is! Can you hear the constant screams of the spider? Imagine how much pain it's in! I love that sound, Andy. It's the sound of dominance. That sound tells me when the spider is going out-of-its-mind crazy with agonizing pain. It's a beautiful sound. Very few people know the thrill of meting out pain to another animal. I made Bob feel pain, Andy. I couldn't hurt him physically, but I made his mind suffer, just like the spider suffers now.

"I kept Bob from getting to a jury trial twice. Yes, I did that. The first time I bribed the judge to dismiss the case. I also had a couple witnesses I bribed to make up some lies about

Bob in case I needed them at trial. I was going to make him out to be some kind of nut that I had to fire, even though he built the company for me. You always need a backup plan, Andy, or as I prefer to call it, a back door out of the problem. You need to see problems before they crop up, Andy. You need to anticipate what your enemy will do, and you need to be sure you have all your moves in place ahead of time.

"The second time I kept Bob from getting to a jury was when I bribed his lawyer. That was actually pretty easy to do. I, my lawyer, and Bob's lawyer were all Conservative Jews. All I needed to do was persuade Bob's lawyer that it was okay to screw his client because Bob wasn't a real Jew. He was just a Reformed Jew, whatever they are. Imagine the torment Bob felt when his own lawyer sold him up the river! After all those appeals wins, I still screwed him!" David laughed uncontrollably.

"Just like the spider is writhing with the insanity of ap-proaching death he can do nothing about, I'm sure Bob went out of his mind with agony." David regained his composure and spoke in a low, serious voice to his protégé. "You need to be unmerciful and cruel in combat. We are rich, Andy, and Bob is poor. I used my money to screw him and to win. That's the beauty of being rich, Andy. We can use our money to bait little people and then screw them later when it suits us. When it comes to a court fight, the guy with the most money, who is intelligent enough to use it properly by bribing the right people at the right time, wins every time."

David poured a fresh glass of whiskey as he launched into the conclusion of Andy's lesson. "The legal system is a farce, Andy. It's a device to make the little people believe there is justice and a way to make things right. But when you understand it like I do, Andy, the legal system is just made up of people, and being morally weak as all humans are, we can bribe the legal system's judges and the lawyers to get whatever we want. You must see money as a big tool to use in combat,

Andy. It's kind of like hitting a little guy with a big bomb from ten miles above when all he has is a rifle.

"Politicians are another farce, Andy. They are useless whores who do the bidding of the Federal Reserve and the bankers. They are merely accomplished in the same sense that female whores, like Susan and Marty, became accomplished. A great female whore learns that success in business doesn't come by catering to the whims and jealousies of other women. The whore knows it matters not who goes to whose parties, who gossips about whom, which woman wears what, whether her selfish needs are being bested by her girlfriends' selfish needs. No, the whore knows that all she needs to do to get ahead is to fuck the right men to get them to do her bidding.

"Politicians are exactly like whores, Andy. You must learn how to harness the politician to benefit the firm. Use them like Dad used Susan and like I used Marty and Bob. Let them do all the fucking of the other guy for you, by passing the right legislation or the right rule-making. Just pay them well enough and they will fuck for you. Unfortunately, their primary client is the Fed and the bankers, and they will always fuck the public and pass laws to squeeze the blood from the public for their masters. But you can still find occasional opportunities for yourself within the bloated government-controlled system they created to screw the little guy. That's when you bribe them to do favors for you and the firm.

"Just chum them up at a gathering. Tell them you need a private moment to discuss something of great importance to your interest. Slip a thousand or two in their pocket while you're talking to them. That's you taking their cue, letting them know that you're willing to pay to play. They'll give you an audience. They like untraceable cash, even if they're rich. That way they can buy a whore and cheat on their wives. They'll appreciate you, Andy. America is sliding into the sewer. In this environment, you have to think and live like a sewer rat to prosper. Remember that. Just learn to think the way I do, Andy. Together, we'll go far."

After another sip, David turned to Andy to give his protégé instructions about how to see the broader world. "Andy, I want you to think of yourself as one of those ants. Just as the ant takes his little bite out of the spider, our business is taking a little bite out of America. See, Andy, we're no different, no better or worse than a corrupt government official who regulates big banks or commodity markets or anything else, then takes a job with the law firm that represents the clients he regulated.

"America will fall to a fascist or communist dictator, Andy. Things can't go on the way they are. The country is failing because of that son of a bitch Woodrow Wilson putting in the Fed and the IRS. He stole the country from the people. He fucked over the concepts of our founding fathers, Ben Franklin, Lincoln, Johnnie Carson, Bob Hope, John Wayne, Mel Gibson, Winston Churchill, and Generals Douglas MacArthur and George Patton.

"Watch out for the Bilderbunkers, the Bank for Internal Settlements and the Diablos crowd, Andy. Their days of power are numbered and the world's banking system will be turned on its head. They sowed the seeds of their own destruction with fractional banking. Their fiat money attempts to suffocate freedom and enslave humanity are ending. You need to be vigilant, Andy. I can't tell you how their power will end, but likely it will either be the Muslims rallying dissenters to their causes, or the Chinese and the Russians will take them head-on in a war, or the mob will get wise to them and overrun their barricaded meeting places with pitchforks.

"War is coming, Andy. It's like the old king of the hill game kids play. There are all sorts of elements that are looking to throw the established powers off the hill. I don't think it will come through the vote. These pricks rig the votes. Votes don't count anymore. Only honest money can save the country, Andy. With honest money, all the tensions that divide the people will end. It's so simple to see, but first the people need to take the scales from their eyes. Just never get into a car with Teddy Kennedy, Andy. He'll drive you off a bridge and drown you, especially if he's drunk. Also, beware of that woman who wears pastel pantsuits and screams like an angry reptile.

"America is dying the same way as that spider. We just need to bite off our piece of the carcass and gobble up all we can. Buy all the gold and silver you can get your hands on, Andy. We've got to be ready. When the end comes, there will be all sorts of destruction. Remember when the Chinese conquered Alexandria and burned that library and replaced all that knowledge with the Little Red Book of Bullshit from Mao? Mao was just a fat nut who liked whores, Andy. Remember when the Nazis took over Cambodia and killed all the Jews? Or when Hitler invaded Tunisia in the Punic Wars and killed all the Carthaginians and the school teachers and burned the books? The Aztecs were the same way, Andy. When they overran France in the First World War, they raped women and cut their heads off. The present tide of socialism-communism has run its course, Andy. Change is coming!" David took another swig of whiskey.

"The Buildyourbunkers and the central bankers they control have gained control of the world, Andy. They meet on the eightieth floor of the Big Stick Tower in Basel, Cuba, or maybe it's in Portugal or Ireland, one of those communist countries. It doesn't matter where it is, because they have telephones. Anyway, Andy, what you need to appreciate is these scammers are trying to control the world for their own personal benefit. They want to use fiat money issued by their controlled governments through their debt-based banking systems so they can suck off the interest from the world's labor and goods production. They want to avoid using honest weights and measures as prescribed in the Torah mitzvahs, so they're doomed to failure. They're jerking off the world.

"In the end all banks will fail. It's not a maybe, Andy. It's a for sure, for sure. The Dodd Frank slime law puts the derivative holders of bad holding company trades first in FDIC liquidation. There's quadrillions of dollars of banker bets and quant software programs that have no idea what values are. It's a levitated roll of the dice shit show. The wealth of the world will implode and impoverish everybody who doesn't get it. People who have assets in brokerage and trust accounts in bank holding companies will lose everything. After the financial crisis of 2008, these clever deviants reorganized themselves into bank holding companies so they could be bank regulated instead of SEC regulated. Now they can reach into client accounts and invoke their hypothecation clauses and steal everything.

"This is a worldwide theft scheme, Andy. It bypasses and circumvents FDIC and SIPIC protections and lets the banks take everything everyone has. The little sticker on the bank window is for confidence purposes only. There's only one drop-of-piss fiat in the ten-gallon fiat money bucket for every dollar that sticker guarantees. It doesn't mean shit. There's nothing behind the sticker. They are set up to steal your money, Andy. Do not trust their shit show.

"And the morons who are bank officers and directors will be screwed along with everyone else, Andy. They can be held personally liable for derivative counterparty losses of the holding companies. So do not be stupid here. Do not go on any bank boards. The bank fraudsters are running scared, Andy. That's why they passed even more legislation after their slimy Dodd Frank Law. They can go back to the public taxpayer for another bailout like TARP.

"Global bank failures on a colossal scale are coming at them at light speed and they're shitting their pants. Their game is over, Andy. They have no teeth, no gold or silver, and no street cred. Just be ready for when fiat becomes worthless. It's coming at you fast, Andy. Buy lots of good toilet paper while you can still get it. The dollar doesn't wipe very well. It won't even be good for toilet paper, Andy. It just kind of smears everything around. I tried it.

"We need to watch the next election carefully, Andy. Both candidates have flaws and vocal detractors, but remember this, Andy. You are an American, and you must give your heart and soul and affections to whichever candidate wins. You must believe that, whatever the flaws, the winner will rule with goodness and benevolence toward all Americans and with malice toward none. Even if the female reptile wins, Andy, we must support her for the common good. We know in our heart of hearts, Andy, that these fucking women are smarter than us men. Just never let them hear that. What goes on in this room stays in this room, Andy. If you ever tell anyone that women are really smart, I'll take you out of your jar and spank you.

"Now, Andy, pay attention! This is important! If America doesn't soon choose honest money over Bilderbunker fiat communism, we'll need to run away before the country descends into a police state. It's going to happen fast." As the alcohol took its effect, David slurred some of his words together and drooled streams of saliva. His vision went into and out of focus and his mind became tipsy as he blabbered incoherently his deepest feelings to his imaginary protégé. "Everything will blow apart at once. Pay attention, Andy. This is important! The hundreds of trillions of undisclosed unaudited Federal Reserve swap lines of Dollars for Pounds, Euros, Yen, Loonies, Aussies, Pesos, Kiwis, Francs, Pesetas, Yuan, Won, Dong, Rupees, Escudos, Lira, Drachma, and other currencies. And with Federal Reserve bank and member bank balance sheets chock-a-block full of no income, no job loans to illegal immigrants who buy cars, disappear and get the car chopped for cash for dope. Money will all fly into chaos. These insane derivative positions holding up phony loans are going to blow apart and the leveraged credit implosion of the banking abortion will fall like the Eiffel Tower standing upside down on its head on a pinpoint, collapsing thousands of trillions in derivatives and collar trades to worthlessness when it all tips over. All this magical financial engineering, the interest rate swaps, currency collars, insurance-guaranteed portfolios, hedges on bonds and bank stocks will all crash and burn. Poof! Whoosh! Gone! Blown away! When it all blows apart we'll watch it together on TV Andy. It will be wonderful!" David drank some more whiskey. He was slobbering all over his shirt and getting drunk.

"The least disturbance, like a butterfly flapping its wings or a Parisian whore spreading her legs too quickly, will set off a breeze that will take the tower of financial babble out of perfect normal and bring the whole façade crashing down. It'll be like the Tower of Babble coming down. The hubris of the banking elite will take a huge drubbing and it won't recover until a new gold- and silver-backed honest money returns. That's called a reset of the bank credit proxy, Andy. See, banks can't make new loans until they have a fresh base of honest money to renew the currency debasing cycle. It's a process they need to go through. The hubris of man against God and nature will end until another John Law, John Maynard Keynes, Alan Greenspan, Mario Draghi, or Robert Rubin comes along playing their Pied Piper meat whistle, the siren sounds of debt creation and money debasement. It's not voodoo rocket science, Andy. It's just a con game. Dark pools and high frequency trades will blow the markets apart and fuck the little guy and his pension and his kids' college funds. Then the gamers will fuck each other. Don't get upset, Andy. This is normal. It happens every hundred or so years. People without ethics or conscience attracted to power and greed will always be with the human species, screwing the little guy with dishonest money.

"Even the vote-switching software in key battleground states' crooked voting machines in vote-stealing precincts won't be enough to stop the peoples' cry for freedom when it comes. The people will rise up against their fascist oppressors and make sure their honest votes are counted. Voting machines will get tossed into lakes in favor of honest paper hand counts. Thugs breaking the law by blocking votes at polling stations with their baseball bats will be met head-on. Honest voters will not be denied by bully thugs. Dead people and illegal immigrants will no longer get to vote. The people will put a stop to communist vote-rigging scam tactics. People have had enough of phony bullshit rigged elections.

"The establishment banking order is going to end in complete destruction because the assholes who play the game don't understand it any better than the agencies that pretend to regulate it. It's going to be a world where only those who own gold and silver survive. People will have to eat their pets and mothers-in-law to stay alive, Andy. No, it will even be worse than that. There won't be any TV! People won't be able to pay for extras. Hollywood will lose its moviegoers. People will have to learn to read books, talk to each other, and go to church again.

"I'm serious, Andy. So far the game has held together because the governments went all-in supplying gold and silver inventory to the market to keep the metal prices down and their scam going. Now they are down to stealing gold from allocated accounts, raiding gold exchange traded funds and begging gold and silver from the Vatican. The pope is pissed off at the liberal secularist commie bastards. It's not good to get the pope pissed off. He wants secularism to end and a return to old-fashioned religion. He's going to get his way. The Imams and the Chinese and the Buddhists all want gold and silver money too. Do you know why the pope and all the rest of the world wants to go back to gold, Andy? It's because they have gold and we don't. Fort Knox gold hasn't been audited for over sixty years. Can you believe they have gold there? There are some real deep pocket players about to show up and change the money game. Dad told me this day would come.

"The fascists that want a single world order will have their nuts removed, Andy. Banks will fail, countries will fail, but we'll keep our nuts on because we're smarter nuts than those other nuts. We'll pick up and move to another country before the roof caves in. We'll find a place where there is real money and honest society. I might have to take you out of your jar and put you in my pocket to get you through Homeland Security, Andy, but don't you worry, son. I never leave a man behind. I'm as trustworthy as the United States Marine Corps, Andy. You can always count on me. You can believe everything I tell you. I'll always take good care of you."

David's mind, polluted with alcohol, began to wander. He skipped from one random subject to another as he spewed advice to his imaginary student. "To become a complete executive, Andy, you need to know all about Europe. I can give you great advice on Europe because I went there once when I was a kid. I'm an expert on Europe. My dad took me there for a five-day trip. He wanted to stay longer, but I kept throwing up over there because the place smelled funny and the people ate fish all the time. What I learned about Europe is that you should never bother going there. It's too far north, too close to the North Pole, so you're always cold over there. It rains all the time in Europe and the people are always coughing because they are cold and they all smoke. It takes forever to get there, even by plane. You risk a terrorist blowing your plane up coming and going, so you worry constantly about surviving the trip.

"When you eventually, finally, get to Europe after five exhausting days on an airplane, you'll find that nobody speaks English except for a couple people in a couple countries, like

England, so it's impossible to make sense out of anything anybody says. But even in England, the people don't speak proper English. They speak with a golf ball stuck up their noses and asses and they use the wrong words for things, like calling a sweater a 'jersey' or a 'pullover.' The entire place is a jumbled mess of people who don't know what the other person is saying. You always have to be careful because they could be trying to steal your money. When it rains the only thing you can do is go to a museum.

"The whole country of Europe is one continuous museum. When you go into one of their museums, you'll stand in front of glass cases where they show you the kinds of clubs guys used a thousand years ago to knock the crap out of other guys. They had some torture racks on display which were really neat, but other than that, nothing I saw in Europe was interesting. After all, who gives a shit about how one guy killed another guy a thousand years ago? And do you know the most insulting thing about those museums, Andy? They make you pay to go in there and get bored out of your mind looking at all that old crap.

"If you grow up liking women, Andy, you especially don't want to go to Europe. The women over there all look undernourished compared to American girls, and all the women in Europe are hairy, smelly, and fat and they all have saggy tits. So my executive advice to you is save your money and stay right where you are. I can tell you all you need to know about the world anyway. Don't go to Europe. It's a waste of time.

"Every now and then you'll encounter someone who is a liberal, Andy. They can't help the way they are or that they can't think logically. That's because they get their news from biased liberal media outlets. Don't get upset with these people Andy. They are useful and we need more of them, because they never know what's going on. When it comes time to dump a stock position we need dummies to buy from us. We need people who believe everything they see on TV.

"There's another really big secret I need to tell you about, Andy. It's about warts. It'll be important to you when you get older. See, there's this special subset of doctor quacks called dermatologists. These guys make a fortune going around with little nitrogen spray cans zapping warts. They charge fifty to a hundred dollars a wart. Now, if you're like me with dozens of warts that adds up to real money. You need to be really smart when it comes to money, Andy. Warts are the perfect example.

"I discovered that I can get rid of them just as easily by biting them off and then digging out the residual wart residue with my fingernails. But, when your warts are on your chest, your back, your feet, or your ass, you need a wart removal buddy who will cut your warts off in exchange for you cutting his off, like I do with my lifelong friend Hirsh. Hirsh and I have saved thousands by cutting off each other's warts. All you need is a simple pocket knife. It's important to think about these things, Andy, because with all the money you save by cutting off your own warts you can buy shares in UGGA instead of throwing it away on some quack doctor.

"But I want to be totally honest with you Andy. You know I'd never advise you to do anything that would hurt you. A lot of times when I have Hirsh cut a wart off, later I get two new warts at just about the same place. In fact, my back looks kind of like a wart field. And taking those damn things off is painful. But I'm okay with pain, Andy. I've come to associate life with pain. Life is just never-ending pain that gets more and more unbearable the older you get. Sometimes I wish I was never born in the first place, in the same way Mother wished I'd never been born. She hated me, Andy, and now I even hate myself. Life makes me cry, Andy, and it will make you cry too. It's painful to go through life, but you have to keep fighting life and never give up that fight, Andy. After you've fought life as long and hard as I have, someday you, too, will probably wish you'd never been born."

Andy sat there in his jar of formaldehyde with his tiny head facing the carnage taking place in the glass arena. The ants were massing, their red bodies a living ball of destruction. The tearing and ripping away of spider flesh was approaching the grand finale of the arachnid's agony.

"Andy, there's news! I just heard on the radio that the conservatives won the election! That means the liberals likely won't get to use the Dodd Frank law to seize everybody's assets. Instead, the country will deficit spend its way into hell and oblivion, and the currency will get monetized by the Fed buying up the government debt. That means your money will get more worthless faster than before, Andy. It also means you need to get your hands on as much gold and silver as you can afford to buy. Stick with me, Andy. I'll make you wealthy beyond your wildest dreams!

"I just had a brilliant thought, Andy! You know, the more I drink the smarter I get. The new President wants to build a wall and have Mexico pay for it. He'll do it all right, by putting silver back into U. S. coinage and getting rid of the Federal Reserve. That's it, Andy! We've figured it out! Mexico will make a fortune on rising silver prices, and part of the price rise they'll remit to the U. S. to pay for the border wall. Mexicans will do great because their peso currency will rise. They'll want to stay in Mexico! Americans will do great because they'll have an honest weights and measures country and government again. The government will shrink in size and our economy will soar!"

Andy sat inside his formaldehyde jar and stared at the carnage taking place inside the glass gladiator cage. David changed topics from his executive lessons to events in the combat arena. He whispered breathlessly to his student fetus as the ants tore away a third leg from the spider. "Look how wonderful this is, Andy! Can you see the beauty of it? Look at the spider shaking. He's well into his death throes! Hear the sounds? I'll turn up the volume on the sound translation system. Can you hear him screeching and screaming? It's a unique sound you won't hear anywhere else in the world.

"It's the sound of unrelenting agony. It's beautiful to hear his pain, Andy. He's in horrible unbearable pain. Can't you hear it? He can't escape from it! It's so beautiful to watch him shudder and shake from his pain. I love this part so much, Andy! I love watching creatures in pain. Listen to how much he hates his suffering! It's his plea for mercy, for his pain to stop. He so badly wants to die so his pain and torture will end, but the ants can't give him mercy and end it. They don't even know how to. They just keep tearing his flesh away and eating him. He only gets to die when his body is eaten away so badly that the body can no longer live. This is how life is, Andy. Those dishing out the pain never stop. They hurt you until you die inside.

"Someday the little people are going to hurt the banks, Andy. There will come a time when the little guy gets even, just like ants ganging up on a spider. The ants are like the little people who are killing the big evil banks by buying gold and silver, Andy. It's like they're taking their bites out of the banks! I wanted you to see this. It's class warfare, just like Dad said. Dad said the little people will win in the end. This is very special to watch and hear. It's wonderful, Andy. I love it so much, and I love you too, Andy. It's much more fun than watching reality TV, don't you think? Here, Andy, have a drink with me."

David poured some whiskey over the top of Andy's jar. Then, David took a healthy gulp of whiskey, leaned over and kissed the top of Andy's formaldehyde jar. He then put down his glass of whiskey and drew his pants zipper down to reach his penis with his free hand. His experienced fingers began their familiar work, stroking and coaxing David's truest and trusted longtime friend until its little head ejaculated to the excitement and tortured sounds of arachnid carnage. His mind long gone, an inebriated David experienced nirvana.

Andy was David's perfect protégé. The spider twisted and screeched in spasmodic twitches of agony as the ants executed David's sadistic death sentence. Andy looked on, ever the loyal, unquestioning observer in his formaldehyde jar. He showed no signs of letting emotions cloud his judgment and never got distracted by the silly needs of women. He never talked back to David, nor did he ever question David's wisdom, behaviors, or entertainment preferences. Alex had a promising future with David.

ANTS

Travelers to Rocky Mountain National Park, Yellowstone, or the Tetons noticed little signs along the roadsides of the surrounding towns and in the parks themselves, signs that cautioned the unwary. 'Caution! Bears are active in this area. Avoid all bears!' Those who lived near these parks heeded these warnings. Especially to be avoided was a female bear's cubs. Getting near a cub, playing with it, touching it, getting between it and its mother was not merely a bad idea. It was a terrible idea.

Something instinctual happened when a mother sensed that her cub was threatened. It mattered not a hoot what the cub had done or whether the cub decided to first approach the human. The mother bear had no human capacity to rationalize or tell a good person from a bad person. All momma bear knew was her primordial drive that told her she must kill the intruder, dismember the meddler, and rescue her cub from any dangers real or perceived. All ursine, feline, canine, and most human mothers shared that protective instinct, and woe to anyone who triggered it.

Whatever composure Susan normally maintained was overwhelmed by the gnawing realization that her precious darling Marty had likely been murdered by David. She visualized her daughter being hoisted into the air by the block and tackle apparatus, suspended in midair like a helpless sheep to be slaughtered. Had David taunted her before she died, before he butchered her? Had he dismembered her, fed her guts to his pigs and her bones to his wood chipper, and mulched her with his compost into his flower gardens? *What did you do to my daughter, you sick son of a bitch?* Her motherly instincts cried out for an answer.

Susan was sickened and enraged by the revelations of Muscle Man. It was too late to save Marty, but not too late to avenge her daughter's death. David was a child Susan never liked. He got in the way of her love for Marvin. He disgusted her. His thievery, lack of ethics and morals, and impish pranks nauseated her, but Susan had tolerated him for these many years, leaving Mrs. Rodriguez and Barbara to bear the brunt of his petty annoyances. Marvin provided well for Susan, ensconced her securely in the firm, and now this! Murder!

Her world was thrown into turmoil. *You little bastard!* Susan seethed with rage. She was incensed at David's audacity. As his lifetime sitter, she saw him do many deplorable acts, but he was not going to kill her flesh and blood and get away with it. Going to the authorities was out of the question. He would lawyer up, bribe a judge or a juror and laugh at her as he walked out of a hung jury or a dismissal. Justice could not be trusted to normal bureaucratic channels. The criminal justice system would be too good for him, even if it convicted him and sentenced him to life in prison. This was a matter that needed to be settled the old biblical way, with an eye for an eye and a tooth for a tooth. Revenge through personal vendetta has a finality that punishment meted out by a jury can't approach. When it's personal, only blood answers for blood, and Susan's blood boiled with rage.

There was no body, no witness, just the circumstantial evidence of the shock of Marty's hair. The thought occurred to Susan that the perpetrator could possibly be someone other than David. She doubted that, but her administrator's sense of getting things right told her she needed to take steps to be sure.

David was in his office feeling jovial. He'd just settled his litigation with Bob and was contemplating a long trip to the Caribbean to relax. There were brochures of vacation spots on his desk when Susan walked in. She sensed he was off guard.

"David, I'm trying to create an abstract painting of Marty and I need some help to make her image realistic. Do you remember ever seeing her in blue shorts or do you remember seeing her in red shorts?" The request seemed perfectly straightforward and with no hidden purpose. Susan could have been an actress.

"Blue shorts. I don't recall her ever wearing reds," David said before returning to his brochures.

That clinched it for Susan. Marty only wore shorts on warm weekends. She never wore shorts to the office. She always wore business suits or skirts to the office and company functions. The only way David could have seen Marty in shorts was if he'd been to her home or if she'd gone to David's for some nefarious purpose without mentioning it to her. Marty went missing over a weekend. Probably she was with David while wearing shorts. The reason didn't matter.

It didn't take long for Susan to get her first bit of proof that David was the culprit. After about five minutes, he gave her door his gentle knock before he entered. She was ready for him, working on an acrylic painting of Marty right there in her office. Her inquiry seemed plausible. Still, David continued to blunder into her trap. "You know, Susan, come to think of it, I don't think I ever saw Marty in a pair of shorts, only in a skirt. I must have been thinking of her wearing a blue skirt. I hope that helps you some." David turned and left. Susan watched his movement closely. He walked more deliberate than usual, like he was a child trying to distance himself from her before he broke into a full run.

She had her confirmation with that well-thought-out denial, much more deliberate than his off-the-cuff comment when he was caught off guard. Susan got what she wanted. It was evidence enough for her if not for the police, but the police weren't going to know anything about her plans for David.

David sought to slip away from Susan's trap, as if he didn't know he was already snared and she couldn't see he was rattled by his blundering revelation. She watched him tiptoe from her office like a cat stares after a nervous mouse. It was too late for the little coward David. He didn't fool Susan for a second. Her maternal instincts were triggered and now they brought him sharply into focus. She planned her next move carefully.

Days elapsed after Susan's inquiry about Marty's shorts. David assumed it was all about nothing, but it nagged his conscience that he could be so forgetful and glib. Susan wasn't stupid, but she was getting older. He believed he was in the clear. He rationalized Susan had no reason to suspect anything. He'd gotten away with avenging Bob's rejection and screwing Bob out of the companies. He'd avenged his miserable childhood by murdering his half-sister. He believed all was well in his world.

It was getting on toward dusk. It was late summer and a circus show was moving into town; the downtown would become a bedlam of traffic if he stayed much longer. He went to get his car from the garage. It was his oldest Cadillac, the beat-up car from hell that he used to intimidate other drivers. As he approached his car, he saw the strangest thing. Someone had attached a chain fall to the steel beam above the vehicle, the chain hanging down from a block pulley suspended from the beam. There was a stepladder off to the side of his car. He stood there for a moment, dumbfounded. He couldn't imagine why someone from the garage was working on something so late in the day, nor could he imagine what it was. As he began to gain a dim awareness that something was amiss, he received a conk on the back of his head from a pipe wrench and fell to the ground unconscious.

Susan remembered what Muscle told her, that even a child could lift a mature bull with the chain fall apparatus. She was about to find out. She wrapped a rope around David's waist several times and knotted it, attached the hook at the chain's end to his makeshift rope belt, and then hoisted him into the trunk of his car. She climbed on her stepladder, removed the block pulley and chain, took David's car keys from his pocket, placed the chain fall apparatus and the stepladder into the trunk with David, and drove away. This would be her last day of babysitting.

Susan drove two hours south of Plaintown to the Shadow Mountain range. It was late and the dirt bikers who rode the trails were gone, probably off to the circus show. A logging road she'd scouted days before took her to an isolated clearing crossed with game trails, but no biker trails. She stopped on a high bluff above the Blue River, listening to the peaceful sounds of the river coursing its white ripples over the gentle rapids below. Her mood was in tune with the soothing sounds of the river on that warm midsummer evening. She breathed a sigh of relief as she worked with a calm deliberation, using the full moon's natural light. She'd brought a flashlight, but hesitated to use it. Being seen by campers on the other side of the river or by ranch hands from the bunkhouse far below was not something she wanted.

She used a convenient tree to rig her chain fall and swing David out of the trunk. He was a little groggy, so she conked him a second time. He was out again. After Susan finished arranging his body, she took her chain fall down and returned it to the car's trunk, along with her stepladder. When she had everything prepared for David, she poured some water on his face. He revived to discover his mouth was covered with duct tape. He was also naked. His arms and legs were spread out and staked down tightly against the ground. He couldn't move an inch, and Susan had placed large rocks upon and around his torso so he couldn't do more than breathe. His legs and arms were tied taut to nearby trees, so that if by some miracle he could work loose a leg or arm from a staked-down fastener, he wouldn't be able to use that limb to reach any other limb. Susan thought of everything. She always was a thorough administrator. It was time to say her good-byes.

"I've placed you near an ant hill, David. The big red ones like the ones you used to torture as a child. Also, I selected a spot above the river for you. You have some good neighbors here. There's a yellow jacket nest under a nearby log, and from this high vantage point crows and ravens often sit to watch the river far below. The sun will be up in about seven hours, David. I've made sure you'll have some visitors. I've poured some honey on your penis. You like having your little pee-pee played with, don't you? I've also dabbed some honey in your hair. That's to remind you of Marty's hair. I'm sure you remember the patch of her hair you cut from her scalp, don't you?"

David shook his head slightly.

"That doesn't cut it, David. There's only one way out of this for you. If you admit you killed her, I'll get you out of this and take you to the police. Okay?"

David nodded. Susan opened the duct tape for him to speak, telling him that if he screamed she'd bash his face with a pipe wrench. He didn't scream. He was terrified.

"Answer me, David. How did you kill her?"

"I drugged her. Then I hoisted her in my barn and I sacrificed her to God. She was a sinner, Susan. You know that. Let me go. I'll give you all my money, my father's diamonds. You can have the business, everything. Just name your price."

"Thank you for that, David," she said as she reapplied the duct tape. She now knew for sure she was not making a mistake. David whined and grunted as befitting a man in dire mortal straits. Susan spoke to him in a compassionate voice as she would to a baby she was about to put to sleep for the last time.

"Your father, your mother, and I all tried very hard to bring you up properly, but you failed all of us. You've failed your god as well as all of his creatures. I've watched you from the time you were a little boy pulling wings from flies, pulling legs from ants. How do you think those insects felt? How do you think Bob felt when you took his career from him? How do you think Marty felt when you hung her up and butchered her?"

David puffed his chest out to push off the pile of rocks, but they were big flat ones and he had no success. He twisted his torso as best he could, but there was nothing gained from that effort either. He glowered at Susan with hate-filled eyes. If there were such a thing as a devil, she saw it in those eyes.

"I doubt if you've ever considered anyone's feelings your entire life. You didn't learn your behavior, David. It's just something you were born with. You're not like your father. He was good at heart, just trapped in a marriage by your religion to a woman he didn't love. He never sought to hurt others or be evil for his enjoyment as you did. You're soon going to learn how other people felt when you hurt them without caring. When these ants begin eating your balls, and when they start digging into your scalp and into your eyes, you'll know what it's like to get hurt by someone who just doesn't care. There's no other way to teach you. This is your final lesson. I'm resigning as your babysitter."

Susan ignored David's insistent grunts. He was not going to get his way this night.

"When the sun comes up, the hornets will smell the honey and they'll also come to visit you, David. The crows eat your eyes. You probably didn't know they did that, did you? You don't want to live without being able to see, do you? You're not answering me, David, just nodding. Well, your sitter knows what's best for you. You won't need to live without your sight. Okay then, I guess we have nothing more to discuss. Be a good little boy tonight and remember to say your prayers. Pray to God that he takes you into his bosom and that you've made some good marks in your Book of Life. Good night, baby David. Sleep well, you worthless sack of shit."

Having said her final good-bye to her one-time charge and lover's son, Susan spit in his face and then left and drove back to Plaintown. She'd finally realized one of her long-sought dreams, a life free of David.

Those were the last human sounds David heard. Two Clark's nutcrackers perched in the branches above him took in the scene, waiting for their chance at a meal. As their good fortunes would have it, they beat the crows to David's eyes. As he lay there, he could already feel little bites pinching flesh from his gonads. The ants didn't wait for morning.

David's car was found in the parking garage in the exact same spot where he'd parked it. There were no fingerprints on the car, no chain fall, no stepladder, and no sign of foul play. Susan was forever thorough. David's bones were discovered by a forest ranger on horseback about seven weeks later. The horse was standing off from the edge of the scattered remains when it stopped to evacuate itself; otherwise, the ranger might have ridden past the site without noticing anything. As he took in the widely scattered bones, he realized they were possibly human. There was a lone field mouse gnawing upon one of the bones, drawing its ration of calcium. There was no other sign of life at the site. David's carcass was picked clean of all flesh and tissues; coyotes or possibly bears or mountain lions had scattered the bones, most cracked with their marrow removed. Coyotes likely gleaned the carcass.

There were ropes tied to the trees surrounding the site. Ground stakes indicated it was a homicide and a terrible agonizing death for the victim. How David's body ended up on that bluff above the Platte baffled the authorities, and the case remains unsolved to this day. Susan dutifully made her calls to his home that next day when he didn't arrive at the office. A few days later, she helped his wife file a missing person report. Some teeth from a jaw fragment sufficed to identify the body. What bones could be gathered were placed into a wooden box and given to his widow. She took them for burial in Israel. No obituary of David's death was ever published.

ANCIENT MARKINGS

Bob and Barbara took a trip back to Milltown to visit his mother. Estella was old now but she bore the ravages of age well. She walked with a cane and her eyesight was dimmed, but her feisty nature and her combativeness never yielded to the march of time. Her old eyes beamed at seeing Bob with Barbara, and she greeted the happy couple with forceful lingering hugs. When Estella saw Barbara, she knew Bob and this woman would soon marry. Mothers had a way of knowing those things. She was happy for her son and bluntly told him so.

"I'm glad you are finally going to get your life straightened out," she remarked, as if everything adverse that ever happened in Bob's life was his fault alone. After lunch, she got down to mother's business. There were questions she had to ask, and answers to questions all mothers must learn.

"You don't look like an Indian. Bob said you were an Indian. You're an awful pretty woman for an Indian. She's one of the prettiest women I've ever seen, Bob. Lordy, Lordy."

"I am an Indian. I know the Indian ways and I believe in myself as one of the Great Spirit's creations and a child of Mother Earth. My father is a tribal chief, but my mother was actually a Lebanese Christian woman. She was a small-boned Arab. I believe it was the will of the Great Spirit that they met, and by his will he brought me into this world through them."

"How on Earth did an American Indian get himself married to a Lebanese? She was part Arab you said?"

"Dad was a United States Marine, ma'am. He was stationed in Lebanon for a while. They fell in love. I am part of them both. Mother died seven years ago from cancer. Mother was all Arab, not part Arab."

"That's a lovely pin you're wearing, Barbara. Where on Earth did you find that?"

"Oh, thank you, Estella. That's my butterfly pin. It's a fond reminder of a woman I used to work for before Bob and I went into business together. She had a daughter who died. It was originally a gift from her daughter to her. Before she passed away, she gave the pin to me. She told me I was like a second daughter to her and she wanted me to wear it in memory of her and her daughter."

"Oh, you knew her daughter too, did you? They must have been nice people." Estella knew of whom Barbara spoke, but she didn't let on. Bob had told her of his intentions toward Marty years before.

"Yes. For a while at the UGGA, all three of us worked together."

"I see. Well, that gift was very thoughtful of her. And you two are getting married?"

"Yes," Barbara confirmed what Estella suspected.

"And I take it that you love my son and you will be a good woman to him. You're not one to run around with other men or drink and gamble or smoke. You're not one of those kinds of girls, are you?

"Yes and no, ma'am."

"Well, which is it?"

"Yes, Estella. I love Bob. I love him deeply. I promise you I will be good to him. And no, Estella, I'm not a bad woman. I'm a good one. Bob is getting a good woman."

"I see. And the children, if you have them? How will you raise them?"

"We'll raise them as Reformed Jews with Christian and Indian Spirits blended in, ma'am. You see, we don't actually believe God would choose one people over another, not the God we embrace. We think that's a false message used to help an exclusive clique exclude others who need to believe in something and be led around by the nose. We think it limits those who take the message literally and prevents them from open friendships and understandings with others, like eating the same bowl of mush day in and day out."

"But without religious groupings amongst peoples, you'll have anarchy!"

"Or acceptance that we are all God's children, all equal in his eyes." Barbara was quick of mind and tongue. "The priests and rabbis will just have to catch up with us, Estella. The world is always changing, and peoples' understandings are changing with it."

Estella smiled. Barbara had a ring of truth and confidence about her. Estella felt the same inner happiness she last knew when she was with Paul before he left for the Russian front.

"Well, you're both old enough to do what you want, with or without my blessings, but you have my blessings and best wishes to you both."

After visiting Estella, Bob and Barbara walked the old path down to the dam on Cedar Creek. They sat together on the cement abutment that adjoined the spillway. It was a perfect day for an afternoon outdoors. They looked out over the dam and watched two wood ducks diving upside down in the water, their tail feathers and wings splashing to rid their down of fleas and lice. Their antics made Barbara laugh. Her laugh was mirthful, and pleasing to Bob. "Silly ducks," she said. As they sat looking out over the waters and up the far reaches of the creek to where it disappeared from view under the overhang of pines and its upstream bend, a pair of coupled dragonflies flew right in front of them and paused in midair. The giant insects were suspended just three feet before their eyes, absorbed in their task of mating.

Barbara looked at Bob and smiled. "The dragonflies are telling us something." Then she leaned against him and gave Bob a soft, loving kiss on his lips.

"Is this your Great Spirit speaking to us through his messengers?" Big Horse teased Little Sparrow.

"It must be so." Little Sparrow nodded and smiled. She looked deeply into Bob's eyes and they both understood their futures belonged together.

"Then let's follow their example. Let's go to the special place I used to go to as a young boy." Bob stood and took her hand.

"Take me there. I want to see it with you. I want it to be special. I want it to be special for both of us. I love you. Take me up there with you. Take me away to your secret place."

They waded across Cedar Creek downstream from the dam where Bob played as a child. As the cool fresh waters coursed over her legs, Barbara noticed an inside wetness as well. Anticipation moistened her.

Bob led her up a long fold in the mountain and up to a glen where the mountain briefly leveled off. She felt the exertions from the climb and was glad for a rest. "So this is where you came as a boy?" She smiled, looking at Bob. She was seeing the boy in her man, and she loved his happiness at being together where they were. "Are we almost there?"

"Almost. It's a bit farther, but it's going to be worth it, I promise." Bob's eagerness came through his voice. "The view is spectacular," he assured her. "We just need to climb up this draw to a little spring that gushes out of the mountain about fifty yards from the top."

"Oh, I'd love to see something gushing!" Barbara giggled her suggestive thought for Bob as if he didn't already have the same idea. They resumed their climb to the spring. "Oh, it just gushes and gushes, doesn't it?" she teased again. They fell to their knees and drank the cool water.

After they drank, Bob led her about ten yards farther upslope, where they came to a game trail. "This is deer highway. We follow it west for a while."

Barbara looked at the rutted path. This was the trail the deer used when coming down off the pines on the mountaintop to drink at the spring. From the looks of the trail, it seemed to go off into nowhere. They followed it for a couple hundred yards into a deep dark pine forest. The trees were close together now and the trail itself grew smaller until deer and man needed to crawl through low pine boughs to move forward.

The ground became less compact as they progressed, the soft earth yielding to loose shale. Suddenly, just when it seemed the ordeal of crawling through pine thickets would never end, they came to a boulder-strewn clearing. Up above them was an altered rock wall, the remnants of a sheer, granite face that was disturbed by geologic forces millions of years before. Near the top of the formation were caves visible as dark entrance holes from the base of these cliffs. Hidden by pines and the steep pitch of the slope below, this amazing feature was invisible from the creek or the valley floor below. Seeing it for the first time, Barbara stood speechless. "You found this as a boy? You came to this place as a child? Weren't you afraid to come this far?" She found it hard to imagine a child of four or five would attempt such an adventure.

"I needed a special place to go when I was a boy, a place no one could find me or follow," said Bob, hands in his pockets as he shrugged.

"You could have died up there, or fallen off, and no one would have ever found you."

"I know that now, but when I was a little kid I never thought about the risks. Are you afraid? Are you up for this?"

"I've been up for this all my life." She held Bob close and kissed him full on his mouth. "Let's climb. Lead the way, Big Horse."

They climbed upward through the rock crevices to a near-level transom trail that arrived from nowhere and ended abruptly at the entrance of the Indian Caves. When their eyes became accustomed to the dimmed light, they made their way about ten yards into the largest cave. The cave walls were damp, ground water trickled down the one on Barbara's left. It was a steady rivulet of glistening clear fluid against the black surface. She became aroused. There, inside the eternal cave by that curious trickle of life coursing over the ancient rock wall, her heart fluttered. *I've come back to this place. My spirit was here before. I feel it. I've made love here many times before. This place sheltered my ancestors from storms and predators thousands of years ago. Big Horse's spirit was here with me then as he is here with me now. We are living in our spirits. I am so ready.* Her mind and body were ordained by the spirits for what was about to take place.

"Look, etched in the stone," she exclaimed when she discovered the same markings Bob first saw when he was a boy. "There's an arrow mark pointed up and there's the mark of the 'V' beside it."

"Yeah, I saw those when I was a kid. I wondered what they meant, and I'd forgotten about them. They look very old. Do you know what they mean?"

"Sure do," said Barbara." Follow me!" She was in her very own magical moment as she led Bob out of the cave, beginning to climb in earnest. As she placed one hand above the other, gripping the rock holds, she throbbed inside. This was the perfect time, the perfect place, and her perfect man. She climbed the mountaintop with her man and her dreams. Her life was with him. Their spirits were coming together. She yearned to consummate their beginning.

Outside the cave mouth she climbed higher on the rock face, never looking down, never looking back. She rose steadily upward to the protruding ledge that jutted over the top of the cave. There it was! That was the very spot that Bob came to as a boy, where he sat and looked out over the town, sitting and wondering what the world beyond was like. His spirit came there searching for her spirit from the time he was a boy! He could not know it then, but her spirit also searched for his from the time she was a child alone with her father. She often wondered then who would be with her when Father left, what spirit could have his strength or his love. What future awaited her beyond her father's home and their tribe, and what would become of her?

Barbara was nimble as a mountain goat and equally sure of foot. She had five minutes alone on the rock ledge before Bob caught up to her. She squeezed her legs together, realizing all her dreams were about to come true, all her desires fulfilled. He was such a handsome, muscled pillar of a man. Barbara yearned to have him. "Hurry, hurry and come to me," she whispered to herself, as if that would help him climb faster.

When Bob's eyes reached above the level of the ledge, he saw Barbara standing naked on the very spot Bobby, the boy, contemplated the world. He climbed the final few feet and stood beside her upon the precipice.

This was a special moment for Bob, a moment of transition. All his childhood wonders about what mysteries lay beyond the town were mysteries no more. The truths, lies, hopes, and betrayals were all out there where he'd come from. He'd run the gauntlet of betrayals and survived. He'd defeated his once-dark thoughts of suicide. He'd endured the crushing loss of his father, the beatings from his mother, and the betrayals of his former partner and his second lawyer were all behind him. He'd consorted with the immoral siren Marty, partaken of her sweet lips and nectars, but fate spared him a life of jealousy and turmoil. Murder swallowed her future adulteries and her memory drifted quietly away, like the softly flowing Cedar Creek far below.

Bob had wrestled with evil's many forms but now he was finally free. Life found its way and offered a loving hand to him. Like a little boy who dreamed that God would place a beautiful goddess in his bed, Bob was grateful to the Almighty for hearing his pleas. He spent a silent few seconds in reverence for this heaven-sent creature.

From the first moment Bob met Barbara, he knew there was something about her that enticed him and drew him toward her. He wondered if she'd had feelings for him, even when he was with Marty. In the deepest recesses of his mind, those places a man never talks about, he wondered if he might somehow, someday know Barbara intimately, if there'd ever come a magic moment like this. Her friendship felt much like his childhood friendship with Pam, but Pam wished to take him away from his career interest and was drawn to another man. Barbara only sought to enhance his career interests and had no thoughts of another man. Life unfolded much as Arlene, the nurse who first took an interest in him as a toddler, had prophesized. She told Bob the same wisdom her rabbi told her. The right woman would find him, and she did. Then there were Sharon, Rosie, and Marty. He desired all of them at one time or another, but life raised barriers and prevented them from coming to him.

Life has a way of sorting through questions of relationships. It's a good thing too, because they are too complicated for men to sort through.

She was always off-limits, but now she is mine. She is Little Sparrow, the mysterious silent woman. She is like the enchanted nature of the forest I knew as a boy. I will explore her forever and learn her ways. I will love her forever. I yearn to be one with her and now it is our time. She exudes sex so much that I always crave having her, but she never puts it out there to invite the gawkers. She is always guarded and so discreet, as if she guards a precious jewel. Other men can only salivate and wonder about what they can't have. I will defend her from any harm or untoward advances from other men. They will not belittle her ethnicity or her family—my family. I will always uphold her dignity and honor. If I am challenged to fight for her, I will, just as I fought and bloodied ignorant boys in my school years. I will never tolerate any person who makes her cry or tries to embarrass her. I love her completely and will always give her the fullest measure of my devotion. I will devote my life to her and her causes. She is a special woman and she is to be my wife.

Bob always suspected Sparrow knew more than she ever revealed. He sensed she would never want a man who tried to force a relationship, so he left her alone those years. Besides, she'd told him early on they needed to wait. His heart now pounded with desires to hold her and embrace life with her. An upwelling of joy overwhelmed him. His eyes filled with happiness that gushed up from his soul.

Barbara knew this was the moment, the moment that culminated the vision she'd had for Bob the first day she saw him when he stepped off the elevator at UGGA. Bob was her destiny, her life mate. Soon, so soon, it was all going to come together for both of them. *I look into his eyes and I see happiness. I know he wants me. What will it be like this first time? Will he be gentle? Will I please him?* She would soon lie with him on the moss-covered outcrop, would soon feel him entering her. She was ready now, ready to go forward forever with Bob and never look back, never regret her choice.

As she smiled at the love of her life, a kaleidoscope of white Pieridae butterflies fluttered between them, attracted to the shimmering ultraviolet radiance of Barbara's lustrous dark hair. One briefly lighted upon her hair, as if to give its blessings for what was soon to come. Then it fluttered away to rejoin the others. "So what do those ancient markings mean?" Bob asked, his eyes filled with wonder beholding hers.

"They mean this is a wonderful place for lovers to make love," Barbara replied as she turned to Bob and closed the distance between them. As the daylight between them disappeared, so did the years of abuse in the insane asylum that was UGGA. Barbara took Bob into her arms, her body heat melting the cares of their past. They held each other in a close embrace. Happiness, appreciation, and love bonded them with a unity that would last and sustain them for the rest of their lives.

And so it was. On the secret mountain ledge while the soft voice of Spirits whispered through the fragrant pine forest, Barbara discovered Bob's full measure as a wonderful, unselfish lover. Then the two lovers lay down together on the moss-covered outcrop and their lips met in a long passionate kiss. After a period of tenderness, with Bob lightly touching her inner thighs, Barbara opened her sex to his kisses.

Great Spirit of all Living Things, bless this day and always. Thank you for showing us the way. Our love is good and this will be a good day.

They began their lovemaking slowly. Bob, ever mindful of his mitzvah, began kissing Barbara's pussy. He was painstakingly deliberate and gentle. When he coaxed her clitoris to arousal, he began gently massaging and caressing it with the underside of his tongue. She felt a sensation she had never imagined existed. As she ran her fingers through the shock of wavy blond hair positioned between her legs, she resonated with Bob's loving tongue. She felt her body tremble and quiver as he stroked her clitoris.

I did not know this feeling existed. This is intimacy of the most endearing kind. He is mine now. He is everything I ever wanted in a man. I feel like I am floating on a cloud with happiness flowing out of my sex. I feel wonderful and so deeply loved. I wish this feeling would never end. I am blessed to have my Big Horse. He is sufficient in his own wealth, he earns his own income, and he loves me without selfishness or inhibition. He is a one-woman man and he never has eyes for another. I will give all of myself to him always.

She relaxed and released a full orgasm into Bob's mouth while he continued working the magic of his loving tongue upon her throbbing clitoris.

"Big Horse, tell me, my lover, what made you want to do what you just did?"

"It's mitzvah, a requirement that a man should wet his woman to prepare her for lovemaking. I've thought about kissing you there for a long time. I couldn't hold back. I love you so much. When I kiss you there I don't ever want to stop. I feel good inside knowing you feel my love for you. I wanted to do it to let you know how wonderful and special you are. I can't get enough of you."

"Well, Big Horse, I need to tell you something as a woman to a man."

"Yes, Sparrow?"

"You are welcome to mitzvah with me whenever you wish. I liked mitzvah very much." She giggled.

Bob clasped her buttocks firmly and lifted her toward his waiting penis. Her orgasmic secretions increased and coaxed Bob's thrusts to increase their tempo. She was one with him. She could feel his penis throbbing with her delightful pulsing passions as it yearned to have more and more of her. All her other thoughts vanished from this spiritual moment. She spoke softly to her future husband. "Big Horse, now that I have given myself to you, you may have no others. You will be my husband. Our marriage will last forever and I will never share you."

"I will be your husband, Little Sparrow. I want for no other woman and will never have another, only you. Our marriage will last forever, and I also will never share you with anyone. We will always be as one."

Barbara's inner spirit voice assured her that Big Horse would be faithful to her. He was a man of honor. She finally had all she wanted in a husband and a father for her children. She silently thanked the Great Spirit for the wisdom he bestowed upon Chief, and she thanked Chief for counseling her to be patient. Now she could give herself freely to this man. This Big Horse was now hers, all hers.

Just as Barbara was beginning to feel the onset of her second release, Bob rolled her over on her side while maintaining their connection. She was daunted at first, thinking that perhaps she would lose the sensation she was feeling, but that momentary uncertainty was suddenly swept away.

Bob grabbed her buttocks with his large strong hands and easily lifted Barbara on top of him. The outcrop had a slight down slope, and Bob lay with his head somewhat lower than his legs. The effect of this new position was wildly sensuous for Barbara. His penis, now rock-hard and fully swollen, had an uphill-angled position which placed it firmly against her clitoris. When Bob thrust upward into the deepest part of her sex, it made its presence known.

Never had Barbara experienced a swollen penis pressed firmly against her clitoris that way, with such strength and endurance. She loved the wild sensations she felt and wanted more and more.

She straddled him. He was hers, all of him, only hers. Her knees welcomed the welcome coolness of the thick bed of soft damp moss as she looked out from their mountain perch to the valley floor below. Barbara's arousal was complete. She was with Bob in their new intimate world now. *I belong to him and he belongs to me.*

An ecstasy of pent-up joys she'd saved for years was about to release. It was unlike any feeling she'd ever known before. As their rhythm quickened, Barbara was transported to another time and place.

In her euphoric state, she looked down on the land below. Her mind was in another place and time. She had a vision of the valley below as it was before the whites came, the land as her people knew it. There was the river, its gleaming white ripples over blue water coursing south where it joined the Cedar Creek. Both waters teemed with fish, and two braves were putting out seine nets along the near shore. The land was no longer a town with streets, squares, houses, schools, and churches; it was a wide and vast plateau rising abruptly above the bluffs that footed the river and the creek.

Below her spread out vast forests of chestnut, hickory, oak, walnut, birch, and maple. She could see men in hunting parties scouting for deer and elk with bow and arrow, and there, near the clearing where the tribe camped, was a boy putting out his snares for rabbits. In the camp clearing, she saw teepees and a few women tending a fire while others were bringing wood to fuel it. Still others were about gathering nuts from the forest floor. One woman was scraping an elk hide to prepare it for curing. It would help keep her family warm during the cold damp winter ahead. She could hear the dull chanting melodies of the tribal shaman and the laughter of the children. And there! She could see a woman with a papoose wrap and a bundled baby on her back. This land was her land by heritage, the land of the Munsee, the Unalachtigo, the Algonquin, and the Delaware.

This was land of the people, the land upon which the great chief Seneca once walked. These simple people loved this place, this land, and then, the white man came. The whites were hungry for land. They had to own land, a concept her peoples never understood. The land was, for her people, part of the gift to all from the Great Spirit and the ancestors.

But the white man coveted the land that was the Great Spirit's. The white man wanted to clear off the mighty trees, kill off the animals, and put the land under the plow. He would, if left unchecked, defile the Great Spirit's land. And so her people fought the white man, and the land below her became drenched in the blood of both her people and the whites.

And in the end her people lost these great battles, lost their historic usage of these lands. They moved west to the Ohio Valley, fought the whites again and again, and lost again and again. Her people were sickened by the white man's diseases and the white man's greed. They would move far to the west, become subsumed by larger tribes, and eventually even the larger tribes would be conquered by the palefaces.

Her people were gone now, but their love of this place would never leave it. The valley below was tranquil again, with the town's houses melting away to rich rolling farmlands. It was, once again, her place too. In the grand scheme of life, her presence there was symbolic of the permanence of the spirit of the people, her people. Barbara felt their presence now as she made passionate love with a descendent of her people's conquerors.

But her lovemaking and her life with Bob would not be a contest of conquests. Their life together would be a wondrous unison of past cultures and traditions with modernity, and it would always bask in the glory of their love. She would be a good woman for this man, and she knew he would be a good man for her. On this mountain ledge, Barbara became a being larger than her own life.

I surrender myself to the Great Spirit of All Living Things. This day I fulfill his will. I will be Earth Goddess of all my people. I will triumph with the will of the Spirit. My soul sings with joy. I am serene and joyous. This is my Spirit moment. I will conceive our first child this day. I release myself to the wonders of my man and the Spirit within us.

Barbara's orgasm began with a low moaning sound that rose from deep inside her. She felt her dam of juices about to burst in an even more powerful release. She moaned louder now, uninhibited, alone with Bob in the wilds on their mountain. Her body trembled uncontrollably, and then—Barbara bloomed!

Her swollen vagina could no longer hold back her bursting flood. Her deep moaning changed to a low-pitched "Ohhh" when her release commenced. It was a small release at first, but then she gained her full voice. She howled out, unrestrained as her flower fully opened. Her joy resounded over the mountainside and her sounds reached the creek below as she entered the throes of her massive orgasm. She threw her head back and looked skyward, her body trembling violently as she slammed her eager pelvis hard against Bob. It was the most wondrous moment of her life. She was alive as never before, and she was creating life.

She shouted out in a full voice for the world to hear, "Yes, yes, yes! Oh, yeeeeeesssss! Don't stop! Don't stop!"

Barbara cried, "More, more. That's it, my Big Horse. Keep going. Don't stop. Ohhh that feels soooo good. I love you soooo much. Oh how I love you. Oh hold me close. Hold me very close." She kissed him wildly on the lips and all over the face. She was in love out of her mind.

Bob's penis throbbed as his thrusts quickened. The stream of semen released was strong and full, pulsing and shooting forcefully. As his sperm frantically searched for her ovulated egg, Barbara felt her stomach and chest heave with her love.

Her thoughts lifted into rapture. *This is so wonderful! With each kiss he's telling me that he can never get enough of me. No woman was ever treasured more. If I could imagine creating the perfect man from clays with my own hands, he could not be as wonderful as this man who holds me now.* Barbara closed her eyes in her delirious state of ecstasy. She had a vision and said to the spirit there, "With this man I will help the people of the world put aside their divisions and hatreds. They will know the wonders of nature and peace as did my forbearers. They will feel the harmony of the Great Spirit of All Living Things."

Multiple visions flashed through her mind. She imagined her future with Big Horse. *I am naked riding a big sorrel mustang stallion. We are racing across the prairie scouting a herd of buffalo. With each forward thrust of his mighty haunches, Big Horse's huge member reaches even deeper into me and becomes more engorged. He strains to please me and go faster and faster.*

There's a teepee on the plains overlooking a long valley. The flap is open and I look out. The Rosebud River courses by below me. A pale full orange moon begins to lift in the sky as the sunset glows behind a bluff. I am faced outward looking at all the creation works of the Great Spirit of All Living Things. I see a flock of Canadian geese flying across the face of the moon. Big Horse is under me and I straddle him. His hands cup my breasts and pinch my nipples. His huge member grows inside me as he raises his head and kisses my back in many places. Tingles of desire shoot through my entire body. I will have Big Horse this night and we will make love for hours until the moon rises high and bright in the night sky. I am crazy with passions for what he is about to do with me next. He places his big hands around my slender waist. Now he's lifting me up and guiding my love place over his gigantic member. Slowly at first, he lifts me up and holds me perfectly before guiding me down over it. I am hot and wet inside and I want him to move me faster and faster. I am juicy like a fully ripened peach. I want him to probe all of me until I am delirious with joys of being his woman. We make love this way for hours and he makes me come many times. A cool prairie breeze flows over me and I know I am one with nature and my man. I know I am a complete woman now. I am happy. I collapse onto him and sleep the night in his arms. I have endless nights like this with my Big Horse. I am woman. I know love.

I stand on the porch of the ranch house looking across the prairie toward the hills. Two little children, a boy and a girl, are racing each other and laughing in the tall grass. The children fall down and get up laughing, and then they race some more. Big Horse stands beside me and wraps his huge arms around me. He holds me tightly to him and kisses my neck. He cups my breasts. I know he wants me. He pushes his pelvis against my behind. It's time to take him inside to our bedroom and push him down on our king-sized bed. He lies there on the bed while I undress slowly in front of him, his member standing upright, waiting for me. This is all very good. I tease him by slowly taking off each piece of my clothing. I cup my breasts and smile at him and stoke his appetite for me. I face him on my knees and hover over him, rubbing his member over my mound. He can feel how slippery wet and ready I am. Now our moment is right. His massive hands come to my waist and he lifts me gently up before slowly lowering me onto his mighty column.

I am back in the present, making love with Big Horse on a ledge on a mountainside. We are surrounded by a beautiful fragrant pine forest. I can hear a river moving far below us. The soft winds are rippling its waters which are lapping against the river bank below. I hear the soft yips of a female coyote searching the marsh bank for her meal. Her female spirit must know we are making love above her on the mountain. She must be telling us that it is good. Yes, surely she is telling us that. I know I am in love forever now. I know that I want this Big Horse's member in me many times. I do love him so. When Barbara opened her eyes again, the kaleidoscope of white Pieridaes had returned. They now fluttered all about her head. They lingered, suspended in the mountain sky, as if to fix a magical blend of Barbara's pheromones with the ultraviolet radiance from her hair forever in their collective memory, as only butterflies can do. Then they fluttered away, descending through the forest below and making their way to the river. *I am eternally satisfied. This is good love. This is the love Chief promised I would discover if I were patient. This is the love my man needs from me.*

Barbara and Bob married in the fall at the Pepke Park Gazebo in Aspen. It was a traditional Indian ceremony, with several of the little girls from the tribe acting as flower bearers. It was also a Jewish wedding ceremony and had elements of a Catholic ceremony. Barbara wore an elegant white gown with raised embossed red-throated sparrows hand-sewn in their natural colors around its fringe. Her hair was done up in plaits wrapped high upon her head and stayed with silver ribbons.

She held her head high throughout the ceremony. Those who attended said she looked like a beautiful princess goddess. She was, after all, royalty.

Bob wore a black tuxedo with tails. A judge presided in his fly fishing boots. He showed up, understandably late, with the marriage license from the Pitkin County Courthouse. He'd been fishing a good hatch on Frying Pan Creek. Chief counseled the waiting guests that it was good and right to wait for a man who was having good luck fishing.

The guests included many of Chief's friends, including some of the Italians from the casino businesses. They came to express their support. Chief gave Little Sparrow away to Big Horse. He joined their hands in his giant strong paws and squeezed their hands together before the judge.

Chief and friends wore their buckskin and jeweled finery, and their best headdresses. The Jews all wore colorful yarmulkes and the Catholics, mostly Italian-Americans, brought flowers and many cases of wine. Everyone danced together in a big circle. It was an original combination dance, a blend of the Jewish wedding dance and the Indian spirit dance. It was the first time the dance was ever performed. It was uplifting and beautiful. The smiles and laughter from all the guests were captured brilliantly in the photos taken by the wedding photographer.

Pictures of Barbara's wedding ceremony were preserved in perpetuity in two photo albums. Barbara kept one copy under her bed, and the other was stored in the vault of one of Aspen's favorite old hotels. Aspen Mountain stood tall in the background, making for splendid, inspiring photos. A light early snow graced the revelers, and many of the photos showed sparkling snow spots. Chief gave Bob a crushing bear hug and spoke only one word after the judge pronounced them married.

"Good."

All the men took turns kissing the bride. Some were overly enthusiastic and had to be pulled away from her by Chief.

Then Chief lit himself a fine Cuban cigar and passed one out to each male in attendance, saying, "You smoke."

All the men smoked in honor of the new couple. Barbara threw her wedding bouquet high into the air. It was caught by a gust from a snow squall and lifted skyward onto Aspen Mountain where it landed upon the antlers of an eight-point bull elk. The elk swiftly disappeared into the forest with the bouquet stuck in his massive rack. Would-be brides still search for Little Sparrow's bridal bouquet on Aspen Mountain to this very day.

In the many years they had together, Barbara and Bob shared a secret code. Whenever they were at a social function and she grew tired of the pleasantries, or when they were at home alone or away somewhere together, she knew how to let him know when she wanted him. She would turn to him and whisper: "It's a good time, Big Horse."

Bob always looked into her eyes, smiled with anticipation, and asked, "For what, sweetheart?"

And she would very softly whisper in his ear, "When the butterflies come."

BONES AND BLOODLINES

After David died, Susan resigned from her position at the firm and turned over her files and records to the new owners. She later wrote two letters to The Mount of Olives Cemetery in Jerusalem seeking permission to be buried as near as possible to Marvin and Eloweiss. Both her requests were refused. Susan then became religious for the first time in her life. She attended Catholic Mass every single day until she became infirm. She prayed her Rosary twice daily. She gave up smoking her slim cigars after she was diagnosed with emphysema.

She had a slow, agonizing death and gasped her last breath for oxygen her lungs failed to absorb. When she passed away, she was given a Catholic funeral mass and buried next to her parents at Mount Holy Ghost of Mary's Sacred Blood Catholic Cemetery in Plaintown. She was later joined there by her younger brothers and sisters.

Mrs. Rodriguez resigned her post as the firm's chief guard dog when the new generation of owners took over. She took a new position as the assistant warden for prisoner monitoring at the U.S. Federal Penitentiary in Canyon City, Colorado. After her retirement there, she left the United States forever to live out her days with her brothers and sisters, and eventually died in Torreon, Durango State, Mexico.

Bob and Barbara built an investment advisory practice in Plaintown. Barbara bore two children, a boy and a girl. They named their son Ehud, or Hud, for the Benjaminite of Judges who slew the evil King Eglon of Moab. They named their daughter Deborah, for the judge who, with Barak, drove the Canaanites and their evil leader, Sisera, from the land of Israel. Each year the four made a trip to Israel, and when their children were in their teens, they annually made three-month sojourns to Israel. Their two children eventually married Israeli Jews and gave Bob and Barbara six grandchildren. The new bloodlines from Bob and Barbara's grandchildren strengthened the bloodlines of the Tribes of Israel and helped to ensure its strength and survival for the next five thousand years. Bob eventually healed and became free from David's emotional bondage and personal betrayal. Barbara's love helped make that happen.

Barbara—or Little Sparrow, as she preferred—realized her childhood dream and the dream of Chief, her father. She established Following the Path of the Buffalo Foundation and dedicated it to restoring America. As the foundation raised monies, it acquired land. Acre by acre, section by section, farmhouse by farmhouse, town by town, road by road, the foundation returned the vast American prairie to its natural state and returned the buffalo, the elk, the deer, the antelope, all manner of birds that spread seeds and all manner of birds of prey, and the great Sandhill cranes, the wolf, the coyote, the badger, the prairie dog, and all the other native animals to the lands which were once theirs.

The native people were permitted to roam free upon the lands with their horses, but no wheeled vehicles of any kind were allowed. White and black and yellow Americans who wished to live the ways of the true Americans were invited to live upon the lands along with the native peoples. They were permitted to come and go as they pleased, but they were not allowed to build upon the land or own any part of it. The foundation took in refugees from America's urban blight, its castoffs and demented.

Sparrow always believed the Great Spirit and his natural blessings would heal all manners of mental conflicts created by the white man's ways. Only hunting and fishing with naturally made materials was allowed, no guns or fishing poles, no steel traps or artificial metal lures of any kind. As the foundation grew to swallow up the white man's world from the Canadian prairies to the Rio Grande, the American plain of fifty thousand years ago returned to its natural rhythm of life.

Chief lived to see the progress of the foundation with his wise old eyes. He saw little Indian girls laughing and running through the prairie grasses. He saw braves on bareback horse with bow and arrow resuming the buffalo hunt, and he saw squaws tanning hides, gathering wood, making fish hooks, arrowheads, pottery, jewelry, tapestries and weavings, music, babies, and family happiness. The products of the foundation were highly sought after. Only the honest monies of gold or silver were accepted in exchange for their goods. The tribal council wisely invested in start-up enterprises and all tribal members became interested shareowners. The foundation prospered because the people were able to integrate their ways of life with the land with the ways of modernity. Chief saw Sparrow's work and proclaimed it good. His old eyes cried with joy before he left his people to join the Great Spirit.

Bob and Barbara's son, Hud, completed a circle of corporate life for the family. He became interested in geology when searching for arrowheads with Chief as a young boy. Later he went to the Colorado School of Mines and earned his degree in geology. He formed a company for mineral exploration and in the course of his prospecting in northern British Columbia, he discovered some irregular rocks and staked claims to his discovery. Following his father's footsteps, he also earned a degree in business administration and learned investment company management at his mother's hand.

Deb married Richard Stone, or Dick, a stockbroker with a wealthy clientele. As fate would have it, conditions at UGGA deteriorated after Bob and Barbara left and after David and Susan died. UGGA was charged by federal prosecutors for violations of the Racketeer Influenced and Corrupt Organization Act, and David's co-conspirators in bribery and extortion were imprisoned. The firm was placed in trusteeship of a federal judge until injured parties were compensated and fines were paid. The only surviving heirs to the firm were David's distant cousins, and they were eager to sell the beleaguered asset. Dick, Deb, Hud, Barbara, and Bob put their heads and pocketbooks together and acquired the old UGGA. Because of tax considerations, Hud's exploration company was folded into the complex as a subsidiary company of the new UGGA holding company. Thus the new UGGA held claim to Ehud's irregular rock claim group.

In an unexpected development, UGGA's new legal counsel received a call from the British Columbia Department of Mineral Surveys asking permission to run some secret tests upon the strange rocks in cooperation with the United States Department of Defense. Testing revealed the rocks had unique properties related to electromagnetism and, with the proper molecular combinatorial binding, these rocks could be invaluable to NATO's defense needs. But, of course, much work needed to be done before this could be confirmed.

Shortly after the call from B.C. Minerals, UGGA's new corporate counsel received a call from a lawyer in New York who said he had an undisclosed client, a bank from New York, who wished to make a friendly tender offer for the UGGA. After a Seder dinner, the family discussed the matter of the potential takeover offer, and it was decided that they would heed the wisdom of Bob and Barbara, their elders. Bob and Barbara recounted the wisdom of Chief in such matters and advised the family to be patient. More would be forthcoming in all likelihood.

Then the matter of the takeover offer went silent until ten years after Bob died. After he passed, Hud, Dick, and Deborah were informed that the bank from New York had renewed its interest in the acquisition of the UGGA. Hud opined that enough time had passed for the chemical tests and molecular studies to bear out the potential of the rocks. Out of respect for Barbara, who was in failing health, the next generation decided to rule out any discussion of merger or acquisition talks until a year after their mother's death. The spirit of Chief, the wise one, observed the patience of the new generation and opined to the other spirits that it was good.

When Bob died, he was buried next to Nevin, the man he'd always believed was his father, in Milltown. Estella never told Bob about Paul, his true paternal father. Before Estella's death, she made futile inquires to the German government about Paul but received no answers. She assumed he'd died in a Soviet concentration camp, and every evening until her death she prayed to God for mercy on his soul. Estella was buried on Nevins's opposite side. Her headstone bore a Christian cross; Bob's had the Star of David with the inscription 'Here Big Horse rests in eternal peace.'

Barbara continued her work on her Following the Path of the Buffalo Foundation after Big Horse died. Many who knew her remarked that she worked at a feverish pitch, constantly flitting about the world, raising money and giving presentations about the foundation's work and the beauty of wilderness and native grasslands. She made Chief's former ranch her headquarters. There she regularly invited children from participating schools to come visit for a week on the prairie.

On one such day, Barbara was sitting on the ranch's massive porch in her rocking chair. She covered her legs with a shawl when she rocked that summer day because her thin legs noticed the cool afternoon mountain air. Her hair was gray now and her face showed the wrinkles of her age and tireless dedication to her work, but her eyes still glowed with the fire of a woman determined to make the world a better place for her family and her people.

Off in the distance, children were playing a game of capture the flag in the high prairie grass. There was a soft breeze from the mountains to the west dancing through the grasses. The corral near the ranch house held several wild mustangs Barbara adopted. She saved them from slaughter so they could be tamed and eventually ridden by the children, or given away to new owners and outfitters Barbara knew would be good to them.

One proud, well-muscled mustang caught her eye and held her gaze. He was a big horse, a chestnut-colored sorrel stallion. His ears turned forward toward her as if he noticed her for the first time before he moved closer. The big horse eyed her steadily from the nearest edge of the corral. Now it seemed as if the big horse was inviting her to come and ride with him. Just then a little sparrow wren alighted upon the log porch rail in front of Barbara. It chirped and flicked its tail twice, and then it flew off to the corral. It alighted a second time upon the rail of the corral right next to the big horse and chirped a long melodious warble call. It seemed the sparrow was calling to her.

Barbara smiled at the wren at the same time the tightness in her chest seized hold of her heart. Her last vision was the little sparrow chirping a few final notes as it hopped onto the back haunches of the big horse. She saw that the sparrow belonged with him. It faced her once more and chirped again, and then it flew away over the grasslands. Little Deer, Barbara's granddaughter, was laughing and running through the prairie grasses apart from the other children. She was a natural leader whom many said was much like her grandmother, Little Sparrow. Her beautiful soft hair lifted on the breeze as the little sparrow flew over her head and disappeared into the late afternoon twilight. Barbara knew the Great Spirit had given her a final sign and called for her to come away. It was her time.

Little Sparrow's body departed from her life that day and her spirit went away to join the spirit of her beloved Big Horse. Over her last eleven years, Sparrow missed Big Horse terribly. Many nights she cried in her terrible loneliness. Nothing could ever replace a love like theirs. She held fast to her wonderful memories with Big Horse, which gave her strength to go on with her work. As she surrendered to death's grasp, she knew with certainty that her spirit would be reunited with his in some other place and time. A foundation worker found her sitting in her favorite rocking chair with her eyes closed and a faint smile on her face. She'd lived the life chosen for her by the Great Spirit and lived it well.

Hud and Deb arranged to give their extraordinary mother an extraordinary remembrance. A bronze statue of Little Sparrow standing next to Big Horse was erected on the ranch, now the foundation's headquarters where the work she began continues to this day. A memorial service was held two weeks after Sparrow died. For the service, Hud and Deb arranged to have the entire Plaintown Philharmonic Orchestra flown to Montana to perform on the lawn of the foundation's headquarters.

The music selected was Symphony Number Nine in E minor, opus ninety-five, *From the New World* by Dvorak. The first movement recalled the forest funeral of the Indian princess Minnehaha, or 'laughing water.' Deb loved that piece because it so personified her mother who, like moving water tumbling down a mountain stream, was high-spirited and life-giving. The 'going home' theme of the second movement helped everyone reflect that it was finally Little Sparrow's time to rest. The finale represented the frenzied energy and boundless spirit of Little Sparrow, which would continue the work she started.

When they heard the final movement, the animals and birds that lived on the surrounding prairie all stopped what they were doing and listened with rapt attention. They sensed something special and wonderful had changed their fortunes for the better, and all the animals were happy. More than a thousand people from all over the world attended the service to honor the life of Little Sparrow.

Barbara's body was flown to Milltown and buried next to Bob's. Her headstone also bore a Star of David, along with an inscription. 'Here, together with her beloved Big Horse, our beloved Little Sparrow is reposed with the Great Spirit.'

The Milltown Cemetery is a quiet peaceful place on a small plateau above Cedar Creek with views to Cedar Mountain and Broad Mountain. The rains somehow fall more softly there than they do on other parts of the surrounding valley, and the raindrops linger longer on the leaves of the occasional maple trees than they do in other places before they fall quietly to the ground. Pleasant breezes gently caress the gravestones in the spring and fall, their force blunted by the bluff as they rise from the valley floor below. Birds sing their tweets and warbles there, and honeybees drone about the perennials which seem brighter and more cheerful than the flora in the valley. Rabbits hop about and mate there, and squirrels scamper about, gathering up their nuts from the assorted pine and acorn trees that surround the grounds.

The spirits of the original German settlers and the Hackatopas Indians, who died together with them in the bloody horrors of the Great Segan Treffpunkt Massacre, knew that Bob and Barbara came home and joined them in eternal peace. The bodies of the two true and faithful lovers and their good souls were warmly welcomed by the ancients, and all the bones were pleased.

SPIRITS AND WONDERS

It was a still half-moon night with passing clouds. The barn owl flew up to the Milltown Cemetery from the forest beyond and perched high above the grounds on the outstretched limb of a maple. It was a good spot to hunt mice and small squirrels. Off by the ringed mass grave of the settlers and Indians, there were two high school boys, about fifteen years of age. They were sharing a quart of stolen beer when a strange wind came up. It came at the boys from all directions. Some said the bluffs caused it sometimes, but it never happened anywhere else.

The boys crouched behind a headstone and peered over it as they heard the eerie sound of people talking. The owl hooted when he saw something rise up from the ground. They were white, misty figures that wavered in the air. There were two of them, a naked man and a naked woman. The spirits shimmered magically in the light breezes. The woman took the man by his hand and made a whooping sound, like an Indian woman calling her children. The spirits spiraled together upward into the sky for a bit, and then they flew away in beautiful graceful flight toward the northwest.

The boys ran from the graveyard that night, shaken to their core. No one believed them when they told what they saw. The owl lifted off and followed the spirits for a bit before he returned to his limb, but he knew what only an owl of the night could know. The spirit of the Indian woman took the spirit of her man with her to the happy hunting ground that night. The owl knew that only happened when there was true

531

love, and he knew those two spirits would live happily together forever.

A few days later, Slim and Wayne, two grave diggers, were sitting on the ground with their backs against the cemetery's equipment building. They'd spent the entire day digging three graves for a family who died in an auto accident. Wayne pulled out a bottle of whiskey while Slim took off his shoes to air out his feet. They faced the setting sun and the warmth of the cement wall heated their backs. As Wayne took a sip, he observed a Monarch butterfly come up from the creek below and flutter toward the northwest section of the cemetery.

"See dat butterfly?" Wayne said.

"Where?"

"Dere," Wayne pointed to the northwest section.

"What of it?" Slim was rubbing his feet.

"I seed it befur. It comes up from the crik late afternoons. I knows it's da same butterfly. It's one of dem Monarch butterflies, bigger and purtier den da rest of 'em. It comes up with da oder butterflies like its ones of 'em, den it seprates from da oders and it goes to da same place about dis time. Den all oder butterflies is gone for da night, but it stays a while. I watched it real close after I seed it come up about four times befur."

"You're nuts. Dere's lots of butterflies."

"No, I's ain't nuts, Slim. Dere's somepin goin' on about dat butterfly. Watch. It will go to dat one headstone, the one of dat guy dat had the Injun wife. Watch it."

"Oh I sees it. You're right. Der it sits on dat headstone, like you sez. It's like putting on a show for all to see. How'd you know it'd do dat?"

"It always does dat. Fans its wings open and closed like a whore opens 'er legs. I went there once and it leaves behind a drop of moisture, a tiny drop on that headstone. Then, just as the sun sets, it flutters off west and goes back down to the crik.

I think it's got somepin goin' on with that headstone or the body dat's in dat grave, maybe."

"All dem headstones in dat plot is fucked up. Mudder and fadder gots crosses, son and Injun wife gots Chew stars. How'd dat happen?"

"Maybe mum went into da hospital an' dey got a Christun baby mixed up wid a Chew baby. Maybe it's da Suckulists."

"Whatcha mean Sucultits?"

"Not Sucultits, Suckulists. Pay 'tention 'for I smack you upside da head! Suckulists is dem dat don't give a shit 'bout religion. Dem's da ones dat want all us dumb shits mixed together, like fish in a big fuckin' food blender machine. Ya goes in Christun, ya comes out a Chew. You's a Christun or a Chew, you marries an Injun. You's an Injun and you switch to Chew. You can even goes into da U.S. Senate as Christun and you flips a switch in der, in da Senate, and presto, you's an Injun!"

"No shit! Dey can do dat? In U.S. Senate, dey cans do dat?"

"I tink so. I heered it on da raddio. Some gal gots herself 'lected into U.S. Senate, an' when she gots dere, she flipped a switch an became an Injun!"

"What? She change her name too? Is she Pocahontas or Sacawageesus?"

"Nah, dis gal is totally fucked up. She's an insult to real Injuns. She's jest nuts is all."

"No shit. Cans we go dere to dis Senate place too an becomes sompin oder dan whats we is?"

"Maybe. I heerd it on da raddio bout dat switch in da U.S. Senate all dem Senators do. We's could flip dat same switch an becomes rich!"

"Yah, why'd she flip the Injun switch instead of da rich switch? Why da fuck she wanna be an Injun anyway?"

"How da fuck do I know? Maybe she jest likes to fuck Injuns. Like I told ye, she's all fucked up. Some people jest don't know der own minds is all."

"You's drinkin' too much whiskey. Gimme some."

Wayne handed the bottle to Slim, who took a swig.

"You think dem butterflies got brains, Wayne?" Slim asked.

"More'n you got, dumb fuck. Hell, you's so dumb your wife bought you dat motion movie pitcher kamer and you put it on da tree wheres you was huntin, and you fell ta sleep dere whiles deers walk by right in front of ya. Dey even hump-fucked and made house right in front of ya an ya dumb shit slept through it all. Then ya dropped a lit c-gar in da woods and torched evra thing up. Lucky ya wasn't jailed. Ain't no butterfly dumb as you, Slim."

"Yeah, well, yer kid bought ya a compooter an' all ya use it fer is to sit your ammo reload 'quipment on it. You ain't smart, neither. What makes ya think dat butterfly's smart?"

"I tink dat one's got a brain and it's got somepin in its head dat it can't lay off and go aways from. Maybe it's had a life frem befur and it's come back to somepin it didn't git right in its oder life. Here, gimme dat whiskey back. I needs a swig."

"You tink so?"

"Could be. Dere's a story about dat guy buried der. Before he married the Injun, he was hot and heavy with some high-class hooker way out west somewheres. Maybe the butterfly is her. Gimme back dat whiskey."

"Why ya tink it leaves a water drop on da headstone?"

"It ain't water, you asshole. I smeared my finger in it once't. It's sticky, has a spicy sweet smell, like dem gardeenya flowers. I tinks it's pussy juice. I tink dat butterfly is somehow dat hooker's pussy come back to life, an' it still wants to fuck 'im."

"You knows a lot about da bodies in here, don't cha?"

"Yep, I doos. They's all got stories. Dat's why I tinks like I do. Dere's stuff goes on in here dat makes me knows dere's other lifes dan da ones we's got now."

"Dat so?"

"Damn right dat's so. Dat butterfly proves it to ya right now. Know how I'm sure it's 'is long-lost lover?"

"No. How can ya know?"

"Dat butterfly does other things dat dem other butterflies don't do. It opens an' spreads its wings real wide like, holds 'em opin fer da longest time, like she's a whore spreadin' her legs wide 'cause she's itchin' to fuck. Den when it leaves dat headstone, it always flies away to da west."

"I never seed butterflies dat way. Why ya tink it goes west?"

"It keeps comin' back to 'im 'cause it wants 'im to go wit her. Wants to take 'im back west."

"Well, how'd ya know he ain't gone with it just now?"

"I don'ts know. I just figure he wants to be with da Injun girl. I heered she was out-of-dis-world beautiful, even more beautiful den 'is whore."

"'Cause they's buried together?"

"Yeah, I tink so. He loved her, he loved the Injun."

"But da Injun girl got buried next to 'im, years later'n 'im."

"Well, maybe spirits can love two womens, be in two places at once't. Maybe his spirit waited for the Injun and finally she came to 'im. But anyways, I knows dat butterfly proves one thing fer sure."

"What's dat?"

"A great pussy never quits! Ha Ha!"

"Yeah, you're right! Pass back the whiskey."

MIDNIGHT AT
MOUNT OF OLIVES

Susan's soul continued yearning for Marvin forever after they died. Every Shabbat evening, and every evening during High Holy Days, her soul's spirit wisped across the hemispheres to the Mount of Olives Cemetery in Jerusalem. There it hovered over Marvin's grave and beckoned his soul to arise and join with hers.

"Be happy. Know my eternal love. Hold me in your arms and kiss my sweetness," it whispered to its dead spirit companion.

Occasionally, a bird would hear the haunting disturbance and would startle from the sounds of the whispering spirit, but the bird could not see the maker of the sounds. Then the bird would jump up and look around, for the spirit's urgings were answered by the faint voice of yet a second spirit. It was Marvin, calling to Susan to wait for him, saying he would try again to arise that very night, as he had tried so many nights before.

Then, the bird would hear the faintest, almost indiscernible rattle of a chain. It was Marvin's chain which bonded his soul to Eloweiss's as they waited to be called up together at the end of days. Marvin's soul tried mightily to follow its yearning heart to Susan's soul. But despite its exertions, it could not break its chain, not that night. It told Susan's soul it would try again soon. Then it fell back into its grave to suffer in torment next to Eloweiss.

The bird cocked its head when it heard a moan of exhaustion, an anguished whimpering cry from a soul that was condemned to be joined to its betrothed, wedded both in life and forever after in eternal paired suffering. And then, like the ghostly Shabbat visitor, the bird flew away.

COYOTE ON A RIDGE

Some ranch hands were in their bunkhouse playing poker one night. It was a full moon and the air was cool, with the Rocky Mountain stillness and light breeze coming from the west teasing the fall aspens on the mountainsides above the valley floor.

Suddenly, a coyote howled.

"Listen to that fella. He's a bigun. Howls deep and mournful. Didn't hear 'im last night," said Big Jim, the first hand, looking at the other three hands through a dim cloud of cigar smoke.

"I heered he's the same coyote, real big fella, comes ever night when dere's a full moon. He yelps up on da ridge top. Rancher Bud says he's seen da animal early in da mornin up dere sometimes. Bud says there's a huge lobo up on the ridge, half wolf and half coyote, that wasn't around these parts before dey found those bones up there. A ranger saw it too, said it was a monster lobo from Wyoming, a killer, come down from Canada or Yellowstone through the Wind River Basin an' down here to Colrada. Ranger said the lobo must have smelled da poor devil's body all the way from Wyo and comed to feed on it. Sometimes dey's three or four of dem coyotes in dat same spot wid da lobo. They runs round in circles and yelps like dey's insane, and deir eyes flashes red and yella in da moonlight, like da devil's inside 'em. Bud says dey do dat 'til mornin' twilight gits bright. Dey runs in circles round in dat aspen grove up on top, dat spot where they found da bones of dat poor bastard dat got killt up dere," said John, the second hand.

"You don't say. I never heard this. What guy?" asked Jack, the third hand, as he popped open another can of beer.

"Well, da rangers found bones scattered all ober da place. The man'd been dead a while. Coyotes cracked da bones, ate out 'is marrow. Bones was chewed by da rodents, not much left of 'im. Dey was stakes in da ground, some leather straps an' ropes. He was tied down to die, looks like. From da teeth they figgered it was some big investment guy," said John.

"Oh yeah, I think I read sompin bout that in the paper once't," Jim said. "It said he left some money to some homosexual foundation or sompin. He was one of them gay guys."

"Somebody musta had it in for dis one, but they ain't never found out who done it. He was into all kinds of bad shit, had enmies. Now, my own theory is dat big dog coyote was into eatin' off 'im and he comes back 'ere and howls to da coyote gods to send 'im another helpin'. Rancher Bud says he's seen them coyotes up dere in the mornin' pissin' all over da place, pissin' on the ground where dat poor bastard was staked down and pissin' on da trees all bout dat place," said John.

"Well, sometimes the animals know what's what. They knows, I tells ya," said the fourth hand, Jake, as he took a swig of whiskey from the open bottle on the table.

"Whatcha mean?" asked Jack.

"I means they knows, damn it. I means what I says, that's all. They's smart. Maybe those coyotes knows that this big shot was some no-good son of a bitch and he got what was coming to 'im, so they ate on 'im while he was still alive, chewed off his ass, chewed off his legs and arms and face, and now they goes back during the full moons to celebrate what they done to 'im, and they celebrate by howling and pissing all over the place, pissing on his remains where he died."

"Ya think so, John?" asked Jim.

"Damn right I think so." The other hands stared at John, amazed by his wisdom. "Dem coyotes are smart as hell. They's smarter'n we is. I always avoid 'em, never fuck with 'em, no sir. I never shoots at 'em, no sir. I jest avoid them sons a bitches. You don't want to go fucking with no coyotes, 'specially no lobo. Noooo sir. No way! They can get the best of you. Take a bite outta you when you least expects it, 'specially a lobo. They's got those watchin', cunnin' yeller eyes, always measuring, figgerin' when you's weak. I seen a guy once't, he was a homeless one and he slept out with a bedroll. One night a coyote got 'im while he slept, bit a cheek right off dis poor bastard's face. A lone coyote did it. Blood everywhere, screamin' crazy like a mad man, he was. Poor son a bitch he was. Coyotes kill, I tells ya. Dey kills anythin'."

"Sometimes," said Jake, "I gets to thinking, which ain't too often. But one day I had this thinking spell about coyotes. I thinked they was God's voice for all the animals of the world, that they yips and howls for all the sufferings of all the animals of the world and for all the bad shit people do to all the animals. They got hearts, them coyotes. And they's there waitin' to get even with humans for all the animals we hurt. They's killers! John's right, I tell ya. They's out there now, watchin' us, measurin' us. 'Specially the big lobo. He's watchin' us all right with them big red and yellow eyes and he's lollin' his tongue and flickin' his tongue over those huge canine teeth. He's droolin' and tastin' the air for us. Don't go out the cabin alone with the big lobo out there, no sir. Once he's et human flesh, ranger says he's gonna want more."

"Jesus H. Christ," yelled big Jim. "I don't want to hear no goddamn more shit 'bout no fucking goddamn coyotes or I ain't gonna be able to sleep! I'm gittin' shivers up my backside an' chills all over. All you jest shat ap! It's my turn. Over to you, Jack. I'm raising you three bucks, and pass me the whiskey."

HUD WITH THE SPIRITS

Hud was camped near the base of two glaciers in northwest British Columbia. He and his exploration crew had been taking stream sediment samples and searching for gold for the past four months. Fall was in the air. Geese were seen flying south, leaves were falling, and bears were fattening themselves for winter. They would break camp in another week and go to the lower forty-eight before the snows came. He slept alone in the giant wall tent that held the boxes of sediment samples. The rest of the crew had a tent nearby. It was nearly three in the morning. He'd worked hard the day before. He was in a deep restful sleep when they came.

A pair of huge hands took hold of his shoulders and gently shook him until he awoke. He propped himself up on an elbow and rubbed sleepers from his eyes. When his vision cleared, he sat bolt upright. There before him stood his grandfather, Big Chief Eagle Feather. Chief was dressed in his majestic ceremonial finery, a white buckskin fringed coat and riding chaps, and his head was adorned with his ceremonial headdress of eagle feathers that trailed down his back. Standing next to Chief was Hud's mother and father. All three appeared to be in their early thirties. Standing next to Chief was an intense wiry man with bony hands and black hair. The man wore wire-rimmed glasses. Hud had never seen this man before.

"Hud, my grandson, we were sent by the Great Spirit of All Living Things to come and visit with you. I bring with me your father, Big Horse, and your mother, Little Sparrow. I also bring the spirit of Mr. Nicola Tesla, a man I met in the realm of spirits. He and I have had many talks and we are good friends now. I wanted you to meet him."

The spirit of Nicola Tesla stepped forward and shook his hand. Hud felt a sudden warmth throughout his entire body and he felt a slight burning on his right arm. He looked down at the source of the burning sensation and noticed there were three brown dots the size of paper punch holes arranged in triangular order slightly above his elbow. Then the spirits of Big Horse and Little Sparrow moved nearer to Hud and hugged him closely. The spirits all stood back and Chief stood alone before him.

"Hud, we have been sent to guide you in a new direction. The Great Spirit of All Living Things is unhappy with the path you are on. You have a gift of intelligence, but you spend all your waking hours in your quest for gold. You work hard but you live like an animal for months at a time. Every two or three weeks you go to the town of Stewart, drink alcohol, clean yourself up, and bed with a whore for a few nights before you return to camp. There is a better path for you, Hud.

"You have a claim group further to the south with some unusual rocks on them. The rocks have properties that open the universe and allow mankind to travel into and out of life among the spirits. Mr. Tesla's spirit can tell you more about their properties."

"The rocks on your claim group were placed there by universal electrical energy transition mechanisms," Tesla's spirit began. "In my papers I explained the methods whereby large quantities of energy can be transmitted wirelessly. This mechanism is universal. The rocks on your claim group can take the normal eight hertz resonance of the Earth and focus Earth's energy into an amplified magnetic force field. The sun resonates at four hundred-forty hertz. That force field can be amplified as well. The amplified Earth's field can flow within the Sun's amplified field and those fields can be directed to other stars and galaxies and universes as amplified fields fold into ever stronger fields. Selected pairs of living persons can use the fields to move freely among the galaxies and universes, and they can visit all the planets in the universes as if they were swimming from one spot in a swimming pool to another. The rocks enable you to be in endless universes in endless galaxies with endless swimming pools of stars and planets. Each drop of water is a planet you can enter and live on, and take a human form if you choose. The rocks hold the key to end all wars, strife, hunger, and unhappiness. Every human person pair can own millions of planets to do with as they choose. There are endless habitable planets available for endless human pairs. There is no need for frictions among the peoples of Earth."

He was dumbfounded by what he heard. He looked at Chief, who moved closer to him and spoke again. "Hud, I bring you this message from the Great Spirit of All Living Things. You are to leave this place and go to Plaintown. You are to study the Tesla papers and the principals Mr. Tesla explained in them, and you are to give up your whoring and marry a good woman and have children. You are the uncle of Sparrow's grandchild, Little Deer, and you must set a good example for her. The Spirit demands it for he has great plans for her. You will take Deborah, Rick, Little Deer, and your woman with you and go on a journey. The Spirit commands that you live a righteous life, Hud. It is necessary to prepare you for your journey."

"But how will I find the Tesla papers? And where will I find a good woman?" He was in quandary. The Spirit wanted him to change his whole life.

"You will begin your search for knowledge of energy fields in Plaintown. There is a bookstore called The Ragged Cover. In the basement of the bookstore, there is a science section where you will find books about Mr. Tesla's papers. Get the books, read them, and understand them. You must follow wherever they lead you. They will take you on a journey where you will travel freely in the company of your woman, your sister and her husband and children, your mother, and your father. Your life and the life of your partner will never die."

"And how will I find a good woman to marry, Big Chief? All women I know are whores."

"You are not to concern yourself with that. We have met the spirit of your future woman. The Great Spirit of All Living Things brought all of us together for a meeting. The Spirit is in her now. Her spirit is that of a very fine and good woman. Your woman will find you when you have made yourself ready for her. That is the way with women. Now waste no time. Go to the bookstore as the Spirit commands you, get the Tesla papers, and read them."

With that last message, the spirits disappeared. Hud went to the entrance flap of his tent, searching all around and up into the sky. There was no sign of his visitors, and they left no footprints. The first rays of morning twilight pierced the black night as a meteor streaked away over the horizon. A shiver shot through his body and the hair on the back of his head bristled as if rubbed by an electrostatic charge. It was the start of a new day.

REST

Before we flutter on, dear reader, like our little Monarch Poon, I must rest for a while. I must knit a sweater and a pair of baby booties for my new granddaughter. There's so much to do! When we continue, we will meet a very special woman and travel with her as she searches for her new life with Hud. We will discover the wondrous rebirth of Marty's spirit when she reawakens in her new home and her new body. Will she be the woman Miss Promiscuity encouraged her to be, or will she be the woman she promised Bob she would be when she joined him again? Or will the magical properties of the rocks that lie on Hud's claim group allow her to simultaneously live parallel lives in multiple parallel universes? And how would that happen, exactly? Does Mr. Tesla's spirit know something that he didn't tell the Earthlings while living amongst them in their universe? Will Hud and our special woman travel well with the spirits of Little Sparrow, Big Chief, Big Horse, and Mr. Tesla?

In writing the butterfly books, the thought occurred to me that God might have inadvertently forgotten to add an eleventh commandment. That commandment, I think, should be that "Parents shall love your children and love them with unbounded love with all your hearts, for they need that love to become a glory unto me."

Until we resume, dear reader, please remember these important things: A butterfly will never lie to you. A butterfly will always love you. When you open your heart to the love and beauty of a butterfly, your spirit will be in a very good place. And when you love a butterfly, your heart is pure and you are beautiful.

Goodbye for now,
Rosemary

For information, contact: rosemarylightfootnessbitner@aol.com

www.ingramcontent.com/pod-product-compliance
Lightning Source LLC
Chambersburg PA
CBHW020822030726
47496CB00001B/39